THE MAGE'S SIN

DRAGONERA: THE DARK ONE CHRONICLES BOOK 3

CHARLIE ROSE

BROKEN
TOWER
P R E S S

CONTENTS

PROLOGUE

An unearthly roar echoed throughout the once pristine halls of the famed academy. Bodies, both human and non-human, littered the floor, painting a horrific, bloody scene. This place, once a safe haven for those with "The Gift" had been twisted into utter chaos.

A young man, possibly in his late teens, ran through the halls carrying a long staff in his right hand. Behind him he heard another loud, unholy roar. The sound sent shivers down his spine; it was the sound of some inexplicable nightmare, more terrifying than his darkest imaginings. It was the sound of whatever had been unleashed in the school.

It didn't take a genius to figure out this was no ordinary school, but one for those connected to the energies of the world. Some might call it a school of trickery and illusions, but the truth was far simpler. It taught an art normal people took for granted these days, an art long since relegated to the pages of fantasy books. An art holding a mighty, but invisible, sway over the modern world: magic, the most ancient form of power the world has ever known. Though much of the world had long since forgotten it, there were a chosen few who had devoted their lives to uncovering its secrets. The fleeing man was one of those chosen few.

The young man glanced back over his shoulder as the unholy roar finished. A pair of formless shadows rushed towards him, with a strange mix of hisses and growls emitting from the shadows as they struck out at him!

Fortunately this young man was not defenseless. As the shadows lunged he stood his ground and turned to face them, spinning his staff! After the fifth spin, the young man struck out with a mighty "thwack" knocking several teeth from the charging beast! The second shadow leapt into the air above its fallen comrade, a mighty roar erupting from its gaping maw, teeth glistening with saliva.

But the shadow made a fatal flaw in assuming the young man had nothing else up his sleeve. As the creature descended on him, he pointed his staff in its direction and began to mumble under his breath. With a great flash a blast of blue lightning erupted from the tip of his staff, piercing through his attacker's maw!

The result was instantaneous. A surge of lightning tore through the shadow, causing its body to dissolve in a shower of crackling sparks. A lifeless pile of ash landed at the young man's feet. With a sigh he rested his staff on his shoulder.

"I love using that spell."

Before he could celebrate his victory, an even louder roar came from deep within the academy. This wasn't a warning roar though, it was a signal. The man groaned as he turned and began to run once again. He cursed himself for momentarily forgetting that killing one of the shadows would draw the attention of the others.

As he started running the shadows gave chase. They were like an unstoppable sea of hellish insects, crawling across the walls and ceiling in pursuit of their prey. Each one hissing as they chased the young man. The hissing sounds were mixed with the loud clanking of their claws scratching against the metal of the hall.

There was no time for the young mage to think. Given how many shadows were chasing him, he stood no chance of defeating the alone. If there was any hope for survival he needed to get to the safe zone where the other students, and the Grand Mage, had retreated.

Thankfully, luck was on his side. The door to the safe zone was just ahead, but he couldn't go there while being followed by a hoard of shadow creatures. He glanced over his shoulder. He might not have been able to destroy them or stop them entirely, but he could sure as hell slow them down.

The young man skidded to a halt and turned on a dime to face the shadows. As they grew closer and closer he held out his staff and began chanting under his breath. The more he chanted the brighter his staff glowed, pulsating with power. With a final word the young man rammed the bottom of his staff into the floor.

A giant sheet of ice rose up between him and the shadows. Any of the beasts unfortunate enough to touch the frigid wall were frozen on the spot! This bought him the chance he needed to get away. He pulled his staff out of the floor and rushed off towards the door. He didn't have long before his wall would begin to melt.

The ice bought him just the time he needed. The safe zone, within his reach, greeted him with warm light and an immediate peace of mind. He stepped through the door, taking deep breathes as the holy magic keeping the door safe sealed behind him, just as the ice melted.

Though they could not get into the room, the shadows tried to tear down the barrier of light standing between them and their targets. Each time they touched the barrier they let out an evil hiss before slowly backing off.

"Thank all that is holy..." The young man said with a tired gasp. "I was certain that I was going to die in that hall."

He took a few seconds to catch his breath. Even for one gifted with incredible power like magic, it took a lot of mental power and physical strength to escape destructive monsters like the shadows. Once he'd managed to relax and settle his breathing, he turned to face several other students. Many of them were injured from the attack; some of them looked as if they were close to death itself.

"How many survivors ?" He asked as he turned to a young woman.

"About thirty of us in this corridor, Head Student." She replied. "At least fifteen of us have been injured, and those who aren't are too terrified to go back out there."

"Dammit... And where's the Grand Mage?"

"He's in his quarters trying to figure a way to get us out of this mess."

The young man gave a scornful sigh as he shook his head. This was not the time to hide in private quarters. Their school, no, their very home was in danger of not only being destroyed, but their existence was at risk of being revealed to the world. The shadows, and the horror controlling them, were too dangerous for them to just sit by and do nothing.

"How many of the survivors are still capable of fighting back?"

"Not many, the strongest students are busy using healing magic to save the lives of the dying."

The young man let out a frustrated groan and slammed the end of his staff into the ground. As if their situation wasn't already bad enough. He needed the most powerful students to even stand a chance against the monsters, but he understood that their talents were needed to save the wounded. Without their help, he was going to have to settle for whomever was left he could get his hands on.

"Get anyone who isn't busy with healing to reinforce the barrier. If that falls, we won't have anything to protect us from the monsters. No matter what happens, we must maintain this safe zone. Am I clear?"

"Yes Head Student!"

The student ran off to find help. As she left, the young man sighed as he tightened his grip around the staff. How did things get so bad? Where did it all go wrong? Their magic arts had never before failed to help them defend their home, even against previous demonic attacks.

But now, well, things looked hopeless. If there was any chance for them to overcome the shadows, it would have to come from outside of the academy.

But...who could possibly aid them, when they'd hidden their existence from the rest of the world?

CHAPTER 1 - ONE YEAR

*B*efore High School Aiden Russel was a lanky kid with one true friend. He was quiet, just keeping to himself, reading fantasy and daydreaming. That awkward boy was gone, burned away by his experiences over the last year.

For Aiden it has been a full year since his adventures at Skyward Camp. That lanky boy paled in comparison to the fifteen-year old attending Wolf Pack High School. A year spent in training since the harpy incident brought huge improvements, both physically and mentally. Not even his old nemesis Eric would recognize him now.

While he wasn't any taller, Aiden was much more muscular than he had been in middle school. Though the training he went through under Garrett was indeed tough, Aiden could not argue with the results. His arms had transformed from noodles to toned, solid muscles. And the improvements did not stop with just his arms. Aiden's calves and thighs had become a solid foundation for the teen's more powerful frame.

Even Aiden's parents were surprised at the sudden change in their son's physical condition. His mother, when she began to notice the changes, could have sworn that some stranger had replaced the son she knew and loved. His father, though also surprised at the sudden change, was proud to see his son taking physical fitness more seriously.

Their surprise didn't bug him too much, at least - at first. It had gotten old after awhile, though. Now Aiden rolled his eyes in annoyance whenever someone looked surprised at his appearance. He'd gotten used to muttering to himself, asking if they'd never seen someone start to exercise before.

The last year didn't just bring an improvement to his body. Aiden's magic training took him from being a slow amateur to a much more controlled rookie. Those were Seamus' words, not his own. Aiden was far more confident in using magic. Now he could cast spells without running out of mana after just a few simple incantations.

Swordsmanship, though, had quickly become his true forte. Theresa worked Aiden to the bone nearly every single day. It came with a lot of bruises, light cuts, and a LOT of falling down, but, he was slowly reaching the point of keeping up with Theresa without making himself look like a complete fool. Theresa had even mentioned how proud she was of the progress he was making.

The past year wasn't all sunshine and rainbows though, it also brought hardship to Aiden's life. After summer came and went Aiden began his new high school life as a freshman. He quickly learned that his rose colored glasses view of high school, based on what he'd seen on television and the movies, was nothing like the real thing. The schedules were tighter, the classes longer and tougher, and the social interactions were...confusing and unfair. It seemed like you were assigned to a category that was either popular or unpopular on day one, and no matter how hard you tried, you couldn't break through to the other side.

It didn't help that, along with harder courses, came lengthier, and more time consuming, homework. Aiden wasn't lazy, but the amount of busy work his teachers loved to assign, multiple classes each assigning "just one hour" of homework, quickly piled up. To make matters worse, after having his eyes opened to the fantastic other world that everyone else was blind to, normal, everyday life just seemed dull and tedious. Every minute spent solving equations or conjugating verbs made him long for the clash of steel or the feeling of magic erupting from his fingertips.

But, he still didn't know why all this happening. Why did his life turn around so suddenly? Why was it that he, a normal kid, had ended up with the sword of the ancient King of All Dragons? Every time he tried to prod his father for answers, he always got the same response: he'd been abroad and saw the figurine in a shop. That was it, just a simple, boring answer. His father seemed to never remember the name of the shop, or just where he had found it. That, or he refused to say. With his dad you could never tell.

Regardless of how his father discovered the artifact, Aiden spent the entire summer training with the blade, becoming familiar with its powers. Theresa's training had been so intense, in just a few months time he'd learned to summon the blade by sheer force of will, without even needing the "Ladbe" incantation.

He still had trouble mastering one attack, the mysterious, unstoppable power he had manifested during the battle to protect the Harpy's Den from Dimitri and Raven. He could still feel the words of the attack echoing in his mind. It helped deliver a decisive finish to Raven and Dimitri's plans: The Draconic Firestorm. Aiden remembered the fiery vortex with the head of a great dragon he somehow summoned last year. He brought it up with Theresa one time during practice and her reaction caught him off guard. She was impressed, confused, and worried that he had somehow used what she called "Warfang's Ultimate Attack." When Theresa asked him how he summoned the attack, Aiden answered truthfully.

He had no flipping idea.

While he didn't mean to be rude, it was the truth. All Aiden remembered was that when he was using the attack he was angry and he felt useless in a battle because others had to come save him. His anger streamed into the blade, somehow summoning the great fiery dragon from within. Ever since that day, he'd not been able to summon the Draconic Firestorm.

Garrett scoffed at the idea of Aiden being able to summon the attack again. As far as he was concerned, Aiden had done nothing: Warfang simply recognized its power was needed. That the whelp had managed the mighty attack was nothing more than a fluke. Aiden had grown used to listening to the mighty dragon's disparaging comments. He'd finally learned to do what Theresa and Seamus did, simply ignore Garrett.

Seamus, on the other hand, was fascinated by how Aiden summoned the blade's immense power. Whenever his partner's words began to cut into Aiden's confidence, he was quick to remind his student how proud he was of him. No human could survive the might of the Firestorm, at least not by chance. Aiden tried to explain that the spell had come forth on its own, that his body had simply been acting without his input, but Seamus waved off his concerns, insisting that it was a sign of Aiden's "true potential." Whatever that meant. Aiden didn't even bother to ask.

After what seemed like an eternity, the last day of Aiden's freshmen year arrived. His last few weeks were an onslaught of final exams, so much so that Theresa had agreed to call off their training as she found herself buried in studies too. Compared to middle school, his high school exams felt like an ordeal, some great gauntlet of challenges that pushed his mental faculties to the breaking point. Not one, but three days of nonstop writing, calculating, and racking his brain, all building up to the final day. After a grueling four hours of testing, his first year of high school was finally over.

As the last bell rang, Aiden sighed and ran a hand through his hair. He was finally free and able to catch up with Theresa and Liza, whom he hadn't seen much of over the last week. The three didn't share many classes, but they were lucky enough to have three together.

He and Liza managed to catch up with each other first, since Theresa's final exam was in a different room. Knowing Theresa, though, the pair were certain she was already power walking her way to where they agreed to meet up.

"I thought those exams would never end. My brain feels like it was just stretched across every single state." Aiden said with a groan as he fell into step beside Liza.

"You and me both, Aiden." Liza said. "Some of those topics, I swear I think the teachers just made up on the spot to get us to freak out during the exam."

Aiden gave a dry laugh. He hadn't thought of it that way, but to hear Liza say it, he could believe it was true. She had a funny way of voicing her thoughts a bit more bluntly than the rest of them. It was an endearing trait, though sometimes Aiden felt she tried a bit too hard.

Much like Aiden, Liza's year of training had done wonders for her physical fitness. She had always been the more athletic of the two, and the dragon's training had only emphasized her fit form. She'd grown taller, her already strong legs even more well-defined. Her arms may not have grown quite as impressive as his, but Aiden knew first hand not to underestimate her strength. She'd chosen to keep her hair short, though nowadays it seemed more untamed.

Aiden yawned and rested his hands behind his head, glancing at Liza's legs absentmindedly. He'd learned, during their training, that as strong as he'd become, he just couldn't keep up with her when it came speed. Her somewhat clumsy fighting style from last year had evolved into a lightning-quick hit and run technique, tearing at her opponent with agile strikes that seemed to come out of nowhere. That, combined with her seemingly endless stamina, made her use of Gitanel something of a wonder to behold.

"Aiden! Liza!" A new voice called out to them.

The two of them turned to the voice, both of them grinning despite their fatigue. Their new friend, Hannah, waved and hurried toward them, clutching a book to her chest. Hannah, or as she was more correctly known, Aello, was the newest addition to their bizarre entourage. While on the outside she seemed like a somewhat-shy, but occasionally snarky, girl, she was actually the youngest princess of the long-forgotten Harpy race.

In spite of the rather perilous journey that led her to them, Aello had adjusted to the Human world with far greater ease than the two expected. That being said, her first few days had been filled with a hefty degree of awkward questions and confusion. The most notorious being the existence of different locker rooms for boys and girls. Coming from an all-female race, Aello was understandably curious about the need for them to change in separate rooms.

Her antics didn't begin with school, though. Before she enrolled she would often sneak into Aiden's room when he was away and play his video games. She'd quickly become obsessed with the games, though she didn't quite grasp the concept of save files. One time, she sheepishly admitted to saving over one of Aiden's files that had over two hundred hours logged. Once he'd recovered from his disbelief, thinking about the countless late nights he'd spent gathering every last collectible and filling out every last bestiary entry, he refused to speak to her for several weeks.

While Aello adapted to the human world by rummaging through her friends' rooms and, eventually going to school, her Guardians, Mia and Gabriella, occupied their time watching over their princess, and by getting their first human jobs to pay for an apartment for the trio. Mia, ever the optimist, was more than content with her waitressing job, but her partner was infinitely impatient with the "rude, obnoxious, lazy" humans she had to deal with while working for a call center. When Aello offered to get a job to help them, the two unanimously refused, giving her a million reasons why they were happy to suffer such indignities to provide for their princess.

The two guardians were, shockingly, not the only harpies constantly hovering around the adventurous princess. Much to the utter shock of her three friends, Aello's older sisters seemed to frequently appear when they least expected them. Aiden couldn't hide his shock the first time he saw the pair working as substitute teachers at their school.

Aiden dreaded the days when he'd find Ocypete substituting for the gym teacher. She was a merciless instructor, pushing even her little sister to her absolute limits with harsh exercises and even harsher activities. Any day he saw her decked out in a gray track suit, her long hair tied into an immaculate bun by one of her many, many guardians, Aiden knew he was going to be sore for the rest of the week. It had reached the point where he found himself longing for Garrett's strength training over Ocypete and gym. He had come to notice that, for some reason, Ocypete, or whichever Guardian was accompanying her, would have a different cell phone every time she appeared. When he asked Aello about it, she just laughed and explained that Ocypete would frequently get too emotional or excited when she texted her and would end up destroying her phone.

Celaeno, by contrast, was interesting as an art teacher. True to her title as the "odd princess" Celaeno would show up in mismatched clothes that she claimed were "all the rage in France about forty years ago." Truthfully, Aiden found her classes insightful. The Harpy Princess knew everything about artistic style and history, able to name hundreds of famous and non-famous artists and the impact they had on the evolution of their craft. Then she would try to draw something herself. For all her artistic knowledge, Celaeno could spend an entire class trying to draw a stick figure and somehow still end up with, well not a stick figure. When anyone questioned her clear lack of any artistic ability, she'd just laugh and reply that intent mattered more than execution.

Aello's big sisters weren't the only ones that came to the school to keep an eye on the princess. Her guardians had also taken up spots as students as well. With how many harpies, in the guise of humans, who seemed to flock around Aello, it had led many of the students to believe she was either exceedingly popular, or some kind of foreign royalty. While their suspicions weren't entirely wrong, Aello frequently grumbled about how much she wished the attention would stop. This feeling only got worse the first time someone tried to ask her out on a date and was met with a rather colorful rejection in the form of a very irate Gabriella.

"Hey Elly." Liza said as Aello pouted at the nickname they had chosen for her. "Where are your stalkers?"

"Probably trying to find me," Aello complained. She sighed and glared off to the side, pursing her lips, "I can never lose them for very long, no matter how many windows I climb through..."

Aiden gave a short laugh, flashing her a grin.

"To be fair, they are your guardians. And it is their sworn duty to protect you at all costs." Aello rolled her shoulders, a gesture she used when she couldn't flap her wings, and gave him a short glare.

"Oh yeah, and what's Theresa's excuse for babying you?" She asked with a mocking tone. Aiden coughed, turning his head to hide the slight blush on his cheeks.

"I have no idea what you're talking about."

"Anyway!" Liza interrupted them, drawing the word out as long as she could, "How'd your finals go, Elly?"

"Terrible!" Aello whined as she held her book closer to her. "I mean I'd heard that humans were terrible, but why in the world did they come up with this kind of torture for their kids? How in the world am I supposed to remember all of your countries?!"

"With a lot of studying," Aiden groaned. At the same time, Liza piped up saying, "A lot of praying!" The two traded a glance, then the trio turned, hearing a soft chuckle from behind Aiden.

"Honestly, you guys make it out to be way worse than it really is," Theresa laughed as she walked up to the group, "Sure, sure, some of the tests are tricky, but at least you only have one species to worry about studying."

"Yeah, yeah, yeah. Well, some of us aren't 'gifted' with ancient draconic knowledge," Liza retorted, throwing an arm around Aello's shoulders, "Some of us are flutter brains," she said, sticking her tongue out. Aello snorted and dissolved into a giggle fit.

"I think I detect a hint of jealousy," Theresa replied.

Liza rolled her eyes and mumbled in annoyance as the four of them walked towards the buses together. The hallways were filled with students that desperately wanted to get away from the school and begin their summer vacations. Aiden couldn't argue them, though his idea of a summer vacation was completely different from theirs due to how his life had changed so much.

As they approached the buses Aello's guardians caught up to them in the nick of time. The young harpy princess groaned a bit as they took up defensive spots around her to keep her protected from anyone they thought were too rude or were making any kind of threat towards her. Aiden almost let a small chuckle escape his lips but stopped when Liza gave him a small glare.

After all he was in the same kind of boat as Aello was when it came to Theresa watching his every single step.

"Should we meet at the local spot today?" Theresa asked.

"Well, it is kinda the first day of summer." Liza said, "We should enjoy it for what it is and relax for a bit. Training every day without a break can get pretty overwhelming after all."

"Training is also important, like studying." Theresa folded her arms. "The less you train the less you'll remember."

"Can't we enjoy our freedom for a day first?" Aello pouted. "I spent like nine months in this school wanting to do other things. I want to have at least one day of relaxation before we start training in that place you call a forest."

"If you can even call it that." Mia grumbled.

"All right, let's take it back a bit here." Aiden said, cutting off any chance of an argument. "All three of you have good points. It is summer vacation and we've been working so hard during the weekends with training and holidays that we need some time to relax. But at the same time we shouldn't become lazy."

He smiled.

"So how about we find a way to balance it out?"

Both Theresa and Liza nodded in agreement. Aello smiled. You could count on Aiden to stop an argument from breaking out. While he knew both Theresa and Liza would have preferred to do what they wanted, Aiden's suggestion was the best option. Besides, it was the first day of summer vacation tomorrow. Today was just a prelude to that summer.

As their group walked towards the buses, Aiden couldn't help but watch the student body. Like middle school the social hierarchy, as he liked to call it, was the same. The popular kids were at the top and the not so popular kids were often chastised or made fun of for being completely different from the 'status quo' the popular kids believed in.

If there was one thing Aiden hated about high school, and society as a whole, was how often those with power abused that power, hurting those who didn't have the ability to fight back. He had started calling out those popular students during his first year of high school - if they tried to use their status as an excuse to hurt someone. Most of the time they turned their attention on him and tried to put him down, but there were a couple of times where they actually backed off when he called them out. As long as the behavior stopped Aiden was satisfied.

Aiden now had a bit of a reputation among the popular students in high school as someone that stood up to them when no one else would. Theresa, a part of that popular circle, always laughed whenever she heard that Aiden started something with one of the popular students. She laughed even harder when one of the popular male students swore that if he tried it with them they would hit him.

The perks of being trained by a dragon, or in this case three of them, had changed the playing field if one of the popular boys tried to start anything with Aiden. After spending a year being trained Aiden was faster, stronger and quicker than most of the class. He almost went all out one time when Eric was being a jerk to someone who had a disability that made it hard for them to get around. The only reason he didn't go into a full on fight was because Theresa warned him that if he hit a normal human being with a single strong punch he could kill them.

Aiden clenched his fists in annoyance as he watched the popular football players gather together as they headed towards their cars. Theresa, sensing Aiden's frustration and annoyance, grabbed hold of his arm firmly. It was how she kept him from flying off the handle, attacking someone if they angered him or insulted those he was close to. He glanced atTheresa, watching her face. A small smile was on her lips.

"They're not worth it." She said. "They never are."

Aiden sighed and unclenched his fists. Theresa was right. Besides, Aiden would get very little satisfaction beating a bunch of meat heads like the football players.

"Remind me again how you always keep me from losing it?"

"I'm your best friend and teacher. I know a thing or two about keeping you calm."

Aiden laughed as he, Theresa, and Liza arrived at the buses. The first bus was Liza's, who before getting on the bus turned to Aiden and Liza one last time. Aello and her guardians hopped onto it as well. Their apartment was close to Liza's house. Liza rolled her eyes at their antics before turning back to them.

"I'll bring Aello and the others with me to the training grounds tomorrow. I'll be sure to keep them from flying."

"Sounds good to me." Theresa said. "Just make certain no one follows you either."

"Always Theresa." Liza stuck her tongue out before heading onto her bus.

This left Aiden and Theresa alone as they headed towards their own bus. Aiden frowned.

"Honestly Theresa? I'm a little concerned about the three harpies joining the training grounds. Remember the last time that Aello's guardians were with us? They ended up starting an argument with a bunch of gossip girls at the freaking mall."

Theresa sighed.

"It's been a year since Aello joined our little group, Aiden." She spoke in a soft tone. "While she has adjusted well to the way humans live, her guardians are still trying to find their place in this confusing world. Try to imagine yourself in their place if you had to leave everything you've ever known behind to follow someone you were devoted to. It's the Guardian's way of life."

Aiden frowned at Theresa's answer. Aello, the youngest princess of the Harpy Queen Lilith, joined their group after Aiden and his friends saved the den from being overrun by Dimitri and Raven's demonic forces. Despite this rough start to her new life away from the flock, Aello had managed to adjust to the outside world quite well.

While their relationship with her wasn't exactly perfect, she made a great addition to their group. The relationships that

Theresa and Aiden worried about when it came to Aello were her relationships with Seamus and Garrett. Aello got along better with Seamus. Made sense since the largest dragon didn't want anything to do with her.

The person that grew the closest to Aello though was Liza, and that greatly annoyed Aello's guardians. She spent every moment she could with the harpy princess when there was no school or when they were training. The two of them seemed to get along better than Theresa ever thought they would. While Aiden was busy continuing his training with the dragons, Liza spent her time teaching Aello about the outside world and how humans reacted to certain emotions.

Even with all she had learned, Aello was still new to the way the world worked and often asked lots of questions. Though the group answered as best they could, the princess would often ask the same question again. Sometimes it seemed no answer was truly good enough for her!

Nonetheless the young princess was a valuable member of the team, especially with her signature weapon, a lance that transformed into a chain like whip. Her skills were invaluable and she helped Theresa demonstrate powerful, and graceful, sword techniques Aiden was just beginning to learn. While she was not as graceful as her sister, Celaeno when using weapons, she was fast enough to keep up with Theresa when demonstrating a new technique, and that was no small feat.

"You're right; she has grown over the last year. Her guardians have been trying their best to adjust as well." Aiden admitted. "But do you think she'll ever truly get used to the way things are done here? It took me at least fifteen times to explain to her what a cell phone does."

Theresa smiled as she and Aiden walked onto the bus.

"I've told you before, Aiden, don't underestimate others. I'm sure you'll find Aello is a lot stronger than you think she is." Aiden knew that if he tried to push the issue Theresa would just ignore him. It was best he just let it go for now and enjoy the long bus ride home. Summer vacation was finally about to begin.

The bus ride home was uneventful. Traffic was crowded; the bus driver took too long to drop off students. Aiden did what he usually did when the bus ride took that long - sleep, and sometimes dream. Lately though his dreams were becoming cryptic and foreboding.

The first time it happened, he dreamt about the other two dragons. This time a strange shapeless darkness appeared before him. In front of that darkness were several lights holding long poles of some kind....

This voice was a guiding force that set everything up for him to follow. A predetermined path that Aiden couldn't simply ignore. The newest message left to him concerned him though. A threat? What kind of threat? Why did the voice have to be so cryptic?

"A threat is coming." The voice from his dreams said, *"A threat that will reveal to the entire world the hidden secrets they are not yet ready to know."*

"Aiden, Aiden wake up." Theresa's voice called out to him in his dreams.

He grumbled as Theresa shook his shoulder. The shaking was enough to wake him up. The white dragoness smiled at him.

"If it was up to you, you wouldn't be sleeping the day away wouldn't you?"

"Oi, it's not my fault that the school decides to have some bull crap early hours..."

Theresa rolled her eyes as the bus came to a complete stop.

"Well we're back now, so you might as well get up and head for home." She smiled. "And Aiden? Do try to go to bed at a reasonable hour tonight."

"Funny lady."

The two of them smiled as they stood up and got off the bus. Aiden had a feeling that tomorrow would be an eventful day, even though in the back of his mind, he felt something was wrong, and he was worried about what the future might bring.

He was right to feel that way. Even a full year of training was not enough to prepare Aiden for what he and his friends were going to face. An adventure that would forever change his outlook on life itself.

CHAPTER 2 - RAVEN'S WARNING

*A*iden's first day of summer vacation was an interesting one to say the least. At the time he had no way of knowing that the day would send him on an adventure that would open his eyes to the darkest secrets of the world. But that was in the future on the first day of summer. For now Aiden saw the world as a positive place, where black was black and white was white. Good people are good and do good things and evil people are evil and do evil things. That was a key component of a lot of the fantasy stories he loved, surely things were the same in his now forever changed life. Right?

Of course the future has a way of making every plan and belief change. But for now, today was the first official day of summer vacation and Aiden took great delight in sleeping in to at least nine thirty. After everything he had been through during his first year of high school and the endless training, he felt he deserved to sleep in. All of that ended when a familiar voice called out in the morning.

"Son! Son are you going to sleep the day away? Get up and have breakfast!"

The voice of his father, Connor Russell. Aiden groaned as

he slowly rose from bed. His hair a mess from sleeping funny on his pillow, he rubbed his eyes with one hand before standing up.

"Leave it to my dad to ruin a perfect sleep." He grumbled under his breath.

As much as Aiden complained, he actually appreciated the "dad" alarm clock. If he was late meeting up with the others Theresa would grill him about it for hours. That was something that he absolutely did not want to deal with on the first day of summer vacation. The fact that they were training outside in the summer, the hottest season of the year, was another added reason for Aiden to not want to get on Theresa's bad side. She could be brutal during training at the best of times, and if she had a reason to be upset.... No way was Aiden going through that!

He dressed in his regular training clothes, really just exercise clothes that Aiden always kept at the ready because you never knew, it was almost becoming his super hero outfit. He headed out the door as his mother and father sat at the dinner table.

"Are you heading out to be with your friends again, dear?" His mother, Helena, asked.

"Only for a few hours." He replied in a quick response. "We're just gonna be exploring the forest for a bit."

"As long as you aren't doing anything wrong, my dear son."

"I for one think it's a good thing that you're out of the house more often." His father said, looking up from his electronic tablet. "It's better that you're outside and not always stuck inside reading or playing video games."

Aiden gave a small eye roll at his dad's statement. But in a way his father was right. His life had completely changed since the day he had gotten Warfang. Aiden believed his life now was much better than any video game or book he's ever read. He was living a reality he'd always wanted to live in. Except for the fact that he had to hide the truth from his parents it was a life he loved now.

"Aiden." His father said, preventing him from leaving for a few more seconds. "Don't be gone for too long today."

Aiden turned to his father at that strange request. Why in the world would his dad ask him that? A look of confusion was plastered across Aiden's face as his dad's attention was brought back to his tablet.

"You might be on summer vacation, but don't think that means you get to do nothing but hang out with them every day."

The look on Aiden's face went from confusion to insulted. He did more than his fair share around the house and his dad decided that what he did with his group was nothing? How he longed to tell him that he was dead wrong about something for once in his life. But Aiden knew better. If he dared to speak out in an angry tone to his parents, there would be hell to pay.

"Why's that, dad?" He asked. He did his very best to keep his frustration and anger from seeping out of his throat. It must have worked because his parents didn't correct him on his tone.

"We have some chores that you need to do today. Some of those chores being yard work."

Aiden felt like his body was about to fall apart at the mere mention of those two words. The dread he felt was probably the most he's ever felt in his life. Sure he's faced demons, harpies, and nightmarish training with Garrett. But yard work was the absolute worst chore that he could be given by his parents.

"Oh wipe that look of dread off your face." His dad ordered. "It won't take that long and you know it. I'm going to be busy all day when I head out to work and your mother has her book club to go too today. So if you could do the yard work for us while we are away you would be doing us a great favor."

"I..." Aiden started to speak, he wanted to cry out in anger, but he swallowed that pride. "I understand, dad. It'll be done today when I get back."

"Thank you, Aiden." His mother said with a kind smile. "I

know it's your least favorite chore but it means so much that you're helping us take care of the house."

Aiden smiled at those words. After he got a nod from his dad that it was okay for him to head out, he opened the door and trotted off towards the forest. Theresa was most likely ahead of him and the others had to be there by now.

"Augh, Theresa and the dragons are gonna get pissed at me when I tell them what my parents want me to do..." He grumbled as he entered the forest.

A cooling breeze from the forest greeted him as he walked in silence. Aiden knew the path to the training grounds by heart at this point. He often found himself enjoying the silence that seemed so rare in his life right now. He couldn't help but smile at the nice summer day laid out before him and the absolute silence from what was normally the outside world. Aiden sighed because he knew that this kind of peace would not last for him or the others. After all, peace was a fleeting that thing lasted for the briefest of moments before it was lost.

"...I know you're there." He said, stopping suddenly, in the middle of the forest. "It's been a full year since we last met. I know when I'm being spied on."

It didn't seem like was anyone else around in the forest at first. But Aiden knew better. He couldn't afford to just assume no one was truly watching him. With so many attacks thrown at him by the trinity during training rounds, he was more aware of his surroundings than he ever had been. All of the attacks by Seamus and Theresa when they were teaching him had taught him to always be aware.

"Either you come out now..." Aiden took out Warfang, summoning the blade from the dragon figurine. "Or I'll just cut down the tree branch that you're watching me from."

A dark chuckle could be heard from the branch. Aiden's eyes narrowed at the sound of the chuckle. He was becoming all too familiar with the chuckle of someone that had become his rival.

"Looks like you're finally learning."

Aiden had no time to answer as someone jumped down from the tree branch. The dark hair and all too familiar face of Raven were all he needed to see to know that trouble was here. His grip on Warfang tightened as Raven landed in front of him.

Raven, much like Aiden, had changed over the last year. His black hair had grown a bit longer, right to the back of his neck. Just like Aiden as well, he had grown physically stronger. While his muscles were a bit bigger than Aiden's, the two of them shared the same height. A toothy evil grin crossed his lips as he stared directly at him.

"It's been awhile, hasn't it?" Raven asked. "Since we last saw each other, Aiden Russell."

"Obviously not long enough..." Aiden growled as he held Warfang out in front. "You have five seconds to get out of my face, before I slice off that ugly excuse of a mug."

Raven chuckled at Aiden's threat. He shook his head as he held his hands up. With a snap of his fingers his weapons, the Claws of the Tyrant, formed around both hands. Aiden scowled as he took a combative position. It was one he had learned from Theresa during their training sessions. He rested the flat back of his weapon on his shoulder, while the blade faced upwards. It was a position that reduced arm fatigue, allowing Aiden to save some strength when blades weren't clashing.

Raven also took a battle position as he bent both of his knees down. His claws pointed towards Aiden, in an upper position. His eyes glinted with danger as the two of them squared off against one another once more.

"You want a fight do you?" Raven asked. "You haven't heard what I came here for yet."

"I don't think I need to know what YOU want, Raven." Aiden

snarled. "The last few times we've faced each other in combat you made it perfectly clear."

"Then let's see how much you've grown in swordplay, fool."

The two said nothing else as their blades clashed briefly in midair. Warfang and the Claws of the Tyrant created a sinister tune of clashing metal that rang throughout the forest. The clashing metal caused sparks to explode each time they met, some singeing the tips of Raven's hair.

Aiden and Raven's faces were completely different each time their weapons locked. Raven's face was confident, downright sadistic looking. Aiden's face was the exact opposite. While he was confident he wasn't letting his ego get in the way. He was focused.

The two once again pulled their weapons back as they began to circle each other once more. Aiden had the flat of his blade against his right shoulder, helping to reduce arm fatigue as he never let Raven out of his sight. The latter did the same, but continued to hold his arms out to the side, the blue metal of the claws seemed to crave blood.

The first one to reinitiate combat was Raven, fast and furious with his strikes. Aiden didn't back down though, blocking each strike without trouble. His training had given him a new edge in combat. He continued to block each swing of Raven's claws with Warfang, looking for an opening.

Aiden began to take notice that each time he blocked one of the claws, Raven had a patterned response. Whenever Aiden blocked one attack with Warfang, the arm with the claw he just blocked would spin backwards as the next claw would rush towards him. Raven was forcing Aiden to continue to block to prevent any chance of counterattacking Raven's attacks.

This tactic wasn't going to stop Aiden. His eyes narrowed as he pulled back his left hand. His palm turned red as a large fire-ball formed there. Aiden noticed Raven's surprise. With a movement of his left arm towards Raven, the fireball in Aiden's hand turned into a fiery beam that slammed into his rival.

Did he mention that he loved the training that he was getting from the dragons?

Raven gritted his teeth as the beam pushed him away from Aiden. With a quick hand gesture, one of his demons, Zeratar, formed in front of him. The demon of grey flames took the beam quite well, with the fire having little to no effect on him. Aiden gritted his teeth as he Zeratar stand tall between him and Raven. It wasn't anything that he had not expected from Raven. He was a demon summoning mage after all. He usually let the demons do all the hard work for him. Aiden was a little surprised it took Raven so long to summon one.

As his demon took a deep breath after taking the fireball attack, Raven laughed, shaking his head. Aiden placed the back of his blade on his shoulder once more. Not once did he take his eyes off of Raven and Zeratar.

"Well, seems like you've learned a new attack. I'm glad that you haven't been wasting your time since the last time we faced each other in combat. It makes my eventual victory all the sweeter."

"I really didn't have much of a choice you know." Aiden retorted. "What you got there was a simple spell Theresa and Seamus taught me. They call it the Dragon's Fury." He held his hand up, smiling. "As you can see, I've gotten quite good at using it."

Raven smiled. "Why not use it more often in this fight, hmm?"

"I'm not an idiot, Raven." Aiden and his rival continued to circle each other, Zeratar still in front of his master. "I know full well that your little demon absorbs my fire like attacks and the only thing that could really harm it is either dragon fire or the attack I used on you in the Harpy's Den."

Raven's scowled at the mention of the Harpy's Den. A moral victory for Aiden, but an almost near death experience for Raven.

"A fluke, Aiden Russell, I assure you that's all that was." He said. "You haven't been able to summon that attack since, am I correct?"

"You're right, I haven't been able to call upon the Draconic Firestorm since that battle." Aiden admitted. "But just because I haven't doesn't mean that I can't."

He pointed the tip of his blade towards Zeratar. The demon of grey flames narrowed his unholy eyes as he took a battle position. Raven held up one hand.

"Enough, Zeratar. He's proven himself ready for the next challenge."

Zeratar turned back to his master, if he had lips they would be frowning. Aiden blinked in confusion. What did he mean by the words 'ready for the next challenge?' Was this all just a ploy?

Raven walked passed Zeratar, the demon of grey flames kept his eyes on him as the latter stood in front of Aiden, smiling. Aiden stood, dumbfounded.

"I was hoping that you would have gotten stronger, Aiden Russell." He said. "After all, what is threatening the very existence of your dragons, the harpies, and even my master and I, requires great strength to repel."

"A threat?" Aiden asked, scoffing. "The only threat I see before me is you and your demon. Once I'm done with you, your master is next."

Raven sighed as he dismissed his weapons. This caught Aiden completely off guard as his rival shook his head.

"Tell me, do you even know HOW I learned I was a mage?" He asked. "On second thought, don't answer that. You obviously don't know."

Aiden scowled at Raven's remark. The latter looked up at the sky, almost absent mindlessly, he began to talk.

"I was a young boy, an orphan, left to fend for myself after my blood parents abandoned me when I was five years old. That first cold winter I almost died. I scavenged for food, warmth, and stole to survive. You can't imagine how horrible it was. Knowing that any moment could be your very last."

Raven glanced back to Aiden.

"The winter had gotten so bad that at one point, I should have died from being so cold. I still remember that night, the night that changed my life forever. It was under a small bridge, where two homeless people were fighting for the last bit of warmth from a trash can they had lit on fire. I was young, stupid, and I thought they would share their fire." His hands clenched, "Do you know what they did? They kicked me away. Ran me off like a dog. I remember how painful it felt, how cold, it was the first time I cried as a child."

Aiden didn't want to believe what he was hearing from Raven. For as long as he's known him, he always assumed his rival was someone who did not know how to cry. Still, his grip on Warfang did not lessen. He knew if he let down his guard Raven would attack, it was what he does.

"I don't recall how it happened but all I could think during that cold night was 'Warm. Make me warm.' As those homeless morons fought over the heat, I begged, pleaded, to be warm. Until finally, it happened." He held his hands up, fire rising up from the palms. "My magic activated for the first time, setting my hands ablaze. Needless to say, this scared the homeless men away. I was a 'monster child' to them. Like any child exposed to magic without knowing what it was the first time around, I was terrified. I thought I was going to die if my hands didn't stop burning. But, on the contrary, they kept me alive."

Raven smiled as he stared at his two hands.

"I still don't know how I was able to access that kind of power, but I survived because of that first spell." His eyes turned back to Aiden. "And that's when I was discovered by them."

"Them?"

"Yes." Raven dismissed the flames in his hands. "Tell me, have your dragons told you where the mages are today in this modern world of ours?"

"For your information? Yes, jerk." Aiden said. "Seamus told me all about how they have a safe haven away from the busy world of humans. It looks like a local school."

"Looks can be deceiving." Raven said. "But you are correct. It is a school, but I doubt that your dragons told you the name of this school. That's one thing you have yet to learn about your little group of friends. Dragons tend to keep the finer points out when they teach others. If they spoke the entire truth, they'd lose any control they have over you. It's how they stayed the ruling power of the ancient kingdoms."

"I fail to see how this leads to the name of the school, Raven." Aiden spat, becoming angry at what Raven was saying about his friends, the things he now found himself questioning.

"Hmph, very well. Ignore what I have to say about your dragons for now." Raven mused. "The name of the school is Rosemary, the Private School for the Gifted. But in reality, its real name is the Arcana Academy. It the last safe haven for those who can learn the art of magic without endangering their existence."

He gave an effortless laugh that would have fooled someone who didn't know his genuine laugh. But Aiden knew better at this point. It was a laugh of pity.

"I'm amazed at how fast they came to get me you know." He continued, "The moment my hands caught fire they were in front of me in an instant. Three of them, one of which was the headmaster of the Academy at the time, found me. Brought me to their school, and gave me a home. Allowed me to hone my skills as a mage, how to control my powers."

"Sounds like you had it all." Aiden said, "So tell me, why did you throw it all away?"

Raven grinned darkly at his question.

"I found a much better way of life, obviously?" He motioned his right hand towards Zeratar. "My master taught me the strength of demonic magic. Those fools at the Academy have no idea the kind of power that comes from controling demons."

Zeratar emitted a dark, gurgling laugh. This seemed odd when you considered the fact that the demon, along with the other demon, Zantul, had no lips at all. Aiden felt a shiver run down his spine as he listened to the demon laugh.

"The point though Aiden, is that Arcana is the last safe haven for mages in this world of ours. And right now, it is at great risk of being exposed to the public."

Aiden quirked an eyebrow. Was Raven trying to trick him?

"Someone has messed up royally within the Academy. Demons and shadows run amuck and the defensive magic the school uses are at risk of failing. When those magics fail, Arcana will be revealed and the shadows within it will escape, causing massive havoc among the world of men. Not only will this bring the world's attention to the fact that magic exists, but it will ruin the lives of those who want nothing to do with the outside world."

"Why the hell should I believe you?" Aiden asked. "If the mages are that powerful why should I worry?"

"You know how our kind is with things they don't understand. Things that they fear." Raven stated. "They tear it apart, study it, and turn prejudice towards it. Those who have magic will be outcasts and become the targets of those consumed by their fear and hatred. And the worst part it is, they will find out about ALL things from the Ancient Kingdoms. The elves that hide, the mages, the harpies, the lesser races...and that includes your dragons."

With a snap of his fingers a portal appeared behind Raven and Zeratar. Aiden hoped it would reveal where he and his master, Dimitri, lived but there was no chance of that. This kind of portal wasn't the one that showed where they were going. He glared right back to his foe, a look of disgust on his face.

"Running away, Raven?"

"Believe me, Aiden Russell, if I had more time to play with you I wouldn't be leaving so soon. But time is of the essence now. I give the magical wards of Arcana at least…three days before they dispel. When those wards fail, the monsters inside the school will be let loose upon the world. If you want to avoid that, heed my warning. Otherwise, say goodbye to your little secret."

Raven glanced back to Zeratar and motioned his head towards the portal. The demon of grey fire nodded slowly as he entered the portal before his master. Once Zeratar entered the portal and disappeared, Raven followed suit. Before he left though, he looked back.

"Choose well, Aiden."

With that said Raven vanished into the portal. Once he disappeared the portal closed entirely. Aiden stood alone in the forest, with nothing but the sounds of birds chirping. He glanced at Warfang, the blade retracting into the figurine, Raven's last words echoing in his head.

On one hand, he had a feeling Raven was lying to him. But on the other hand the situation sounded really dire. If what he was saying was true, then everything was at risk. Everything.

"…What the hell am I gonna tell Theresa?" He asked himself as he looked up at the sky above.

No one answered him.

CHAPTER 3 - BACK TO SCHOOL

"So lemme get this straight." Liza said as she sat on an old tree log. "Raven appeared before you, fought with you, then told you about this school for mages being in trouble?"

Aiden sighed. He expected folks to doubt his story, but he thought it would be Theresa, Seamus, or even Garrett doubting him. But the three dragons didn't react the way he thought they would. Instead they were just quiet. Odd.

"Yes, Liza, it's like I said. Raven appeared before me, told me how the school for mages, Arcana, is in trouble, and claimed everything we know is at risk."

"I dunno if I would buy that, Aide." Liza frowned. "I mean, this is that jerkface Raven we're talking about. The guy and his master wanted to control the Harpy Queen because of her powers, and they weren't exactly against the idea of slaughtering some of her people when she refused."

"You think I don't know that?" Aiden said. "Liz, as much as I dislike the asshole, and as much as I want to not believe him, I saw the look in his eyes. He was genuinely worried about Arcana."

"Aide, you're missing the bigger point here." Liza interrupted. "What if this whole thing is a trap? What if he made this entire thing up just to get us there to be killed by a giant horde of monsters?"

"You think I didn't consider that?" He rubbed his forehead. "But you weren't there, Liza. You didn't hear the concern in his voice. He was upset and...genuinely worried about what could happen if the Academy is revealed."

"That or he's thinking we'll do something for him and his master!"

Liza jumped up from her tree log and landed in front of Aiden. The two of them exchanged glances with each other. Liza shook her head from side to side.

"I want to believe you, Aide. It's that jerk off that I don't trust." She said. "Even if it's true, what's stopping him from coming up from behind and stabbing us in the back after the mess is dealt with?"

"Dammit Liz! You're asking me questions I don't have the answers to!"

"Would you two please stop?" A new voice spoke up. It was Aello in her harpy form. The entire time she had been perched on a tree branch alongside her two guardians. "You've been having this same argument for at least five minutes now."

"It's not an argument!" Aiden and Liza said together. Aello tilted her head in confusion.

"It sure looks like an argument to me. If it's not an argument then how come you're still yelling?"

"That's enough, both of you."

Aiden and Liza jumped in surprise at the sound of Theresa's voice. The two of them were so into their argument they had completely forgotten that she and the other dragons were still there. The look in Theresa's eyes was stoic, and it looked like she had just reached a critical decision.

"Arcana Academy..." She mused, "Seamus, you know of this Academy do you not?"

Seamus gave a small nod towards Theresa. The second dragon took out his staff and leaned against it.

"Yes indeed, Rexkin." He said. "It is as Raven says. It's the last safe haven for human mages to live in peace. They're taught everything about the old kingdoms, magic, and the dangers of being found out by the rest of humanity before they are truly ready to know that the things in fantasy are actually real."

He turned his glance back to Aiden. A small frown came to his lips.

"It's also a place that is very strict about rules. If what Raven said is really true, that dark magic now seeps out of that place, then someone has really screwed up."

"Why's that?"

"Kiddo, let's just say that Arcana is a firm believer that all forms of dark magic, and demon summoning for that matter, is always evil. No excuses. So the only way dark magic happened in that school is either someone decided to turn against the head honcho of the place, or they decided to try something it would be completely stupid to attempt."

Aiden noticed how Seamus' grip on his staff became tighter. The green dragon didn't have the same physical strength Garrett possessed, but it was clear to see that he was bothered by the news.

"And I know a lot of good people in that Academy. None of them would use dark magic."

"Wait wait wait." Liza shouted. She was comically waving her arms back and forth in an attempt to get everyone to look at her. "How in the world do you know people in this Academy? I know you can take different human forms, but how do they even know you?"

Seamus puffed out his chest.

"I, young Liza Hollingsworth, happen to be one of the people who helped create that school. Hell, I guess you could say that I was unofficially the headmaster of the school for awhile."

"**You** were a headmaster of a school?!" Aiden and Liza asked together. They were shocked at the words coming out of Seamus' mouth. The green dragon gave them both a really perplexed look.

"Why is it that when I say I did something in my past the two of you get all bent out of shape?"

"Seamus, you DO realize that tat Aide and I are shocked to hear you did things that we don't expect from you." Liza put her hands on her hips, an annoyed look on her face. "So tell me, how is it that a flirt like you managed to get, let alone keep, that position?"

"Hey hey hey!" Seamus waved his left hand back and forth. "Just because I'm a flirt doesn't mean I ever flirted with any female mages that came to the Academy when I was there!"

Theresa and Garrett gave Seamus looks of annoyance. Garrett's was more of a 'stop lying' face while Theresa's face simply said one word. 'Really?' Seamus gave a dry chuckle at the two of them before clearing his throat.

"Seriously though, I would never do that to female students. Plus back then a lot of the students that we did have were young adults so flirting with them was not really a crime…"

"SEAMUS!" The entire group shouted together.

"All right all right!" Seamus shouted back. "I'll get to the point! Jeez you people I swear."

The green dragon cleared his throat once more. His eyes turned serious about the matter at hand.

"I believe it was back in the nineteen thirties, after the First World War. I knew that there were magically talented people in America. I could sense their magical skills with just one sniff. I knew that humanity was not truly ready for the return of magic in their lives. Especially in some of the big countries like America. This country still had trouble with certain issues that I dare not bring up here because of how sensitive they are. Imagine the uprising humanity would have had back then when those who are magically talented are exposed? You know those cases of people being burnt at the stake, being accused of witchcraft? Well that was one of the possibilities that could have happened."

Seamus sighed as he looked up at the sky for a moment. Then he turned his attention back towards his friends.

"I, a dragon, knew all too well that they needed a safe haven to hide. It was the only chance that they really had to not only stay safe, but to also learn that their gift was not a curse. So I began to do what had to be done. I began to gather resources, and called a few people up for certain favors that they owed me, and found a building where no one would even expect magical arts being practiced. After that, I began looking for those who were interested in learning to master their powers."

"I can guess they were really shocked to find out that you were a giant flying fire breathing lizard." Liza said with a tiny smile.

"I admit, there were some complications when they found out I was a dragon." Seamus said. "But that didn't stop them from wanting to learn. I didn't pick humans that wanted to expose what they could do for their own personal gain. I picked humans that were naturally curious, who wanted to know if magic truly existed."

With a twirl of his staff Seamus created a magical mirror into his past. It revealed him in his true form, as a dragon, behind four people in cloaks. Aiden couldn't make out their facial features as the hoods of their cloaks covered their faces quite well.

"The first four, who later became the ones who ran the school after I left, became known as the Arcane Masters. A title I gave them because they were my first students in the magical arts. After they learned from me, I gave them a simple mission. Find those who were talented, or had hidden talent, in the magic arts and bring them to the Academy." Seamus had a small smile of pride on his lips. It didn't take eagle eyes to see that he was proud of the four students he had trained.

"Needless to say the four of them were very good at finding new students and they taught them quite well. Hell, that school has been around for so long that it amazes me that it didn't have an incident before this." He held his chin with his left hand. "But why in the world would the Grand Mage allow this to happen to the Academy?"

"If our time being warriors has taught us anything, Seamus, it's that peace does not last forever." Theresa said. The leader of the small group stood up from where she was sitting and dispelled the magical mirror. "Time changes everything. The current Grand Mage might not have the same views as those from the past Grand Mages."

"Then what the hell do we do?" Liza asked. "This Academy isn't in our state, and we can't just vanish on our parents for this."

"We can have magic clones take our place when we're away." Theresa said. "I don't know how long we'll be gone though. I doubt we can get this mission done before summer ends." She folded her arms across her chest. "It all depends on how bad the situation has gotten in Arcana."

"And from what Raven told me, it sounds really bad." Aiden mused. "Theresa, we need to do something. If we don't, you guys are at risk of being exposed!"

"Calm yourself, welp." Garrett finally spoke. The sound of his booming voice was enough to catch everyone off guard. "Information might travel faster in this age than it ever has before, but we will be able to adjust to changes if worst comes to worst. Besides, maybe it's time the rest of your kind actually learns that you're not the only sentient life forms on this planet."

"Garrett!" Theresa and Seamus snapped.

Aiden and Liza rolled their eyes as another argument began. Aello and her guardians looked on as the three dragons bickered amongst themselves.

"Why does the big headed dragon like to start things like that?" Mia asked in confusion.

"Let's just say that Garrett has a slight bias against humans that he won't let go of because he's a butt." Liza answered.

"I'll second that." Aiden agreed.

Mia quirked an eyebrow at their answers before shrugging her shoulders. She began to groom Aello's left wing carefully. Gabriella just scoffed in annoyance at the dragon's arguing. Aello though, was in deep thought as she scratched her chin. Aiden could have sworn he was seeing the gears in her head spin as she considered the risk of the Academy being discovered if left unchecked.

"I...I think we should go today." She said. "If things are that bad it can't be ignored."

Theresa snapped her fingers to gather everyone's attention. Aiden noticed that Garrett looked like he had a few lumps on the top of his head. Theresa probably whacked him pretty hard on the head during the argument.

"Aello is right." She said. "This is something that we cannot ignore. Action must be taken. The risk of the magic being discovered now is too great."

"Then what's the plan?" Aiden asked.

Theresa turned to Seamus and gave him a short nod. The green dragon didn't need to respond with words as he took his staff out and began to chant in the draconic language.

"Seamus will conjure up a portal that will allow us to travel to the academy. At the most we have at least a whole day to fix the mess that's within it."

"But what about our parents?" Liza asked. "We can't be gone for more than twenty four hours!"

"Calm yourself, Liza." Theresa gave a small smile. "If I know how mages are, they will have already cast a spell over their academy to make time slower there than outside the school."

"Wait, what?" Aiden and Liza asked together.

"It's complicated magic, whelps." Garrett said suddenly. "For the sake of keeping your mind at ease, let's say that the magic makes a single minute there feel like a day."

Both Aiden and Liza looked dumbfounded. There was magic that could do that? The sudden urge to keep Arcana safe from the rest of the world was now more apparent than before. That kind of magic would be extremely dangerous in the hands of the wrong people.

"Wait a minute." Aiden frowned. "How come you never told me about this spell before?"

"What do you mean?" Theresa responded.

"It's just that when we were searching for Garrett, you had us fly over several states and land in a random forest. How come you didn't use a Teleport spell?"

"That's a different situation in itself, Kiddo." Seamus explained. "See, teleport spells don't lock onto a person's location. Only a location that the user is aware of. If Theresa and I knew Garrett's exact spot a year ago I would have used the spell right then and there to find him. But since our big lug tends to wander around you can never truly know where he'll be at any given time."

"In other words, you can only use the Teleport spell for locations you are aware of?" Liza asked.

"Yes, and no." Seamus frowned. "That's where it gets tricky. Teleports can only work if a certain area has a strong enough presence of magic in the area to allow teleportation. That happens when someone with enough mana leaves behind a considerable amount of it for those with the Teleportation spell to lock onto, almost like a homing beacon."

"So...it's like fast travel in Aiden's game?" Aello asked. Aiden felt himself tensing up at the mention of his game, but also proud that Aello had made the obvious inference.

He still was a bit sore about her deleting his saved game though.

"In a way? Yes." Seamus replied. "And before you ask about how it is that Dimitri and Raven are capable of doing that without such a spell, the answer is kinda simple. Dark Magic gets around those requirements by paying a very big price. Though with the way Dimitri seems to be able to appear anywhere he wants, it's like he's broken even those rules somehow given the power he seems to have."

With a flick of his left wrist, Seamus fired out a small bolt of lighting into the air as a tear began to form. Aiden knew right away that this was the very same Teleport spell he was telling the group about a few moments ago.

As the portal began to grow in front of Seamus, the group gathered behind the green dragon. It was like a mini vacuum of sorts as it began to pull the group towards the portal as it grew in size. The portal itself had a greenish hue of sorts on the outer rim, while the inside of the portal looked dark green, with possibly no end in sight. Aiden felt a lump in his throat grow before he swallowed it.

"Listen up!" Theresa shouted over the howling wind of the portal. "This portal is like traveling at the speed of sound! It will feel like your body is being stretched beyond its limits, but don't let that fool you! That is just how your mind perceives it! But whatever you do, do not try to move as the portal teleports you! If you move even one muscle, you could disrupt the portal and end up in an entirely different location!"

As she finished speaking the portal completely opened up in front of them. The energy that the portal was exerting was immense. While the vacuum like feeling Aiden felt before was great, it wasn't enough to suck the group up on its own. Theresa placed a hand on Aiden's shoulder. He could tell that her grip was strong enough to keep him close to her should he start to drift away.

Liza and Aello stood by each other as well, the former grabbing onto the wrist of the latter with all the strength she could muster. Mia and Gabriella weren't too far behind their princess though glaring at Liza for taking their princess' wrist so brazenly. If they could shoot daggers from their eyes they would. Garrett meanwhile stood perfectly still, his eyes closed. Seamus stopped his chanting as he pulled his staff up and spoke a single word.

"Teleport!"

It all happened within the blink of an eye. The portal pulled them from their feet, and into its gaping maw. It happened so fast, Aiden didn't have time to even feel his feet leave the ground! None of them could utter so much as a gasp of shock before they were pulled right into the portal as it sealed itself away.

Soaring through the portal's strange, unearthly depths, Aiden could scarcely understand his surroundings. At best, he could describe it as a tunnel, a swirling green amalgam of countless different locations, some familiar, some indescribable. And as more flew by, they seemed to be gathering speed.

Theresa was right about one thing. His entire body felt like it was being stretched, torn beyond what should have been possible. Though she'd said it was simply an illusion, he could swear his legs had stretched several feet longer. His muscles felt stiff and unresponsive, displaced from where they should be.

The feeling of his muscles not responding would continue for at least a few seconds. At the very end, he could see it. A bright light. That had to be the ending of the portal's seemingly endless tunnel. Once more his mind must have been playing a trick on him. It seemed the portal's end looked like it was miles away. Aiden wanted to grit his teeth, move his muscles, do something while flying through the vacuum of the portal. He just wanted it to finally come to a stop so that they could arrive.

And then within a matter of five seconds, the end finally arrived. The portal's end had opened up in front of Arcana Academy. When they arrived, the group's feet returned to solid ground below them. Each of them was in a completely different state.

The three dragons were fine. There was absolutely no change to their facial expressions. All of them just seemed rather annoyed with the portal, but not bothered by the effects it caused. Aello and her guardians were trembling from the intense force of the magic they had just experienced. Mia clung to Elizabeth's arm, shaking like a leaf, as her eyes were as wide as saucer plates.

Aello was far better off than either of her guardians. While she still was trembling, her wings were the one body part that trembled the most. The princess clenched and unclenched her talons into the ground as she took in a deep breath of air.

Liza's eyes could have spun out her head with how much they were twirling. Her body wasn't trembling like Aello's but it was clear to see that the portal's travel speeds affected her as well. She promptly fell onto her rear end the moment her feet touched the ground.

Aiden didn't have the dizzy eyes like Liza, but he did have the trembling body and muscles like Aello. He would have toppled over onto his hands and knees, but Theresa's firm grip held him in place.

"That. Was. Crazy." Aello suddenly spoke out. "I think my eyes are about to explode from how fast we were travelling in that...THING."

"Heh, sorry, I kinda forgot to mention that the first time you travel through a portal it's a very tiring experience." Seamus said with a cheesy grin. "But if it makes you feel any better, everyone that uses a portal feels like that the first time around."

"H-How come we didn't just fly?" Mia asked. Her body still trembling.

"This school isn't anywhere near Virginia." Seamus explained. "Hell, we're in one of California's cities. Los Angeles."

Aiden and Liza immediately stared at Seamus with shock in their eyes. Los Angeles? They were in freaking Los Angeles? The look in their eyes didn't go unnoticed by Seamus and the other dragons.

"What? You're surprised that we're here of all places?"

"Why in the world would you establish a school in California?!" Aiden and Liza asked at the same time.

"Simple. It's the most obvious place to hide a school for magical people."

Theresa rolled her eyes at Seamus statement. Before Aiden and Liza could continue to ask questions though, the white dragoness snapped her fingers to get everyone's attention.

"Enough. We've already wasted time talking." She turned her attention to Seamus. "Get us into the school, Seamus. The sooner we enter the school the better."

Seamus nodded slowly as he turned towards the front door of the academy. The green dragon sighed as he walked ahead of the group. Aiden frowned but followed after Seamus with Liza. Both of them would have preferred to get answers as to why the school was located in California of all places, but Theresa was right. They had already wasted enough time coming to an agreement to help the school.

A few tense seconds passed as they approached the door. The doors slowly opened for the group. At first, Aiden only saw a regular waiting room and a table with a single person, a young woman with glasses, sitting at said desk, typing away at a computer. Aiden turned to Seamus, an eyebrow quirked at the seemingly ordinary room. The green dragon didn't respond as he continued to approach the desk.

"Excuse me, miss?" Seamus spoke out. "I'm here to take a look at some of the classrooms?"

"Do you have an appointment?" The woman asked, her voice a bit nasally.

"Er, not really." Seamus responded. "We're kind walk on students, if that makes sense."

"If you don't have an appointment, then you can't apply to the school. Please move along now. We're not accepting applications right now anyway."

Seamus sighed as he leaned forward on the desk. Aiden thought at first that he was planning to hit on the woman, but the next moment completely caught him off guard. The green dragon's eyes, though naturally friendly, or in the case for women that he eyed flirty, turned dead serious.

"Our true bonds are the source of our strength." He said. "The source of how we control the magic that flows through our veins. Should I forsake these bonds…"

The woman at the desk looked up in shock at Seamus. She removed her glasses slowly, and then nodded her head once at him.

"Then I give up the title of mage." She said. Aiden took notice that her nasally voice was gone. Slowly she stood up. "How is it that you know the creed of mages?"

Seamus smiled at the woman.

"Come on now, did the Grand Enchanter not teach you how this school was founded? Who it was that taught the mages the creed in the first place?"

The woman gasped right before she bowed her head to Seamus. The green dragon cleared his throat though as she kept her head lowered.

"Forgive me, I did not think you were still alive, Dragon of Magic."

"Well, the last time I visited this place was at least a few years ago." Seamus admitted. "Anyway, lass, we need to get into the Academy. We've heard that there's a problem here and we need to get it fixed as soon as possible."

"I…I don't know what you mean, sir."

"Don't play dumb with me." Seamus' eyes narrowed. "We

were told by a former student of this Academy that something has gone horribly wrong, and it's taking every last ounce of magical power to maintain the beasts within. If the situation isn't taken care of now? You can kiss this pretty job good bye. Along with the secrecy of the hidden world."

The woman went dead quiet for several seconds. With a heavy sigh she snapped her fingers once. A large red book slowly floated over towards her. Once the book was in her hands, she opened it up to a page number that was too fast for Aiden to read.

"Mineos Tyra." She said.

At the command of those words, a new door slowly revealed itself to the group. It formed from the very wall itself, like it had been camouflaged the entire time. The door was tall, dark blue, and had golden door knobs in the shape of a wizard's staff. The outer rims of the door were also painted a golden color as well. The door itself was quite a magnificent sight to behold.

"The head of our Academy is beyond these doors with the students who managed to get away." She turned back towards Seamus. "Great Green Dragon, if you and your friends can fix this mess we have gotten ourselves into, please do so soon."

Seamus didn't answer. All he did was simply nod his head once to her before walking towards the door. Something about Seamus seemed different to Aiden. He no longer had the joking persona he would usually have, or even the flirting persona he wore even more often. He seemed extremely serious about the situation.

As Seamus grabbed the door knob, he slowly pulled the doors open. A bright light shown from the door. As the light enveloped him, he turned towards the group. He beckoned them to follow after him.

"Ladies and gentlemen, it's time that we head back to school."

With that said, Seamus entered the door, disappearing into

the light. Before Aiden or Liza could say something, Theresa pushed them both gently from behind into the door. The bright light wasn't as bad as the portal, but it did hurt his eyes for a moment.

The light slowly began to die down, allowing Aiden's eyes to readjust once more. What he saw made his mouth drop. The inside of the Academy was far larger than he could have imagined it to be. He turned to Seamus, who smiled playfully at his shock.

"What do you think, kiddo? Does my school impress you?"

CHAPTER 4 - THE GRAND MAGE

The real main hall of Arcana Academy was by far the most impressive main hall that Aiden had ever seen in his life. All over the hallway tomes were floating, each one a different color that resembled the type of magic they were affiliated with. Spiral stairways lead to several different floors. Each one with different rooms. Many of them being either classrooms, from what Aiden could tell, or libraries for different spells. The golden color of the door that lead them into the main hall was also present in the main hallway.

It was also the color for the hand rails for the stairs. It decorated the book shelves with the same color that were on each floor. Bright gold. The actual stairs themselves were colored a silvery color. Aiden could have sworn that each step that as each step was taken on the stairs they actually lit up.

Perhaps the biggest surprise of the Arcana Academy's main hall was the star like ceiling above their heads. Each major constellation hung over their heads, shining brightly with amazement. There were a few of them that Aiden didn't even recognize, like one that looked like a dragon's head.

"Look at this place!" Aiden whispered to Liza. "All the gold, all the books, and the ceiling looks amazing!"

"Aide, not now." Liza whispered back.

Before he could ask why, Liza pointed ahead of her. Aiden turned his head towards where she was pointing and immediately wished that he hadn't looked. Several body bags were in front of them. Each one attended to by what Aiden had to guess was a student or a teacher of the Academy. Many of them looked young, too young, to be attending to the injured and dead bodies that littered the floor.

The students, from what Aiden could tell, were all his age. A few of them looked like they were in their late teens though. All of them wore casual modern day clothes as well too. There weren't any long robes or frilly dresses that most mages were associated with in fictional stories. Many of them wore regular jean pants and short sleeved, and sometimes long sleeved, shirts. The ratio ranged from several young men and many young women. In fact the amount of female students greatly outnumbered the male students.

Aiden and Liza both looked surprised at what they saw. Even the harpies, who grew up in a colony of nothing but females, was also surprised to see that the female ratio was greater than the male ratio. Though the students didn't notice them at first, the three confused younger members of the group turned to Seamus.

"What's up?" He asked, nonchalant like.

"How…how come there's more female students than male students?" Aiden asked.

"Oh. That? Well let's just say that when it comes to humans the females tend to be more in tune with the magical energies than the males." Seamus explained. "That doesn't mean that there aren't a lot of male mages around though. It's just that females have a much easier time becoming mages."

"Heh, I guess that's something else women can be better at than men." Liza said.

"Liza, not now." Theresa ordered. "We're here to fix a problem, not learn why the female student body is larger than the male student body."

Liza nodded her head before turning back to the students. Many of them now had their attention. Most of them looked confused while others had looks of mistrust on their faces. Aiden took notice that several of the mages had grabbed ahold of the staffs that laid beside them.

One of the students, a young woman with short brown hair and brown eyes, wearing a sleeveless red tank top and blue jean shorts, stepped towards the group. Her magical staff, with a purple gem in the top piece, spinning behind her. Even though he was not incredibly gifted with magic, Aiden could sense that she alone was enough to outclass him in magical combat.

Thankfully for him though, Seamus was there with the group.

"Hold, apprentice." He ordered. "We're not your enemies here."

"Give me one good reason not to blast you into ashes right now." She responded, aiming her staff's tip towards Seamus.

"I'd put that down, if I were you." Seamus replied, looking rather displeased. "You don't know who you point that staff at."

The young woman growled as she swung her staff at Seamus' head. The green dragon could have avoided the hit with a quick dodge, but instead his eyes turned bright white. An unseen force field rose up around Seamus, knocking the attack from the young mage away slightly.

She looked up at Seamus in confusion for a brief moment, but then began to charge at him once more with more staff swings. Each time the force field would block any of those attacks and force the mage away from the group. The frustration that was building up in her eyes was clear to see. Meanwhile Seamus' serious look remained on his face.

"Who. Are. YOU?" The mage asked as she took her staff and fired out a blast of magical fire towards Seamus.

Once again Seamus did not move as the blast of magic came towards him. The moment the attack came close enough to hit him; the green dragon summoned his own staff. Aiden let a small smile come to his face as he watched Seamus take his weapon and blocked the flames with just the very tip of his staff. The blast's direction was re-aimed towards the ceiling of the main hall. The moment the blast hit the ceiling the magical energies that created the fire blast began to dispel.

Aiden and Liza's jaws dropped to the ground.

"How in the..." Liza started.

"That, my friends, is one of the perks about this academy. The ceiling is able to dispel any spells that go out of control, it keeps the magic within from escaping or destroying the school." Seamus said, "The entire school is made up of magical energies like this as well. Though if it was at maximum power, we wouldn't have to be here right now."

He turned his attention back to the young woman.

"You there. You have some power in your attacks, that's a good quality to have in your spells. However, you put too much into one attack." He smiled. "That one blast took a lot of your mana, didn't it?"

"How...how did you..." The young woman asked. It was then Aiden realized that she was indeed tired from using her attack like that.

"How did I know?" Seamus finished her question. "Simple, I taught that lesson to the very first few Grand Mages of this academy a very long time ago. I'm surprised that no one has enforced that lesson on you newbies."

The young woman's angry look was immediately replaced by a look of shock at those words. Several of the students stood up at those words. Many of them began to murmur amongst themselves for a few seconds. The young woman's eyes however never left the eyes of Seamus.

"Are you saying that you are..."

"You got it." Seamus replied, stopping her question halfway. "I'm the Spellweaver, the one who helped establish this fine Academy itself."

The students all blinked in amazement at that. Some of them even tried to kneel down on one knee towards him. The young woman that had attacked Seamus also bowed her head in respect.

"Forgive me, Sir." She said. "It's just that we are all high strung right now. "

"I gathered that from the attacks." Seamus frowned. "I did not come here to merely visit this school you know. We've been tipped off from a source that this school is facing a great problem right now. One that requires the attention of me and my associates."

The look on the woman's face turned pale at those words. Seamus walked up towards her and placed a hand on her shoulder.

"Tell me, young one. What the hell happened at this academy?"

"I believe I can answer that." A new voice suddenly said from one of the upper levels of the main hall.

Aiden, along with the rest of the group, glanced up towards where the voice had come from. The owner of the voice actually fit the image of what Aiden thought a mage would be, in this case it was more stereotypical than the students' outfits.

The voice's owner was an older man, perhaps in his late forties or early fifties. There seemed to be an air of power about him, as the edges of his dark cerulean robe wafted in some unseen, unfelt breeze. His pale green eyes were narrowed, gleaming with power that could be felt in a stare. A simple glance into his eyes and Aiden felt his body going numb. There was no doubt about it: this man's magical powers were immense, something not to be trifled with.

Aiden managed to tear his eyes away from the man's gaze. Instead, he caught sight of the man's staff, a strange, garish weapon that seemed unworldly in its design. A staff made of meticulously blended silver and gold, capped by a bizarre ornament: a golden tome, decorated in a number of sparkling gems. Each glittering in the dark, humming with mystical energies. Aiden swallowed nervously. His hunch was correct: no normal man could wield an instrument of such power

"G-Grand Mage Ivan!" The young woman cried out.

"That is enough, Rebecca." The Grand Mage said. "Allow me to explain to our guests what has happened here."

Before Rebecca could respond, Ivan disappeared from where he stood. It took Aiden and Liza a few seconds to figure out that he had teleported in front of the group. Seamus didn't seem too impressed at the magic from the Grand Mage though. Instead he just stared directly at Ivan with narrowed eyes.

"I must admit, I did not expect that you would appear in this school once more." Ivan said slowly. "The last time you visited our school was quite some time ago, wasn't it sir? I was still a young mage that was the best of his class."

"Young, good, and arrogant." Seamus responded. "I am surprised to see that you are the Grand Mage here, Ivan."

Ivan gave a short laugh as he shook his head.

"Let's just say that I stayed after graduation, I wanted to pass skills down to the next generation of mages. As you can see, I have turned this academy into something even greater than when it was started."

Aiden couldn't put his finger on it, but part of Seamus felt like it was trying his best not to attack Ivan in anger. Something about the way the two interacted seemed to indicate that they were not on the best of terms. Aiden swallowed a lump in his throat as Seamus and Ivan shared looks with one another.

"What happened to the old Grand Mage?" Seamus asked. "Last time I checked Gerald was still healthy."

"I'm afraid that's no longer the case, Seamus." Ivan responded.

"Grand Mage Gerald fell ill a few years ago. Sadly he is no longer with us."

"…I see." Seamus closed his eyes. "He was a good man, and a wise leader. If memory serves correctly, he was a fine student as well."

"That he was." Ivan turned. "Come, you and your associates will learn what is happening in my office."

Seamus gave a slow nod to Ivan as he walked away from the group. Theresa and Aiden shared the same concerned frown as their friend watched Ivan walk away. Even Garrett showed some worry for the green dragon. It wasn't like Seamus to be so hostile to someone, or rather not trusting of them right away.

"Is there something you want to tell us, Seamus?" Theresa asked.

"…Rexkin." Seamus spoke in their draconic tongue, "Gan ot ki fraw kalen."

No one asked what he said. It was clear that Seamus felt like the Grand Mage was a colossal fool.

Despite that feeling of distrust for the Grand Mage, they did follow after Ivan to his quarters. The entire time, the students looked down at the ground. Almost as if they were ashamed. Aiden wanted to ask them if there was anything really wrong, but every time he tried to speak out to one mage, that mage would turn away from him.

One thing was for certain, these mages were not the trusting kind. It was either that or they were ordered not to talk to outsiders. Liza quirked her eyebrows at how some of them didn't even bother trying to talk to them. They were either tending to their own wounds, the wounded, or looking through large tomes of spells.

"And I thought high school life looked rough." She muttered to Aiden.

"No kidding." Aiden muttered back. "This guy must not allow a lot of free time here."

Finally they arrived at the Grand Mage's office. It was by far the most orderly kept room in the Academy that Aiden would come across in his time in Arcana Academy. Unlike the unruly main hall, which to be fair was only unruly because of how disastrous the situation was, the office of Grand Mage Ivan had kept several tomes in the book shelves, all in alphabetical order, and several jars holding body parts of different creatures were on the lower levels of the book shelves. These jars contained jaws of manticores, wings of Hornet Men, feet of goblins, and several heads of demons that Aiden had never encountered before.

The wall behind Ivan's desk were several different staffs. Each one was made out of a different material. There was a wooden staff, an iron staff, a gold staff, a black staff, and a platinum staff. Each staff was decorated with different jewels, but unlike Ivan's staff they all kept one singular color. The wooden staff had emeralds, the iron staff had topazes, the gold staff had sapphires, and the platinum staff had rubies.

The desk was also another very large decoration for the room as well. It was made of mahogany and had a green marble top. On the top of the desk were several more tomes, all kept in neatly order, and a few more jars with several other creatures, tiny ones that Aiden didn't recognize, floating. The one that caught his attention the most though, was a dragon tooth in one of them.

Ivan took his seat behind his desk before snapping his fingers. Several chairs formed out of midair for the group. The entire time Seamus kept his eyes on Ivan, before eventually taking a seat.

"I do hope you find this an acceptable place for us to discuss matters." Ivan said coolly. Aiden's neck hair stood up on edge at the sound of his voice.

"You've redecorated." Seamus said quietly. "You made this office more orderly, less inspirational."

"Order keeps thing in check, Spellweaver."

"And order also keeps inspiration and creativity down."

The room felt like it had gotten a lot colder than it had already felt before. The tension was so thick that it felt that all it took to start an argument was something stupid said by either of them.

"We can discuss my methods of being Grand Mage later." Ivan finally said. "What matters is, that we are in desperate need of your assistance, Dragon of Magic."

"I've heard that there's a situation here." Seamus replied. "Don't look so surprised, one of your old students found out that this school is in danger of being exposed."

Seamus pointed towards Aiden with his thumb.

"The kiddo here was told by that said student. Let's just say that he and this old student have a rivalry of sorts. And that said old student actually wants to make sure that the secrets of the old world don't get out."

Ivan slowly turned his attention to Aiden. The latter felt like he was suddenly put on the spot as the Grand Mage examined him carefully. Aiden felt his palms getting damp with sweat. But he kept his composure as Ivan continued to watch him closely.

"You look familiar, boy..." He mused, "Did you attend this school before?"

Aiden blinked a couple of times at that question. Even Theresa looked confused at that statement.

"Um, no sir." Aiden responded. "This is my first time being here."

"I see, did this old student mention any other details?"

"Cut the crap, Ivan." Seamus suddenly said with a dark tone. "I didn't come here to play games, I want you to tell me exactly what the hell you were doing that causes demons running amok in the halls of the academy."

Ivan turned his eyes back to Seamus. The Grand Mage could have given Seamus a dark scowl, but he didn't. Instead he simply nodded as he leaned back in his chair.

"Very well, you deserve to know what has happened. After all, Great Dragon, you helped create this established school."

Ivan snapped his fingers as several tomes flew out from the book shelves. Each one was entitled 'The Study of Demons' with several volume numbers. The tomes gently floated down onto the table. As they landed, Ivan took the first volume as he opened it.

"One of the lessons we were taught was that to use demonic magic was giving yourself over to demons themselves. Becoming corrupt with their evil influence to the point where we could be controlled by them. But yet two mages are now running out in the open world with control over their own personal demons." Ivan said. "We don't know how they are able to do it, but the demons they summon have not completely destroyed their minds."

"You attempted to control demons..." Seamus said quietly. "A foolish mistake, Ivan."

"We came so close, Seamus. We came close to achieving this goal." Ivan continued. "We knew the risks, we knew that trying to control demons without resorting to dark magic was a foolish mistake, but we had to take that risk."

"Do you mind telling me why?" Theresa suddenly asked out. "If you're the Grand Mage of this Academy, than you should know that demons only answer to those who allow dark magic to run through their veins. Like Dimitri and his apprentice."

Ivan sighed as he rubbed his fore brow with his left index finger and thumb. The frustration was building up greatly within the Grand Mage.

"We had our reasons, young lady." He resumed. "For thousands of years we were taught that the ability to control demons was an act of evil. An art of magic that was forbidden from all to learn. But yet there have always existed demon mages, who command the utmost loyalty from the demonic beasts that they summon to their side. How did they do it? Without falling to the temptation of the demons they summon? We had to find the answer."

The Grand Mage turned to a picture frame on his table. He smiled a bit as he brought it forth with just a motion of his right index finger. Seamus quirked an eyebrow as Ivan took hold of the picture fame in his hands.

"My youngest of my two sons, Lewis, is gifted in many ways. While others might see him as someone who is, for lack of a better word, not right in the head he has a hidden brilliance to him that people do not understand." Ivan closed his eyes. "He volunteered for a project that we called, Project Overmind."

"Pardon?" Liza suddenly asked. "Did you just say that your special needs kid volunteered for a dangerous project?"

"Liza!" Aello gasped in shock.

"What? I'm not condemning the kid!" She glared back over to Ivan. "I'm asking a legitimate question about using someone who has a disorder for something like some kind of project to control demons!"

Ivan glared right back at Liza as his left hand clenched itself tightly. A magical bubble appeared over Liza's head. Her reaction to the bubble was one that anyone would have done as she tried shouting loudly. But the bubble kept the noise from escaping, completely making Liza's voice, for the moment, mute.

Aello and Aiden tried to help pop the bubble open with the tips of their weapons, but the bubble would not pop. Even Gabriella and Mia attempted to pop the bubble around her her but their sharp talons weren't enough to destroy it. Liza continued to shout, using her hands as a way to communicate with them.

"I did not ask for your judgment, **girl**." Ivan said coldly. "I know very well that I was putting my son in great risk for the project. I would suggest that you keep that mouth of yours shut or I will leave that bubble around your head forever."

"That's enough, Ivan." Seamus barked. Small flames erupted from nostrils. "Let the girl breathe."

Ivan scoffed as he motioned his hand once. The bubble surrounding Liza's head suddenly popping quite quickly. Aiden and Aello both kept Liza from falling over from the sudden lack of air. Needless to say, Liza was not happy with what happened. She began reaching for Gitanel on her hip, but her right wrist was grabbed by Theresa before she could do so.

"Don't." She said sternly. "Ivan is beyond any of you three in power. Let Seamus and us handle this."

Liza let out a small growl of frustration, but nodded her head in reluctance. Aiden couldn't blame her though. Ivan had just humiliated her in a very embarrassing way.

"As I was saying, Project Overmind was a project to attempt to control the demons without resorting to dark magic." Ivan said. "Our recent studies of demons from old tomes and from recent discoveries shows that many demons, like the Wall Demons, share the same mind pattern of say an ant colony or a bee hive. Where they are all drones taking orders from one source. In the case of the ants and bees, it's their queens. For demons, there is something called the Overmind for each species of lower class demon. The humanoid or giant ones you see don't require Overminds to keep things in order you see, it's the beast like ones that require someone to direct them."

Ivan turned a page in one of his tomes with his magic. The page that he stopped at revealed notes on the project and what Aiden expected to be what the Overmind was meant to look like. Though it was completely blotched out by what looked like a giant ink spill.

"This, was to be our Overmind. The image, as you can see here, is gone due to an accidental spill of ink, but the main purpose of the project was to not control entirely, but to direct the demons away from settlements. With enough magic, it was possible to achieve this. No mages would be at risk and we would have a way to combat against the demons without risking the lives of those who have the talent to become mages."

The Grand Mage closed the tome with a small 'slam.' The anger and frustration that built up from within him beginning to boil over quietly.

"But something went wrong. Lewis is still in the room that we began the project, and now shadow demons have begun taking over each section of the school piece by bloody piece."

Seamus sighed as he rubbed his forehead. The story weighing heavily on his mind now.

"The only thing keeping them from entering the main hall is a spell I put up. It will hold them back, but I have a feeling that the Overmind that we've created will eventually find a way around that barrier. And when that barrier falls, then this entire school is lost."

"And the world will know about magic." Seamus finished. "Ivan, this is probably the biggest mistake that this school has ever made, trying to control demons with a mock Overmind, but we can argue about the ethics later."

He stood up from his chair. Ivan watched carefully as Seamus clenched and unclenched his hands back and forth.

"Right now, we have something more important to deal with. So get up out of that chair, Ivan. You're going to lower that barrier and let us deal with the problem that you created."

CHAPTER 5 - ENTERING HELL

"*Y*ou want me to do WHAT?" Ivan asked hoarsely. "Do you have a death wish, you fool? Why in the world would I allow you to venture into the Academy when there are thousands of demons within the walls?"

"You heard me." Seamus replied. "You're taking that barrier down, we're entering the Academy, and we will make certain that the demons that you brought here will be destroyed."

"Um, Seamus?" Aiden suddenly spoke out. "How do you think we'll stop them? They could literally be hundreds of them within the school."

"Ah now that, my young kiddo, is a very good point." Seamus replied. "But I know just what exactly the main problem is. You see, what the mages did here was create a fake Overmind. Now despite the fact that this thing they made is not right, but they did manage to get one key aspect of the Overmind right. It controls and creates the demons in the school now. Destroy the Overmind, and those demons will disappear completely."

He turned back to face Ivan now.

"But so long as this man right here has his barrier up to

keep the demons from escaping, we can't enter the Academy to make our way to the room where the Overmind has taken root. And just as with bees and ants, you kill the main source of the infestation. In this case, it's the Overmind. Once that's taken care of, the rest of the demons here will either die off instantly or will retreat back into the shadows."

Seamus folded his arms across his chest and looked down on the Grand Mage. Ivan's eyes narrowed in anger before he stood up from his chair. The hair on the back of Aiden's neck seemed to rise up from the intense pressure of magical energy that came from Ivan. As if he was greatly insulted and wanted to show just how upset he truly was.

Thankfully, Theresa was there with the group. Aiden noticed that she immediately stood up from her chair as smoke from her nostrils.

"Enough. Grand Mage." She said with a deep growl in her throat. "You are to do what Seamus has ordered you to do. The six of us will enter the Academy, and we will undo the problem that has befallen this Academy."

Ivan's eyes darted back towards Theresa. The pressure that he was giving off slowly began to die down as he stared right into her eyes. Seamus glanced back to Theresa, than right back to Ivan.

"I suggest you listen to her." He said. "You see, I have some patience when it comes to waiting for you to agree. But this young woman right here? She's the white dragoness. My superior. And when she wants something done, she will see it done. So either you undo the barrier that you've put up and allow us to go in, or she will find a way to take it down herself. And trust me when I tell you, you don't want my Rexkin to lose her patience."

Ivan growled in frustration, but eventually let out a sigh of defeat as he began to nod his head. It seemed like the group had reached an agreement with the Grand Mage that felt like it could have turned into a long drawn out argument, and time was not on their side, even with the magic energies that slowed time down in the school.

"Very well." Ivan said. "You are twisting my arm here, dragons. But I shall lower the barrier that protects what remains of my students and teachers. But know this, when I put the barrier back up I will not lower it until you have defeated the Overmind. I suggest you gather supplies from us here before you head off into what has become a hell on earth."

"Supplies?" Aello asked.

"Yes. Supplies, harpy." Ivan answered, though his tone towards her sounded rather bigoted. "You will not survive long in the halls of the academy without food, water, and even some potions."

"This doesn't sound like a video game at all." Aiden thought in the back of his mind. There were multiple role-playing video games that had the scenario that he had found himself in.

"Hey!" Liza suddenly spoke out. "I would not talk to Aello like that you jerk!"

"She's not just some kind of regular harpy!" Mia added as her feathers ruffled up. "She's one of the princesses and you will show her the respect she deserves!"

Ivan scoffed as he promptly ignored the cries from the two of them. Liza gritted her teeth in anger as she reached for Gitanel once again at the actions of the Grand Mage. However Theresa shot her a look.

"Liza. Hush." Theresa ordered. Liza grumbled under her breath as she folded her arms.

Aiden fully expected Ivan to put another magic bubble around Liza's head like last time, but luckily for her that wasn't the case as he left his office. Seamus kept his eyes on Ivan the entire time, before taking a deep breath of air and sighing out of frustration.

"I know this is a very strange situation to be in right now, but wait for me to explain to all of you why I don't trust him." He said. "This is not the place to speak of such reasons."

The rest of the group gave Seamus a simple nod. Without saying another word the green dragon left the room to follow Ivan. With nothing left for them in the Grand Mage's room, the team left it. They had a long trial ahead of them. One that would test their very limits.

Several of the students watched them wait in one area together as Ivan fetched the supplies for them. Aiden took notice that several of the students seemed almost too intimidated by them to even approach. He wasn't the only one that took notice of this attitude either. Seamus had been watching the students very carefully ever since Ivan left.

"You know that none of you have any real reason to fear us." He said to the students watching them. "I don't know why all of you are looking at us like we're about to suddenly attack you for no reason."

"They're not afraid." Garrett said. "They're watching us, making sure that we don't do anything that they could use to justify a reason to not trust us."

"In other words, Ivan must have taught them that outsiders are too dangerous to trust." Seamus' face contorted to one of disgust. "Dammit. That is no way to live a life. To never trust anyone? When we made this school we made sure that the students understood that their entire lives did not have to be completely tied to this Academy. Only that they learn about their abilities and how to control them without being exposed."

"And Ivan didn't seem like the kind of Grand Mage that would hold those ideals." Theresa said. "I don't know how he came to be the leader of this Academy, but I hope for the sake of the students here he knows what he's doing."

Aiden sighed as he listened to the dragons go on about the

Grand Mage and the way the students were acting towards them. He had to admit that while the Academy was in shambles, things were not what he expected them to be. Sure the school was probably the only school in the world where he would willingly go if he ever got the chance to. But on the other hand, to be told to never trust anyone from the outside would be an absolute hell.

Rebecca, the girl from before, was the only one who did not seem intimidated by their presence. In fact, she was the only one that got up the nerve to approach them.

Seamus quirked an eyebrow as she approached them.

"What do you want, little one?" He asked. "I thought your Grand Mage ordered you to not talk with us."

"To hell with what the Grand Mage ordered." Rebecca replied. "The school hasn't been the same ever since he took over."

The tone in Rebecca's voice was not like it once was before. Instead of respect that she should have had for the Grand Mage, it was filled with contempt and resentment.

"Listen to me. You must put an end to this. While the Grand Mage does nothing but have us sit behind this barrier he put up the demons inside the Academy are growing stronger and stronger. Soon enough, one of them will be strong enough to destroy the barrier and escape to the world."

"You're telling us information that we already know, girl." Garrett responded. "Unless you have a reason why you're talking to us, I suggest you leave."

"The Grand Mage hasn't told you everything though." Rebecca continued. "He told you about this project, yes, but he hasn't told you that his eldest son is already within the Academy by himself."

This caught the group's attention. Seamus in particular had his interest tweaked once more.

"What else do you know that the Grand Mage did not reveal to us?"

"I only know that the Grand Mage refuses to tell any of us exactly how Project Overmind worked, but I do know that the location of the Overmind."

"Where is it?" Theresa asked.

"The one place I thought they would never place such an ambitious project." Rebecca said, gritting her teeth. "They placed it in the Arcane Lab."

"He did **what**?" Seamus asked in a dark tone. "Is he mad?"

"Um, could you like, explain to us why this is such a big deal?" Liza asked.

"The Arcane Lab is the very source of all the school's magic." Seamus explained. "While it doesn't affect any of the people here that can use magic, it does effect the very source of power within this school. If the Overmind gets its claws into the magical energies that the Lab has, then the barrier won't matter anymore. The Overmind could very well increase the power of the demons it controls so much that one hit is all it takes to destroy the barrier that's protecting the students now."

"Oh. That's just PERFECT." Aiden groaned. "But what's stopping the Overmind from doing so now?"

"We don't know." Rebecca admitted. "I've begun to wonder myself why the Overmind simply doesn't do that, but something is preventing it from doing so. But I worry that it's only a matter of time before it does find the power. And when it does…everything we know will come to an end."

Aiden turned to Seamus just in time to witness the look of anger in his eyes. Never before had he seen his friend get so angry about something. At least, not like this. Sure he didn't seem as angry as Garrett did all the time, but he was still very upset.

"That idiot. I'll confront him about what he's done right now!"

"No don't!" Rebecca pleaded. "If he finds out that you know the true stakes here he'll immediately know that one of us told you! And we're already on a strict schedule with him as it is!"

Theresa nodded her head as she grabbed Seamus' shoulder from behind and squeezed it tightly. The green dragon gave her a small glare of sorts, but eventually calmed himself down when he saw the stern look that was forming in Theresa's eyes. Once he was calm, the white dragoness turned back to Rebecca with a frown on her lips.

"And you did not tell us this before the Grand Mage talked to us because?"

"You saw how fast he appeared." Rebecca replied. "He doesn't want you to know everything. If he did, he would have told you exactly what happened with the protect."

She glanced around the room, making sure that Ivan was nowhere near them. Once she was certain that he wasn't there she resumed.

"You know that one of the Grand Mage's sons, Lewis, helped with the protect. Well his eldest son, Ryan, is within the Academy now. Trying to find his way to the Lab to stop the Overmind. He did it in secret and his father has no idea that he has entered the school without his permission."

"I'm not surprised." Liza said with a mocking tone. "If I had a dad like that jerkass I would probably do the same thing."

Aiden and Aello both turned to Liza with surprised looks on their faces. More specifically, Aello seemed more surprised at what Liza had said, more so than Aiden.

"Jerk...ass?" She repeated.

"Yeah, you know. He's a jerk. And he's an ass. Therefore, a jerkass." Liza explained.

"That's...that's kind of the same thing." Aiden pointed out.

"Oh bite me, Aide." Liza replied with pursed up lips. "It's a word that I'm going to use more often anyway."

"Would you three be quiet for a moment?" Seamus asked with a small glare. Before they could respond, he turned his attention right back to Rebecca. "You seem to really want us to find this Ryan in the school, why's that?"

Rebecca blinked at Seamus question. A small blush started to come to her cheeks as she realized what it was that he really wanted to know. The young mage looked towards the ground, hiding her blush from the others as best as she could. Before she barely managed to speak out.

"He's...he's my boyfriend."

"The Grand Mage's eldest son and one of his students together?" Garrett asked, eye rolling. "Why do I get a feeling that you allowed open relationships in this school, Seamus?"

Seamus turned back to Garrett with a mocked shock expression on his face.

"Me? Have it so that the students could have relationships with each other? I would never! This is a place of learning, not for exchanging kisses!"

"Seamus..." Theresa said with an annoyed tone in her throat.

"Oh hush." Seamus responded. "Sometimes it's best to let young ones fall in love and get close to one another."

"I'm afraid to tell you this, Green Dragon, but those rules were dropped when Ryan's father took over as Grand Mage." Rebecca said. Seamus turned back to her with a somewhat surprised expression on his face. "He said that relationships distracted us from our studies. And that any student that was caught having a relationship would be immediately mind whipped from this place, and all their magical abilities would be taken away."

"Goddammit..." Seamus growled. "He really is trying to change everything that we strived to have for this school."

Aiden wanted to ask if Seamus only cared about the students being able to date or not, but decided against it as Theresa gave him a look to not bring up that question. Rebecca looked up at them once more, though the blush on her face was still there.

"You don't understand though, Ryan is not like his father.

He wants to take over as Grand Mage and fix everything that his father has placed into the Academy. And he believes that will become a reality when he left in secret to stop the Overmind."

Rebecca took out her staff and began speaking in a different language, one that Aiden didn't completely understand yet, before the tip of her staff glowed with power. Before anyone could ask what was going on, the magical energies from the staff spread out and a beam of light hit them in their foreheads.

Aiden's mind began to see things. He assumed it was just days before they arrived at the Academy, because in front of Rebecca was a tall young man, who was at least in his late teens, glancing down at her. It was hard to make out the details of the tall young man, for he was covered in shadows. Though Aiden could see that his eyes were dark green and he had a kind smile. The two of them shared a small smile before kissing one another on the lips. There was an exchange of words, though it was if someone had hit a mute button on the duo, as Aiden could not hear a word of what they were saying.

Finally, the tall young man turned back to the barrier; with his powerful staff he distorted the barrier for a few moments before he walked into the shadow covered halls of the school alone.

When the memory came to an end, they all looked at Rebecca. The young mage girl sighed as she closed her eyes.

"That was over two days ago." She said. "He told me that he was going to end the Overmind, stop the problem, and if he could, end his father's control over the Academy once and for all."

Rebecca slowly got onto both of her knees as she bowed towards Seamus. The green dragon blinked as she did so. Even Garrett had a somewhat surprised look on his face as Rebecca bowed before him.

"I'm begging you, Great Dragon of Magic, please...please

find Ryan. Please lift the terrible dark cloud that has been brought upon this great academy of ours...please..."

Aiden, Liza, Aello, Mia, Gabriella and Theresa all watched Seamus' for his next move. It was all about how he responded to such a request. It didn't take long to know Seamus, and those who did know him would say that no one would ever truly bow down to him out of respect. But here was Rebecca, a girl that they barely even knew, bowing before Seamus asking him a huge favor.

The green dragon gave a kind smile.

"First off, stand up, you don't have to get on both of your knees to ask me for a favor." Seamus said as he made Rebecca stand up. "Second off, this school is one of my pride and joys. So of course I'll help return it to the way it was before. And third off? Yes. I'll be sure to find Ryan and set things straight, for all of you."

A grateful smile came to Rebecca's face at Seamus' words. Aiden could scarcely believe what he just heard from Seamus's mouth. The green dragon, the one who would always take a chance to hit on women, was actually showing a different side he did not expect.

"Dragon of Magic." Ivan's voice suddenly said. The group looked up towards where his voice came from, one of the upper levels of the main hall. But suddenly within an instant, thanks to his magic, the Grand Mage teleported down in front of Seamus. In his left hand was a big bag of supplies. When he jiggled it Aiden heard a distinct sound of glass banging against each other from within.

"I've gathered all the best potions and elixirs I can spare. Several of them are from my own personal supply. The rest have to stay here for the injured staff and student body."

Seamus quirked an eyebrow as he took the bag from Ivan with a swift movement of his hands. Not wasting any time he opened the bag and began to count how many bottles and vials that Ivan had placed into the bag.

"Six potion bottles, and four elixir vials?" Seamus asked, dryly. "Are you trying to jerk us off here?"

"Come now, dragon, these bottles will be more than enough for your party." Ivan replied. "One potion for each of you. A single sip of it will heal your injuries. One bottle should last all of you long enough should you need it."

Aiden frowned as he watched Seamus close the bag once more. The frustration in his friend's eyes was clear as day to see. He honestly was quite surprised to see Seamus restrain himself from attacking Ivan where he stood. If it had been Aiden, he would have taken the chance to slug Ivan right where he stood. But then he thought about how bad that would have made him look in front of not only the student body, but also his friends.

He turned to Theresa to see what she thought of what Ivan was doing to them. Just like Seamus, he could see the same frustration in her eyes. He could even see a put of smoke coming out from her nostrils. Though just like Seamus, she kept her cool and refused to cause an outburst in front of everyone.

Aiden glanced over to Garrett. Just as he expected, the strongest member of their party was not even paying attention to Ivan. Though he didn't expect him to really care about the history between Ivan and Seamus.

"Thank you." Seamus said, with a taste of scorn for the Grand Mage. "I'll make sure that each of us use these little gifts you gave us wisely."

Ivan nodded his head slowly before he walked off towards the barrier. Seamus turned his head back to the party, and motioned his head once. Saying no more the team followed after him as they chased after Ivan. As they approached the barrier, Aiden's eyes darted around the main hall as the students in turn watched them. Many of them looked nervous, or rather concerned, for the party as Ivan lead them to the barrier.

Once at the barrier, Ivan held his staff up high over his head. The very top of the staff glowed with immense magical power as each of the jewels within the staff shined one after another in perfect order. After all the gems shined with power, Ivan's staff fired out a white beam of magic into the barrier. The effect the beam had on the barrier was like a stone had been thrown into a body of water causing a ripple effect.

The barrier began to slowly open up in front of the team and Ivan. Aiden was amazed at how it looked like someone had just opened up a hole in a body of water, allowing one to travel through if they so wished it. Once it was open, the Grand Mage turned back to Seamus.

"Tread lightly, dragon of magic, the shadows are strong and will continue to grow in strength the further you progress into the Academy."

"I've dealt with shadows before." Seamus replied, Aiden could have sworn his voice was so close that he saw ice for the briefest of moments. "I suggest you remember that I am older than you can imagine."

"And I suggest you remember not to underestimate your enemies." Ivan retorted.

"Enough." Theresa said with a strict tone. "We are running out of time here. Ivan, bring the barrier up the moment we leave. Do not bring it down until you know for a fact that it is safe for you, your staff, and your students again."

Before either of them could argue with her, Theresa immediately stepped forward through the open barrier and summoned her two blades, Snow and Fire, before glancing back to her team.

"Let's move it. Now."

No one dared argued with Theresa. When she was in 'the zone' she was without a doubt the undisputed leader of the team. Aiden followed after her, summoning Warfang to his side as soon as he walked through the hole. Garrett, Seamus, Liza, and Aello did the same as well.

Once they were all through the barrier, Theresa glanced back over at Ivan. She didn't have to say anything as Ivan saw the dangerous look in her eyes. Not wasting a moment the Grand Mage quickly brought the barrier up once more.

They were on their own now. And what was within the Academy's walls would forever change Aiden Russell.

CHAPTER 6 - SHADOW DEMONS

The neatness of the Great Hall behind them, not including the injured students and staff members they saw, nothing could have prepared Aiden for the absolute destruction and chaotic mess of the rest of the Academy. What was once nice and orderly, was now destroyed and disorganized. Shadowy claw marks were everywhere on the walls and dead bodies, of what looked like staff members, littered the ground.

Aiden glanced back over to Seamus. It came as no surprise that he was livid. His grip around his staff tightened so hard it could have crushed his weapon with just pure force. His eyes were filled with disgust, anger, and disappointment at what had been the school he helped established.

"Ivan you bastard." He muttered under his breath. "This is a thousand times worse than you let on."

"Seamus." Theresa squeezed his shoulder with a firm grip. "We can't afford to let ourselves be overtaken by our emotions by what he's done. We must make our way to the lab."

Seamus nodded his head at Theresa's words. Even with the illusion that time was much slower in the Academy than the outside world they were on a short time limit. Aiden let a small smile come to his face as he saw his friend calm down. It wasn't like Seamus to get so upset.

"Come on, all of you." Seamus said as he walked ahead of them. "We need to get this situation under control and keep this mess from getting even bigger than it is now."

No one argued with Seamus as they followed after him. The hallway was not only covered in claw marks, but from what Aiden could tell, dried blood. He couldn't tell if it was the blood of the students, staff, or the demons that the Overmind had released onto the Academy, but it painted a nightmare picture.

Mia let out a whimper as they progressed down the hallway. She was not used to seeing such things. She wasn't the only one either. Both Aiden and Liza looked like they were about to pass out from the dried blood on the walls. What kept the three of them going though, was the safety the three dragons seemed to provide. When one of them almost stopped walking, Theresa, Seamus, or Garrett would immediately be at their side and convince them to continue walking.

Several times Aiden came to a complete stop as they followed after Seamus. The blood covered walls and fallen bodies on the floor were starting to get to him mentally. And each time he felt like he couldn't progress any further, Theresa was there to help him continue. Every time she did, there was always the kind smile she would always have on her face when he needed support.

"I know it's hard to continue walking on through this hell." She said after the third time seeing another dead body. "But I promise you, we will get to the Overmind, and we will end this nightmare."

Those words alone were comforting enough for Aiden. He didn't know what it was about Theresa but she always seemed to know what to say when he had difficulty continuing. Even though they were walking through destroyed hallways together, the kindness that Theresa had in her smile was enough for Aiden to keep pushing through the horrible things that had happened.

He had no idea what he would truly encounter within the academy though. And it was quite possible that even Theresa's comfort would probably never make him feel truly happy ever again. But that was a while off for now. For now, Theresa and his friends were there for the morale support that they needed to continue through the destroyed halls.

The further they progressed, the more destructive things became in the hallways. Bookshelves were knocked over, broken glass littered the floor with razor sharp edges that could easily pierce through skin, and the broken bodies of students and staff alike were everywhere. Some of the bodies were lying on the floor while others were thrown into the walls.

It took every bit of mental strength Aiden could muster to not be sickened by the bodies. The dragons didn't seem too bothered by it, minus Seamus due to his personal connection with the Academy. The dragon of magic muttered something in the draconic tongue that Aiden couldn't properly translate until he was more familiar with the word so all he could do was assume that it was a draconic swear word.

Liza, much like Aiden, was having a much more difficult time taking in the sights they were seeing. He didn't know how she did it, Liza was still rather new to the harsh reality of things in the world much like he was. Their training couldn't have prepared them for something like this. Not even after they fought against demons and harpies were they prepared for the true state of Arcana.

Aello and her guardians were having just as hard a time themselves. Unlike her sisters and their guardians the youngest princess was not used to seeing so many fallen bodies. Aiden wasn't surprised. The only action that they saw in combat was during Dimitri's attempt to use Queen Lilith's incredible power for himself. And even then by some miracle none of their flock had perished in battle against the Wall Demons that they had summoned.

Aiden clenched his fists and hands as they continued to trek through the halls. How could anyone allow such destruction to get out of control like this? That was the one question Aiden would not be able to find the answer to during his time in the Academy. All that mattered now though was that they had to stop the Overmind before the damage got out of control.

"How are you kids holding up?" Seamus finally asked.

"I…" Aiden started to say, but the former cut him off.

"Don't answer that question." Seamus said. "I know the rest of you are having a hard time looking at all this. You're like babies to us."

Aiden wanted to argue with him but relented the moment Seamus sighed. The frustration, anger, and disappointment in his eyes blended together. But yet, at the same time, Aiden could sense that Seamus was sad. It was like he was heart broken by the carnage that had happened to his school.

"You shouldn't have to see such destruction. Such death like this…hell, you shouldn't even be here right now. Not when the school is like this."

Before either Aiden or Liza could argue with him a dark roar came from one of the rooms of the Academy. The roar was unholy, like a mixture between a lion's roar and a woman's high-pitched scream. Seamus immediately turned on a dime and entered a defensive stance.

"W-Was that a woman?!" Liza asked.

"No." Seamus replied. "That's a Shadow Demon…"

Theresa's eyes narrowed at those words. She didn't waste any time as she immediately stood in front of Aiden protectively, her swords raised high into a combat stance.

"W-What's the difference between Shadow Demons and demons?" Aiden asked.

"Whelp, I'm telling you this right now. Shut your trap and

don't ask questions." Garrett said harshly. "This is not the time to ask them."

"Garrett I swear to God-" Aiden started to retort, but he didn't have a chance to finish as a different roar came from another room. It was the same kind of roar as the last one.

Aello placed her hands over her ears in an attempt to shut out the horrible sounds. Liza gritted her teeth in pain. Aiden felt like his ears were going to begin bleeding from the sound. It was chilling to hear such a roar the first time, but it was painful to hear it a second time.

"The four of you stay close to us." Seamus said as he held his staff out in front of him. "These demons can attack from anywhere."

"A-Anywhere?" Mia squeaked out.

"It's one of their abilities." Seamus gritted his teeth. "These aren't like wall demons that can only crawl on walls. They are literally beings that can arrive from any shadow."

Aiden swallowed the lump in his throat before he held out Warfang in a defensive stance. If what Seamus said was true, they were vulnerable to attack at all times now. The gold and silver of Warfang shined brightly in the darkness. The sword itself seemed to give off a radiant glow that banished the fears of its wielder.

"I ain't scared." Liza said as she drew out Gitanel from its sheathe. "I've fought demons before, these won't be ANY different."

As she said those exact words, a loud bang sound was heard. The team turned towards the source of the banging sound. One of the classroom doors shook violently as it was rammed repeatedly from the other side. Each time it was rammed, cracks began to show on the door.

"Everyone duck!" Theresa ordered.

Her order arrived just in time, as the next impact was enough to shatter the door. Thanks to Theresa's warning Aiden was able to avoid a very sharp piece of broken wood from impaling his face. It flew right over his head into the wall behind him.

A bead of sweat rolled down Aiden's forehead as he watched the destroyed doorway carefully. Then he saw it, for a very brief moment, he saw it. A life form that didn't look like any other kind of demon that he had seen before rushed onto the wall and seemed to merge with it.

"W-What the hell?!" Liza stuttered.

"Dammit..." Theresa snarled as she pointed to the walls. "Watch for ANY kind of shadow, even if it's your own!"

The three dragons immediately got out in front of the young group. They each wore looks of anger and concern on their faces. Even Garrett seemed very concerned.

The Trinity of Dragons watched each corner they could. Their powerful weapons glowing with power as their eyes scouted every corner they could spot. Something had to give though. Either the dragons' keen eyesight would miss their target, or this Shadow Demon would be struck down.

No one had to wait very long though. What erupted from the shadows on the floor was a creature that Aiden's imagination could not have come up with in years. This new demon was far different from any of the other demons that Aiden had seen Raven or Dimitri summon before.

It was the very first Shadow Demon that Aiden had ever seen. And it was a monstrous looking creature. The shadow demon had a large body in the shape of one of the big cats that roamed the world today, probably as large as a lion's body. In fact it looked much larger than a big cat, but retained similar traits from the breeds of big cats! It had the same snout and teeth like a big cat, and its paws were filled with razor sharp claws like those of the big cats.

The major difference setting this beast apart from them though, was it's outer appearance. Unlike the big cats, this Shadow Demon was not covered in fur. In fact, it had a reptilian like pale blue skin covering its body. If that wasn't enough though, the Shadow Demon had these weird tendril like spikes on its back, tail, chin, and ankles of its front and back legs. These spiky tendrils were a dark orange color, each one brimming with a violent display.

But what made this beast truly terrifying though, were its eyes. The eyes were the most disturbing things about the Shadow Demon. They were filled with the intention of malice and dismembering body parts from its prey. The pale yellow eyes shown like a dim flashlight in the darkness. Aiden took notice that the eyes had no pupils at all, which made the beast look even more terrifying than it already did.

A low growl came from the Shadow Demon as it observed the group. Aiden swallowed another lump in his throat as he noticed that the Shadow Demon was drooling a green ooze like substance from its jaws.

Aiden felt a pinch of downright terror rise up from his soul at the sight of the Shadow Demon.

He turned his gaze towards Liza to see if she was having the same reaction that he was having. Not surprisingly, Liza was wide eyed in fear at the sight of this new monster. Gitanel shook briefly in her trembling hands, but somehow she was able to hold onto her blade.

"W-What is that?!" Mia shouted, a noticeable quiver of fear lingered in her voice. Gabriella grabbed ahold of her shoulder and squeezed it as hard as she could.

"Get a hold of yourself, Mia!" She snapped. "Remember that we're Guardians for Princess Aello! We can't be afraid now!"

"All of you listen very carefully," Theresa said in a very quiet voice. "This one is known as a dakgrul. It relies heavily on its eyesight and hearing. Do not make any loud noises, and always keep your eyes on it."

It took Aiden every single ounce of control to not ask why the creature was called a dakgrul, but he managed to do so.

Despite all his training over the last year, he still couldn't help but ask questions about such things. He could only hope that his one annoying flaw would not end up costing them this battle.

The dakgrul growled in a low tremor once more as its claws extended from its paws. The green ooze it was drooling hit the floor. When it did steam rose up from the spot it hit. When the steam disappeared, there were only small holes where the ooze had been.

Acid salvia.

That's when the dakgrul let out the same roar that Aiden and his friends had heard before. Seamus didn't waste any time with attacking the demon as he fired out a powerful stream of fire from his staff into the mouth of the dakgrul. The fire began to incinerate everything from within the dakgrul, destroying much of its insides.

The dakgrul had already called forth the rest of its kind within the vicinity. As it fell over burning to death the rest of the dakgruls in the area rushed to the spot that their fallen kin had cried out from. Aiden had a brief moment to count the amount of dakgruls to measure up their chances at winning against this pack. There were at least seven of them, Garrett would have to take two of them to make things easier.

At the sight of their fallen comrade the dakgrul pack glared towards the group of friends. They let out the same kind of roar the fallen dakgrul did all at once, causing the very walls of the hallway to tremble at the sound.

"Ready your weapons!" Theresa ordered. "Don't even bother slicing at their skin with standard strikes!"

That was all the time Theresa had to warn Aiden, Liza, Aello and her guardians. The pack charged straight at them. Their speed could have caught them off guard if it wasn't for the intense training that they had gone through. Aiden immediately dodged one dakgrul charge and slashed at the hide of the passing shadow demon.

The impact from his sword caused Warfang to bounce back from the skin. Aiden almost fell over onto his back before he regained his balance. The dakgrul that he struck turned its body back towards Aiden. Though it didn't seem possible Aiden could have sworn it had some kind of sick smile on its face.

Unlike before though, Aiden wasn't intimidated and went right into a defensive stance again. The dakgrul let out a short roar as it pounced at him. The sharp claws of the dakgrul raced towards him with the intent to stab his chest. Aiden's response was quick to the attack. His blade rose up to block the claws, right before he used his upper body strength to throw the shadow demon into a wall.

The shadow beast growled in annoyance as it glared at Aiden. He smiled as he held Warfang out in an attack stance. He would not be beaten by this demon.

Aiden charged towards the dakgrul, confident that he could harm the beast this time, and pulled Warfang back for another quick strike. The sword once again made contact with the demon's skin. The same effect happened once more though as his blade bounced back from making contact with the dakgrul's skin.

The dakgrul let out a small snarl at Aiden's attempts to cut its skin. Its sharp claws dug right into the floor of the hallway before it lunged out and tried to bite him. Aiden dodged to the left to avoid the bite, but wasn't fast enough to avoid a slash across his left arm.

Back in the past year Aiden would have fallen down to one knee in pain from being slashed. But unlike when Raven's demon slashed into his arm, Aiden only gave a small grunt of pain. With the intensive training exercises over the summer, he was able to not let the new pain overcome his mind.

It still hurt, but it wasn't mind-numbing.

The dakgul didn't stop attacking though. Its sharp claws raised high once more in an attempt to slash into Aiden again. This time though, Aiden was ready for the attack. With his newfound strength, Aiden swung Warfang straight at the rising claw of the dakgrul and sliced it right off. The strike was so fierce that the dakgrul didn't even know its claw was sliced off before it landed on the ground with a thud.

Aiden expected blood to erupt from the wound he inflicted on the shadow demon. But surprisingly no blood came. Instead a stream of shadows spilled out from the wound of the dakgrul. As it stumbled to get back up from its injury, Aiden heard Theresa yell from behind him.

"Blast a flame into its mouth or thrust your sword into the mouth!"

At first Aiden was about to ask what she wanted him to do again but he stopped himself from doing so. Without a second thought he pulled back Warfang and rammed the tip of the blade into the mouth of the dakgrul.

Within an instant the shadow demon stopped struggling as the blade pierced right through its soft inside. Aiden watched as its pale yellow eyes rolled back into its skull before its lifeless limp body fell down.

There was a time Aiden would have hesitated at taking the life of a creature, but he couldn't afford that now. The dakgrul was out to kill him and would have if he didn't defend himself. Instead he just pulled his blade out of the mouth of the fallen demon and turned his attention back to his friends to see how they were fairing against the dakgruls.

It wasn't a big surprise to see that the dragons were holding their own against the dakgruls. Liza and Aello were both fighting against two dakgruls together. Nearby Aello's guardians were flying above one dakgrul and dive bombing it with their sharp talons. Theresa was breathing a stream of white fire onto the dakgrul she faced. Seamus was using magic to slam the dakgrul that he was facing off with into the floor and walls over and over again. And Garrett, being Garrett, used his bare hands to choke the life from the dakgruls he faced.

Aiden smiled at how his friends were handling their fights. True Aello and Liza were having a bit of a more difficult problem killing the dakgruls that they were facing, but they were putting up a good fight. Or at least the beast they could do against demons that had some of the toughest skin either of them had seen.

Aello's guardians proved to have a much harder time than they thought against the one dakgrul they faced though. Their sharp talons, which had been enough to slice into the hides of the prey they hunted back at the den, weren't even making so much as a dent on the hide of the Shadow Demon. Mia flinched for a brief moment as one attempted strike sent her back a few feet in the air.

"Dammit!" She cursed as the dakgrul merged with the shadows and moved on the walls towards her. Mia gasped as she glanced around her, waiting for the right moment to dodge that dakgrul's attack.

"Behind you!" Gabriella shouted.

Mia turned right the very last second to see the dakgrul lunging at her with its claws down out and acidic covered mouth wide hope. The guardian braced herself for impact as the claws of the demon dug their way into her shoulders. She let out a loud cry of pain from the claws before the two of them fell to the ground together, with the dakgrul pinning her. Before it could bite down on her throat though, a loud screech erupted from above them.

"MIA!" Gabriella roared out as she dive bombed at the dakgrul in fury. Her talons shined in the dark hallway of the room before they stabbed right into the back neck of the dakgul's neck. If the dakgrul had pupils, they would have shrunk in both surprise and pain.

"No one harms my sister!" Gabriella shouted as she dug her talons deeper into the Shadow Demon's skin.

With all the strength she could muster up, Gabriella forced

her talons right at what would be the Shadow Demon equivalent of an artery and sliced it open. The instant she did so the dakgrul froze on spot before falling over onto its side. Mia jumped off from the ground and kicked the fallen demon in the stomach a couple of times.

"Stupid, ugly, demon!" She spat out.

"Mia, focus!" Gabriella snapped at her. "We need to help the princess!"

Not far away from the duo, Aello and Liza were cornered by their own dakgrul foes. The Shadow Demons circled them, like sharks, as their claws left marks in the floor below them. One let out a roar at the two of them as its acid saliva dripped from its jaw. Steam rose from the drops as they ate away at the floor beneath them.

Aello glanced back to Liza as they stood back to back as they faced off against the surviving dakgruls. Liza nodded her head at the harpy princess before she held Gitanel backwards in her right hand. No words had to be spoken as the two of them faced the dakgrul facing them.

The dakgrul facing Liza charged at her in a fury. Before it was within inches of her, Liza immediately bent her knees and jumped as high as she could into the air. Aello, almost as if their minds were in sync, flapped her wings once and flew up into the air alongside Liza.

The charging dakgrul couldn't come to a complete stop as it rammed its head into the head of its fellow demon. The two beasts staggered a bit from their collision, staggering around for a few moments.

That's when Liza and Aello struck.

Aello flew down from above onto the back of one dakgrul with her sharp talons, actually digging into the hide with little to no effort compared to Mia and Gabriella's attempts to pierce the hide of just one. The dakgrul let out a surprised yelp in pain as it lifted its head into the air to let out a pained roar. Aello wasted no time as she summoned her weapon.

Aiden and Liza had learned from their training with her, Aello was a beast with the spear. But she was also quite skilled using a whip as well. The harpy princess flicked her wrist once as the spear transformed into a chain whip like form. With a shout she wrapped the chain whip around the dakgrul's neck and pulled with all her might.

The sudden presence of the chain around its neck caused the demon to begin to buck as hard as it could to toss Aello off its body. But the princess' sharp talons kept her in place, refusing to let the dakgrul go.With a sneer she let out a short harpy cry before the tight whip around the dakgrul choked the very life out of its body. *

Liza meanwhile had jumped onto the back of her dakgrul. While she didn't have talons to keep her footing into the shadow demon, she was able to maintain her balance. Aiden watched as a confident grin came to Liza's lips before she jumped into the air and dive kicked the skull of the dakgrul hard into the floor.

The demon's eyes widened in pain. It slumped down, twitching a bit from what had just happened. This gave Liza enough time to jump off the dakgrul victoriously before she placed Gitanel back into its sheathe.

"Game, set, and match." She said. Aello flew right over to Liza and the two of them gave each other a high five. "That was awesome!"

"I can't believe that actually worked!" Aello said with a big smile. "I thought for certain that something like that would be impossible!"

"Princess!" Both guardians shouted as shouted together as they flew over towards Aello.

"Princess Aello, you must be more careful!"

"Your talons aren't hurt at they? Did you chip one of them

digging into the hide of that brute?!"

Aello had a flabbergasted look on her face as her two guardians bombarded her with questions. She looked to Liza for help in calming the two of them down.

"B-Both of you, please." Aello grumbled. "I'm not some small fledgling anymore."

"You shouldn't have to do such fighting!" Mia cried out as she pulled up the princess leg up to look at her talons. "They're not chipped? Oh thank the Gods she's not injured!"

"That's just one talon you dip!" Gabriella cried out. "Check the other one!"

"Knock it off already!" Aello cried out, blushing. "You two are embarrassing me!"

"Um excuse me ladies." Aiden interrupted, "But would you two mind telling me what the hell that was?" Aiden asked, a little flabbergasted at what he saw.

Liza smiled with pride as she put her hands on her hips and puffed out her chest in an attempt to look cool.

"That, Aiden, was what I'd like to call the mind synchroniza- tion." She said. "Me and Aello have been practicing it for a few weeks now."

"Mind synchronization?" Aiden asked with a flat voice. "That was just some back dodging and jumping onto other creature's backs."

"Yes, but, the important thing to note here is to know when to move along with your partner." Liza continued. "When the two of us knew that the situation was right we jumped into the air at the same time, completely catching those ugly things off guard!"

"Mind synchronization my ass!" Aiden spat back. "You two got lucky!"

"That can be reckless." Theresa said as she walked up now. "The two of you could have gotten hurt if that dakgrul was able to jump in the middle of its charge."

A smile came to the white dragoness' lips.

"But I am proud that the two of you were so in sync with each other that you were able to catch both of them off guard."

The injured dakgrul twitched a bit on the ground. Liza glanced back over to the fallen beast. She began to draw out Gitanel but Seamus' staff suddenly stopped her from moving forward.

"Wait." He said. "This beast could be an advantage for us."

"Um, what?" Liza asked. "I thought you just said that shadow demons all had to die."

"Yes, they do." Seamus responded. "But, each of these shadow demons are connected to the Overmind. With any luck, this lil bastard could lead us to the lab with no trouble."

"Shouldn't you be able to find the lab on your own?" Aiden asked. "You basically helped build this school you know."

"Kiddo, you know nothing about Shadow magic. It can warp things and make even the basic hallways turn into something that it's not."

Seamus approached the dakgrul slowly. He held out his staff in front of him horizontally as a yellow hue covered his weapon. The magic rose up from his staff like hot steam from water as it flew over to the ankles and neck of the fallen demon. Seamus snapped his fingers just once.

The magic that formed around the creature's ankles and neck suddenly became solid golden shackles that clamped down hard on the dakgrul. Taken aback by the shackles the surprised demon let out a shocked yelp. Before it could attack any of them though the shackles immediately shocked the dakgrul with electric magic.

"There we go." Seamus spoke with pride. "These lil shackles will keep this bastard under our control until I see fit to get rid of it."

"Isn't that kinda like Raven and Dimitri's magic to control demons though?" Aiden pointed out.

"This isn't magic that summons demons." Seamus explained.

"See, these shackles are meant for us to let us control these creatures without resorting to dark magic. When I say the right word, I'll set this beast free. That or I'll kill him."

The dakgrul slowly stood up from the ground. The electric magic that came from the shackles began to die down as the pale yellow eyes the shadow demon once had were now light blue. Aiden watched with caution as the shadow demon slowly walked towards Seamus, like a dog would greet its owner. Seamus gave a short smile as he patted the head of the dakgrul.

"All right buster, lead the way to the Overmind. And warn us if we're getting closer to any of your kind in these halls."

The dakgrul gave a slow nod before it took the lead. Seamus turned his eyes back to the group and winked at them.

"Don't worry guys, this fellow will be our guide through these messed up halls of my once great academy. And any chance of him betraying us are quiet low."

Theresa sighed as she dismissed Snow and Fire from her hands. A concerned frown was plastered onto her lips as she looked over to Aiden.

"While he is right that the shackles will indeed keep the demon under control, we should exercise caution." She said. "Aiden, if that beast tries to attack us, you will be the one to take it out."

"W-Wha? Why me?"

Theresa gave a small whimsical smile.

"It's a good way for you to do something when we are forced to take breaks from battles in this place. And let's just say that it'll be the pet that you've always wanted."

Aiden groaned at that remark as he slowly began walk with the group. Yeah. A pet that's a demon. That's what all the boys wanted to have as a pet. A pet that could turn on you and eat you within a second if it wanted.

He told himself that Theresa would pay for making the dakgrul his responsibility.

CHAPTER 7 - A TALE OF HER PAST

"*H*ow's your arm, Aiden?" Liza asked.

"Not in as much pain as you think it would be." Aiden responded.

"We should get that patched up before we go any further." Liza frowned. "We don't want it getting infected, right?"

"I'll be fine."

The frown on Liza's face didn't disappear despite Aiden claiming he was okay. Not that he could blame her for being concerned for him. After a full year of getting to know one another, Liza was like a sister. During their middle school years Aiden often dreamt of Liza talking to him a more but he never imagined in his dreams that the two of them would become actual friends.

And like all friends, they often tended to worry about you even when you said you were fine. Aiden had seen that same look of concern on Theresa for years before he and Liza became friends, so he was used to it at this point.

"Come on, you could be bleeding a lot from that arm and not know it." Liza persisted, "You know when you're body's running on adrenaline that your mind makes you think you're not in pain."

Aiden groaned. At this point they were going around in circles about this.

"You're not going to leave me alone if I keep telling you no, aren't you?"

"E-yup."

"Would you two whelps knock it off?"

The two of them nearly fell over at the sound of Garrett's deep voice. The third dragon had barely said anything their entire time in the Academy. It was like he had been completely absent the entire time so his voice had caught them off guard.

"Get his arm patched up and stop bickering about it already." He said, looking more annoyed than ever now. "If it ends up getting infected because he did something stupid like he is now, he has no one else to blame but himself when the arm has to come off."

"H-HEY!" Aiden shouted.

"Garrett, knock it off." Theresa ordered. "There's no reason to scare them into thinking that we cut off limbs like barbarians."

She turned back to Aiden though and grabbed his injured arm. The moment she held his arm in her hand a pain rose up from Aiden's nerves. While it wasn't enough to make his arm feel numb, his arm felt like several knives had just stabbed it. Theresa sighed as she took out a rag from her pocket.

"Let's get this tended to now, then we'll continue to move forward." She gave Aiden a threatening smile. "Unless you want your arm to go blue and fall off?"

Those words alone were a constant reminder that Theresa was not someone to make angry. Sure Garrett was in a state of constant anger whenever he talked to Aiden or Liza, but Theresa's anger was more frightening due to the fact she rarely ever let it show. After deciding that it wasn't worth the risk of becoming a victim of Theresa's own white fire, Aiden reluctantly let his arm be tended too.

"You got lucky you know." Theresa said as she wrapped the bandage around his arm. "Dakgrul claws aren't as sharp as most other demons, but if they had been any sharper you could have been cut a lot worse."

"Let me guess, I could have lost an arm?" Aiden asked with a dry voice.

"Oi, don't give me that lip." Theresa pursed her lips up. "And for the record, no, you wouldn't have lost an arm."

Aiden winced as she tightened the knot around his arm with several knots. While his arm wouldn't have fallen off from it being slashed, it felt like Theresa would cause his arm to fall off with how tight she was making the knot. The pressure was necessary though, as it kept the blood from leaking out of the slash marks.

"Why not use magic to heal it?" Liza asked. "I mean, it shouldn't take that long to heal with it."

"Healing magic takes a lot of mana." Seamus said, Aiden noticed that he had the captured dakgrul sitting like a dog beside him. "And we need what mana we can spare, without using all the potions and elixirs that Ivan gave us."

"So in other words, don't use them all the time." Garrett said. "If I find out that one of you has taken one of them without the consent of the group there will be a price to pay for it."

Theresa rolled her eyes as she finished wrapping the bandage around Aiden's arm. The latter sighed as he tried to lift his arm up to make sure that it was still capable of movement. The pressure from the bandage kept his arm movement limited.

"That wound should be healed within an hour in this place." Theresa explained. "Just keep using your right arm for combat and try not to lift anything heavy with your left arm during that time."

She smiled as she ruffled Aiden's hair up.

"Relax tough guy, they won't leave any scars that you'll have to explain to your parents."

Aiden scoffed, but his attitude was better than it was a few moments ago. Even if he did tell his parents the truth about how a demon cat like beast tried to slice his arm off he doubted that they would even believe him.

"So, where are we exactly?" Aello suddenly asked. "Just how is this school laid out anyway?"

Seamus frowned as he folded his arms across his chest. The entire group turned to him for answers at this point. The green dragon closed his eyes, trying his best to remember every section of his academy like it was yesterday.

"Well, if memory serves right, the lab is still at the very end of the academy. The reason why it's at the very back is because that place is only for the staff and senior students. It's where they practice new theories about magic. It's suppose to be a safe place to keep any damage under control, but as we can see that backfired."

Seamus sighed as he opened his eyes halfway now.

"The main hallway, where we met Ivan, is basically just that. Sure it has several books and the office of the Grand Mage but it's nothing besides that. This hallway we're walking now is towards the dorm rooms. After the dorm rooms, several class-rooms that each excel at one thing. Potion making, elemental magic, shield magic, healing magic, and the history of magic as a whole. Each classroom is rather big, mostly so they can practice their spells."

"How big is each classroom?" Theresa asked.

"Let's just say that room can be about the size of a basket-ball court."

"Hold the phone!" Liza spoke out. "Why in the HELL would you need classrooms to be that huge?! That's like, twice the size of a regular classroom!"

"Picture it like this, girlie." Seamus replied. "Imagine

trying to cast a spell in a tiny room with at least, ten to fifteen other students. People would get hurt and with most of the spells that this academy teaches, it makes more than enough sense to have a big room so that you can cast said spells without worrying about the room being destroyed by a simple Flarenea spell."

A sly smile came across his lips.

"And if you think that being the size of a basketball course is too big, you should have seen the Mage Kingdom back in the old days. Their rooms were mansions."

Aiden and Liza's jaws could have fallen and hit the ground. Theresa and Garrett just rolled their eyes at their fellow dragon's words.

"Quit wasting time, Seamus." Garrett said before anyone could answer Aello's question. "We need to get to the lab as soon as possible, so stop wasting time."

"Hey no need to get testy, jerk." Seamus replied as she turned to the dakgrul. "All right you, lead us to the closest room where we can stock up on supplies."

The dakgrul nodded its' head once and began to walk forward. The feeling of dread about where this demon could be leading them was thankfully absent in Aiden's heart. As long as those golden shackles remained on the ankles of the shadow demon, the beast wouldn't lead them into any danger.

As the group began to move the destroyed hallways became more apparent. Bookshelves, glass, and the floor were damaged past the possibility of repair, but now Aiden saw claws marks in the walls of the Academy itself. These claw marks didn't have any trace of magic though, they were fresh claw marks left in solid stone.

Aiden shuddered at the thought of a demon so physically strong that it left claw marks into something as hard as solid stone. Sure Garrett could do that easily, but Aiden had never faced something in direct combat that had the same strength as the third dragon. To make matters even worse, there were several spots on the wall that shared the same claw marks.

The color in Aiden's face was close to fading away from his cheeks.

"Aiden, Aiden what's wrong?" Theresa asked.

The very sound of her voice was enough to take Aiden out of his imagination before he turned back to her Theresa.

"S-Sorry, I was just trying not to think about what kind of demon could leave claw marks in stone walls." He answered.

Theresa sighed as she whacked him upside the head.

"We really need to work on taming that imagination of yours, Aiden." She said with a tiny smile. "The demon that can do that is most likely far away from us at this point."

It was just like Theresa to make things seem better in a dark situation. He didn't feel a hundred percent better, but he was glad that she attempted to make him feel a bit better.

The dakgrul came to a stop in the middle of the hall way. Its eyes glanced around the room quietly before it turned to the left. The group followed after their new 'member' as it walked several feet in front of them. Aiden took noticed that Theresa had her hands on the hilts of her blade just in case the dakgrul was leading them to a trap. The chances of that happening were low, sure, but those chances were still there.

Before anyone could utter another word, the dakgrul came to a complete stop in the hall. It lifted its massive head up slowly before looking both right and left, deciding to turn right towards one open room. Seamus followed after the dakgrul.

"Good shadow demon." He said. "It lead us right to the supply room."

"Let's hope that there's enough for us here..." Aello said with a frown.

The state of the supply room was surprisingly not as damaged as the rest of the Academy. Yes it had several broken glass pieces as well as broken tables and chairs, but it was far and away the least destroyed room in the academy. For now it was one spot in the school where they could rest without worrying about the shadow demons.

"All right, let's take full advantage of this." Theresa said. "Seamus, start gathering the potions and elixirs that are not destroyed. Have the dakgrul stand guard at the front of the door to make sure that no passing members of it kind don't come after us."

"And what about the rest of us?" Liza asked.

"Garrett will take watch with the dakgrul as well. Liza, Aello, Mia, and Gabriella, you start gathering wood for a campfire." The two guardian harpies wanted to argue with Theresa giving the orders, but Aello just gave them a short nod for them to obey. "As for us, Aiden, we'll tend to that arm more and have you take a sip of one potion bottle."

"I could help gather the firewood you know." Aiden mumbled.

"Not until that wound is treated properly." Theresa responded. "You've trusted me before, Aiden, trust me now."

There was no point in arguing with Theresa at that point. Once she made up her mind on what she wanted to do there was no stopping her. Aiden sighed as he looked for a seat to take in the room before finding a small stool that had not been destroyed. While he much rather would have preferred something more comfortable he didn't complain.

Everyone began on his or her assigned tasks as the white dragoness took a seat besides Aiden. She frowned as she gently began to remove the bandage she had applied to his arm. Once the bandage was removed Theresa placed one hand over the slash marks and began to use her healing magic.

"Dammit, I thought I was better at this…" Aiden grumbled.

"Better at what?" Theresa asked.

"Better at fighting, dodging, using my sword, and not some fool that always has to depend on his friends to bail him out of trouble."

Aiden rubbed his forehead in frustration. That frustration was justifiable though. After spending all those hours in the woods practicing sword attacks, dodging, magic, and even being forced to lift such heavy things under Garrett's training he felt like he should have gotten better. Or at least remember to dodge when it was absolutely necessary. But even with that year of training under his belt he still took a hit from a demon's claw.

"I thought I was better than I was before." He continued. "I thought that after a full year of training that I would be able to fight without making myself look like a fool."

Theresa frowned at his statement, but continued to heal his arm regardless.

"You have gotten better, Aiden." She responded in kind. "You're far better than you were when you first acquired Warfang."

"Apparently not good enough though…"

"Oh stop it." Theresa pursed her lips up. "You have gotten better, yes, but just because you've had a year's worth of training does not mean that you're invincible at any point or time. Hell, even with a hundred years of training for dragons, we tend to get injured and make mistakes as well."

Aiden blinked at Theresa's statement as she applied pressure onto his arm with her hand now. A small smile came to her lips.

"…I don't think I've ever told you this, but I had a little sister."

"Wait…what?" Aiden asked.

"Yeah, you heard me, a little sister. And no, our relationship wasn't like a title that I share with Garrett and Seamus, an actual blood sister. It's something that not a lot of beings knew about me back then during the Age of the Kingdoms."

Theresa sighed as she finished healing Aiden's wound before grabbing several broken pieces of wood before placing them in front of Aiden. She pointed her right index finger at the wood before setting it ablaze. The warmth of the campfire was more than welcoming for Aiden. He didn't notice it at first but the cold air of the academy was starting to slowly get to his body. That's to be expected though when you're fighting to survive against several demons.

"My little sister was a special dragoness, Aiden." Theresa continued her tale. "I know this might sound odd to you, but I was young when she hatched.

"And what's young for a dragon?"

Theresa gave a wryly smile.

"Fifty years old. Which I guess in human terms would be around ten years old for us. I was barely getting to understand the longevity of a dragon's long life span."

Aiden's mouth could have dropped to the ground. Fifty years is considered *young* to a dragon? In the back of his mind he couldn't help but wonder what their secret was to their longevity but he stopped himself from asking. The wryly smile on Theresa's lips had been replaced by a somber expression.

"She was the only one of three eggs to hatch. When I was told by my commanding officer at the time that only one of my mother's eggs had hatched, I was given the chance to go home and meet my newborn sibling. I think, beside the moment when the Dragon Kingdom fell, that was the fastest I ever ran home."

Theresa sighed for a moment as she casually took another broken piece of wood and rammed it into the fire in front of her. Aiden watched in awe as she managed to pull her hand away from the flames without it catching fire. He felt silly for being in awe though. Dragons couldn't be burnt by fire like humans could.

"When I arrived at the hatchery, I could see my mother and father gathered around the clutch of eggs that my sister hatched from. Dragonlings, or as most people call them whelps, are tinier than you think Aiden. They're about the size of a newly hatched chick. But I didn't care about how small she was, I cared about only one thing, and that was to protect my little sister above all else."

"That makes sense, right? I mean, you were her big sister. It was something you were expected to do. Right?" Aiden asked.

"Yes. But it's different with dragons." Theresa responded. "While it's true that human siblings vary about how they interact with their brothers and sisters, for dragons we don't treat our siblings poorly. To us, they are part of us. It's more than just blood that connects us, it's our souls."

She let out a small laugh before shaking her head.

"Though in my case, I had the strongest urge to keep my little sister safe. Unlike many members of our family's bloodline, she was not as powerful as the rest. She was consistently getting into trouble with dragonlings that were twice her size. Starting fights with them whenever they called her weak or said that she was inferior to them and was an embarrassment to our bloodline."

The look on Theresa's face turned somber once more as she closed her eyes. Aiden tried to read what she was thinking about by watching her facial expressions, but he wasn't able to do so.

"I...I had to get her out of a lot of trouble whenever that happened. It was before I became a knight for the Dragon King himself. Mother and father were known as respectable dragons in the ever changing games of politics, if it got out that one of their children was a troublemaker it would make them look bad. But I watched out for my sister because I loved her, and she needed someone to protect her."

Theresa shook her head slowly.

"However, like you she was a gifted person in more ways than one. While she was not the best at combat like most expected her to be, she had a tenacious drive. She refused to give up when it looked like the odds were against her. Even when she knew she got better, it was never enough for her. She always wanted to become better no matter what it took. In a lot of ways, she was like you."

Theresa sighed a bit before leaning back against the wall that was behind them.

"But I lost my sister long before the Dark One destroyed the old kingdoms. I don't want to go into full details, but she was accused of something that I never thought she would have done. Not long after that, the Dark one emerged. You know the rest from there."

Aiden frowned as he reached his left hand up and placed it on Theresa's shoulder. He gently squeezed it once to get her attention. The white dragoness turned back to him before giving a tiny smile.

"In a lot of ways, you remind me of her. You don't like giving up, and you know that you can get stronger. But at the same time you believe that you will become invulnerable when you gain new power. My sister was the same way. And that pride often got her into trouble. So please, Aiden, try to not be too prideful."

The white dragoness turned her attention back to the fire in front of them. As she did Aiden glanced back to the other members of their little group. Garrett remained on guard with their captured dakgrul; Seamus had found several extra bottles of potions and elixirs, and Aello and Liza had brought more firewood for the campfire. A grateful smile came to Aiden's face when they arrived. The fire Theresa had started was slowly starting to run out of wood to feed off of and it was getting a lot colder again.

Still, the story that Theresa told him was one that he truly didn't expect her to reveal. Sure she revealed that she was really close to the Dragon King himself at one point in her life, but she never once talked about her old family with him before.

It just goes to show that even if you thought you knew everything about your best friend that they could always surprise you with another new fact.

Aiden didn't know why, but he felt a little bit closer to Theresa now that she had told him the about her sister.

CHAPTER 8 - HEARING VOICES

"*L*uckily for us, we have a couple more potions and elixirs here that the shadow demons somehow missed." Seamus said. "Some of them are half empty, probably used in a potions class earlier, while the rest of the bottles were either empty completely or they were shattered."

"Are you certain that this stuff is still good to use?" Liza asked as she held one vial in front of her. "Doesn't this have like an expiration date on it?"

Garrett sighed from the doorway at Liza's question. Aiden could have sworn he heard him mutter under his breath 'humans' in disdain. But he decided against causing a scene in front everyone and just ignored the largest of the three dragons.

"Ah my young Liza, I have to teach you a bit more about the properties of making potions and elixirs." Seamus smiled. "See, potions and elixirs have no expiration dates. The materials used in making these things are very powerful magical ingredients."

"Is that why in several stories and movies whenever there's a lab full of potions that are covered in spider webs are suppose to be safe to drink?" Aiden suddenly asked.

Theresa, Seamus, and even Garrett all turned towards Aiden with dead flat expressions on their faces. Aiden felt like he had been put on the spot for saying such a thing as they all shared the same expression with one another. Liza tried not to let a giggle escape her lips and Aello just looked confused.

"Aiden Russell." Theresa slowly said. "Those are bad stereotypes of potions and elixirs that aren't even **close** to being true."

"Aw don't get angry at him, Tes." Seamus said with a grin. "The kiddo didn't know, after all Hollywood and fictional writers have gone out of their way to be dramatic about the old ways."

"The whelp probably reads too many fantasy books." Garrett spoke with a gruff tone.

"I..." Aiden looked down in embarrassment from his question. Now he just felt really silly and put on the spot by everyone.

"Ah don't worry about it kiddo." Seamus waved his hand back and forth, as if he was brushing it off. "A lot of things put into fantasy stories are often exaggerated to an extent. Like how we dragons only hoard gold and kidnap princesses."

"Why do I have a feeling that you caused the latter to be believed?" Liza asked with pursed lips.

"Hey now, I did NOT kidnap princesses during your medieval times." The green dragon grumbled. "They were too fussy to mess with anyway."

"And what's THAT suppose to mean?" Theresa asked with a small growl in her throat.

"Nothing nothing!" Seamus immediately put his hands up in a defensive stance. "I swear that it's nothing like you're thinking!"

Aiden, Liza, and even Aello chuckled at Theresa's definitive death glare towards her fellow dragon. Garrett meanwhile just kept his back to them as his fellow dragons bickered with one another for a few minutes.

Aiden didn't know why but he couldn't keep a smile from cracking onto his lips as he watched Theresa bicker with Seamus. It was moments like these that he realized that the dragons, despite being creatures from another time, weren't that different from any sentient creature that held a bond with one another. Even though Theresa was practically berating Seamus for actions that he might have caused in the past, he could tell that she was merely concerned that he could have gotten hurt.

It dawned on Aiden that even though that their first meeting wasn't exactly the best kind, over the first year of his training he and Seamus had grown to become friends with one another. Which was odd to even admit now due to how they first interacted with one another, clashing their weapons in an alley by the mall.

Then again, Aiden had met all of his friends in the most unexpected ways. With the exception of Theresa who he had known for all his life all of his friends so far came from his father giving him Warfang as a gift. Liza had been the girl that he never in a million years would imagine that she would become his friend and Aello came from a race that lived far away from humans.

The only exception to the friend list was Garrett. No matter how many times he tried to make things seem a little better between him and the dragon of strength it felt like all of his attempts were in vain. Aiden wished he knew why Garrett was so resistant to any attempts at becoming friends with one another. With the way that the large dragon treated him though during their training most might have given up on trying to get on Garrett's good side a long time ago.

But Aiden for some reason would not give up on getting Garrett's approval. He couldn't outright explain it, but it was like a driving force within him that refused to give up on getting to know the large dragon. Even if it would be filled with pain and frustration, Aiden would get what he was after.

And that would be the respect of Garrett.

His mind was brought back to reality though as he Theresa had slapped Seamus up the back of his head rather hard. The force of her blow was strong enough for him to feel the hit himself. Seamus rubbed his head in pain as he grumbled under his breath in the draconic tongue. Aiden was able to translate it in his head, but he dared not repeat the words that Seamus spoke.

"Sometimes I think I should have awakened earlier in order to keep you in line, Seamus." Theresa said with narrowed eyes. "At least when I'm around you don't try to do stupid things."

"Aw come on Theres." Seamus replied, though he kept head lowered. "It's not like I started any wars during my time on this planet."

The white dragoness groaned in annoyance as she turned back to the rest of the group. It was clear to see that the well of her patience with Seamus had gone dry.

"Time is still against us." She spoke. "If we're to get to the Lab and stop this madness, we need to have a route that will take us there without delays. Please tell me you at least know of a few ways to do that."

Seamus, as if he suddenly regained his senses, quickly straightened up. With just a motion of his hand, a three dimensional map of the school formed over the fireplace. Aello looked at it with mesmerized eyes full of wonder. Even Liza looked amazed at the magic map that Seamus had just created before them.

"All right, let's get serious for a moment." He said. "The lab is at the very end of the school, as I've stated before. Now normally the fastest way to get to the lab would be to just walk down the hallway until we came to a big staircase where it would take us to the lab. But like I said before too, only those who have clearance can enter the Lab. Though since the entire school is in a heap of trouble I'm pretty sure we're more than allowed to enter the lab."

Seamus spun the map around with one hand as he used his magic to zoom in on the location they were at. It looked like he was using a touch screen tablet's function of zooming in on a location. Only this looked cooler and was made from magic rather than a tablet. Well, it looked cooler to Aiden at least.

"Right now we're in one of the supply rooms. Probably one of, if not the only one, that didn't get completely destroyed by the shadow demons running amok here. Now normally it'd be a simple walk for us to get to the lab. But as you all know, that's impossible now."

"How many shadow demons can you pinpoint on that map?" Garrett asked.

Without saying a word Seamus held his hand up and cast a spell on the map he created. Suddenly a small red dot appeared in the room they were in, representing the dakgrul that they had under their control. But shortly after their demon's dot appeared, a hundred more followed in many different places in the Academy.

That initial one hundred began to grow into even larger numbers though. The entire map began to become completely covered by the sheer amount of shadow demons that the Overmind had under its control. Aiden, Liza, and Aello's faces turned pale at the numbers. The normally calm expression on Seamus' face turned serious as he watched the numbers grow more and more.

"If I had to put a guess that's nowhere near accurate? I'd say that there's at least a thousand shadow demons in the academy." His eyes narrowed in anger. "But I'm betting that there's a lot more than just a thousand of those things crawling around the school."

"T-This is insane." Liza spoke out. "We're only a group of eight people fighting against numbers that not even you can accurately guess?"

"This is typical, Liz." Seamus responded. "Hell I've lost

count of how many times we had to fight off against a grand number of enemies that had us outnumbered before."

Aello gently tapped Liza's shoulder to get her attention.

"Um, Liza? Don't you remember when you and your friends fought against the wall demons?"

"I'm more than aware of that, but…" Liza frowned.

"The wall demons were mindless for the most part, and we handled them just fine didn't we?" Aiden pointed out.

"Not helping, Aiden!"

Theresa let out a small laugh Aiden's intentional teasing of his friend. It was nice to hear her laugh after being annoyed with Seamus. Liza didn't look too amused at Aiden being difficult with her but thankfully she didn't take it too seriously.

"We need to plan our route." Garrett said. "Where's the next supply room?"

Seamus spun the map around till he was faced by what looked like two large classrooms were in front of him. By simply pointing one finger between the two classrooms another hidden room became visible to the group.

"This right here is a secret stash of supplies." Seamus said. "If we're lucky, it will have remained undetected by the shadow demons."

"Why in the world is it a secret?" Liza asked.

"Well, it's a secret cause it's not meant to be known by the students." The green dragon increased the image's size on the map. "It's usually where the teachers keep their back ups for potions and elixirs when they're teaching students. If we're lucky, we'll find a lot to salvage from it."

Before he could continue explaining though the captured dakgrul perked its head up suddenly before it turned to its left. No one was sitting when they noticed the low growl that it was admitting from its throat. Aiden had Warfang ready, just incase there was a battle to be had.

"Hold it." Theresa whispered. "If there's a chance that we

can avoid a battle we should take a shot on it."

"Rexkin, that chance could be low..." Garrett growled under his breath.

"We're going to end up fighting this things later, Garrett." Theresa retorted. "If we can avoid any loss of our supplies and save our strength for the stronger demons I would rather take that path."

The largest dragon sighed in defeat once more as they quietly stood together. Their dakgrul turned back to them for a moment, as if it was waiting for an order from them. Seamus gave a slow nod of his head.

"Steer whatever it is off." He ordered.

The dakgrul gave a slow nod before it walked out of the room. The captured demon turned towards its left, than sat down as if it was expecting something to arrive. Aiden swallowed a lump in his throat as he watched the dakgrul with tensed muscles in his body. Seamus said that the creature would be loyal to them thanks to his magic, but he couldn't help worrying that the next shadow demon would sense that the dakgrul was under control of someone other than the Overmind.

The ground trembled a bit beneath their feet. Aello almost fell over before Liza caught her from doing so. Aiden nearly did as well, but didn't as Garrett grabbed the back of his shirt and pulled him back up. The young warrior ignored the whispered 'Stupid whelp' from the large dragon.

Though the dakgrul didn't tremble from the ground. Instead it seemed determined to face down what was coming towards it. Aiden took notice of its bare fangs as it stared down into the darkness that was approaching it.

Aiden didn't have to wait long for the creature to reveal itself to their dakgrul. As what emerged from the darkness was one of the strangest looking creatures that Aiden would ever see in his life.

It was some kind behemoth that could have passed off as

a collaboration of different animals. The most noticeable part of this new demon it was a quadruped beast and had four very large legs. Each leg looked like a solid tree trunk, the skin actually looked like it was made out of tree bark with ridges that looked very similar.

Besides its massive legs, the behemoth's face was also a sight to see. From it's jawline Aiden noticed two very large tusks that curved upwards. On these tusks though were several other smaller tusks that curled the same way. The main tusks had to be at least as long as a regular elephant's tusk, if not longer. Each point was just as sharp as the last. They had to have been sharp enough to pierce through steel walls themselves.

But one of the most disturbing things about this beast was that its mouth was not like the one for a mammal. In fact, they weren't even mammalian at all. What took the place of a mouth was a very large pair of insect like mandibles. The mandibles were as black as the night sky was when it seemed like the stars had been stolen away. But at the very end of the mandibles was a light green color of sorts. Aiden realized that the tips of the mandibles were dripping some kind of green goo down onto the ground.

The very first thing Aiden thought what that goo was poison. But the rising steam from the drops of goo proved him wrong when he saw small holes in the floor appear. This was far worse than poison. It was acid.

The behemoth also lacked any kind of long nose in the front of its face. Instead only two large, but thin, slits served as the nose. The eyes of the behemoth, like most creatures that were its size, were small in comparison to the rest of its body. They were black beady eyes that, at first glance, looked like they lacked any kind of pupils.

Aiden's grip around Warfang tightened as they watched the behemoth glare down at their dakgrul. Despite the very obvious size difference, their captured demon did not move an inch from its spot. If it made one wrong move though, Aiden could see that it would meet a very gruesome ending from this larger demon.

"What the hell IS that?" Liza hissed in a whisper.

"A very rare kind of shadow demon." Seamus responded. "It's known as a Kelgrath. Not very smart, but very very dangerous."

The team's captured dakgrul stared right up at the kelgrath with its gleaming eyes. With a slow snarl the dakgrul bared its sharp teeth and claws at the kelgrath. The larger of the demon stared down at the smaller beast. It let out some kind of weird grunt as well.

"Intruders...where?"

Aiden's ears perked up a bit at the sudden voice. At first he glanced over to the rest of his team, as if one of them had suddenly spoken out. None of them were looking in his direction though. All of them were too captivated by the two demons conversing to even question what Aiden thought he heard.

He glanced back to the two demons. Did those two words come from one of the demons?

The dakgrul's upper lip curved into a snarl as it stared down the much larger kelgrath.

"No intruders. Go away."

That was the second time that he heard another voice. Aiden was so close to telling the others that he could understand the demons for some reason, but decided against it. Not only did he theorize that they would not believe him, but even if they did believe him they would have assumed that he had suddenly began to study demon arts in secret.

The kelgrath glared at the smaller shadow demon before stomping one foot down on the ground. The area trembled from the stomp, but not enough to knock over any bookshelves or break glass vials.

"No lying." The Kelgrath 'said,' **"Overmind knows intruders here. Must find. Must squish them flat."**

"The Overmind also stated to bring any intruders to it."

The dakgrul argued back. "**You kelgraths must have very small brains if you forget the orders of the Overmind.**"

That particular insult the Kelgrath did not like. It let out some kind of scratching hissing noise as the insect like mandibles it possessed scrit and scratched against each other. The sound was ear grating as Aiden, Aello, and Liza covered their ears in pain from the sound. The dragons didn't seem to bother to cover their ears, but they were annoyed by the sound of the mandibles.

"**Brain is not small!**" The Kelgrath roared. "**Kelgrath mightier than puny dakgruls!!**"

"**Body muscle does not make up for the lack of brains.**" The dakgrul replied. "**Go away. There's no intruders here.**"

The kelgrath let out some kind of low snarl from its mandibles. As it began to turn around though, it stopped midway before turning back to the dakgrul. A dangerous glint in its eyes as it stared down the smaller demon.

"**Where pack at?**"

Aiden's eyes grew wide at that question. Despite it being a lumbering mass of muscle, the kelgrath had picked up on the fact that their dakgrul did not have any pack members left. He wasn't worried about the dakgrul turning against them, but worried him was if the kelgrath would pick up on the fact the demon it was talking to was under the control of Seamus instead of the Overmind now.

He was caught in a predicament now. If the kelgrath didn't believe the dakgrul's next answer, their demon would be dead. But if he did rush out and attack the kelgrath, he would end up giving away their position to the larger demon. Either way if things went south it would be bad for the capture dakgrul.

But even if Aiden did attack the kelgrath to save the dakgrul from being killed, where would he strike the behemoth? It was a foe that was quite massive and he had no idea where any of its vitals could be located. But a part of Aiden was screaming to do something before the group lost their dakgrul.

The dakgrul however continued to stare up at the kelgrath. It did not appear intimated by the larger demon. Its lips curled back once more to reveal its sharp teeth towards the kelgrath.

"My pack is hunting." It said, **"Like you they seek out the intruders that the Overmind wishes to see."**

The kelgrath however did not move from its spot. Its massive legs slowly began to turn right back to the dakgrul. Aiden saw a glint from the eyes of the behemoth. Had the dakgrul been found out by the massive shadow demon??

After what seemed like forever the kelgrath let out a snort before turning away from the dakgrul. The tension in the room finally left once the kelgrath was out of sight. Aiden's forehead was covered in sweat from how nervous he had become during the exchange between the kelgrath and their dakgrul.

The dakgrul let out a snarl at the retreating kelgrath before it returned back to the group. Seamus stroked the top of the dakgrul's head like a dog owner would when the dog had behaved.

"Good boy." Seamus said. "I don't have a clue on what you told that ugly thing, but it looks like we managed to avoid a fight."

Aiden's suspicion that the others could not understand a word that the demons were saying was confirmed at that very moment. It seemed that for the moment, only he could understand the shadow demons. The perplexed look on his face might have given him away to Theresa's ever watching eyes though. She immediately tapped his shoulder to get his attention.

"What's wrong?"

Aiden didn't answer right away. He just stared at their dakgrul as the once dangerous enemy in silence. As he stared at the beast, the dakgrul slowly turned towards him. The demon's eyes stared right back at his own for a moment. For a moment it felt like the dakgrul knew that Aiden understood it.

"...Nothing's wrong." Aiden said quietly. "Nothing at all."

CHAPTER 9 - PRIME DEMON

"You know, we should give this bugger a name." Seamus said with a smile. "I think he's earned it after all."

"Really?" Liza replied, her lips pursed up. "You're now going to give him a name because of what it managed to do with that thing?"

"Well, truthfully I've been wanting to give him a name since I captured him, but I know that Rexkin here would say it would be a stupid idea."

"You're right. It is a stupid idea to give a name to a shadow demon." Theresa replied.

"Aw come on now, Thes, he needs some kind of name, right?"

"Seamus this is not a pet we're talking about here." The white dragoness growled. "It's a shadow demon, a demon you captured to suit our needs. Once we're done here and the Overmind is dead, he will either go back to the shadows with the rest of his kind of he will die alongside them."

Seamus pouted a bit as he folded his arms across his chest. Aiden, Liza, Aello, and even the dakgrul were surprised to see him make such a face. Theresa however was not amused as she spat a small white fireball at her fellow dragon. Seamus gracefully dodged, but the fireball slammed into the wall behind him.

"Hey! Try not to burn this school down would ya?!"

"Seamus, do not be foolish with this idea that you can keep a demon as a pet." Garrett spoke. "You do not use demonic magic, it would be foolish of you to keep this thing as your own personal pet just because it managed to drive away one of the stupidest breeds of demons."

"You stay out of this." Theresa and Seamus said simultaneously.

Liza had to stiffen a giggle that threatened to escape from her lips. Aiden also had to fight back the urge to laugh as well as Theresa and Seamus went back and forth with each other about naming the dakgrul. Mia however looked confused, tilting her head to the side.

"What's a pet?" She asked.

Both Aiden and Liza almost fell over at the sudden question from the young harpy princess. They had almost forgotten that their newest member to their team was not completely used to human terms.

"Well, Aello, sometimes humans decide to take in some small animals and care for them. Like dogs and cats." Liza explained. "The humans take care of the pets and in exchange for that, the pets give love in return."

Mia's head remained at the tilted angle.

"Does that make Aiden Theresa's pet then?"

Seamus burst out into laughter. Liza joined in right with him at that question. Aiden however was as red as a beet, while Theresa's face only had a minor blush.

"W-Why would you ask something like that?!" Aiden cried out.

"Well...she's always watching out over you during training, and she told me how when you were still new to combat she would often come to your aide to keep you safe." Mia pointed.

"T-That doesn't make me her pet!"

"I dunno, whelp. I think that suits you perfectly. You're always at her beck n call and she's always protecting you even when it's effectively babying you."

"T-Theresa doesn't baby me!"

Before Seamus could respond with a witty retort, a sudden sense of dread came from within the group. Each of them turned to the source, Theresa. The white dragoness' hair was flowing up in the air from the intense heat her body was giving off. Each one of the team began to sweat from the intense heat that her body was pulsing from her human form. Even Garrett was a little bit intimidated from it.

"This. Is not. FUNNY." Theresa growled through her teeth, as Aiden noticed that her teeth had reverted to sharp fangs. "Am I understood?"

"Yes ma'am!" The entire team said in unison.

"Good."

Theresa's long hair suddenly stopped flowing upwards before returning back to its normal straight length. Aiden noticed her pointed fangs returned back to normal human teeth once more. The same kind smile was once again back on her lips.

"Note to self, never ever anger Theresa." Aiden thought as she walked right past him.

"Alright everyone, if you are all rested let's get ready to move. We have a lot of ground to cover and no one besides us is going to stop the Overmind."

As soon as they were rested they began to head back out. Aiden's wound had finally healed up properly, thankfully it did not leave a scar. This was the second time he got lucky and avoided getting a massive scar, he wondered if there would be a third time. He knew that eventually he would end up with a scar, but for now he was just grateful to have been spared such an ugly looking scar.

He was also grateful that he wouldn't have to explain it to his mother or father this time around anyway.

The job of carrying the bag filled with all the potions and elixirs fell to Seamus. Both Aiden and Liza had offered to carry the bag themselves, but Theresa told them that they had no experience carrying delicate things like the contents within the vials. It only made perfect sense for Seamus to carry the bag himself so that there was no chance of the vials being broken in the heat of combat.

It was better than letting Garrett handle the bag. If they were really unlucky, he would have used the bag as some kind of weapon on the next shadow demon that they saw.

The further they progressed down the halls though the more twisted and destroyed they became. Slash marks had become common on the walls now, but what took Aiden completely off guard were the splashes of blood on the wall. Some of it looked fresh, while the rest looked like it had dried after being there for hours.

None of the group wanted to know if it was human blood or demonic blood.

Their captured dakgrul continued to guide them slowly down the halls of the Academy. Any doubt that Aiden once had about the demon betraying them were gone when it managed to convince the kelgrath that it had not betrayed their Overmind. Sure Seamus had said that the beast would not betray them due to the shackles on its ankles, but one had to doubt just a little bit.

The further they walked down the hallway the more claw marks they came across. But they weren't the only things they came across. Large footprints from kelgraths covered the floor. Broken tusks from the giant demons also littered the hallways in every corner. Some stuck out from the walls, others were on top of bookshelves, while many were shattered and left sharp pointed ends stabbing right into the floor itself.

Some of the mages that were trying to escape or the Grand Mage's eldest son must have been responsible for the littering of these tusks.

"Look at these things." Aiden said as they walked. "They're everywhere in this hallway."

"Yeah seriously." Liza scoffed. "You think for such a great academy they would at least have the decency to use magic to clean up this mess."

"Uh, I don't think they could clean this up in the middle of a battle, Liz." Aiden replied.

"Oh Aide, you know that's not what I meant." She waved her back and forth. "I was merely saying that I expect the mages to be able to use their magic to fix up messes like this and make it presentable to say the least."

"Both of you, quiet." Seamus suddenly ordered them. Before either of them could argue back at him, the noticed that their dakgrul's spines began to tremble badly. Aiden glanced back to Seamus. He noticed small beads of sweat were forming on his forehead.

"We're getting dangerously close to something terrible."

Theresa instinctively got in front of Aiden as she summoned her two swords. Even Garrett seemed to get tense as he hefted his large axe onto his shoulders. Aello glanced back to Liza, who gave her a small nod before the harpy princess drew out her falchion.

"All right, the three of you who've never seen the mess we're about to come across stay close to us." Seamus said, Aiden took note that his voice was low. "Do not touch anything, or look around. Got it?"

No words had to be spoken as the youngest members of the team slowly followed after Seamus, Theresa, and Garrett. Everyone felt frightened when the dragons were worried.

Normally the Trinity would be calm, collected, with their emotions kept firmly under control.

But something was getting to them. Something that their battle hardened skills and years of combat experience told them was dangerous, putting them on the edge.

Theresa stood in front of Aiden with one hand holding his tightly. The other held the combination of her two weapons, Snowfyre, as they walked down the hallway. The tight grip she had on his hand became tighter and tighter the further they progressed. Just like Seamus, Theresa seemed clearly intent on keeping Aiden close by her in case things went wrong.

The next room the team walked into was a large square area, filled with long tables and several broken chairs. Littered on the floor were broken utensils - forks, knives, and spoons. It didn't take a second guess to figure out that they had entered the cafeteria for the academy. But that paled in comparison to the true 'show' of the cafeteria.

Before their eyes laid broken dead demon bodies of different kinds. They ranged from the lean dakgrul to the tall and destructive kelgrath they had encountered earlier. Most of them either had been squashed, or in the case of the kelgraths, their tusks had been ripped off their faces completely. Like most of the halls of the academy, the floor and walls had dried blood covering them. It was unclear if it was human or shadow demon blood.

Many of the walls themselves were also destroyed from the center or had large cracks in them. It was a sign that something very powerful had been in this room before the team arrived.

Liza made a very audible gulping sound upon seeing the destruction before her. Aiden didn't blame her for making that sound. His own body began to feel a great sense of dread at the sight. Something, or rather someone, very strong had been here.

"What the hell happened here?" Liza asked.

"Something I was afraid would happen." Seamus answered. His eyes glinted as he pulled his staff, Hurricane, up in front of him. Aiden had never seen the green dragon get this tense. The fact that his teeth were turning sharp, like Theresa's whenever she was upset was a clear give away to the tension that Seamus was feeling. "The culprit behind this, my young friends, is known as a Teleranta. A prime demon."

Chills immediately went up the spines of Aiden, Liza, and Aello. The last three words were said with such disdain and anger that it seemed that Seamus could have passed off as Garrett in that very moment.

"Keep your eyes open, all of you." Theresa ordered. "A Teleranta is not like a kelgrath or dakgrul. They are not beast like. They're sentient and very, very dangerous. More so than most of the other demons here."

Aello let out a very silent 'eep' sound from behind Liza. The latter immediately drew out Gitanel in front of her. Garrett immediately pulled out his axe, which Aiden had come to learn it by the name Worldshaker, as the muscles of the great dragon grew at least a few sizes. Mia and Gabriella surrounded Aello, claws at the ready.

Their captured dakgrul however, was the one who looked the most concerned of the team. While it was now loyal to them, Aiden could see the fear in its eyes. He could have sworn it didn't want to move a single step forward due to the dead bodies of its kind littered all over the ground.

That's when Aiden heard it. A very deep, yet raspy, breathing sound. It was unlike any other kind of sound that he had heard before in his life. The very sound was filled with a lingering danger. It was almost as if the Teleranta was hunting them.

Then it hit Aiden. It <u>was</u> hunting them!

"Guys, we need to move apart, now!" Aiden shouted. Before anyone could argue with him though, they found themselves being pushed away by Aiden himself! "GO!"

At that moment, a massive claw erupted from his right, snatching Aiden in an instant. He felt his entire body being crushed as the monstrous claw lifted him slowly into the air. There, in the darkness of the cafeteria, a pair of baleful, pale yellow orbs gleamed.

The shadows lifted away as it stalked into the light. The beast, so massive even that word seemed to not do it justice, was easily one of the most terrifying things Aiden had ever laid eyes on. The creature was easily the size of Garrett's dragon form, possibly even bigger, judging by the way it hunched over.

The Teleranta, was a horrendous sight to behold. It's harsh scaly skin was black as coal, tainted by streaks of blood red along its arms that pulsed with immense power. As it's tail swished back and forth, Aiden caught site of the same shade of crimson along the underside. It was brief, but he was able to get a glimpse of its powerful hands. They were massive, with four long fingers, each ending in terrifying claws. It stood on massive legs, balanced on three deadly-looking talons. Aiden glanced up, watching as the creature unfurled its burly, bat-like wings, each crowned with a sharp spike.

Worst of all, though, about the Teleranta, was its gargantuan head. While the creature was covered in scales, its head appeared to be striped up to its skull. Two curved horns rose up from the sides of its head, as if guarding the eerie jewel in the center of its forehead. Like its eyes, this gem gleamed pale amber, as if brimming with malevolence.

The Teleranta glanced to Aiden, a demented grin on its face when its baleful eyes met his own. Within those evil eyes he saw it, the intent to harm all life that dared to stand before the prime demon.

"Humans…" It said slowly. "I thought you were all behind that pathetic barrier."

"Yeah? Well you thought wrong!" Aiden replied in kind. He wasted no time as he summoned Warfang into his hand before stabbing his blade into the thumb of the Teleranta. The blade managed to cut through its skin, but the giant prime demon did not release a cry of pain. Instead, the monstrous face just grinned, as its grip around Aiden suddenly grew tighter.

"Oh, you'll be fun to kill, boy."

At that exact moment a brilliant flash of light exploded from the ground below them. Both Aiden and the Prime Demon glanced down to the source of light. Within the blink of an eye Garrett's large dragon head suddenly rammed the three horns, including the broken one, into the abdomen of the Teleranta. The impact from the head butt was enough to force the Teleranta to release Aiden from its iron grip. As Aiden fell, he found himself falling onto the back of Garrett.

"Whelp, grab onto a spike and do NOT let go!" Garrett ordered. It took Aiden a few seconds to adjust to the sudden deeper voice of Garrett, but he did not argue as he held on for dear life on Garrett's back.

The largest member of the dragons continued with his attack. With his immense strength Garrett began to push the Teleranta back. As he did the broken tables and bodies of the dead demons flew into the air as the massive strength of Garrett allowed him to move the Teleranta back.

The Prime Demon growled as after a few seconds of Garrett pushing it, it got its footing. Two large hands suddenly grabbed Garrett's shoulders, forcing the large dragon to come to a complete stop as well. Neither of the large creatures could give up their position, even if they wanted to. The harder the Teleranta pushed back against Garrett's shoulders, the more determined the largest dragon was to keep his three horns in the abdomen of the demon.

The battle of physical power could have lasted forever between these two beasts. For the briefest of moments Aiden believed they would continue this bout until the end of time. But he knew that one of them had to give in.

The Teleranta made some kind of sound as it suddenly pulled its massive right fist back and punched Garrett in the side of his face. The punch was enough to force Garrett to pull his head back; the dragon glared at the Prime Demon. The same glare was returned as the fingers of the Teleranta clenched into fists once more. Again the Teleranta threw another punch at Garrett's face, forcing the great dragon's head to rise up into the air.

Aiden's eyes grew wide at the force of the Prime Demon's strength. Garrett was the strongest member on their team and the Teleranta had just forced the head of the great dragon up with a single punch.

The Teleranta wasted no time with its next attack though. It immediately flung its hand out and grabbed Garrett around his neck and began to squeeze tightly. A demented grin came to its mouth as it held Garrett.

"I shall make you cry out in pain, dragon." It said. "And then I'll break your body in half."

Aiden glances up to Garrett's eyes. At first it looked like the great dragon was in a lot of pain, but then he saw his eyes open slowly. They weren't filled with pain, they were filled with anger and annoyance.

Garrett didn't waste a second in starting his counter attack, opening his mouth at a gradual pace. The Prime Demon took notice of this and began to laugh, but that laugh disappeared when he noticed a spark form in Garrett's mouth. Time slowed down as Garrett unleashed a powerful blast of fire right into the face of the Teleranta. The scorching flames were so intense it forced Aiden to cover his eyes with one arm at the heat.

The fire from Garrett was also affecting the Teleranta as it was forced to use its arms as a shield to hold off the attack. Aiden saw it snarl in the intense heat though as it suddenly swung its massive tail out at Garrett.

"GARRETT!" Aiden shouted to him

He didn't know if Garrett had heard him in time, or if it was because of Garrett's eyes, that the great dragon was able to block the tail swipe with one of his claws. Once Garrett grabbed ahold of the giant tail though, the Prime Demon quickly delivered a powerful kick to his chest.

A loud hissing sound came from Garrett as the kick forced him back a few feet away from the Teleranta. Aiden never thought he would see the strongest member of their team forced back by a kick. He glanced back to the Prime Demon, who despite the burns it had on its body, walked slowly towards Garrett.

"You are strong, dragon." It said through clenched teeth. "But you will never be able to defeat me alone."

Garrett positioned his claws in the ground before firing a larger blast of fire at the Teleranta. The Prime Demon was ready this time though and it used its massive left wing as a shield to prevent the fire from burning into its hide once more.

In that instant, Aiden saw it. The Teleranta had gathered some kind of dark energy into its right hand, a large purple orb of some kind. What looked like some kind of grin on the Prime Demon's face vanished though when he threw the large orb into the fire that Garrett had let loose.

Garrett, who looked like he had been taken by complete surprise, stopped his attack before dodging the attack clumsily. The purple orb flew by the beast, singeing his left hind leg badly though, before making impact with the wall behind him. The great dragon growled as he glanced at his injured leg.

"Dammit..." He growled.

"Garrett, look out!" Aiden shouted.

In that moment, the Teleranta was above the both of them. Both of its hands held two large orbs of dark energy. It wasted no time as it held out both of its hands and fired the two attacks at them. They were slow, but they were also massive in size. Garrett growled as he held his ground and stared directly at the two orbs with the same steely determination as before.

Just before the two orbs could make impact with Aiden and Garrett a white flame flew out from behind them as it slammed into one of the large orbs. Aiden smiled in relief; Theresa's white fire was perhaps the most powerful fire breath around. A second flame, of normal color, joined her flame as well. Seamus' fire breath.

The two flames pushed back against the two orbs. The power behind the flames seemed strong enough to push the orbs completely away from Aiden and Garrett as the four attacks cancelled each other out.

Aiden glanced to his right as he saw Theresa's dragon form land right besides Garrett. Seamus followed suit, landing beside Garrett's left side.

"...the hell were you thinking?" Seamus asked the larger dragon. "Trying to take on a Teleranta without our help?!"

"I can handle my own battles." Garrett replied with a snarl. "Where are those girls?"

"We're right here!" Liza cried out from Seamus' back. She sat on the back of Seamus' neck, grabbing onto his neck for dear life. Aello, however, hovered in place besides Liza as her guardians took to Aello's side.

"Garrett, you can't take this one down by yourself. Not without help!" Seamus argued. The larger dragon spat something onto the floor.

"I've defeated Telerantas in the past, and I can do so again."

"This is different and you know it!" Theresa snapped at him. "Telerantas are not mindless demons, you know that!"

She glared back at their target. The Teleranta stood there with the same demented grin on its face as one finger began to gather energy on its fingertip.

"Garrett, give me Aiden, now." She ordered. The larger dragon gave her a confused look for a moment, but slowly placed his wing over Theresa's back so that Aiden could slide off.

With a soft thud Aiden found himself sitting on the back of Theresa. He didn't complain about switching between the two dragons. Compared to Garrett's rough scales that felt like they were going to cut through his legs, Theresa's were soft and smooth.

"What do we do, Rexkin?" Seamus asked. "The kids are nowhere near ready to do battle with a Prime Demon without our help."

"That's exactly why they aren't taking part of the fight." Theresa replied.

"What the hell are you talking about?!" Liza asked. "The three of you are strong sure, but you'll need our help!"

"Even with the three of us working together, this demon will prove to be incredibly dangerous." Seamus said darkly. "The rest of you are nowhere near the ability to fight a Prime Demon and survive."

"Even with all our training?!" Liza shouted. "You took us under your wings to teach us how to fend for ourselves! What good is that training going to be to us if you don't let us help you?!"

"Against a Teleranta, you three would be crushed in a single swipe of its giant claw." Garrett growled. "You will not enter this battle, no matter what happens."

Aiden turned to Theresa for support, but the white dragoness refused to look him in the eye. She kept her head low, turned away from him as the Trinity faced down the Teleranta. Aiden's fists clenched as he summoned Warfang to his side. To get her attention, he kicked his heels into the sides of her neck.

"Theresa! Let us help you fight this thing!"

"No," she responded, in a tone he couldn't recognize. The warm, kind-hearted voice of his best friend was long gone, replaced by a harsh, hollow combination of anger...and fear? "I lost my family, my home, my friends, and my king. I refuse...I refuse to lose you, too, Aiden!"

"T-Theresa..."

The Teleranta let out an unholy laugh at the group's arguing. The roar was enough to force Aello to land behind Liza. Theresa's lips grew into a snarl at the Prime Demon's laughter. The pale yellow eyes of their enemy gleamed once.

"It matters not if they assist you or not, dragons. All that will happen will be the same result. All of you will die, by my hands alone."

The Teleranta pulled his right arm back and swung it once, letting out a powerful crescent like slash towards the Trinity. The speed it possessed was incredible as it rammed itself into the chests of all three of the dragons at once.

"THERESA!" Aiden shouted as the attack pressed into her hide.

The white dragoness' claws dug themselves into the ground in an attempt to keep her balance, but the energy from the attack was enough to force her off her feet. Aiden nearly fell off her back as she was sent flying backwards. Theresa's eyes snapped open though as she turned around and grabbed him with her right front claw. Though Aiden was safe in her claw, the Teleranta charged from behind her and delivered a deep slash to her back.

The white dragoness let out a short roar of pain from the attack. That was the first time Aiden had ever heard her let out pained roar in her true state. Reality suddenly began to hit him. The Trinity, while powerful, never once said that they were invincible. His eyes widened and he watched as the Teleranta grabbed Theresa's throat with one claw and began to squeeze it tightly.

"Trying to defend the boy, are we dragoness scum?" The Prime Demon asked with a scoff. "It makes no difference, he will die anyway. Even if you defend him he will die."

Another loud roar came from the Telerenta's side, Seamus charged the Prime Demon in fury. The green dragon let loose a powerful blast of its own fire at the Teleranta in a vengeance fueled attack. The Prime Demon growled as it used its free hand to block the fire.

The fire did not stop as Seamus continued to breathe his intense fire at the Prime Demon. Finally a speck of fire got passed the hand of the Teleranta and it landed in the right eye of the great monster. The Prime Demon grunted a bit from the attack as it lowered its guard for a second.

In that one moment, Garrett charged from above and landed on top of the Teleranta. With his massive jaws, he bit down into the hide of the Teleranta with the intention of delivering a killing blow. The force of the bite was enough for the Prime Demon to let out a pained cry as Garrett's sharp teeth dug themselves into its right shoulder. Aiden watched from Theresa's claw in shock as blue blood welled up from Garrett's bite.

"Wretched dragons!" The Teleranta shouted in fury as his free hand reached back and grabbed the upper jaw of Garrett. Despite the Teleranta's incredible strength, one hand was not going to remove Garrett's bite from its shoulder. If anything all it did was make the dragon of strength more determined to keeps his teeth in the Teleranta.

The Prime Demon turned its gaze back towards Theresa. It let out an annoyed sound before pulling back its arm and throwing her away from him. Once its hand was free, it grabbed Garrett by his neck and began to push back as hard as it could against the massive dragon.

As the two giant creatures did battle with each other, Aiden watched as Theresa's lifeless like head did not respond to being thrown. His eyes grew wide as her body began to race towards the wall of the cafeteria.

"THERESA!"

The dragoness' eyes stirred a little bit. Once the gears in her mind began to turn she quickly spun her back towards the wall and held Aiden close to her chest. Aiden closed his eyes tightly as Theresa's dragon form slammed into the wall of the cafeteria at full force.

Time seemed to slow down as debris fell from the wall and hit

Theresa over and over on her back and neck. The white dragoness gritted her teeth though as she took every hit without complaint. But Aiden could see in her emerald green eyes that she was in pain. Something he foolishly thought he would never see Theresa go through.

When the pieces of debris finally stopped falling, Aiden was released from Theresa's claw. The white dragoness' breathing was heavy and her body had suffered multiple wounds from the Teleranta's claw attack and the heavy debris falling onto her, but she was alive. Aiden's eyes shrunk as he ran up to her head. He dropped Warfang along the way as he finally approached Theresa's face.

"T-Theresa!" He cried out as he placed both his hands on her cheek. "C-Come on, I know you can hear me! Theresa, you can't let something like this lick you! Not like this! Theresa!"

Slowly but surely, Aiden's words began to reach the white dragoness. Her eyelids twitched for a moment, but they opened up and glanced towards Aiden.

She pushed herself up from the ground as best as she could. Her once beautiful dragoness form bled badly from the damage she received battling the Prime Demon. Unlike before where her body looked unstoppable, it looked like it was about to fall apart at any moment. Despite the immense pain that she was feeling though Aiden saw it. A smile crept to her lips.

"Aiden…you're….okay?"

"Don't worry about me!" Aiden snapped. "C-Come on, w-we gotta get your wounds h-healed! I'll use Emalla a-and…"

For some reason, Aiden's eyes could not help but well up in tears. The feeling of fear that grew in his chest began to rise up as he glanced back to the battle with the Teleranta. Garrett and Seamus were holding their own, but it was eas to see they were on the defensive.

"O-Once you're h-healed we'll get back into the fight and kill that thing! Come on, w-we need you!"

"...I'm sorry..."

Aiden's heart stopped for a moment at those words. He turned back to Theresa's eyes. In all his life, he never once heard Theresa utter those words.

"I made it seem like...the dragons were invincible. That I was invincible to you." She coughed a bit, some blood coming down her lips. Her breathing becoming more raspy and heavy. "I mislead you, Aiden...because I loved your ideal world of fantasy. And now...now you've been forced to see reality...that even us, the dragons, have a hard time fighting a prime demon...I'm so sorry, Aiden..."

"S-Stop talking!" Aiden shouted. "You didn't let me down! Theresa! You've made my life better than it's ever been! Don't talk like this!"

Theresa gave a small smile as her body faltered for a moment before regaining balance. She grunted in frustration before digging her claws into the ground.

"If things go south...you, Liza, Aello and her guardians...need to run. Do you, understand?" She asked. "We will fight, until this thing is dead, we will fight..."

"No!" Aiden shouted. "You're injured! If you continue to fight like this you'll die!"

The white dragoness glanced back down towards Aiden. A somber look in her eyes as she gently lowered head back down to Aiden's eye level. With a small smile the white dragoness nudged him with her snout.

"You trust me, do you not?"

"I..."

Before he could finish speaking, Theresa's eyes narrowed as she turned her head back towards the Teleranta. Aiden barely saw it happen within that instant. A large shadowy orb had been thrown at the two of them, with the intention of killing them both off in a single blast.

Theresa however stood her ground as she reared her head

back and unleashed a powerful stream of white fire at the orb. The two attacks clashed with one another as a power contest between the attacks began. The sheer force of the shadow orb was enough to contend with the power of Theresa's fire breath. At first it seemed that the two attacks were completely even, but Aiden noticed that Theresa's fire was slowly losing ground with the shadow orb.

Aiden could see it in Theresa's eyes. She was straining herself in order to keep her flame going. The damage from the rocks and debris earlier had taken its toll on the white dragoness. The more she strained herself to keep the attack going, the weaker her fire became.

A new feeling of anger grew within Aiden. It wasn't anger at Theresa, but at the Teleranta. How it had came from out nowhere, endangered their mission, and now it was forcing Theresa to strain herself for his protection. Something that he made a promise to himself that he would never let her do ever again.

His eyes glanced back to the battle away from him and Theresa. The Telranta had Seamus in its claws, squeezing his neck like it had done with Theresa. Garrett himself was covered in cuts as well from the battle, and he looked furious. Above the Telranta Aello carried Liza with her talons. Mia and Gabriella flew beside their princess as well. The two guardians let out a shriek of some kind before they dive bombed the Teleranta with their sharp talons, swiping at its veins on its neck. Aello and Liza made their move next. Both of them struck fast against the prime demon when they flew past its face, but their attacks only seemed to annoy it rather than do any damage.

"Damn you..." Aiden snarled, Warfang appeared in his right hand. "You bastard!!"

A familiar feeling rose up from within Aiden's body once more. It was one that he had not felt in over a year since facing down Raven in the Harpy's Den. The same fiery aura that surrounded Warfang's blade that one moment had returned. Aiden's eyes glinted as he pulled his blade back and swung with all his might.

"Please." He prayed. *"Please come out again, Draconic Firestorm! Please!!"*

Aiden's prayers were answered. The same fiery dragon head that had erupted from his sword one year ago erupted forth once more. It let out a powerful roar as it flew by Theresa's white fire and slammed into the shadow orb alongside it at full power.

The intense power of the Draconic Firestorm was enough to completely shatter the orb with just one hit. With no orb to stop the combined fires of Theresa's white flame and Aiden's attack, the two fiery streams flew towards the Teleranta at full force. Before making contact with the prime demon though, Theresa's white fire suddenly began to merge with Aiden's Draconic Firestorm. When the merging was completely, the white fire swirled around the fiery dragon.

The Teleranta, noticing that something was wrong, turned its head towards the new combined attacks of Theresa and Aiden. Its pale eyes seemed shocked at the sudden attack reaching it at full speed. It wasted no time as it threw Seamus away and held both of its hands up in an attempt to block the attack from slamming into its body.

The very moment its hands made contact with the attack though, a loud 'hiss' came from its palms. It was trying to hold the attack back with all its might. Aiden could see that the force of his attack was forcing the Teleranta to skid back slowly. As it continued to hold the attack back, Aiden could feel his mental strength slowly fading. He had forgotten that using this attack before had nearly drained him. And he was starting to feel weaker just using this one attack.

But he had to give it his all. If he didn't then there was an incredibly high chance that this battle would be his last!

"Ultima!"

Aiden's eyes widened at the sound of a new voice that echoed in the cafeteria. Before he could even ask what was going on, a medium sized white ball that was about the size of a basketball, flew above his and Theresa's combined attacks straight at the head of the Teleranta.

Though it looked small it obviously had a powerful punch to it. The Teleranta's head jerked backwards from the attack so violently that its arms were also forced to go upward as well. This proved to be its final moments, as the combined forces of Aiden's Draconic Firestorm and Theresa's white fire suddenly rammed themselves into the Teleranta's body.

The sheer power from the attacks was more than enough to begin to burn away at the Prime Demon. Aiden couldn't see it burn away, but he was able to hear the Teleranta let out a pained roar one last time before the attacks completely overwhelmed its body.

In an instant, the great Prime Demon that had been there before completely disappeared as the Draconic Firestorm finished its job. The fiery dragon head let out one roar of pride before disappearing into thin air.

As soon as it vanished, Aiden fell to one knee. He was so exhausted from using the attack that it felt like his entire body had just been filled with lead. Aiden took several deep breaths; his eyes watering, blurring his vision.

"Theresa…" He gasped out. Just as he was about to pass out, Theresa reverted to her human form once more before grabbing Aiden in her arms as his vision turned completely back.

CHAPTER 10 - THE ELDEST SON

*A*iden groaned as he heard voices talking beside him. His head was pulsing in pain as he slowly rose up from where he was laying. Much to his surprise, it was on a soft cushion that must have come from one of the couches. He blinked in surprise momentarily as he glanced around him.

"Where am I?" He thought to himself. His vision was still a bit blurry so he couldn't make out exactly where he was.

In that moment he felt a surge of pain rise up in his right arm. Aiden hissed as his left hand immediately went to grab his right arm. In the back of his mind he cursed himself for using the Draconic Firestorm again. His entire body felt like the ultimate attack of Warfang took a lot out of him.

The voices he had heard before continued to talk though, as if they were unaware that he had woken up. Aiden blinked a couple of times, trying to clear his vision of the blurriness that he suddenly had. After the fourth or fifth blink, his vision came back crystal clear to him.

He was surprised to see that he was no longer in the cafeteria, but in what appeared to be another supply closet. Unlike the first one though, which despite a few broken vials was in fine shape, this one leaned more towards being completely destroyed. Shelves were either burnt down to the ground, rammed through the walls, or had broken pieces scattered across the ground.

Unlike the first supply room, there were very few bottles that weren't destroyed. At most Aiden could only count at least three of them that had not been broken. And that was if he was counting correctly.

His right arm pulsed in pain once again, which brought another painful hiss from his throat. This time he caught the attention of those in the room with him.

"Oh thank God, Aiden!" Said Liza, who immediately rushed over to him. "You scared the crap out of us you know!"

"U-Us?" Aiden blinked, glancing over to who was with Liza in the room.

Aello offered a small smile as she saw him. The youngest harpy princess had not been very vocal throughout this journey, but it wasn't hard for Aiden to see the relief in her eyes that he was alive.

"You shouldn't make us worry so much." She said, right before muttering under her breath. "Theresa thought that you had killed yourself..."

Aiden's eyes immediately grew wide at the mere mention of Theresa's name. Despite the pain in his right arm, he slowly pushed himself to stand up from the cushion he was laying on. Liza immediately grabbed him when he was about to fall over.

"Easy there big guy." She said. "You're not completely recovered from using that badass attack just yet."

"Forget about how much I've recovered!" Aiden snapped at her. "What about Theresa? Seamus? Garrett? That Prime Demon fight took a lot out of them!"

"Well now, I know that voice from anywhere." Seamus' familiar tone came from the doorway.

Aiden glanced over to the doorway. There standing together was the Dragon Trinity in their human forms. Seamus had some cuts still on his face from the battle, but he looked like he was going to be okay. Garrett had several bruises on his cheeks and what looked like a gash mark on his arm, but thankfully he wasn't bleeding.

Theresa was the most injured of the trio. Around her neck was a dark mark from where the Teleranta had grabbed her neck in her dragoness form. Aiden noticed several cut marks on her arms, legs, and possibly her back. She looked dead tired as well, as if she was about to pass out at any moment.

However, she still wore the same kind smile that she had since Aiden and her first became friends. Even when she had taken a beating or was in pain, Theresa somehow was always able to give Aiden that smile.

"Hey." She said. Aiden took notice that her voice was much softer than it usually was. "We were wondering when... when you'd wake up."

Aiden felt his arms tremble as he heard Theresa's soft-spoken voice. Never in his life had he ever heard Theresa have such a soft voice. Usually she spoke in a strong tone that seemed defiant, a tone that would never be broken. But hearing Theresa with a quiet voice made him realize that even the mighty dragons were not invincible.

"Theresa you..." Aiden's own voice began to tremble. "Your voice..."

The white dragoness simply let out a small dry chuckle as she shook her head. The same smile still remained on her face before she returned her eyes back to Aiden. Despite the pain her throat was in, she put on the best face she could muster. She was in pain, but that didn't stop the leader of the Trinity from walking towards him.

"My voice will be fine." She said. "A benefit of being a dragon is that we heal from our wounds faster than most other races do. In a few minutes, my voice should be back to the way it was before."

Aiden for some reason just couldn't help but feel relieved to see Theresa standing there before him. During the fight with the Teleranta it looked like he was going to lose her or the other two dragons in that fight. Theresa must have seen the relief in his face as well, as she gently flicked his forehead with one finger.

"It'll take more than just a single Teleranta to kill us." .

"Almost did you in though, Rexkin." Garrett said. Aiden took notice that his tone towards her was vastly different now. "You've not had a close call like that in awhile. What with your power being limited due to your human body's limits."

"I will manage." Theresa responded. "I've managed so far before the Teleranta fight, and I will again."

"Wait, everyone back up a bit here." Aiden quickly said. "What happened after the fight? Why are we in this supply area, who the hell saved us during that battle?!"

"Whoa whoa whoa, take it easy kiddo." Seamus answered as he placed a hand on his shoulder. "You just woke up from being knocked out for at least two hours in Academy time. Take a breather and calm down."

Aiden gave Seamus a bit of a glare, but eventually took a deep breath. The dragon of magic was right about one thing. The use of the Draconic Firestorm did take a lot out of him. He honestly was surprised that the attack even answered his call in that moment. After a full year's worth of training, Aiden had not been able to get the attack to come out no matter how hard the training sessions got.

He wondered if the attack would only answer him when his friends were in grave danger. The last time it appeared, the attack erupted from his blade when he refused to let Aello protect him from Raven. The second time came from a desire to help Theresa defeat the Teleranta.

Aiden groaned as he placed a hand on his head. He suddenly felt a massive headache hit him as his knees began to buckle. In that instant Theresa immediately went to his side and caught him before he fell over. Despite her own wounds, the white dragoness seemed to be as fast as ever. He did catch her grunting in pain though from the wounds the Teleranta left behind, but she simply held him in place the best she could.

"Come on." She said. "We need to get you to back to resting. I promise that we'll explain everything that's happened when you're fully recovered."

He wanted to protest and say that he was fine, but the look in Theresa's eyes was what stopped Aiden from doing so. Her normally confidence eyes were now filled with a demanding tone. He wondered if that was her version of the Dragon's Stare before he eventually allowed himself to be lowered on the cushion by his best friend. His eyelids grew heavy once more as he again drifted off into a slumber.

AIDEN FOUND himself in a strange room. All around him the walls were covered in what appeared to be either black slime or shadows. He couldn't tell exactly what it was but it ran down the walls that surrounded him like running water. All around him he could sense it. A feeling of dread filled the air around him, it made the hairs on the back of his neck slowly rise up.

He tried to call out to see if anyone would respond but nothing came from his mouth. Aiden blinked in surprise as he placed a hand over his mouth. Once more he tried to speak out, but again nothing escaped his lips. Had he suddenly become a mute without knowing it?

No. This had to be some kind of strange dream that he was having. That had to be the answer. A person doesn't just lose their voice instantly the way his voice seemed to have disappeared.

His eyes squinted a bit as he tried to figure out where he was exactly. The room he was in was covered in the blackness that surrounded him. If there was any source of light in this place, he was having a hard time locating it.

But that's when he saw it. A flash of red-white light exploded in front of his face, forcing him to shield his eyes for a moment. When the light died down, Aiden moved his hand away and in that one moment, he wished he had not done so.

Floating in front of him, looked like a spherical mass of pure dark energy. The mass had several tendrils rising up and down all over its mass. The tendrils that didn't rise up and down were already sticking up from the ground. Aiden watched in horror as he watched the center of the spherical mass twitch for a moment, before what looked like an eyelid suddenly opened up slowly. A red orange eye with a slit pupil revealed itself to Aiden.

At first Aiden tried to scream out for help, but once more his voice had disappeared. He realized that he might have been in for a fight he reached for Warfang at his side, but Warfang wasn't there! Aiden cursed in his mind before staring back at the eye.

He fully expected the strange mass to suddenly attack him, but instead what happened completely caught Aiden off guard. Despite the eye's dreadful appearance, it did not look like it wanted to cause him any harm. Instead it just stared at him. Aiden blinked in confusion for a moment. Why did this eye appear like it was ready for a battle, but at the same time would lash out if it were attacked itself? All it did was just stare at Aiden. It's gaze almost felt like it would pierce right through his very soul.

Instead of attacking though, the eye just looked at him. Not once making a threatening gesture towards Aiden. All it did was just stare. The eye's stare itself felt very unnerving to Aiden. Not being able to summon his weapon of speak didn't make it easier for him either too. He felt completely vulnerable in that one moment.

The eye blinked once, and everything turned to black once more.

* * *

AIDEN WOKE with a fright from his strange dream. His face covered in sweat from the ordeal. He glanced down at his hands and he looked around for his weapon. Warfang thankfully was still beside his cushion. He let out a sigh of relief as he realized that he was back in the real world and not some strange nightmare.

"Ah, so you've decided to join us have you?" A new voice spoke out from Aiden's left.

The young warrior blinked in confusion as he turned to the sound of the new voice. Standing in front of his group of friends was a newcomer. He was a human looking much older than the students they had come across before. From what Aiden could tell he looked like he was at least eighteen years old.

Unlike the head of the Academy who wore robes that made him fit the part of a mage, the newcomer's outfit was more like the students of the Academy. He wore casual clothes, but Aiden could tell that they had seen battle due to the slash marks and tears. The new comer's blue jeans, which seemed a bit baggy, had several holes on them, partially in the leg area. His shirt, which was a black short-sleeved t-shirt, had tears in the sleeves and at the bottom of the shirt as well.

The newcomer had a pair of light blue eyes, which unlike Aiden's deep ocean blue eyes, shown in the darkness. He also had brown hair like Aiden, but it was a lighter shade of brown rather than Aiden's dark brown hair color.

The mage smiled as he held out his hand in front of him as he pointed towards Aiden.

"*Emalla.*"

With just that one simple word, the healing magic that erupted spread throughout Aiden's body. The pain in his arm disappearing once again, Aiden felt like he was again at a hundred percent. As soon as the healing spell finished, the young warrior jumped up from the cushion with ease. For some strange reason he felt like his body had become even lighter from that spell. It wasn't like when the dragons cast it, it felt more advanced and more powerful.

"Hope you enjoyed that." The mage said with a knowing smile. "The top notch magic one gets here can work wonders when you know how to use it properly." He turned his gaze over to Seamus. "Though I'm surprised you haven't taught them any of the advanced spells yet."

Seamus shrugged his shoulders a bit before putting his hands behind his head in response.

"Eh, the kiddo's not ready yet. Neither is the girl for that matter. They've only had a full year's worth of training so it's not like they are anything special just yet ya know?"

"Shame. I can sense the potential this boy has within him." The mage turned his attention back towards Aiden. "Name's Ryan, the eldest son of the Grand Mage here at the Academy. And one of the very few people here that is trying to contain this problem before it gets out of hand."

Aiden blinked a couple of times. It took him a few seconds to register what Ryan had just said to him. **He** was the eldest son to the Grand Mage? He acted so different from his father that it was shocking to see it.

"You're the last one of this group to learn my name. Your little group of pals here learned who I was while you slept in dream land."

"How long was I out this time?"

"About three hours." Theresa responded. Aiden took notice that her voice had returned to normal. "We were worried that you wouldn't wake up before we had to move out again." Garrett scoffed. "Well, some of us were worried."

Aiden smiled. It was almost funny to think that he was so use to the large dragon's dislike for him and the rest of the group now. That smile didn't happen though when Garrett gave him a short glare before glancing back out of the supply room.

"Your friends told me that you all came into this place on your own will." Ryan said. "I gotta admit. I'm surprised that you all came into this hell hole while my old man just sits back on his ass not doing a damn thing."

"That's a lil harsh to say about your dad you know." Liza spoke out. "I mean, I do kinda agree that he's an ass but that's because he put a bubble over my head."

"Tch, he did that huh?" Ryan shook his head. "Guess you must have said something to get under his skin."

Ryan flicked his finger once as a chair suddenly appeared from thin air. Aiden, Liza, and the harpies almost fell over in a comedic fashion from the sudden magic that brought a chair into existence. Ryan smiled at their reaction before taking a seat in his chair.

"So, why did you personally come into this Shadow Demon infested Academy of ours?"

"You should know why by now." Seamus responded before folding his arms. "This place has sentimental value to me after all. And it's not just your fellow mages that are at risk of being exposed to the rest of the world."

"Oh don't worry, great dragon of magic." Ryan frowned. "I know all too well that the rest of the old races could be exposed. The elves, the harpies, and of course yourselves would be labeled as monsters while the mages would be called freaks. I know that threat better than my father, but yet he believes that just setting up a barrier will stop the Shadow Demons completely."

Ryan laced his fingers together as he rested his chin on top of them. His smile long gone as a more serious expression took its place.

"And while I know that he's wrong, he sadly is in charge of the school. The only true way to end this Nightmare is to defeat the

Overmind Demon. But as you can imagine, my father refuses to do anything."

"Why?" Aiden suddenly asked. "It's obvious he's incredibly powerful, why would he not bother trying to stop the Overmind?"

"I wish I knew, kid." Ryan sighed. "Either he's incredibly upset about those the fact that people were injured or died, or he's hiding something that he doesn't want the rest of the student body to know."

"I wouldn't put it past your old man to hide something." Seamus' growled, a puff of smoke erupting from his nostrils. "When I was last here he kept trying to hide the progress of his students from me."

Theresa frowned as she put a comforting hand on Seamus' shoulder. The dragon of magic glanced back towards her for a brief moment, smiling as he shrugged his shoulders.

"I know how you feel, green dragon." Ryan replied. "I am frustrated that the old man refuses to do anything about it. One of the reasons why I went in myself, to find a way to stop this mess."

The eldest son of the Grand Mage went silent as he laced his fingers together before staring off at the ceiling.

"That and...there's someone else here that my father either forgot or just left for dead."

This caught the group off guard for a moment. Aiden tilted his head to the side in confusion at those words.

"Is it someone that we know?" He asked. Ryan glanced up to Aiden as if he had just asked the million-dollar question. A small smile came to the mage's lips as he shook his head.

"Sorry there, newbie. But it's not someone you know. But he is an important person. At least, to me and my father he is."

A look of melancholy filled Ryan's eyes. The mage seemed to drift off into his own memories. It was a completely different man that took the place of the friendly mage that saved them in the battle against the Teleranta. After what seemed like a good five minutes, Ryan spoke once more.

"The person I'm looking for in this hell hole is my younger brother. Lewis." Ryan had a small frown on his face. "My dad was always hard on him growing up. Lewis was different from the rest of us."

Theresa frowned as she folded her arms across her chest as Ryan spoke. Neither one of the team wanted to ask what made him different to the other mages. The way Ryan's tone sounded made it explicitly clear it was a sensitive matter to talk about. Even Garrett, who Aiden fully believed would say something inappropriate, said nothing insulting to the mage.

"In the eyes of my father, Lewis was not as talented as the rest of the students. He hated how he would just drift off into his own little world and not pay attention during lessons. Mom would always tell dad off whenever he was being too hard on him for not learning the way he wanted Lewis to learn, but when she passed away sometime ago, defending Lewis fell to me." Ryan gave a small smile. "And I saw what she saw, true talent. Talent that my stupid old man couldn't see because Lewis had a different way of learning than what we've been taught."

"What kind of talent?" Liza asked, but the way she asked was kind, not intrusive. Ryan sighed as he leaned back in his chair.

"My brother doesn't learn from reading something over and over, like most students do. It took me awhile to figure that out, but when I figured out that he learned from seeing examples rather than reading several thousand books on how to cast fire-balls and lighting, he has to see them cast before understanding. It makes him unique. Hell after the classes that I have, I spend most of my time teaching him the basic spells so that he can see how they work."

The mage smiled as he glanced back to the group.

"He's not the best mage in the world due to his, condition, but I know for certain that he has a true talent."

Garrett scoffed a bit, but then turned back to face Ryan.

"If your brother is truly as talented as you say he is, then he should have been able to escape on his own. So why is he lost?"

"Garrett!" Theresa snapped. Ryan put a hand up to stop Theresa from berating the larger dragon.

"No, it is all right to ask this question, my lady." He said, the 'lady' part caught Aiden off guard as no one he knew ever called Theresa that. "Your muscular dragon friend is correct. Lewis is talented, and he knows this school like the back of his hand, just like I do. He should have been able to escape easily. But when the shadow demons attacked, I couldn't find him anywhere in the main hall."

Ryan leaned back in his chair once again as he rubbed his forehead in frustration. Aiden couldn't help but wonder if they actually did hit a sensitive issue with the subject of Ryan's little brother.

"I know he's somewhere in this damn place. I don't know where, but I know that he would not just be left behind in the dust. My little brother isn't some newbie that can't cast the most basic spell."

Theresa frowned at Ryan's story. She glanced back to the other dragons for a moment, then nodded at them before turning her attention back to Ryan.

"We are seeking the Overmind of this place. You have been here longer than most humans would dare to be in this hell that your academy has become. I hate to ask this of you, due to the fact that you have your own mission, but it would be in the best interests that we join forces to save this school from falling."

Ryan glanced up to Theresa. For the briefest of moments, their eyes met in a deadlock. Aiden swallowed as he felt a lump in his throat form. Even though he could barely tell just how strong the two beings truly were, it was the first time that Aiden felt like someone could actually contend with the immense power Theresa held within her body.

After what felt like an eternity of silence from the mage, Ryan gave a dry laugh as he stood up.

"You bring up a good point, dragoness. The chances of this succeeding are greater if we do join forces." Ryan frowned. "However, how do I know that you're not after anything else in this place?"

"Never doubt the word of a dragon, boy." Seamus quickly retorted. "You probably studied us in your classes, and you know that when a dragon gives his or her word, they will not break it."

"And you promise that you're not after anything else in this school?"

"On the honor of the dragon race itself."

Ryan just sat there for a few short moments to himself as he thought quietly. The entire mission depended on his answer. With a mage of his strength on their side, they would have a much better time going through the academy's twisted halls. If they didn't join forces than the mission got a lot more challenging.

"All right, great dragons." Ryan finally said. "We'll work together, but keep in mind, do not expect me to bail you out of everything like I did with that Teleranta."

CHAPTER 11 - VISIONS

*A*iden felt like the group had just gotten much stronger with the addition of Ryan to their cause. Not only did it feel stronger, but it also felt more diverse than it did before. He couldn't help but feel that he was in one of the classic role-playing games that were turn based. He had a team of characters that were each unique and excelled at their own skills. It made him think that they had a much better chance of getting through the mess of the academy together.

With Ryan added to their little party, they had another person that excelled in incredible magical abilities. While Aiden knew that Ryan was by far a more powerful mage than any of the mages they came across in the main hallway, he couldn't help but imagine what would happen if the Grand Mage's eldest son went toe to toe with Seamus.

Speaking of Seamus, the green dragon was busy looking through an old book he had brought back from the space he had created with his magic. While Aiden remembered him mentioning it before, Seamus had never really brought him to that place. Aiden and Liza had given it the nickname "The Library" due to how whenever Seamus entered it he vanished and when he returned he usually had scrolls or books with him. Just another thing about magic that was truly amazing.

Aiden had approached Seamus with the intent of seeing what the book had written inside it, but the moment he caught a glimpse of a page Seamus would smack him up the back of his head and tell him that he couldn't understand the book even if he did get a chance to read it.

It must have been written completely in the draconic tongue if that was the reason why Seamus always stopped him from reading it. Though to Aiden that felt like a pretty weak reason to keep him from reading the book. He had slowly begun to get a hold of the draconic language since he first learned of the dragons, not enough to fully speak it, but enough to understand a good majority of the words.

Seamus often spent hours with Aiden teaching him several words over and over again. If Aiden mispronounced a word, Seamus would whack him up the head with his tail. Theresa didn't like how Seamus taught Aiden the language, and would often snap at Seamus for the way the dragon of magic would teach him how to speak draconic. Not that Aiden complained about how Seamus taught him of course. Garrett's training had proven to be a thousand times worse with each passing day.

Speaking of the largest dragon, Aiden glanced to where he was currently standing. Like before, he stood in the doorway, on guard with the dakgrul once again. It was almost kind of funny to see the two of them get along so well when a few hours ago the dakgrul was trying to kill them. If Aiden was someone who believed that everyone could get along, he would have sworn that Garrett and the dakgrul had become friends in the short time they've known each other.

But if there's one thing Aiden learned during his time with the dragons though was that things were never what they seemed to be. The state of the academy was a prime example of that. It was a long list of things that had happened that Aiden had witnessed with his own eyes during his strange adventures. Of course things would just get more complicated for the young man as his time with the dragons continued to go on.

While Theresa recovered from the battle with the Teleranta, they were allowed a small break. Aiden felt bad that they had to come to a stop because of that, but he understood that fighting enemies with injuries was too risky. Even for the mighty dragons, there were enemies that they had to be careful with. And if the Teleranta was any indication, there was going to be a lot more of his kind in the academy waiting for them.

Try as he might, Aiden could not get the image of Theresa being injured out of his mind during the fight against that demon. The strong dragoness that he had come to look up to when things got rough, his lifelong friend, had got injured during the fight. Sure it wasn't anything life threatening to her, but he did not like think of Theresa in a battle that she ended up getting hurt from, much less a battle that she couldn't win.

The funny thing was that Theresa had told him multiple times during training that even she had moments when she wasn't always going to win a battle. Aiden knew he heard her say it before to him, but yet the very thought of his best friend injured in a battle with a foe just as strong as she was bothered him. Sure her wounds had not been extremely bad, but it was obvious to see that the Telranta's grip on her neck had not only injured her voice for a time, but left several bruise marks on it.

Aiden thankfully wasn't alone in worrying about the white dragoness. Liza and Aello would frequently walk up to Theresa and offer her one of the potions to drink or to just talk with her for a bit. Theresa gave her familiar kind smile as the two of them did their best to talk with the white dragoness. It might have been hard to see Theresa deal with pain, but it did bring a smile to Aiden's face whenever he saw his best friend smile.

While Liza and Aello chatted with Theresa nearby, Seamus took a seat beside Aiden with a tiny frown on his lips.

"It's taking you awhile to come to terms with it, isn't it?" He asked. Aiden didn't need to ask what he meant.

"Yeah. I am still having a hard time just imagining her in a battle that she ended up getting hurt in." He admitted before staring down at the ground. "My entire life Theresa's been that one person that never got hurt doing anything, and she just continues to show she's stronger than I think with each day we train. So just seeing her have bruise marks on her neck...it just disturbs me, Seamus."

Seamus sighed at Aiden before shaking his head a bit. The dragon of magic placed a hand on Aiden's shoulder for a few seconds before giving a small smile.

"Truth be told kid? I know exactly how you feel."

"You do?"

"Of course." Seamus turned his eyes back to Theresa. "I know what's going through your mind right now kid, you think that she's so powerful that you can't even imagine her being injured in combat. That no one could take her on. That she's the most powerful being in the world and that she has no weaknesses." The dragon gave a small dry laugh. "But that's just a dream, even the mightiest warriors have moments when they are injured greatly. It's something that happens in battle, hell I could tell you that it's happened to me more times than I can count."

Aiden glanced over to Seamus in confusion for a second. His expression must have given his confusion away though. Seamus just smiled a bit as he pulled up his left sleeve on his shirt, revealing a jagged scar on his shoulder's side.

"See this kiddo?" He asked. "This is from an old battle I got into a few thousand years ago when the Great Kingdoms were still around. It was probably one of the biggest battles I ever had in my life. A local demon was waging a raid on the nearby human town that was in our protection. While it is a puppy compared to the Telranta that you, Liza, and Aello had the unfortunate pleasure of seeing when you're no where near ready, it was a nasty creature."

Aiden blinked a couple of times during Seamus' tale. The Telranta that Seamus mentioned was one of the strongest demons that they could have possibly encountered, but the way that Seamus spoke of the demon that gave him his his scar made it sound like it was a monster on its own right.

"I won't say its name, but I can tell you that this demon was a threat. I was still new to the dragon army at the time, and my squad had been picked to be the squad to take care of the demon. So you can imagine that I felt like we would be invincible fighting against it, especially with Thes as our leader."

Seamus grew quiet, solemn as he continued to speak. Once again, Aiden saw the old wisdom that the dragon of magic tended to hide from the others. Compared to Theresa or Garrett, Seamus always seemed so high-spirited, so impossible to impossible to phase. But...when he spoke about his past, or of the Great Kingdoms at all, Aiden always noticed a hint of real wisdom. Something Seamus always seemed to hide from the group

Unlike Theresa or Garrett, who had no problem talking about the past, Seamus always seemed reluctant to talk about his own memories If Aiden had been a bit ruder, maybe he would have harassed Seamus, tried to get the reasons why until he cracked and told him. But, Aiden respected the dragon of magic too much to break the trust between them, especially after their rocky beginning.

"When we got there the entire town was on fire. Not like dragon fire mind you, this kind of fire was...cold. Like it had sapped the life energy out of all the people that lived there. And for the first time, I felt unsure that'd we'd win the battle."

Seamus placed a hand over the scar as he gritted his teeth. Though Aiden could not understand what the battle was like, he saw the pained memory in Seamus' eyes. A battle that Aiden could not even begin to comprehend or hope to.

"In that battle, we lost at least a few young dragonlings. They gave their lives to defend the small human town, while I somehow survived with a gaping wound in my shoulder." Seamus continued. "I'll never forget that battle. It was the one moment in my life that reminded me that no matter how powerful we believe we are, there are beings that match our power. Hell, there could be even stronger beings that could be greater than even us. Remember Queen Lilith's brother? How he was quite a handful even with all of us?"

Aiden felt a shiver go down his spine at those words. The Harpy Queen's brother, Samael, was one of the most deadly opponents he had faced. While the fight had no true winners, thanks mostly to Queen Lilith interrupting the battle, it was clear that Samael was far stronger than Aiden had believed him to be. Seamus smiled a little bit as he noticed Aiden shiver for a moment. The dragon simply gave him a small punch in the shoulder.

"Ah relax, kiddo. Don't let the stories of an old dragon bother you too much. Besides, you know that you three have some of the best protection you can ask for. As you've said before, dragons can do anything right?"

Aiden felt like Seamus was forcing himself to say those words. After the close battle with Samael last year he was fully aware that there could be enemies that could match Theresa's skills with a blade, Seamus' ability with magic, and possess the same kind of strength Garrett had. Even though Aiden still believed that the dragons were the most amazing things in the world, he had a hard time imagining other beings that were just as strong if not stronger than they were.

"Hey Seamus? What kind of spell did Ryan use to help us kill the Teleranta?" Aiden asked. He hoped that the dragon would see that he was desperate to change the subject. Seamus frowned at that question before sighing.

"That spell, kiddo, was an attack. It's an attack that is to be used in extreme situations. A spell that I thought humankind would never use." Seamus gritted his teeth for a second. Aiden was taken aback in that moment as he saw that the green dragon's teeth turned sharp. He was so used to only seeing Theresa's teeth turn sharp in extreme moments that it caught him by surprise. "The Ultima Spell. One of the highest level spells to be created."

Aiden felt a chill run down his spine at those words. The tone in Seamus' voice somehow was able to maintain a balance of wisdom and, if Aiden was guessing it, pride. Just the very sound of the spell's name though was enough to make him feel like his body was about to explode from anticipation.

"I won't go into extreme details, kid, but I'll tell you this. The Ultima Spell is the most powerful spell that a human can cast. One of the few attacks that can exceed it in power was the Dragon King's ultimate attack." He pointed towards Warfang. "And you already know the name of that attack."

Aiden's eyes glanced down to his weapon. Seamus was right. He knew exactly what attack it was. The Draconic Firestorm, Warfang's most powerful attack. Last year he was able to summon the attack after he let his frustration of having to be protected by everyone got the better of his senses. And then came the very recent summoning of the attack against the Teleranta, and even then it took the help of the Ultima Spell to fell the foul Prime Demon.

If only Aiden knew how to use the attack at will and not at random chance. The attack was obviously powerful and it certainly would have made their missions easier. But then again, even when Aiden did get the attack to work, the backlash of using it made his entire body feel like it had been drained of all its strength.

In that moment as Aiden pondered on how to bring out Warfang's ultimate attack, he felt a smack on the back of his head.

"Ow!" He turned to Seamus. "What was that for?"

"That was for getting lost in your own thoughts." The latter replied. "You're letting yourself worry too much about one attack. Right now we have to keep in mind where we are."

Seamus was right. Their situation at the moment was still dangerous. With the shadow demons running around the school the chances of recovering seemed to dwindle more. Aiden gave a short nod as he stood up from his spot.

"I should check up on the others too." He said. "I have a feeling that Theresa will want to move out soon."

The green dragon gave a short laugh before shaking his head. Aiden blinked in confusion at the laugh from his friend.

"You should consider yourself lucky, kiddo." He replied. "Back in the day, Theresa would only let us rest for at least a few minutes at the most. She must really care about your well being if she is letting us rest for more than just a couple of minutes."

Aiden blushed a bit at that comment before dismissing said blush. He had to focus. Now was not the time to get embarrassed by Seamus or a compliment. After he put the blush aside he headed towards where Theresa, Liza, and Aello were. Thankfully the trio of ladies didn't notice that his face went red as they greeted him with kind smiles.

"Hey." Theresa said with that same kind smile she always had when the two of them talked. "How are you feeling?"

"I could ask you the same question." Aiden replied with a smile of his own before sitting down across from her. "Is your throat feeling better?"

"I'll be fine." Theresa pursed her lips up. "Did you forget that I am a dragoness that has had more experience in battle than you have?"

"Believe me, Seamus just got done telling me all about his scar on his shoulder." Aiden frowned. "I'd rather not hear anymore stories about scars from my best friend."

Theresa's lips turned into a tiny frown as she reached up and ruffled his hair a bit. Aello couldn't help but giggle at Aiden's reaction from his hair getting ruffled like that.

"You worry way too much." Theresa simply responded. "One hurt throat is not going to be the end of me, and neither were any of the battles I experienced years ago. You can't keep this dragoness down."

"Still, that was a pretty nasty battle you guys had with that thing." Liza said. "If I know any better, I'd say that you weren't expecting one of those Tel things at all."

Theresa went silent for a few seconds before taking a deep breath and sighing. Aiden took not that when she breathed out that she let a small puff of smoke escape from her lips.

"In all honesty, Liza?" The white dragoness turned back to her. "I was not expecting a Teleranta to be here. They are such a rare and powerful species of demon that I never imagined that one of them would be under the control of an Overmind."

"W-Why's that?" Aello asked, then mumbled aside. "It's not like they're any different from other demons…"

Theresa shook her head at Aello's question before responding to it.

"That's exactly the point though, Aello. Prime Demons like the Teleranta, are truly sentient beings. Only those who are masters in the dark arts can control them and even then it's a dangerous pact between mage and demon. Prime Demons usually do not heed the call of Overminds because they view Shadow Demons as an inferior species of demons."

"Why doesn't that surprise me?" Liza asked.

"Not now, Liza." Aiden quickly said to stop her from going on a rant. Theresa leaned forward a bit as she locked her fingers together before getting lost in a deep thought.

"Why would a Telranta be here? Why would it take the

orders of an Overmind? Maybe it never was following orders from the start. Maybe...maybe it was here before the Shadow Demons broke out."

Those words sent an icy chill down Aiden's spine. Not because of the tone that Theresa had, but because of the very idea that the Prime Demon was brought here not by the Overmind but by the mages didn't set well with him. Seamus had talked non-stop about how glorious this academy was since he lent a hand in founding it. Aiden did not want to picture the look of devastation on his face that the mages had captured a Prime Demon on their own volition.

"Are you serious about that?" Liza asked. "I mean that's a very gutsy statement to make, Thes. What if you're wrong about it?"

"Like I said, Prime Demons don't work the same as other demons do." Theresa replied. "They are solitary beasts, they never follow the orders of Overminds. The only chance that one would be here in an Overmind infested place is if it was already here."

"But...that doesn't make sense." Aello frowned, before mumbling to herself. "Why would mages that aren't part of the dark arts capture a prime demon?"

"I wish I knew the answer to that." Theresa sighed as she stared into the fire in front of her. "Humanity is always seeking out new ways to further progress themselves. To control that which they shouldn't control. It's a trait that sadly is integrated into their blood. They aren't the only ones who try to control that which they shouldn't. All races have that curse sadly. But to think that they would be able to allow an Overmind to control a Prime Demon is a fool's errand."

The white dragoness sighed as she let out a puff of smoke escape from her nostrils, but this time a small spark of white fire followed after the smoke. Aiden knew that she must have been incredibly stressed by the situation if she had let a spark of fire escape from her nostrils. It wasn't often that she would allow a spark escape that easily.

"You three should get some sleep." Theresa ordered. "We'll be in this place for a couple of more hours, which thanks to the time shield around here, we can spare a few moments of rest."

Aiden and Liza seemed reluctant to obey Theresa's direct order, but Aello wasted no time in falling promptly asleep in the spot she was sitting at. Liza giggled a bit as she stood up.

"I'll get her to a different spot to nap at. Try not to lose sleep, Aiden."

"Same to you."

As Liza walked away, dragging a sleeping Aello with her, Aiden found his own eyelids getting heavier as well. Theresa gave him her kind warm smile before taking him up from his seat and guiding him towards the makeshift bed they had made earlier.

"Rest your eyes, Aiden. When the time comes to move out, I'll wake you up."

"But..."

"No buts. Remember when I started your training when I told you to always listen to me? Well don't start disobeying me now."

Aiden let out a sigh of defeat as he felt himself placed down on the makeshift bed. His mind drifted back to the incident with the Harpies once more though as he thought about Theresa being injured. The duel between her and Samael, and how she forced her limits to battle him before Aello's mother stopped the battle.

While it was true that her human body's limits had grown stronger over the year with Aiden and Liza's own growth, a part of Aiden could not help but worry about his best friend. She had pushed herself so hard in that fight that he was worried that she had injured herself somehow.

He shuddered for a moment as he remembered those

battles within the harpy's den. How Theresa nearly lost to Samael, how she pushed herself in battle against Zeratar and Zantul, and her transformation.

Theresa had accepted that she was a human with the soul of a dragon, and by that extent her powers were still the same, but he always worried that Theresa felt like she was lesser because of her limits. Aiden glanced back over to where she sat. He could see in her eyes, the same planning mind set that she would have whenever she came up with a plan. But at the same time, he could see that she was mentally debating with herself about their next move.

The stress of being Rexkin must have weighed heavily on her mind.

As much as he wanted to stay up and be by her side though, Aiden felt his eyelids slowly getting heavier. He sighed in defeat as he quietly laid on the makeshift bed once more before drifting off into a deep slumber.

* * *

THE NEXT TIME Aiden opened his eyes, he found himself in a completely different room. It was not like their small base camp. But instead it was neat and filled with endless books and what looked like a giant vial in the center of the room where a mass of dark energy floated. At least, it looked like dark energy to Aiden.

The young teenager glanced around the room, trying to find any of the other members of his group. They weren't in eyesight, much to his disappointment.

"Where the hell is everyone?" He thought to himself as he continued to look around the room.

As if to answer his question, a door to the room slowly opened. Aiden squinted his eyes as he saw what looked like a tall man walk into the room towards the giant vial of dark energy. Aiden couldn't make out his face's details, but something about him just really put him off. Like a bad itch that you couldn't reach even though it was aggravating.

The man reached up towards the vial and placed his hand on the glass that contained the dark energy swirling around. When he spoke, Aiden felt a chill run down his spine that made him completely uncomfortable.

"Do not let me down." The man said, his voice distorted and hard to make out. "Everything is riding on your shoulders."

Those words brought nothing but confusion to Aiden. What did he mean by that? Why was he talking to the dark energy? Just who was this man? There were so many questions that left him completely confused as to what was going on.

Aiden tried to speak out to the man, but when he tried to speak he found that his voice was non-existent. His eyes grew in surprise as he brought his hand to his throat. Once again he tried to say a simple hello, but nothing came from his mouth.

A confused look crossed Aiden's face as he glanced down at his body. To his shock he could see through his entire body. His mind raced a thousand thoughts at a moment's notice. At first he felt like he was in some kind of scene in a movie where the hero was a see through image and couldn't interact with anything. But this wasn't a movie, this was actually happening to him.

The second thing that came to his mind was a question. Why? Why was he seeing this? Just like that weird dream with that mass of shadows, this one came out of nowhere and brought him nothing but confusion. And of course he had to wonder, why was it that he couldn't speak out in his own dream?

However, before Aiden could continue to form questions that he probably would never get the answer to, another being walked into the room behind the first man. The former turned towards the newcomer and gave the figure a short nod.

"Let's begin." He said. "And...close the door."

Aiden's eyes began to feel droopy once again. As hard as

he fought to stay awake, he couldn't. He wanted to see who this person was. Why he was talking to what just appeared to be dark energy, and what the man meant that everything rode on the shoulders of said energy. But the harder he fought to stay awake, the more he found himself drifting off to sleep once more.

CHAPTER 12 - SNAKE EYES

*A*iden woke from his strange dream with a fright. His hands felt clammy and drenched in sweat. This was the second time he had a strange dream like that. No. Not a dream. Dreams never made a person feel like that they were actually there in the events that happened.

He knew what the dreams truly were. Something he thought only happened in the movies. These weren't dreams. They were visions. Visions that he knew he couldn't deny that it felt like they were important. But why? Why was he having them?

A part of Aiden felt like they were important to what caused the events that happened at the Academy. But he had nothing to prove that they were. All he knew was that someone had captured a lot of dark energy and was using the energy to do something.

Aiden let out a frustrated growl before rubbing his forehead in annoyance. Maybe he was wrong about it all. Maybe the visions he was getting didn't have anything to do with what happened at the school. It could very well be that the stress of having to save this place was starting to get to him as well.

Those distracting thoughts disappeared slowly as he felt a

comforting hand on his shoulder. He glanced over to the owner of the hand and smiled. Theresa, with the same kind smile, greeted him with eyes that shown with happiness.

"Hey. You all right?" She asked. "You were twitching and turning a little bit in your sleep."

"Yeah...didn't have a good dream." Aiden told her. A part of him felt bad for lying to her, but he doubted she would believe him. Theresa just kept her hand on his shoulder and gave it a squeeze.

"You know you could always wake up and bother me about them if you want, Aiden." She said. Aiden glanced away for a moment, staring down at the ground below him before turning his eyes back to her own.

"I don't wanna make you feel more stressed, Thes. I mean, last year in the den you were so stressed from the fight against Samael and Raven's demons that you entered that burning state and...I thought you weren't there anymore."

Theresa frowned when he mentioned his concern for her because of what happened last year. The white haired dragoness removed her hand from his shoulder, only to pull him close to her in a comforting hug. Aiden blinked a bit as he felt her chin on top of his head.

"Last year was an eye opener for me, Aiden." She simply stroked the back of his head with one hand as she spoke. "I over-estimated my own abilities so much that I overlooked the fact that my human body does not have the same capabilities that my old body did before. But now that I know my limits, I will do what I can to improve my body's capabilities and achieve the same kind of strength I had years ago."

The same smile that Aiden had always seen on Theresa's lips returned once more as she held him close. He could feel his cheeks turning a little warm from her hug as she just sat there holding him in her arms. It wasn't uncommon for the two to share hugs, though this one felt more comforting than the others.

He could feel just how much strength that she was using in order to keep him in place too. Granted she wasn't using a lot of it, but he wasn't going anywhere until she deemed otherwise.

"But that's okay. I will not give up on getting that kind of control again. To be the dragoness of white fire once more. Maybe then, you'll be able to keep up with the rest of us."

Aiden stuck his tongue at her. She just stuck her own tongue back out at him before releasing her grip that she had over him.

"Now come on, get up, we got to get moving soon." Aiden grunted a bit as he stood up. His legs no longer feeling wobbly or weak anymore as he stretched his back out. "And for the record, we still have time to get to the lab."

"That Ryan guy's coming with us, right?" Aiden asked, Theresa gave him a quick nod.

"Yes. He knows the school better than the rest of us do, or rather he knows it better because of the damaged condition that it is in." Theresa sighed a bit before shaking her head. "I'm worried though. The Teleranta we faced is one of the strongest kinds of Prime Demons there are."

"There are other kinds?" Aiden asked as he followed Theresa towards the others.

"Yes. Prime Demons don't have a single species of demon, much like other races there are different branches of their kind. Each one is put into a category of strength. They range from C Rank, B Rank, A Rank, and the strongest of them all, are S Ranks." The white dragoness let a scowl come to her lips. "Do you remember what I told you about the Obsidian Demon? That monster was an S Rank beast, even the King had a hard time fighting him. The Teleranta that we fought was in an A Rank category."

Aiden almost felt his heart drop out of his chest hearing those exact words from Theresa. The monster that they fought was the second highest-ranking demon and they just barely managed to win? He shuddered to think about what an S Rank demon could possibly do with the immense power it held in its body. Hell he was having a hard time just imagining a demon stronger than the Teleranta they just fought.

"How does a demon grow in rank?" Aiden asked hastily. He mentally smacked himself for asking a question about a subject that already sent shivers down his spine thinking about it. Theresa just smiled at his question.

"Prime Demons tend to get stronger when they age. Sometimes it takes them thousands of years to even achieve an A Rank level of strength. S Rank Demons are very rare to find, due to how powerful they can become." Theresa explained. "Of course there are other ways that a Prime Demon could achieve a new rank, and that's by absorbing massive amounts of energy. Or in this case, mana."

Aiden blinked.

"Wait, is that why so many demons try to take over mages?" He asked. "Because they have mana?" Theresa slowly nodded her head at his question with a grim look on her face.

"Demons, especially prime ones, will do whatever they can to grow stronger. Unless the mage that they are summoned by has an incredible will, they will never allow themselves to be controlled willingly by the mages who summon them. Which is why Dimitri and Raven are so dangerous if they can control demons without being tempted by lies that demons often spin."

If a pin dropped Aiden could have heard it landing on the ground. It was that quiet in the room when Theresa finished explaining how Prime Demons grew stronger. All the scuffles that Aiden had been in before when he first held Warfang, even the incident with the harpies, didn't compare to how dangerous the situation was with the Shadow Demons.

But those thoughts were put aside for now as he and Theresa met up with the rest of their party. Each one was doing something different to pass their time.

Their newest member, Ryan, was reading a levitating book to

pass the time. Aiden took notice that he was turning the pages with his own magic. Seamus was busy tending to the group's captive dakgrul. It was weird to see one of those monstrous creatures act so docile and relaxed as Seamus healed any injuries that it might have had from their battle with the Teleranta. Garrett, as Aiden expected, did nothing but stand watch at the doorway with narrowed eyes. Liza had just finished eating and talking with Aello.

Speaking of Aello, Aiden noticed that her two personal guardians were fussing over the state of the harpy princess' wings. They were trying to groom Aello as she talked with Liza about their mission. Aiden noticed that out of the two of them, Gabriella, seemed to glare daggers at Liza for even daring to talk to Aello. The other guardian, Mia, was too busy stroking Aello's hair while humming a small tune to pass the time. Though he could have just been guess as to who was who. After all, the two guardians looked so alike that it was rather hard to tell either one apart.

Aiden couldn't help but smile at how his group of friends seemed to just grow a bit bigger with each adventure that they took. Sure he couldn't exactly call Ryan a friend yet, seeing as how they just met the guy, but he at least seemed more trust worthy than his father, Ivan, did.

Just thinking of that man made Aiden's spine shiver out of disgust for him. Here his son was risking his life to find his little brother and to stop the Overmind from breaking out of the academy, and the Grand Mage did nothing but hide back in his office. The thought of the leader of the school that his friend had founded was not doing anything to fix the problem made him just feel furious.

"Rexkin." Garrett called out from the doorway. "The coast is clear, no shadow demons have been spotted."

"Right. Well then, everyone gather around so that we can talk about what we need to do." Theresa ordered. At the moment she gave that order, the team gathered around in a circle. Even though there were some glares from Mia and Gabriella about taking orders from a dragoness, Aello gave them both a short nod to listen.

"What's the plan, Rexkin?" Seamus asked as he held Hurricane in his hand. "Are we rushing straight to the lab to take care of this mess?"

"No." Theresa replied simply. "As simple as it would have been to do that when the academy was in perfect shape, Seamus, that luxury is lost to us now."

"Your Rexkin is right." Ryan spoke up. "This school's changed greatly because of the Overmind's influence. Making our way down to the lab will prove to be more complicated than you think, Dragon of Magic."

Seamus sighed as he rubbed his eyebrows in frustration. What they said was true, but he couldn't help but hope that they would be able to do that and fix the problem at its source. Aiden didn't blame him for wanting to rush to the lab and stop the Overmind, but there was no telling what kind of dangers there were waiting for them.

Theresa turned to Ryan and gave him a short nod to take over. The mage moved his hand gently as he brought up a map of the entire school in front of the crew. Each section was defined by a color. The colors were red and green, much like the maps in Aiden's video games where areas that he hadn't explored were red while areas that he did explore were green.

"As you can see, all the areas marked by the red are infested with Shadow Demons. The areas that you came through, here and here," He pointed towards the various parts of the academy that the group came through. "Are the least infected areas. You guys are strong, there's no denying that. But you're lucky that you didn't have thousands upon thousands of Shadow Demons trying to rush you down without remorse."

"Spare us the logistics, mage." Garrett spoke out. "We're not here to talk about what areas are infected. What would be the quickest way to the labs?"

Ryan sighed as he used his right index finger and began to draw a line on the map from their correct location through several parts of the academy. Aello's guardians watched with amazement at the magic before them as the lines that Ryan used from magic itself. Even Aello looked a little impressed by the magic that he was using before them. Aiden and Liza didn't share the same amazement from watching him use the magic; they had seen enough of it from Seamus over their time training after all.

Still. It was really cool to see him make a line with just one finger.

"The path I just lit up is the one that could possibly be the one with the least resistance." Ryan explained. "The thing is though, we still have several shadow demons to face there. And I don't know if there will be any more Prime Demons waiting for us during the trek. What I do know though is that there's at least one spot where we can set up another camp area."

Ryan pointed to a rather large section on the map. Aiden quirked an eyebrow at it.

"What's so special about this area?"

"It's the room where we usually hang the honorable mentions in the school. Mages before our time are remembered there. They range from Grand Mages to the best teachers that our Academy's ever had. We call it, the Hall of Memorial." Seamus nodded at the mention of the name. He stroked his chin a bit as he recalled it being placed up.

"Yeah, I remember when I put that Hall up with the original mages that I found. It was to remind future generations of the mages that came before them." He laughed a little bit, "I also remember there being a picture of me up there with a different form that I took."

"Was it one of your fat camp councilor forms?" Liza asked. Seamus gave her a short glare with a VERY coy smile.

"That was a one time thing, you know."

"Focus." Theresa ordered. "We have a mission to think about." Ryan sighed as he began to speak up once more to the group.

"We'll still face some demons, but luckily for us the Hall of Memorial isn't too far from us. The demons that we'll will probably be the dakgruls and kelgraths that you've already spotted. But be warned, there's a lot more than just those two subspecies of Shadow Demons." The eye color Ryan's eyes seemed to turn a darker hue as he dismissed the map. "You do not want to see the worms, or as their species known as, Turkskas."

Theresa, Seamus, and Garrett all gave slow nods at the mention of the name of this other Shadow Demon species. Aiden, Liza, Aello and her two guardians all shared the same look of confusion but decided it was best not to ask about this other Shadow Demon species just yet. In the back of Aiden's mind he tried to imagine what they would look like, but there were more pressing matters to deal with.

"One question." Liza spoke out. "You said that in order to disperse the Shadow Demons, the Overmind has to be defeated, right?" Ryan and Seamus nodded in response to her question. "Well then, what happens to OUR dakgrul? I mean, we're using him to find the Overmind. Will he disappear if the Overmind goes down?"

"This guy here," Seamus replied before patting the demon's head. "Is completely under our control. Remember when I placed the lil cuffs around his ankles? Well those are meant to cut off his connection to the Overmind entirely. So even if the Overmind is defeated, our lil dakgrul here won't be going anywhere."

Aello pursed her lips up before speaking up.

"You're making him a pet?" She asked, and then mumbled to the side. "A little hypocritical…"

"More like we're giving him freedom from the Overmind." Seamus replied. "Think of it like this, if he stays with us he's not only free from the control over Overmind but he doesn't fall at risk at becoming one of Dimitri's personal demons as well."

The dakgrul snarled a bit at the idea of being a personal servant to any kind of mage that summoned demons. Garrett, for the first time that Aiden could remember, actually smiled at the dakgrul's display of disgust.

"Seems like our little demon here shares my disgust being a servant." He said. The dakgrul's response to Garrett was to give him a short nod before stretching its body out, like a cat would. Theresa cleared her throat to catch the attention of Garrett and their dakgrul.

"We have our objective people." She said, taking charge once more. "We head to the Hall of Memorial. Once we're there, we begin forming a plan on taking down the Overmind without damaging the school even further."

No one argued with the order. Not even Aello's two guardians argued with Theresa about what they were about to do. Aiden was sure that out of the group that they would be the ones to argue with Theresa's orders. Last year a similar thing nearly happened between Theresa and Garrett, where the latter was starting to question Theresa's orders before she proved that she was worth following.

Aiden told himself that the two of the harpies were probably told to follow Theresa's orders by Aello herself. If there was one-thing guardians were, it was being fiercely loyal to their princess and they wouldn't dare question her.

Without saying another word, the group began to head out once more towards the Hall of Memorial. Aiden being the fantasy lover that he was, couldn't help but picture large painted portraits of powerful mages that wore strange garments and carried powerful staves in their hands. Images of men with long beards and whimsical eyes also came to his mind as he thought of one of his favorite wizards. A wizard who wore a grey robe and had a particular dry sense of humor that made him a favorite amongst fantasy lovers.

Aiden felt Theresa pull him by the shirt when he found himself lost in his imagination about what the Hall of Memorial could possibly have within it. He blushed a bit in embarrassment from being dragged by her. It wasn't the first time that Theresa had to drag him to get him out of his day dreaming state before. When they were much younger, she would often had to pull him along to get his attention.

Thankfully, with Ryan's guidance, the trek was not as long to get towards the Hall of Memorial. Whenever their path seemed blocked by broken wall pieces of what looked like dead demon bodies, or at least that's what Aiden HOPED they were, Ryan would direct them to a different direction and cut avoid any straggling Shadow Demons that they heard nearby.

The further they progressed though, the more dead bodies they found. Of both Shadow Demon and mages, they littered the area. The amount of Shadow Demons out did the mages' body count, but the mages that they did find were either sprawled across the ground, or thrown against the walls, leaving behind a trail of blood where they fell. Aiden almost lost his lunch seeing such disgusting things, but somehow he was able to keep moving forward.

After about fifteen minutes passed, the crew arrived at a large door that had several gems decorating the outer rim of the door-way. The doors that were placed in said doorway though, were shattered and jagged all over. Ryan looked absolutely shocked to see that something had broken the doors into the sacred Hall.

"These doors were protected by some incredible magic…" He whispered quietly. "I placed several enchantments to keep Shadow Demons out."

Theresa turned to the group and gave them a short nod. Without wasting time, all of those capable of using weapons summoned their respective weapons in their hands. Ryan spoke a single word to illuminate his hand before throwing a ball of light into the hallway to light their path.

The state of the hall was a gigantic mess. Broken picture frames that were crooked covered the walls, shattered glass was all over the ground, and there were several tears into the wallpaper. The hall had seen much better days for sure, and the condition that it was in was absolutely disappointing to see from the Academy.

Aiden turned to see Seamus' reaction, and for a brief moment he could have sworn that he saw Seamus' dragonhead take the pace of his human head. The fury that was in Seamus' eyes was almost enough to rival that of Theresa's fury when she became enraged.

To make matters look even worse for the hall, several tables looked like they had been crushed by something massive. The shape that they were in was a strange curved position. Like something just either punched it really hard or had placed something with incredible weight down onto those tables.

That's when they heard something none of them expected to hear. A voice. A rather LOUD voice for that matter.

"Look at this mess! Ugh, how can any creature be expected to work in such conditions? It's so...filthy and nasty! Humans are such horridly disgusting creatures. How dare they expect my radiance and beauty to shed light on their putrid darkness?"

Theresa's eyes narrowed as she held Fire and Snow up in front of her. The rest of the group that carried weapons also brought their weapons up for combat in case they had to battle. The only one who didn't prepare for a battle was Ryan. The mage looked incredibly confused by the fact that there was someone else in the demon-infested area beside himself. Based on the voice's high pitch, that the owner of the voice was a female.

As the group continued to approach the source of the voice, they could hear it rant about multiple things. Like how the being was a 'delicate flower' and how the academy, or in her own words 'pitiful excuse of a beauty parlor' was unfit for a being such as her because she held her own being up so high. Seamus looked like he was about to snap at someone insulting his school like the way she was doing.

That's when Aiden noticed something massive to his left. A large, snake like, tail. He nearly let out a shout in surprise at the size of the tail, but held fast. He glanced back to Aello, hoping to see that she didn't see the tail either. It might have been a year ago, but he still remembers when his friend was using the Hannah persona to fake having a fear of snakes. Or did she really have one?

Aiden wasn't the only one who noticed the large snake tail either. Theresa was the second one to see the massive tail as well. She glanced over to Garrett and gave him a short nod. The largest member of the Trinity hefted his axe up slowly above his head as he prepared to bring it down on the massive tail.

"Wait!" Liza hissed out to him. "You hack that tail off, and whatever it belongs to will get pissed!" Seamus sighed as he tapped Liza's shoulder.

"That's a tail of a Lamia." He said. "They're a demon species that has a long ass snake tail, but they keep the body of a human to deceive their foes."

"S-Snake?" Aello whimpered, then muttered to the side. "Why did she have to be a s-snake?"

Before Theresa could tell them to remain while, Garret slammed his axe into the ground rather hard. Then without meeting a beat he grabbed ahold of the large tail with both of his hands easily. Aiden could have sworn he heard a 'yelp' kind of sound from the lamia before Garrett effortlessly pulled her with just a single pull. Never in his life had Aiden seen something move so fast from a simple tug as the form of the lamia was finally revealed to the group.

She was a bit over fifteen feet long and her human half was that of a grown woman. However her human half looked nothing like any kind of human that Aiden had ever seen before. She had venomous green eyes, long red hair, and bluish-purple skin. As for her most eye catching feature, it was her tail. Her tail was a shade of dark blue with a yellow stripe outlined in black. The lamia's fingernails were also very long and painted a red color that Aiden hoped wasn't blood. She also had a pair of visibly large fangs that Aiden could only imagine were even larger when she opened her mouth. He shuddered at the very thought that she could even possibly dislocate her jaw to eat anything. And despite Garrett effortlessly pulling her towards them by her tail, the tail itself looked obscenely strong. It could probably smash through metal with a simple movement.

The look in the lamia's eyes went from shocked to complete rage when she stared right into Garrett's own unrelenting eyes.

"What. the. HELL IS WRONG WITH YOU?!" The lamia shouted, in a very high pitched shriek, as she pulled her tail out of Garrett's grip before holding it in her hands. "My poor tail! Did he hurt you?! How dare he tug the tail of a radiant, beautiful creature such as myself?!"

"You can quit calling yourself that." Garrett responded. "I can just tell by looking at you that you're the only one who thinks of yourself as those things." The lamia stopped tending to her tail before glaring daggers right at the large dragon.

"How dare you? What are you to even gaze upon a creature such as myself?" She asked. Aiden took notice that her voice went from a very high pitch down to a low dripping arrogant tone. Garrett scoffed.

"If you think I'm a lowly human, than you have another thing coming, demon."

The lamia blinked a bit as she leaned forward towards Garrett. Her venomous green orbs examining his body carefully. Aiden could have sworn that he heard a sniff come from her as Garrett didn't flinch from her approach. A sly grin came to her lips as she let out an amused hiss.

"Ooooh I see. You're one of those high and mighty dragons from years ago, aren't you?" She laughed. "Well, well…that's a surpriiiiiiise." Aiden noticed that she let her tongue slip out of her mouth and just like other snakes, it two was forked.

"Spare me from your pitiful attempts to look impressive." Garrett responded, still not intimidated by the demon at all. The Lamia frowned as she folded her arms.

"You know, you should have some more respect for a radiant creature like myself." She huffed. "It's not every day that you aren't killed by a Prime Demon, wittle dragon."

"Wait, YOU'RE a Prime Demon?" Liza asked with a mocking tone. "No offense, lady, but you don't look scary enough to be one of those Telerantas we just fought. I mean, you look more like you're a member of these little Shadow Demons."

This caused the lamia to turn slowly towards Liza. A look of disgust on her face could be seen as she scoffed rudely.

"Excuse me? I'm sorry, it's normally so hard to hear anything more than whimpering from creatures so far beneath me…but, did you just compare me to those mindless drones? How dare you! I am the most beautiful and radiant creature to have ever come forth from the circles of Hell and you dare to compare me to such trash? You miserable, ill-begotten, hideous little thing! The Teleranta you fought is a hulking, idiotic brute with no true understanding of grace and beauty. How dare you even mention one in my presence?!"

Aiden didn't know whether to be afraid of this lamia or just to be flat out perplexed by her attitude and appearance. She said that she was a prime demon, but she didn't act like the Telranta. She seemed very open about her status, and the glare she gave Liza was a clear indicator that she viewed humans very poorly.

"She's not wrong." Theresa finally spoke out. "Lamias are a Prime Demon race. Some of them have been known to be incredibly powerful." She turned towards the lamia and gave her a dirty look. "Though I'm guessing you're a low rank, judging by your arrogance, lamia."

The lamia, rising up on her tail, curls back around to face Theresa. She flicks her tongue, a wry smile spreading across her pouting lips.

"My, my, my, another dragon? This day is becoming just sooooo interesting..." Slithering closer to Theresa, she rests on her tail and daintily covered her mouth, "You're not near as cute as the little angry one..." She leans forward, locking eyes with Theresa, flicking her tongue. "Such a special day...dragons, back from their well-deserved grave..."

"Better a grave than spending thousands of years in a place where you do nothing but enjoy the very idea of waging a war with mortals because they exist." Theresa responded. She, just like Garrett, didn't seem intimidated by the lamia's advances. Aiden took notice that Theresa seemed to be giving her what looked like The Stare into the lamia's eyes. But at the same time, the lamia returned the said stare without flinching. A shiver ran down his spine when he realized why Lamias were considered prime demons. They could resist The Stare!

"And for that matter, why are you not in Hell to begin with, demon?" Theresa asked.

The lamia finally broke the staring contest, turning away dramatically, slithering back to where she had come from.

"Why indeed? I would never dream of setting foot in this horrid, filthy realm. Those miserable mages ripped me from my home by accident..." she sighed and places her fingers on her chin, flicking her tongue, "They aren't exactly working swiftly to return me, it seems..."

"That's a flat out lie, demon witch." Ryan finally spoke out. Though he did his best to hide it, everyone could hear the displeasure of even having to speak to her in his voice. "The Academy never preaches practicing summoning demons from your accursed realm. And even if we did bring you here, we certainly wouldn't want anything to do with slime like yourself."

Like a switch flipping on the demon's mood, quicker than the eye could see, she was suddenly in front of Ryan, reared back on her tail, eyes now glowing like poison. Her fangs were clearly visible. Whatever playfulness she'd exhibited before seemed to vanish the moment Ryan spoke.

"You self-righteous little magician! Your order tore me from my realm and imprisoned me in this disgusting, tacky school for spell flickers. Why would I EVER willingly subject myself to such horrid accommodations?"

"How about you start by telling me how you got into this place, demon?" Ryan asked, his voice just as icy. "This Hall is protected by strong magical barriers represented by those gems on the door way. How did you break in here?!"

The lamia flicked her tongue, her eyes still blazing as she leaned in closer to Ryan. Her voice raises and becomes more like a hiss as she whispers to him.

"You make it sound like it was hard."

Ryan nearly took out his staff to strike at the lamia, but he stopped the moment he felt the ground shake. The entire group nearly fell over when they turned towards the source of the interruption. Garrett had stomped his right foot into the ground rather hard, to get the attention of the lamia once again.

"Stop wasting your breath on a human." He said. "You want out of here, then you speak to me alone. Why? Simple. You don't like dealing with lesser creatures. While my fellow dragons would suffice to deal with you, I alone am best for the job of reaching an agreement with you, lamia."

Theresa gave Garrett a nasty look. The larger dragon held one hand up to her, giving her a short nod between the two of them. Theresa was the Rexin that was fact.

"Relax, Rexin." Garrett spoke to her. "I know how to deal with attitudes like this lamia's. After all, she doesn't put up with crap as well."

The glow in the lamia's eyes faded and her fangs shrank. With a little grin, she slithered over to the dragon, rising up on her tail until she was just a few inches taller than him.

"My, my...the big strong dragon takes orders from the little girl with such stringy hair...you must be. So. Whipped." she hissed, flicking her tongue at his nose.

"You wouldn't know anything about loyalty, demon." Garrett responded. "Then again, you lamias enjoy back stabbing your kind so much I doubt you would even know loyalty if it bit you in your ass."

The dragon's muscles tightened up slightly as he stared into the lamia's eyes. Just like her, he was not intimidated by her presence. Aiden swallowed a lump in his throat as he realized someone other than Theresa was standing up to Garrett.

"What is it that you really seek here, demon? Materials here are pitiful and not worth your time."

The lamia leaned in until her nose was pressed against his. Her eyes lit up and her fangs grew a bit more.

"I want to go home...but first, I want to see every single one of the people who dragged me into this world suffer."

"A quest for revenge then...I can respect revenge." The large dragon nodded his head. "Do you know who brought you here then?"

"Garrett!"

"Trust me on this, Rexkin." He said, and then turned back to the lamia. "What did these mages look like, demon?"

Just the mention of the ones who captured her caused the lamia's eyes to burn again. Her fangs grew out more and her voice rose to a vicious hiss.

"I didn't bother to look at the ugly creature, but I could feel their magical power. For humans? They were...noteworthy. Not like your little spellflicker over there, no. These humans were powerful." Her eyes narrowed and she hissed again, "The humiliation of being trapped in a cage...can you even imagine, dragon? A creature such as me deserves to be revered and worshipped, not...poked and prodded like some rodent!"

"Then we have a common dislike. Humans are far too greedy for their own good and they put their noses where they don't belong." Garrett responded, ignoring the glares from Liza, Aiden, and Ryan. The dragon folded his arms across his chest.

"Odds are, these humans might be the ones who brought in the Overmind and its horde here. Now, a prideful demon like you cannot stand the sight of these Shadow Demons, correct? Help us destroy them, and we'll find you the men who summoned you from Hell. In exchange, you get to destroy those lesser demons you hate so much."

The lamia pulled away and crossed her arms across her chest. The light in her eyes faded and her fangs shrank. With a sigh, she flicked her tongue and glanced at Garrett.

"I wouldn't dream of dirtying my hands on those worthless creatures. But, you have a point...I've been unsuccessful in finding my way through this dump. You have one of the little spell-flickers to guide you. Fine, as long as I get to see that wretched human burn, I'll join you," She suddenly slithered closer, wrapping her body around Garrett and grinning close to his face, "Just don't get any ideas, dragon...a creature such as myself is far above a dragon who takes orders from a stringy haired child."

Garrett's eyes didn't move once as he stared right into the lamia's eyes. How he was able to keep his cool for so long and NOT be intimidated by a giant snake woman amazed Aiden. After a second of letting the lamia wrap itself around him, he simply pushed her off.

"And know this, I will personally see to it that if you turn against us, I'll have your head." Garrett motioned his thumb to the group. "Besides myself, my Rexkin, and fellow dragon brother, are three humans and three harpies. I will make one thing clear to you now. They are to not be touched. Especially the whelp. He wouldn't even be able to harm you if he tried."

Aiden almost wanted to shout at Garrett for calling him that nickname again, but stopped when Theresa instinctively put one of her hands on his shoulder. The leader of the group then turned back to face the lamia. A look of displeasure in her eyes

"Your name. Lamia. What is your name?" The white haired dragoness asked.

The lamia rose up, clearing her throat as she coiled around and sat back on her tail.

"I am called many things in the circles of Hell. Goddess, Enchantress, Beauty, Radiant...but, as a sign of my endless benevolence, I will allow you lesser creatures the true wonder of my name." She hisses, flicking her tongue, "I am Kali."

CHAPTER 13 - THE SECOND PIECE

*A*iden wasn't exactly sure how to feel about working with a demon like Kali. Sure, their dakgrul wasn't going to turn on them any time soon but that was because Seamus' magic allowed him to keep it under control. Kali though, was not a Shadow Demon. She was a prime demon and when Garrett said that lamias tended to backstab their own kind he could only be cautious of Kali's actions.

She also was very rude to the group during their first meeting. She made it very clear that she despised humans and saw them as a lower form of life. What amazed Aiden though was that Kali was able to not only resist The Stare from Theresa, but she didn't even show a hint of intimidation when she confronted Garrett. The only other person to confront Garrett and not back down was Theresa.

Once again Aiden couldn't help but let his imagination get the best of him. He wondered what kind of abilities a Prime Demon like Kali had that would allow her to resist the dragon's stare ability. He would have asked, but he had seen the kind of personality she had and he did not want an insult thrown in his face.

"While I'm sure you've nothing more than base garbage, I am unfortunately famished to the point I'll graciously accept your petty charity."

"Why the hell should we give you any food?" Liza asked with a flat expression. Theresa placed a hand on her shoulder to stop her from attacking the prime demon.

"We are about to set up camp here for awhile, then we'll head out for the next safe spot." She said to Kali. "If we give you some food, you will tell us if you've seen Turkskas, am I clear?"

Kali scowled a bit at Theresa's order, but she gave a short nod to the white dragoness. Theresa turned back to Ryan, a frown on her face.

"Go on, conjure up a meal for her." She ordered. Ryan looked very displeased at that order.

"You gotta be kidding me."

"Look, she's been in here longer than you have, she knows how many Shadow Demons are here and she could quite possibly know how many Prime Demons are here as well. Just do it so we can save your Academy."

Ryan groaned at this argument, but he eventually relented by flicking his wrist as a large roasted chicken with several fried potatoes and broccoli stalks. He gritted his teeth as the plate floated over towards Kali for her to devour.

"Enjoy, snake."

"Such an adorable trick for such a young spellflicker. In a few more years, you might be able to hurt an icicle with that dull tongue."

Without wasting another word the lamia began to dig into her meal. Though she didn't eat it in a disgusting manner. She surprised Aiden by eating it very regally and posh like. For a demon like herself, Kali held herself in high enough regard as she ate. Aiden figured that it was because she saw herself as such a radiant being that she didn't eat like a lower class demon.

At least she stayed true to the trait that she believed herself to be so high and mighty.

"Right, now that I've had such a regular meal, let's talk." Kali uncoiled herself as she slithered up towards the door that lead out of the Hall of Memorial. "The low classed drones you keep talking about, or in this case the worms, are not too far from this area. There's at least ten burrowing underground right now, trying to avoid being caught by another Prime Demon like myself. That doesn't mean that your weak humans and the spell-flicker will be safe though. The worms tended to sense when something is walking right above them. That's when they strike."

"And how do you suggest we avoid them then?" Aiden asked. "We kinda don't have a choice but to take that path to get to the next safe room."

"Sorry, did someone hear something?" Kali asked. Theresa let a snarl come from her lips. "Oh my, is he yours? Well, if you'd keep him under control, I'd be able to finish."

"T-That's not how it is!" Aiden stammered.

"Leave him alone." Theresa grumbled as she pulled Aiden back by his shirt. Kali let out a short laugh before clearing her throat.

"All right, peasants, "If you want to survive stick close to me and don't touch anything. That includes myself since you're all unworthy of such a feat."

"Spare us the pain of it all." Garrett mocked. "We're not allowed to touch the scales of a Prime Demon. I think I'll live."

"Glad to see you know the rules, dragon."

Garrett rolled his eyes at Kali's response before the large lamia slithered away. Ryan turned back to Seamus for support on not relying on a Prime Demon but he had no luck with him. Seamus wasn't please as well, but they DID need someone to tell them when danger was ahead or not.

Theresa said nothing as she took Aiden's wrist and dragged him out of the room. He almost stumbled a bit as she dragged him away, causing chuckles to come from Aello's two guardians behind him.

"Just what I needed. Another mystical creature making fun of me." He thought to himself.

That negative thought melted as quickly as it came though as he felt Theresa give his wrist a friendly squeeze. A small smile came to his lips as he felt the reassurance from Theresa's grip. It was nice to know that at least one of the mystical creatures didn't make fun of him behind his back like Garrett, Aello's guardians, or Kali did.

The moment that they entered the next hallway though, a rotten smell hit Aiden's nose at full force. His stomach nearly churned as the decaying smell crept its way into his nostrils and refused to leave them. His eyes began to water so bad that he could barely see and his arm hair rose up on end from how wretched the smell was.

"What the hell man?!" Liza asked. "This smell is even worse than that awful stench we came across in the harpies' den!"

"H-Hey, don't make fun of our home!" Mia shouted at Liza. The former rolled her eyes as she covered her mouth. Aiden, though his vision was blurry, turned back towards Seamus as he did his best to fight off the stench of the hall.

"Why does it smell so bad?" He asked.

"That is the stench of decay. Living decay." Seamus answered him. "When you and Liza entered the den last year through their waste channel you experienced decay of creatures that had already died. The Turkskas are a type of Shadow Demon that is constantly in a state of dying. They're alive, but their bodies produce the scent of a body that is about to die."

"He's not wrong." Kali said from the front of the group. "They can pop out of nowhere and don't stop twice to chew their food, let alone take prisoners. Ugh, they're such base, mindless creatures."

Aiden decided that asking Kali why the Turkskas taking no prisoners made them mindless beasts, but decided against it when he remembered that she would just literally ignore him like she had been doing since they met. Because of how she viewed humans and mages, he couldn't trust her as far as he could throw her.

He did however; trust the words of the dragons. So far their experience with demons was what kept the group alive throughout this mission. And now because of how far they came the group had two more members to their small little party. One was a very powerful human mage, and the other was basically a female version of Garrett with her attitude.

Aiden let out a small chuckle when he thought of Kali being exactly like Garrett was. But then realized that it was an actual reality that the two of them were so alike. He felt a groan escape his lips which earned him a look from Theresa.

"What's wrong?" She asked. Aiden frowned as he turned to Theresa.

"Did you notice that Kali and Garrett are similar? They're both arrogant, hateful of humans, and tend to argue with you about orders."

Theresa laughed a little bit before shaking her head at Aiden. The latter looked confused for a moment.

"While it's true that Garrett can be arrogant, Aiden, he has one advantage over the lamia. When he's truly loyal to someone, he will not disobey. Kali though? I doubt she knows what it means to be loyal at all."

The white dragoness' eyes glared at the slithering lamia ahead of them. Aiden noticed that she let two balls of smoke escape from her nostrils. The only time she let that happen was when she was either really irritated or was angry with someone. It didn't take much to guess that it was the latter.

"Hey, Theresa?" Aiden quickly spoke out to get her mind off of Kali. "These Turkskas, they're not as bad as Telrantas or

Kelgraths, right?" Theresa turned her attention back to him and gave a reassuring smile.

"Relax, Aiden. The Turkskas are dangerous but they're predictable. They have a hunting pattern that is very much like a Great White Shark's. They try to ambush their prey from below before the prey can react." She gave a wink. "But because of their smell and how predictable they are, we know when they'll strike."

"Hey, love birds." Kali spoke out rather loudly. "When you're done talking about the stupid drones how about you take a notice of something in front of us?"

Aiden and Theresa turned around at the same time to chew Kali out for calling them lovebirds, but that thought left their mind as they noticed the large gaping hole in front of the group. The giant hole itself must have been about fourteen feet wide and at least seven feet tall.

There was little to no doubt about it. This hole was the source of the smell.

At that moment, Kali simply slithered across the wall nearest to her and reached the other side of the hole. She turned back to the group as she coiled her body together and gave them a dry cocky smile. Aiden knew that she was giving him and Liza that dry smile alone.

The next to make it across the giant hole was the Trinity. Each one had a different way to get across. Theresa jumped effortlessly across it and in the middle of the jump did an acrobatic spin before landing without trouble. Seamus used a magic spell to teleport himself and the dakgrul across the hole. Garrett simply ran on the side of the walls to reach the others before turning back to the rest of the team.

"I don't suppose you can use your magic to get us over there, can you?" Aiden asked Ryan.

"I have only one spell that lets a person get across. It can only teleport the person casting it as well. So you and Liza are on your own." Ryan frowned as he placed a hand on their shoulders and gave them a short squeeze.

"How do we get across?" Liza asked. "Even if the dragons came back over for us this area's too small for their true states to fit in."

"It's a shame that you don't have wings." Gabriella said. That smug expression disappeared from her lips though when Aello gave her a nasty look.

"We don't have time to waste here," The harpy princess spoke. "we need to get across and quickly. Mia, you'll carry Aiden across while I carry Liza. And that's an order."

Mia blinked in surprise at the order from her princess, but there was little to no time to argue with the choice. Aello flapped her wings once and flew just above Liza as she used her talons to grab ahold of the latter's shoulders. Not enough to pierce through Liza's skin, but enough to keep her from falling out of her grip.

"I've got you." Aello gave a tiny smile, before she mumbled to the side. "Don't look down."

Liza let out a yelp as Aello effortlessly picked Liza up from the ground. Aiden gave a small laugh as his friend's legs kicked back and forth a bit in a vain effort to find ground beneath her feet. It admittedly did look pretty silly to see Aello carry Liza like this, but it stopped being silly when Aello effortlessly flew across the hole with Liza intact. Once they reached the other side, Aello placed Liza back down with no effort before landing herself.

"That. Was crazy." Liza said, stumbling over a bit before regaining her balance. "Don't do that again, Elly."

"Her name is Princess Aello!" Gabriella shouted from across the hole. Liza glared at Gabriella before folding her arms.

"Hey, flutterbrains! Would you hurry up and bring Aiden over here?!"

"S-Shut up!" Mia shouted. Her plumage rising up greatly. "You're the flutterbrain, flutterbrain!"

Aiden slapped his left palm against his head in annoyance. There was a time and place to call each other names like that, and this was not the time.

"Could you just pick me up before we lose any more valuable time?" He asked dryly.

Mia grumbled a bit before floating over Aiden and opening her talons. The harpy floated downwards and grabbed his shoulders with a sharp grip into his skin. The hiss that escaped Aiden's lips was a clear signal showing his discomfort at being grabbed like that.

The harpy didn't seem all too concerned with his discomfort though as she lifted him into the air with a fierce tug. Aiden had to mentally will himself not to kick his legs like a raving lunatic when she carried him over the hole slowly. Not far behind them Gabriella followed them. Her eyes glanced down towards the hole for a second; thankfully there was no sign of a Turska nearby. The harpy flew ahead of Mia and Aiden, landing quickly beside Aello before giving Liza a glare for even calling Aello a nickname.

Aiden had to groan as Mia flapped her wings very slowly on purpose as she carried him. The young teenager glared up at the harpy as he folded his arms across his chest.

"Do you mind picking the speed up a little bit?" He asked with disdain. "By the time we're over this dumb hole they're already gonna be gone."

"Shut your face!" Mia snapped at him. "Maybe if you didn't eat so much junk food you wouldn't be so hard to carry over."

"I'm worked to the bone everyday with training, there's no way I'm heavy enough for you to make that comment."

"Muscles are heavier than fat you know." Mia grumbled.

Before Aiden could respond in kind though, Aello cleared her throat to get their attention.

"Would you two stop fighting?" She asked, mumbling to the side. "You're both in a position where you could end up as worm food…"

The moment Aello finished speaking Mia quickly flapped her wings even faster than before to race over towards the group. Aiden felt his head bounce back and forth with how fast she was flapping her wings to reach the group. If there was one thing Aiden had to give Mia and Gabriella it was that they were, as guardian harpies, incredibly loyal to their princess.

Aiden felt relief when his feet made contact with the ground once more. He didn't particularly enjoy the idea of being over a giant hole where demonic worms once were. He glared a bit at Mia as she hovered over to Aello and landed beside her.

"Forgive me for the delay, Princess Aello." She spoke, glaring daggers at Aiden. "Someone was too heavy for his own good."

"Mia it's okay! Aiden is my friend too…try to be nice."

The guardian harpy mumbled under her breath for a moment, but didn't speak out against her princess' order. Aiden just brushed the incident off his shoulder before turning back to Theresa and Kali.

"Any idea on how close we are?" He asked. "If we come across more of those holes, we could be in trouble." Theresa frowned as she placed her hands on her lips.

"The chances of more holes like that are slim, Aiden. Turkskas aren't very bright creatures, they only move by instinct and when the Overmind gives an order."

"Ugh, such pathetic demons really. If there was a morsel above me and I had to take an order not to attack it, I would have already devoured the poor soul."

"Touching. Really touching." Seamus growled at the lamia. Kali just shook her hand up and down at him.

"Blah blah, spare me your righteous 'honor.' Last I checked you dragons ate meat too ya know."

"We didn't HUNT sentient creatures though." Garrett responded as he glared down a hallway. "Rexkin, there are more ahead. Lying in wait."

Theresa put a hand up to silence anyone from talking. Her eyes narrowed as she took a deep breath of air. Much like Seamus and Garrett, her sense of smell was greater than a human's, so she and the other dragons were the best bets they had at finding the worms.

Theresa wasted no time as she walked ahead of the group into the hallway before her. No one second-guessed her direction as they quickly followed after here. Garrett gave Kali a glare for not moving at first, to which the lamia responded with her own glare before she slithered after the team.

"They'd make a lovely couple if they weren't so exactly alike one another." Aiden thought to himself as he watched the two share glares with one another.

It had gotten incredibly quiet as Theresa sniffed the area out. The further down the hall they traveled, the darker it became. Seamus held his hand up, casting an illumination spell so that they wouldn't be completely wandering in the dark. Aiden noticed that Mia and Gabriella flinched a bit at the bright light. Their first encounter last year with the guardians resulted in Seamus using the same spell in their den's prison.

"Hold." Theresa ordered. The group came to a stop; all save for Kali who continued to slither on. "I said, **hold.**"

Kali stopped for a moment before she coiled herself back up and leaning forward, glaring at Theresa.

"I don't take orders from you, dragon girly." She said with a hint of disdain in her throat.

"And do you think I care if you take orders or not?" Theresa retorted. "Unless you want to be attacked by the worm that's circling underground beneath us right now, I suggest you don't move."

The group immediately got tense at those words before each of them drew out their weapons. Kali didn't look intimidated though, in fact she looked more annoyed at Theresa instead. The lamia pulled herself back into her coiled position before placing her arms over her chest.

"And what makes you think that I, a goddess in my own right, fear these things?"

"I thought you were suppose to be a Prime Demon?" Theresa responded. "After all, you all should know that Turskas strike when your guard is completely down. Even the most cunning and skilled warriors could fall victim to their massive jaws if they're not careful."

Kali let a hiss escape her lips, her forked tongue slipping through her teeth as she and Theresa continued to stare each other. Theresa cornered Kali with her argument. The lamia didn't seem to back down though as she pulled back.

"I don't take orders, dragon, remember that before I decide to bite off your pretty little head-"

The ground began to rumble beneath the team before Kali could finish. Liza almost fell over onto her face but Aello grabbed her shirt just in time. Aiden nearly landed on his back, but used Warfang as an anchor in the wall. The more experienced members of the team didn't seem to lose their balance at all.

"One's coming." Theresa said very quietly. "Watch all over, don't make any sudden movements."

The very idea that one of the Turskas was near the group was a bit unnerving. Each member of the team readied themselves for the arrival of the shadow demon in their own way. The harpies floated above the group, talons at the ready, while Aello held her personal lance. The dragons each held their respective weapons out, Ryan had a spell ready at the get go, and Aiden and Liza stood back to back with one another.

Aiden glimpsed to his right just for a second and nearly dropped his weapon in shock at what he saw.

The ground bulged, nearly splitting in half from the massive beast from below. It was like a shark was swimming below them as it approached them. The faster it came, the more the ground threatened to open up.

"Incoming!" Aiden shouted.

The group immediately moved out of the way as the ground suddenly exploded in front of where Aiden once was. What emerged turned out to be one of the most hideous demons that he had seen yet in his life.

The Turska was nothing like what Aiden had imagined. The beast was living decay; it's skin was pale gray, with patches missing completely or threatening to fall off. Beneath the skin, Aiden could see pale red muscles, tinted green with rot. Just looking at the creature was enough to make his stomach churn.

The most disturbing part of the beast, though, was its head. When it reared its head back, Aiden saw that its face was almost entirely a gaping mouth. Within the maw were rows and rows of jagged spikes, which Aiden could only assume were its teeth. Atop its head were several bulging eyeballs, near twenty of them, twisting turning and looking in every direction. The moment one caught sight of the group, they all turned to them, twitching with feral rage.

"T-That's a WORM?" Liza asked in shock. "It looks like something only a sick bastard would come up with!"

The dakgrul growled at the Turska that threatened them. It was a warning to the beast to stay away from the group. But the larger demon didn't seem to even acknowledge the dakgrul's threat as it turned its head towards a specific target. Aiden.

What erupted from the Turska was an unholy roar. It wasn't like a dakgrul, kelgrath, or even a Teleranta's roar. Aiden could only describe it as some kind of mixture between a high-pitched scream and a low grotesque gargle. It was a combination of sounds that should never have been.

Aiden nearly forgot where he was for a moment when the Turska roared. But his senses came back to him when the large worm began to slither towards him at a quick speed. The ground bulging up once more as the demon rushed towards its target choice of prey. Its massive mouth open as it got closer and closer to Aiden.

"Kiddo!" Seamus shouted. "You're gonna have to blast it with a magic spell!" Aiden turned to Seamus, looking absolutely lost at that statement.

"Blast it with what?! I can't summon the Draconic Firestorm on a whim yet!"

"Then use another attack! The Flarenea spell!" Theresa told him. "Until the Turska is dead it'll just keep coming after you, even if we attack it! Hurry dammit!"

Aiden turned towards the large demon worm as it slithered right towards him. Its large mouth gaping open as if it expected to swallow him whole when it got close.

"AIDEN!" Theresa shouted at him. "If you don't now, you'll die!"

Those words were enough to snap Aiden out of his uncertainty. Without wasting a second he put Warfang in his left hand before gathering the necessary mana required to gather for the Flarenea spell. He felt the familiar fire magic from before build up in his hand. It was strong, but he didn't know if it would be enough to slay the Turska charging at him.

A sudden rush of power, rising up from his feet to the tips of his hair. It wasn't like the Draconic Firestorm, but it was dangerously close. For the first time since he summoned that awesome power in the Harpy's Den, Aiden felt like he could do anything.

At first, he looked around in confusion. The sudden surge left him dizzy and confused. But, that feeling passed when he turned his attention back to the worm. Wasting no time, he took aim with his palm pointed out towards the giant beast.

"Flarnea!' His words exploded from his lips, emboldened by the swelling of his power and confidence. And then, what erupted from his hand was not a fireball, but something else entirely. His entire body jerked, his eyes widening as a concentrated ray of raw fire exploded from his palm, the heat searing the air as it careened toward its target. Aiden stumbled, reaching out and grabbing his wrist to hold the beam steady.

Once the beam penetrated the skin, it began to burn away the rotten flesh of the demon. The monster didn't even have time to let out a dying cry as the beam tore it apart, leaving nothing but ashes where it once was.

"Wha…What just happened?" Aiden asked as he pulled his hand back to glance at his palm. The fire spell that he used was indeed Flarenea, but it was different. Theresa walked up and took his hand, examining it herself. For once the wise and powerful Theresa was just as confused.

"Aiden how did…how did you make the Flarenea that powerful?" She asked.

"I…I don't know." Aiden truthfully answered. "I just felt some kind of power surge erupt in my body that just came from out of no where."

"Power like that doesn't erupt so suddenly like that, kiddo." Seamus stepped up. "That was some advanced magic that was pulled from your body. It strengthened the power of your ability to use the Flarenea to another level. In other words, with some more practice you can make it on your own without outside assistance."

He wondered who it was, looking around blankly at first. He quickly noticed the way Seamus was staring right at Kali.

"That was some pretty high end magic there, demon. There's been a few cases of enhance magic recorded before, but that? That was something else. Just what did you do?"

Kali gently covered her mouth and laughed softly. She slowly unfolded her arm and stared at her nails. Her eyes gleamed and a sly smile came to her lips.

"Oh, that? That was just a little gift, from me to the worm," she replied. "I couldn't help myself, I wanted to see how the little boy would react to his first taste of true power." Her eyes glittered and a sly smile came to her lip, "And, by the by? That's all that was. A taste of what a goddess like myself is capable of."

Kali slithered closer to Aiden, rising up on her tail and leaning close to him. She cocked her head as her tongue flicking through her slightly parted lips.

"I'll admit, I'm impressed...most humans would have lost at least an arm drawing on that much magic. You're an interesting little human, aren't you?"

Aiden's cheeks turned a crimson red as Kali leaned in close to him. Not from attraction to the lamia or from her compliment, but from something else. He didn't notice it when they met her, but there was a power that the prime demon was hiding from the group. With just a simple boost to his magical capabilities, Aiden could sense how much magical power flowed within the lamia.

Theresa frowned as she grabbed his shoulder, pulling him away from Kali's eyesight as she gave her own glare back at the demon. A soft chuckle escaped the demon's lips as Theresa held Aiden back.

"Oh that's right, this one's suppose to be yours, right?" She reared back a bit. "Sorry, dragoness, I forgot how possessive your kind can be about their belongings."

"He is not a belonging. He is my treasured friend and I will not have you corrupting him with your magic." Theresa snapped back. Kali just smiled as her eyes glittered.

"Corrupted? Oh that's not the word I would use. He's already felt a small taste of my magic. He could probably use the spell again and the results would be the same."

Aiden felt his cheeks nearly going red again as Theresa's grip on his shoulder became stronger. Even after the events from last year with the Harpy's Den Theresa just couldn't seem but be protective of him. Though that was a trait of hers that he was glad that she had always kept.

"I hate to interrupt people, but we should get moving." Ryan spoke out. "The next rest area is close by, and I'd rather we not get attacked by another one of those worms."

Kali just scoffed at his proposal before slithering away. Theresa sighed as her grip on Aiden's shoulder began to lighten up before turning back to him with a tiny smile.

"I'm surprised, Aiden. You managed to maintain that spell very well even if the power came from a demon. It shows just how far you've come." Seamus gave a short nod, a smile on his own lips. Even Garrett seemed mildly impressed.

"Maybe you're not such a whelp after all." The large dragon said. This almost made Aiden and Liza's mouths drop in shock. If they didn't know any better they could have sworn that Garrett wouldn't ever give one of them a compliment.

Nobody wasted time anymore as they immediately went after Kali. If there was another Turska waiting under the ground then there was no time to waste. Aiden didn't complain about moving though, he'd rather be moving fast than face off with one of those worms again.

Their trek eventually led them to another room. Much like most of the rooms, it had destroyed walls, furniture, and broken floor pieces. Ryan frowned as he walked into the room and glanced over the destruction. The sorrow in his eyes was clear to see, as he ran his fingers across the wall of the room.

"This was one of the study rooms." He whispered. "Students would spend hours reading, practicing, and making friends here. It was one of the happiest places that this Academy ever had…and now it's a shell of its former glory." Seamus' low growls could be heard from the side as Ryan talked.

"I will personally make certain that your father fixes my school, Ryan. This tragedy will be answered for what has happened." Ryan turned back to Seamus, giving him a short nod of approval.

"If you will allow me to, I'll also make certain that my father responds to the destruction of this school. Though if we are able to defeat the Overmind and rid this place of the Shadow Demons, I fear this school will never reclaim its former glory."

"Everyone, see what you can find." Theresa ordered. "We won't spend as much time at this room, so be certain to use your time well."

The group gave a short nod, minus Kali, as they each separated to a different part of the safe room. The only one who didn't bother was Kali as she had made it clear that she did not want to work with anyone. To make the search easier they split up into different groups to find what they could. Seamus and Ryan searched one part of the room, Liza, Aello, Mia, and Gabriella searched another, while Theresa and Garrett took up guard duty at the entrance.

Aiden took the opportunity to look at one section of the safe room, as everyone seemed distracted. After what had happened with the Turska he needed time to go over what he just did thanks to Kali's helpful boost in magic power.

Even though the lamia stated that the boost that she gave him was only temporary he could still feel the lingering effects of the magic she had used on him. Did his body adjust to the power boost from their uneasy ally? Or was there just a pinch of her magic left that filled his veins? All questions that he didn't have the answers to.

Before he could ponder further on these thoughts though his attention changed when he saw a familiar golden glint not far away from him. Aiden noticed that the glint had come from a pile of books that had fallen over into a pile. There was only one thing that glinted like that. It was the shoulder pauldron from the harpy den.

Aiden glanced around, making certain that no one was watching him. If last year taught him anything, that same mysterious voice from before would speak to him once again the moment he approached the next piece. Once he was certain that no one was watching him, Aiden hurried over to the pile.

The sudden drive to find this piece of armor was an intoxicating force. Aiden couldn't describe why the urge to get this piece was so strong but he wasn't going to deny himself the desire for it. The last piece of armor had the same kind of effect over him when he obtained the piece.

Finally, Aiden saw his prize waiting before him underneath all the books he had pushed aside. Just like the pauldron that he found before it was another crimson dragon head with golden outlines to it. It was all the same when he reached his hand out towards the pauldron. The surge of heat, the sensation of power that came from it, and the same mysterious shadowed figure that appeared before his mind.

"Good job, lad." An all too familiar tone spoke out. *"You found the second piece, three more to go."*

Aiden looked at the mysterious figure with confusion in his eyes as he tried to speak out. The shadowy being just held up one finger to stop him from speaking.

"Say nothing." It demanded. The tone it took was powerful and demanding him. *"Keep it known only to yourself. No one must know. Not even the person whom you most cherish."*

The figure began to disappear from Aiden's sight once again. The second pauldron appearing on his other shoulder just as the first one did one year ago. Aiden hissed a bit as he felt a surge of heat seem to form over his shoulders as spectral images of the shoulder pauldrons. Just as soon as they appeared over his shoulders though, they vanished. The mysterious figure slowly pulling away as it nodded its head at Aiden.

"Aiden?" Theresa's voice called out to him. "Aiden, what are you looking at?"

The voice of his best friend brought him back to reality within a heartbeat. Aiden glanced back over to Theresa. He wasn't exactly keen on telling her a lie...but the voice that had spoke to him from the mysterious figure was so controlling that he feared what would happen if he did speak out at what he found.

"I thought I saw something." He said in a hasty response. Though as Theresa approached him, Aiden's eyes couldn't help but glance to the large pile of books that had just fallen.

"Did you find anything?" Theresa asked. He simply shook his head no before placing his hands in his pockets.

"Nothing. There was nothing at all."

For Aiden though, the mysterious being would stick in his mind long after this experience was over.

CHAPTER 14 - MORE VISIONS

"*L*ook at this," Ryan said as he picked up a particularly large book, with several pages ripped out of it and the back cover nearly torn in half. "This was a tome of knowledge. Mages of all ages could come to this particular tome and study it for hours. They could learn everything from the basics of being a mage to casting some of the most powerful spells. And now, it's not even a shell of its former self."

It was subtle, but Aiden could hear Ryan's tone begin to change from calm to enraged. What was once a place of learning, understanding, and familiarity for the mage had become a living hell full of demons that the average human would never dream of. The young mage didn't seem to acknowledge the others as they tried to comfort him. Except for one.

"Ryan." Seamus' voice snapped whatever trance Ryan was once in. "Is there anything that you can find here that we could use to reach the Overmind?"

The eldest son of the Grand Mage frowned as he placed the tome down. With a flick of his wrist, another book flew down from a shelf into his hands. The mage didn't even have to move his fingers to open the book as the page he was looking for opened right before him.

"If there's any chance of finding the Overmind with a spell, it'll be in this chapter of this particular book." He answered the dragon of magic. He must have noticed Aiden and Liza's confused looks as he continued to explain. "In case you're wondering how a spell like the one I'm talking about works, it's all based on finding the strongest source of magic in a location. Aside from the Dragon of Magic and my father, the Overmind is the most powerful being in this academy."

"Um, excuse me?" Kali scoffed. "I believe you're forgetting about my skills and grace? Then again, I had a feeling you would forget about a creature such as myself, spell wicker."

"No one was talking to you, snake." Garrett coldly responded. Kali feigned being heartbroken as she placed her hands over her chest.

"Oh! How could you say such a thing?! I'm a delicate creature, you brute!" Garrett rolled his eyes as Kali let her forked tongue slip between her teeth. Theresa growled at the two of them as puffs of smoke escaped her nostrils.

"Focus. Both of you. Ryan, how long will it take for you to locate the Overmind with this spell?"

"If I'm lucky, the spell might find it immediately. But the Overmind's magic is so powerful that it could very well have masked itself from being spotted. The only way to know is to try it and see."

Ryan sighed as he turned to a page that looked like it was written in a language Aiden couldn't make out. The language was different from the Draconic language that he had learned, but it probably was just as old as the language of the dragons. Like a curious child, Aiden poked his head over the book.

"What kind of language is this?" He asked. Ryan just smiled before shaking his head.

"It's not really a language, newbie. They're old spells.

Back in the days of the old kingdoms, the great masters of magic developed spells that only they could use. As a way to keep the most powerful spells humans and elves could master out of the hands of those whom they did not deem worthy to wield them." He cleared his throat. "The pronunciation of these words can be tricky, if even one vowel is said wrong it could result in the spell completely backfiring on the caster."

"And what's the backlash of this spell suppose to be?" Liza asked suddenly. Ryan glanced back over to her for a moment and frowned.

"The worst? It reveals our location to the Overmind and its demons. The minimum damage it could do is send us off on a wild goose chase."

Ryan wasted no more time with idle chat as he held out his hand to the book in front of him. A yellowish aura formed itself around the book as streaks of it rose up into the air. The sight of the aura held Aiden in awe, as Ryan's own body was covered by a blue aura of his own magic. The auras were transparent, but there were moments when their solid colors appeared briefly. Aiden could just feel the magical power rising off the two of them.

The two auras began to meld together as their colors united to form a greenish glow around both Ryan and the book. Once the two auras had melded into one, the mage's eyes turned completely white before he spoke out the spell.

"Tragateostrum!"

A flash of green white light came from the point of Ryan's staff. The intense light forced Aiden to shield his eyes momentarily. Sound seemed to die momentarily as Aiden felt as if his mind had just left his body. The last thing he heard was Theresa crying out to him for a moment...

* * *

"UGH, MY HEAD…" Aiden groaned as he began to slowly come to. His entire body felt like it had just been hit by cart filled with bricks as he slowly stood up.

"Hey, is anyone else feeling like they just had the worst migraine ever?"

Aiden expected Theresa, Garrett, Seamus, or even Kali, to respond to his question with a quick retort. But to his surprise, no one answered. Confused, Aiden spoke out once more.

"Guys? Is no one gonna say that it's because I'm inexperienced?" He asked.

Again, no one responded. Aiden slowly began to open his eyes, trying to adjust his blurry vision. Whatever that spell did it must have knocked his head against the floor rather hard to make his vision blurry. The bright light didn't help either.

Wait, bright light?

Aiden blinked in confusion as his eyes finally adjusted to the light around him. What greeted him was a complete shock. The damage that had been done to the room he was in had been undone. Several students sat at different tables with different books open and their staffs either in their hands or on the tables. There was laughter, joy, gossip, talks about the upcoming exams that the head mages were planning, and even bickering amongst rival students.

It didn't dawn on Aiden when they first entered the Academy, but these students were just like any other high schooler. They had a group of friends that they hung out with everyday, there were classes that they each attended, tests that they had to take, and even young romance. He had been so drawn in by the fact that he had seen mages that he didn't realize that the students that attended the Academy were like any other group of students.

He remembered when he and Liza first heard the harpies gossip in the den one year ago. What he thought he knew about them was completely eradicated when he learned that the harpies weren't as monstrous as previously thought. Had the Modern world forced the older races and kingdoms to adjust so much? What would the elves be like if he ever encountered them?

All those questions he had in his mind were completely abandoned when one even bigger question had to be answered. Had the others defeated the Overmind without him? The school looked like it was brand new once more! And he missed out on the battle against the Overmind!

"Oh Theresa, if I find out you guys left me here to deal with the Overmind without me I am going to be SO angry with you!" He shouted.

To his shock, none of the students reacted to his sudden shout. They just kept talking with one another as if nothing had disrupted their daily lives. The next words from Aiden's mouth fit his confusion perfectly.

"What the hell is going on?"

No one answered his question. Typical. But he already knew what was happening to him. He was having another vision.

"Hey, Lewis!" One student shouted across the room. Aiden's attention immediately turned to where the shout came from.

He sighed when he saw the source of the voice. He should have figured that just like any other school, there was some brawny tall student who used his size and power to intimidate the other students. This student had messy dark hair, hazel colored eyes, and a tan. His staff's top resembled a goat head, with the goat's mouth open and tongue sticking out.

The brawny student reminded him of Eric in a way. It wasn't uncommon for a student body to have at least one student who had to take up the oh so 'classic' bully role to mess with the other students. It was something Aiden had been terrified of, but was now incredibly irritated by after being trained by the Trinity for a year.

The student that the brawny one had called out, Lewis, sat at a table alone. He had messy blonde hair, very light blue eyes, and a pair of black glasses that sat on his nose. His physique was nothing special either. His arms were skinny, almost branch like, barely any muscle on them. Aiden felt sorry for him, he just painted the picture of being completely pathetic.

His surroundings weren't that special either. With nothing but a pile of books beside him and a short staff that honestly, was probably the plainest looking staff Aiden had seen yet from any of the mages. It hardly passed off as a staff too. It looked like someone had taken it from a grey colored withered tree that had just recently been cut down. There wasn't any kind of magical decorations to this staff.

While he would never admit it, Aiden always felt like as cool as his sword. But even Aiden wouldn't want a staff that looked so brittle that it had almost no purpose left other than to break apart.

Lewis just glanced up to the brawny mage momentarily, then quietly glanced back down to his book. His meek appearance clearly indicated that he did not want a confrontation with this bully, showing almost no interest in responding to the brawny mage. However, as most things go in life, the brawny mage did not back down from his prey. Strutting over to Lewis with a sense of pride and confidence, the brawny student grinned darkly.

"You deaf or something? I was talking to you." He said to Lewis. The latter student just kept his face down in his book.

SLAM.

The brawny student had suddenly used his magic to slam the book in front of Lewis down tightly. Thankfully the meeker student was able to pull his hands away from the book in time before his fingers were crushed. The look of not caring about the bully had been replaced by terror.

"Yeah, got your attention now don't I?" The brawny mage said with an evil grin. "You know you getting special treatment is starting to piss me off. You think you're some hotshot that you get clearance to some of the better books because of your mind huh? I should just flat out kick your ass."

Lewis didn't respond as he wrapped his arms around himself. His breathing turning heavy as he tried to look away from his attacker. Aiden snarled in anger at the scene playing out before him. The other students could clearly see that the bully was about to torment the poor boy, but they were all too terrified to do anything to stop him.

"What's wrong?" The brawny mage asked as he pulled Lewis over with his magic. The meeker mage almost let out a cry of terror as his face was inches away from the bully's. "Not gonna fight back, runt?"

"You really didn't think this through, did you?" A familiar voice asked.

Aiden turned on a dime to see the new comer that had just arrived on the scene. His eyes almost jumped out of his head when he saw the new comer was Ryan.

Ryan didn't look like he did when Aiden first met him. His clothes were much cleaner, more refined, and he was not covered in scratches. His hair wasn't a mess either.

Aiden knew that he was experiencing a vision of some kind. And it had to be Ryan's spell causing it.

The brawny mage scoffed as he turned his wrath on Ryan with the flick of his staff. Ryan's eyes narrowed as he used his own staff to block the unseen magic with little effort.

"Why don't you back off, Ryan?" The big mage asked. "Your brother and I here were having a personal conversation."

"Conversation eh? Cause from the way it looks from where I'm standing, you're directly antagonizing him for no reason."

Lewis whimpered a bit as he covered his head with his hands as his older brother took a step forward towards the attacker. Aiden had heard Ryan speak strongly in defense of his little brother before but he did not know just how protective he would be for Lewis. The fire in his eyes was possibly enough to rival the fury of Theresa herself when she was enraged.

"And if you mess with my little brother, you mess with me. You can bet that I will not only single handily kick your ass but after I'm done kicking it, I'll drag it back to the Grand Mage so that he can deal out the final punishment to you himself for trying to antagonize one of his sons." Ryan pointed the top of his staff towards the brawny mage, eyes filled with determination. "What's it going to be, jerkwad? Either way, you're screwed."

The tension in the room grew as Ryan stared down his little brother's aggressor. Aiden swallowed a lump in his throat as he watched the confrontation as neither the bully nor Lewis' older brother made a single move. After what felt like an eternity, the brawny mage turned around and left the two brothers. Once he was out of sight, Ryan let out a sigh as he dismissed his staff.

"Punk ass. I knew he was going to back off." He grumbled. "He talks big and acts like he's a hotshot but in reality he's nothing but a coward."

Ryan turned his attention to Lewis, who still had his hands over his head and tears forming in his eyes. The older brother gave a soft smile as he took a seat beside him and placed a hand on his shoulder.

"Hey. Hey it's okay. The asshole's gone now." Ryan said with a gentler voice. Lewis gave a short whimper as he glanced up to his brother.

"R-Ryan…" He said quietly. Aiden took notice that Lewis' voice was soft and high as it could be for a teenager that was roughly Aiden's age. "I-I'm sorry. I-It was my fault…"

"Stop that right now." Ryan cut his brother off. His eye brow had furrowed in anger. "You did not start anything. That punk was just being an asshole because he thought he could get away with it."

"But…but I know what he and the others say about me." Lewis protested, glancing down. "I'm terrible at being a mage. I can't even do the most basic spells without screwing i-it up somehow..."

Lewis pulled his legs up to his chest and held them in his arms. His eyes still wet with tears as he let a slight hiccup escape his lips.

"I'm n-not like you or f-father, R-Ryan..."

The elder brother frowned at his little brother's self doubt before putting one of his hands on Lewis' shoulder. Ryan just gave his shoulder a tight squeeze, attempting to comfort the younger mage.

"You're right, you're not like our father or me." He said, a small smile coming to his lips. "You're your own unique self. And that's all you'll ever need to be."

"But you and d-dad are so good with casting s-spells and are so powerful!" Lewis frowned. "I can barely even cast the most basic spells."

"So?" Ryan asked with a smile. "Just because dad and I are good at casting spells doesn't mean that you're not powerful, Lew." The elder mage ruffled his brother's hair up. "You just haven't discovered what it is that you're incredible at yet. And I'm willing to bet that whatever it is will make you even greater than our old man."

Lewis gave a short sniff as he raised his glasses up to dry his eyes with his sleeve. When his placed his glasses back down he glanced back up to his older brother with a small glimmer of hope in his eyes.

"D-Do you really think so?"

"I know so, little bro." Ryan replied, gently flicking his index finger against Lewis' forehead. "And has your big brother ever been wrong before?"

"N-No..." Lewis muttered, looking embarrassed. "Don't flick my head in public..." Ryan responded just by simply flicking his little brother's forehead once more.

"Or what? You're gonna smack me with your sissy hands, lil bro?" Lewis covered his forehead with one of his hands.

"Knock it off, big bro!"

The two brothers shared a quick laugh with each other. Once the laughter died down, Ryan flicked his wrist to close the books that Lewis had placed on the table. The younger mage looked up at him in confusion.

"Come on." Ryan ordered. "I didn't just come here to save you from that punk. Our old man wants to see the both of us for something." The color in Lewis face disappeared as he grabbed his left shoulder and squeezed it tightly.

"I don't like it when he wants to see the both of us." He muttered, "Whenever he does that he usually wants to chastise me in front of you."

"Well that won't happen this time." Ryan replied. "Come on, I've got your back little brother."

Aiden gave a soft smile at the scene between the two brothers as they both rose up at the same time. It was nice to see something happy for once in the Academy after what he had witnessed. But just as he was getting used to the scene between the two brothers another flash of light went off.

Forced to shield his eyes once more Aiden waited for the bright light to die down. As the light dimmed around him, Aiden found himself in a different room. His brain quickly recognized the room as the Grand Mage's office. Aiden felt like he could just spit at the sight of this office. The Grand Mage, Ivan, had given them the rudest welcome and acted higher and mightier than any of them during the entire time the spoke.

But he forced that desire to get upset back as he noticed the two people sitting in the room. Ivan, with a rather large book open in front of him, sat in his office chair with a dissatisfied expression. The other person, Lewis, sat at a small desk writing down notes into a book and constantly looking back and forth between the source material that he was copying notes down from to his notes.

Lewis looked miserable while working non-stop on copying notes back and forth. Again, Aiden had to sympathize with him. In his own high school Aiden had to work with little to no rest on notes during class and preparing for the upcoming tests and exams that all students had to take. But the way that Lewis was writing down notes and by the size of the large books in front of him made Aiden want to vomit at the disgusting amount of work.

"How far are you, Lewis?" Ivan asked from his book. He still wore a vexed expression as he glanced over to his son. "I do hope you're not slacking off."

"N-No sir." Responded the young mage as he continued to write. "I-I'm on chapter one hundred and thirty seven n-now."

"One hundred and thirty seven." Ivan repeated, almost in a mocking tone. "Your brother was at chapter two hundred when he was your age. I expect you to do better, Lewis."

"Yes, f-father." Lewis responded as he continued to work on his notes. Aiden noticed that his wrist had turned red from writing non-stop. Every time Lewis began to write another paragraph a pained hiss escaped his lips.

The silence between father and son resumed once more as they both went back to the different activities. That silence lasted at the most five minutes though, as Ivan closed his book with a sudden 'slam.'

"Lewis." He spoke out, nearly making his son flinch at the sound of his own name. "Do you remember the notes I took down the other day?"

"U-Um, which ones, father?"

"The ones regarding the work I am doing with the other teachers at this Academy."

"O-Oh, right. Those." Lewis cleared his throat. "You came back, looking irritated from a failed experiment. When you sat down in your chair you began to rant about how the mages here are incompetent and failed to deliver any kind of development for the project you're so secret about." Ivan leaned forward in his chair, his fingers interlocked with each other as he placed his chin on top of his hands.

"Yes, yes. That I remember. But do you remember the kind of magic I wanted them to look into?"

"Mind magic. A type of magic that hasn't been studied in years." Lewis quickly responded. Ivan gave a short nod of his head, and Aiden could have sworn he saw a glint in the Grand Mage's eyes.

"Well done, son. That is exactly what I hoped you would remember."

As Ivan finished speaking the imagery began to change once more. Aiden groaned as he brought his hand back up to block the bright light that exploded in his face. Once more the scene had changed to a different room as the light died down. Aiden's eyes grew wide, as it was a room that he had previously had seen before.

The laboratory.

Aiden was at a loss of words as he glanced around the room. Several large and giant tubes filled with the dark magic that he had seen before were everywhere in the room. They were not the only things, however, as Aiden noticed that the room also had several demons locked behind jail cells made of magic. Several of them were dakgruls and kelgraths, but he noticed a sleeping Kali behind one force field. Aiden had to guess that she had to be put to sleep before being put behind that field.

In the back of his mind Aiden wondered if this was the work of her magic once again the moment he saw Kali. After what she had done to increase the power of his Flarenera, he wouldn't be surprised if she was capable of casting magic letting him seeing the past. But he doubted that her magic was strong enough that he could see into the past of someone other than the caster.

"Work, dammit!" Ivan's voice shouted from behind Aiden. "Let me see what you are hiding!"

Aiden turned to see what the Grand Mage was attempting to do and gasped. There, strapped to a table, was one of the dakgruls. It had made some kind gurgling noise as it tried to lunge at Ivan's hand with its mouth. The grand mage glared at the beast as he moved his hand out of the beast's way before he slapped it across the face rather hard.

"Disgusting demon filth. You WILL listen!"

The dakgrul just gave a snort as it rested its head down on the table once more. Several mages frowned as Ivan turned to face them.

"Why is it that we have not made any progress?" One of the older mages approached Ivan. Aiden noticed that she was an older mage, almost in her twilight years, but had a streak of blonde in her hair.

"What you're asking for, Grand Mage, is for us to discover a way to worm our way into the mind of demons." She answered. "It is practically impossible to do that."

"Don't you give me that crap." Ivan responded, his upper lip curling up into a snarl. "Those who go to the dark arts are able to control the demons, we will find a way to do so without turning to the power of dark magic."

"What you're asking for is physically impossible, you fool." The woman responded. "The Dark arts don't allow the mages to control the demons they make the fools who use that damn magic believe that they do. In reality, the demons control them and you know it!"

"Then tell me, Iris, why is it that it is hard for us to discover a way to control the demons without dark magic?" Ivan spat back. "We have over thousands of years of research and magical studies in this academy. And you're telling me that there was never not one instant when the thought of controlling demons without dark magic came across their minds?"

The grand mage flicked his wrist once as an unseen force of magic blasted into a pile of books, the fell over with no grace at all. The mages behind Iris flinched at his power, but Iris stood tall. The same look of defiance was in her eyes as she stared right back at the display of power from Ivan.

"Yes. That is the truth, and you just have to accept it."

Pure fury was plastered all over the grand mage's face. Never before had Aiden seen such anger from an adult. Ivan held his staff up high and blasted a nearby table with books in his rage, causing the books and table to fly apart from the concussive blast of magic. Once more, Iris stood tall in front of Ivan's rage, unflinching as the Grand Mage turned away from her.

"Throwing a tantrum is not going to bring you anything." Iris said, her tone unimpressed by the Grand Mage's magic. "You're going to have to let this project die, Ivan."

A defeated sigh escaped the lips of Ivan at those words. He clenched his hands once more before glaring at the dakgrul that was strapped to the table beside him. The demon just stared right up at him with defiant eyes. The shadow demon gave a short snarl at the grand mage before making a strange kind of clicking noise in its throat.

Silence filled the room for the briefest of moments. Then, like a drinking glass, it was shattered by a new voice.

"I understood it."

"AIDEN!" Theresa shouted as she shook him up and down by the collar of his shirt. "Aiden, wake up!"

The entire group, with the exception of Kali, had gathered around the knocked out Aiden. Each of their faces expressed a different expression for their friend as Theresa continued to shake him. Finally, after what seemed like forever, her attempts to awaken him succeeded.

"T-Theresa, you can stop shaking me!" He managed to spit out before his best friend pulled him into a massive hug. Aiden blinked as she felt the warmth of her cheek against her own.

"Thank goodness, you're awake again…" She whispered. "I was afraid Ryan's spell affected you for the worst."

Aiden's eyes widened at those words. He glanced around, before spotting the eldest son of the Grand Mage. Ryan blinked in confusion as he saw the solemn look that Aiden was giving him.

"What?" Ryan asked in confusion. Aiden shook his head a bit before standing up with Theresa. The white haired girl also looked confused as she watched Aiden take a deep breath before speaking right to Ryan.

"I have something to tell you that I think you're going to hate to hear…"

CHAPTER 15 - CHRYSALIS

"*H*e. WHAT?"

Aiden flinched from the question. He had told everything that he had seen from the vision that he just witnessed. At first the eldest son of the Grand Mage didn't say anything. Instead, he just listened to every single detail that Aiden told him. What he saw in the lab, how Ryan's father and Iris argued right down to the demons imprisoned by magic cells.

The fury that was in Ryan's eyes grew during Aiden's story. Finally, the straw broke the camel's back as the eldest son took his staff and blasted a large fireball into a broken bookshelf. Aiden could have sworn that the grip around his staff was just about to break his weapon in half.

"Are you positive about what you saw?" Ryan asked. Aiden just nodded once at him. "Goddammit…I don't want to believe this. I don't want to believe any of this…"

"What's your deal?" Mia asked. "If your dad is trying to control demons doesn't that mean that you guys don't have to fight them all the time then?" Gabriella frowned as she turned to her fellow harpy.

"Don't you remember last year at our den, MiMi? What with

those two mages and their demons? We had a hard enough time fighting back against two mages with an army of demons."

"You two know that the situation is different." Aello said. "Those big jerks used dark arts."

"And you can be damn sure that I would never stand for the school I helped found using the dark arts as a means of gaining power." Seamus growled. "The moment we defeat the Overmind, I will have words with your father about what he has done as the Grand Mage, Ryan. This will NOT go unanswered."

The entire group seemed to share the same mind. What Ivan had done, the experiments to control the Shadow Demons, was unacceptable. He had to be dealt with the moment they were done defeating the Overmind. One member, however, did not share the same mind.

"You….YOU!" Kali screeched as she slithered up to Aiden with a disgusted and horrified look in her expression.

"You did what? H-How dare you! It...it makes my scales crawl to even consider a filthy, disgusting thing like you dared to gaze at my beauty in its most vulnerable state! You had no right, you wretched little beast!"

Aiden nearly fell onto his rear when Kali slithered up to him. He forgot in that moment about how prissy the prime demon was. He nearly flinched when Kali's forked tongue slipped through her clenched teeth as she glared right at him. Just when he could have sworn that the giant snake demon was about to eat him, her face suddenly began to back away from his own.

"That's enough of that." Garrett said as he literally dragged Kali away from Aiden. "If anyone is going to chastise the whelp for stupid decisions, it's going to be me, snake."

"I feel sick! I feel so sick!" Kali cried out as she held her face. "Sick, sick to the bones!"

"Just...ignore her." Theresa said with an exasperated sigh. "Right now, let's get back to the matter at hand. If what Aiden saw was indeed true, then this school is in need of more than repairs. It will need a new leader." The white dragoness turned to Aiden. The look of Theresa Goldwin replaced by her Rexkin nature once more. "Are you positive of what you saw, Aiden?" He slowly nodded at his best friend. A steely look in his eyes met Theresa's emerald green eyes.

"A hundred percent." His tone was confidence. "It was like I was right there the moment it happened, Thes."

"...I see." Theresa sighed. "Visions like this are often tricky, Aiden. If the group had experienced the vision with you, I would not be questioning you like this."

"Why do you think it only affected him?" Aello asked. "I mean, Ryan's spell was bright sure but it didn't exactly have an affect on anyone else here."

Theresa brought her hand to her chin, scratching it a few times as she thought deeply for a few moments. With only a few seconds into her thoughts she turned her attention to Seamus.

"Is it possible for one person to experience a vision alone without others experiencing it?" She asked. The green dragon frowned as he folded his arms across his chest.

"It is possible, yes. But that's only if the person who experienced it has a heightened sense of magic. And I can guarantee you that Ryan and I have the higher magical senses here in our group." Kali hissed at Seamus for forgetting her name. He cleared his throat. "Well...us and Kali."

"Wait a minute, Kali." Ryan quickly turned to the lamia. "You said that you can increase a being's ability to use magic if you wished. Is it possible that your magic might have allowed Aiden to see the vision of my father?"

The lamia scoffed as she coiled herself up and perched herself over her long body. Aiden flinched a bit as he watched her tongue flick out from her teeth once more.

"It is possible that a sliver of the magic I used on this nobody is still within his body. But I highly doubt that such a low creature has the ability to glance into the past. Especially if it's to violate something as graceful as myself."

The lamia turned her attention back to Ryan. Her eyes shown darkly in the room as she eyed him carefully.

"But let's not forget that the spell weaver here said that the spell he just cast could have any kind of side effect on anyone. Maybe it was his magic that allowed the runt to see into the past instead of mine?" Ryan sighed at her suggestion in frustration. There was truth in the words that she spoke.

"I did say that." He admitted. "I guess that out of the group he was the one who was the most effected by the side effects of the location spell."

Aiden's eyes widened. In the heat of the conversation he had completely forgotten about the spell that Ryan had cast. He quickly jumped up from the spot before rushing over to the taller mage.

"The spell! Did it work? Do you know exactly where the Overmind is?!"

Ryan gave a slow nod. A grim look was on his face.

"It's as I feared, newbie. The Overmind IS in the lab like my father said it would be." Ryan folded his arms across his chest. "But I don't like the path we have to take to get to it."

"Ah what's the big deal?" Liza asked, her hands behind her head. "We've fought our way through dakgruls, came across a kelgrath, survived an encounter with a Prime Demon and the Shadow Worms. We can handle whatever else is coming up."

"Because the spell showed me what kind of Shadow Demons are in the hall before the laboratory." Ryan replied as his eyes closed in union with his hands that clenched. "In the hall are the deadly assassin Shadow Demons, the Zonaws."

The dragons went deadly silent at the mere mention of the demon name. Even Kali, who would often scoff at the names of the other demons, seemed to take the news seriously. Aiden and the rest of the younger members of the group blinked in confusion as the older members looked grim.

"What's a...zonaw?" Mia asked. Ryan sighed as he turned his attention towards her. The look on his face painted one emotion. Fear.

"Zonaws are not like the Shadow Demons that we have faced so far. Even compared to the Prime Demons they are to be feared."

"Disgusting maggots. That's what they are." Kali added in. "They have the audacity to try and turn Prime Demons into one of their own! Even for us demons they are utterly vile repulsive things!"

"All right, snake, you've made your point." Garrett said as he pulled her away from the group once again. Theresa sighed as she took a turn to speak up.

"I'm certain that you five are familiar with butterflies, right?" She was answer by a nod of all the younger members of the group. "Konaws are almost like them. They too emerge from a chrysalis much like a butterfly does. But that doesn't mean that they form their chrysalis from their own bodies."

Aiden and Liza's faces went pale at that statement. Theresa continued to explain even though she noticed how their faces changed color at a moment's notice.

"Zonaws initially start out as spores. They burrow into the skin of their host, and forcibly make a chrysalis around the host. When they emerge from the chrysalis, they are incredibly strong and resilient. And they can use ANY kind of host."

"T-Then what do we do?" Liza asked. "What if these spores come into contact with us?!"

"We shouldn't have to worry about that." Seamus continued on for Theresa. "When Zonaws emerge from their chrysalides, they don't spread out spores. Zonaws only release spores when their natural lifespan comes to an end."

"In other words, we can kill them and not worry about being

infected by the spores." Garrett concluded. "That being said, Zonaws are not like the beast like Dakgruls, Kelgraths, or Turskas that you have seen. They are sleek, fast, and agile. Out of all the demons you've faced here today, they are the most dangerous after the Overmind."

"And there's at least several of them in the main hallway that leads right to the lab." Ryan finished, rubbing his eyebrows in frustration. "Zonaws. Why did it have to employ them of all things?"

Aiden began to feel nervous again as he noticed that even all of the experienced members of the team seemed to be bothered by the upcoming encounter. Just how horrifying were these Zonaws that even the dragons seemed uncertain about coming across them? Up to this point the biggest threat that they all faced was the Teleranta. And it was one of the most terrifying creatures Aiden had ever seen.

"Wh...what should we expect from them?" Liza asked. Just as Theresa was about to answer her, Garrett spoke out before she could answer.

"Whelps, you listen to me now and you listen well. The Zonaws are not like the past demons you have faced. They are not mindless creatures, they are strategic, alethic, and very strong. If even one of those Chrysalides hatches you let us know immediately before they strike at you. Do you understand?"

This sudden concern for the younger members of the group caught Aiden off guard. Before Garrett would just tell them off if they were caught in danger or just barely even help. This was the first time that Aiden could ever remember Garrett showing genuine concern for their well being with the new threat.

"Garrett." Theresa's voice caught their attention. "Your concern for them is touching, but we don't have time to waste. We must get to the lab." Garrett gave her a short nod before summoning his axe into his hand.

"Ready when you are, Rexkin."

No one said any words as the trek into the school resumed. Not even the prissy Kali had any quick comments about the Zonaws. And she was a Prime Demon herself. Aiden could only imagine that even among demon kind, Zonaws were seen as monsters for what they do to their hosts.

They must have looked terrifying to those who laid eyes on them. Aiden couldn't help but imagine them as the most grotesque and vile beings to ever walk the earth. In his mind he pictured them to have elongated jaws with rows of razor sharp teeth, soulless black eyes, rancid breath, and disproportionate limbs that did not match its body size. Zonaws probably even made terrible sounds that were absolutely sickening to hear like disgusting gurgles that could have been mistaken for drowning on the blood of others.

Just thinking about that kind of creature made a shiver run down Aiden's spine in absolute terror.

The trek went on in silence for a good solid while. But the closer they got towards the lab, the more destruction Aiden noticed the school had suffered. Walls were completely broken, ceilings in several rooms had collapsed, and the most disturbing bit was seeing the dead bodies of the mages who had fought off the shadow demons to protect their fellow students or teachers.

Aiden had to swallow a lump in his throat when he saw the lifeless bodies of the mages before him. After last year with the Harpy's Den he wanted to never see another dead human body again. What Samael did to the human prisoners was horrible, and Aiden swore to himself that he would never let another life die under his watch.

He admitted that it was a foolish thing to swear to though. But it made him feel a little better with dealing with dead human bodies. But the amount of dead mages was beginning to test him. Aiden shook his head as the group walked past the dead bodies with a heavy heart. He felt incredibly bad about their deaths, as they could have been avoided if Ivan was not experimenting with Shadow Demons.

The group's trek came to a stop when they arrived at the entrance to the hallway. The sight that Aiden saw was almost made his stomach turn upside down. What lay on the ground were several fallen mages, hollow and lifeless. Each of their eyeless faces wore the same expressions though. Fear for what had happened to their bodies.

Behind the vacant husks of the human skins were several large ovals that hung on the sides of the walls. Aiden had to mentally will himself from throwing up at the sight of them. They were massive chrysalides about six feet tall in height. How they were formed from a single human body Aiden did not want to know, the terrible sight of the shed human skins were enough to make him not want to learn about these demons.

The most disturbing thing about the chrysalides were their offsetting colors. While Aiden had seen a monarch butterfly's chrysalis before in books they were at least a warm green color that felt peaceful to look at. The color of a Zonaw's chrysalis was the exact opposite. In place of a warm green was a sickly white color with black veins made out the blood of the demon that rested inside the chrysalis.

An audible hiss of hatred and disgust escaped Kali's lips from behind the group. If Aiden were a giant snake like her he would have made the same kind of sound. It created an uneasy feeling just looking at them for too long. Even the dragons were on guard as an eerie silence filled the room.

In the blink of an eye, the stillness and quiet of the room came to an abrupt end. One of the chrysalides began to move, violently, back and forth from its perch. There was an audible gasp that came from the harpies as something suddenly burst out from the chrysalis as black blood spilt onto the ground. What had burst out of the chrysalis was a large claw.

If there were a way to describe the claw best, it would be that it was shaped like a giant fiddle crab's claw. Unlike a fiddle crab though, this claw was not frail like a fiddle crab. Its upper half was a shade of dark sickly yellow with jagged, rough skin that was very strong. What drew Aiden's attention to it though wasn't the size of the claw, but the way the blades of the claw were shaped. The top half were serrated. Perfect for slicing through meat like a hot knife through butter. The bottom blade, however, was smooth and razor sharp. Perfect for stabbing without difficulty.

In the blink of an eye the second claw emerged from the chrysalis as well. Like the first it too was covered in black blood. The claws wasted no time in slicing open the chrysalis that contained the demon resting inside. After a very loud ripping sound the demon gracefully jumped out of the chrysalis with a soft 'thud' from its feet.

The zonaw was not what Aiden had suspected it to be. In his mind he was picturing a hideous looking monster with several mouths all over its face and skin so disgusting that just looking at it would have made a person feel sick. Because the zonaw used a human as its host it was very humanoid like, with a few exceptions like the lack of any kind of hair on its body. In fact, its skin looked almost reptilian like with small dark green scales cover its body. Aiden noticed that much like Raven's two demons, it too lacked a mouth but instead had two slits right where a human nose would be. But out of all the words that Aiden could have used to describe the Zonaws, sleek and graceful were the furthest ones. Its body lacked any representation of what gender it was, but the feminine form it had could have deceived anyone at a first glance.

The hatching of the first zonaw was like a chain reaction. Soon the rest of the chrysalides began to hatch as well. Each one shook just as violently as the last before the same claws sliced through the chrysalis holding them. Just like the first one that hatched, they too landed with a soft 'thud' and readied their claws for battle.

Aiden tried to count how many of them there were, but he lost count when the fifteenth zonaw hatched out. Once he was certain that all the zonaws had finished hatching he wasted no time in summoning Warfang to his hand. When the figurine appeared in his hand the golden and silver blade immediately erupted from it as he entered a stance.

"Anyone have any bright ideas?" He asked. Theresa just gave a simple nod as her own weapons formed.

"Only one. We have to fight through them." She said. Seamus wasted no time in holding out his staff in hand.

"Kiddo, don't let them get their claws around your limbs. They can slice your arm off with a simple grasp." His eyes narrowed. "Unlike us, you humans and harpies have bones that can break easily. So I'll say this again. Avoid those claws at ALL costs!"

No other words were spoken as the zonaws, almost in unison, all charged towards the team. The first one that hatched had its eyes set dead on Aiden instead of the other members of the group. Aiden felt a bead of sweat drop down his face as he made eye contact with the zonaw.

In an instant the demon leaped at him with a speed that Aiden wasn't prepared for as its right claw swung down at his shoulder. Aiden's reflexes were just barely fast enough to block the attack that swung at him. Warfang's metal rang out in a horrifying sound at the collision with the claw of the demon that was before Aiden. He grunted as he felt the weight of the zonaw's claw press down against his blade. The strength of the zonaw had completely taken him off guard because of its fragile appearance he believed that it would not possess the strength to make him struggle, but in reality it was stronger than it looked.

Even though it had no mouth, he could have sworn that the zonaw was grinning at him! Aiden felt his arm muscles screaming out in pain from the weight. He had to get away from this pressure before either of his arms broke.

"Ugh, little worm." Kali said from behind the group. "Do I have to help you with everything?"

Aiden suddenly felt a surge of power flow through his body once more. At first he expected it to be the same kind of surge that increased his magic capabilities, but instead he felt his muscles suddenly harden and gain new strength. The zonaw blinked in confusion for a moment, but that moment of confusion disappeared as it raised one claw up to strike once again.

This time Aiden didn't hesitate as he pulled Warfang back from the first claw and quickly blocked the second claw from striking down. His muscles felt renewed once again as he pulled his sword back once more. This time it was his turn to strike at the demon as he quickly swung his sword in a horizontal slash.

Warfang's metal struck true, slicing part of the top half of the zonaw's claw off as its black blood covered his sword's blade. He held Warfang in front of him. With a strike like that one, any creature would cry out in pain or flinch in anguish.

The zonaw, however, pulled its left claw back and tilted its head, almost curiously, at the injury. Aiden watched as it blinked its eyes as it turned its claw back and forth, examining the wound for a moment. It turned its head back to him at a very slow pace, then tilted its head to the left before holding its claw up once more.

Aiden nearly gasped as he watched the top half of the claw that he sliced off reform on the injured claw. Once the skin had been grown back, the zonaw entered its own combative stance as the blades of its claws shined in the dim light.

"Are these things are like Raven's demons?!" Liza asked, her own voice shocked at the regenerated claw.

"Almost!" Seamus was quick to answer. "The Zonaws are a subspecies of Raven's demons, however like those two these still need a host to hatch from!"

The zonaws quickly raised the rest of their claws as they prepared for combat. Theresa let a small growl escape her throat as she spun her swords in both hands as she spotted one charging from Aiden's left side. With her agility and skills with a sword, the leader of the Trinity was able to block the incoming attacks from the zonaw.

Theresa let an audible grunt of effort escape from her lips as the zonaw's claws pressed against her swords. However unlike Aiden she didn't struggle for long as she pushed the enemy's claws away. She wasted no time as she quickly aimed her swords' tips right at the chest of the demon. In the blink of an eye, the zonaw was able to avoid the death that the swords would have brought to it by back flipping away.

When the zonaw landed away from her, it lifted its head back up and made eye contact with Theresa. With a slow tilt of its head, the eyes of the demon had a glint shine momentarily. It was almost as if it was mocking Theresa for being too slow to stab it. An audible groan came from Theresa's mouth as she spun her swords in her hands.

"Zonaws. Why did the Overmind have to use THEM of all things?" She asked with disgust for the demon.

"Rather than waste time talking, how about we kill these things, dragoness?" Kali asked as she flicked her fingers once more. Aiden felt the same empowering magic flow through his veins once more. But he wasn't the only one that felt the magic empower his body.

In the corner of his eye he saw it. Liza was surrounded by a strange dark green light as well, empowering her body. The light also covered Aello and her guardians as their own abilities were enhanced too. The dragons looked on in surprise at this as the prime demon then turned her attention to them and granted them a power boost as well.

"There." She hissed. "That should be enough to put all of you on the same level as these accursed beasts." Theresa stared in disbelief at the lamia. Her eyes full of amazement at what she had just done.

"Kali…" She spoke out. "What brought this sudden change of attitude?"

"You know damn well why I did that." Kali responded. "These things are a disgusting stain on demon kind. Even among the Prime Demons we would love to see the zonaws wiped out of existence."

The lamia coiled her body upwards as a powerful force of magic covered her hands.

"Now stop wasting time and kill these disgusting things for me!"

Aiden almost felt like he was about to fall over on his face when Kali gave that order. He began to wonder if Kali was just using him and his friends as her own personal way to do her will. Not that he could argue with the power that she had given them momentarily. He spun his sword around in his hand for a moment before taking an offensive stance once more.

"You're all heart, Kali." He said. The large lamia didn't acknowledge his words as she turned over to Garrett.

"Well? What are you waiting for dragon?" She hissed. Garrett's eyes narrowed as he scoffed at her.

"Don't push me, snake." He responded.

When he finished speaking the zonaws attacked. The horde of the assassin type demons in front of them leapt into the air, their sharp claws ready to slash. In the blink of an eye, the Trinity also leaped towards three zonaws that were closest to them as their own weapons were swung directly at the zonaws.

The room was soon filled with the sounds of clashing metal and claw. It all happened in the blink of an eye as the Trinity separated from one another to focus on the zonaw that had confronted each of them. If he weren't a part of the battle, Aiden would have just watched the dragons do battle against the zonaws alone.

The zonaw that had attacked him charged once more, with several more of its kind behind it. Aiden quickly bent his knees and swung his sword at the first zonaw as Warfang's metal clashed with its claws. He gritted his teeth as he felt the demon press back against his own strength, right before noticing two zonaws running towards him from both his left and right. The bottom half of their claws pointed right at him, trying to stab right through his body.

Before the demons could ram through him though, Aiden heard Liza let out a shout of anger. He grinned when he saw Gitanel quickly block one claw from the zonaw from the left. Liza's increased agility gave her the edge she needed to push away the left claw away, right before swinging Gitanel right at the right claw to block it from attacking as well.

From Aiden's right side, Aello had charged out with her lance right to block both claws of the second zonaw. The youngest harpy princess gritted her teeth as she pushed the demon's claws into the air before pulling her lance back. The princess let out a confident laugh before she aimed her lance right at the chest of the zonaw. With a powerful thrust, she rammed her weapon through the demon.

Most beings would have died the moment a sharp and long weapon went straight through them. But the zonaw that Aello had stabbed did not. Instead it started down curiously at the lance. Within the blink of an eye the zonaw grabbed the lance with its two claws and began to push itself off of Aello's weapon.

The young harpy princess let out a shocked gasp as she watched the demon land on its feet. The zonaw once again tilted its head to the side as it stared down Aello as the hole that had been left by her weapon slowly began to heal up.

"Idiot bird!" Kali shouted. "Stab it in the heart this time!"

Aiden could only imagine the dark looks that Gabrielle and Mia were giving Kali for calling their princess a bird. But Aello did not respond in anger at the prime demon as she pulled her arm back and aimed the tip of her lance right at the heart before thrusting it forward.

In the blink of an eye the tip of Aello's lance stabbed right through the heart of the zonaw. The demon's near lifeless eyes flashed for a moment, before closing as it dissolved away. There was no time to celebrate though. After watching one of its brethren fall in battle a second zonaw launched itself towards Aello, slicing into her right shoulder with its right claw's bottom half.

The harpy princess screamed out in pain from the sharp claw of the zonaw. In that one moment, there was a shrill scream of rage from behind Aello. Gabrielle and Mia both opened their wings, and dive-bombed towards the zonaw with unbridle rage in their eyes. Aiden shivered at the looks of pure fury in their eyes. The last time he saw a Guardian Harpy get that upset was when he and Liza watched Ocypete's guardian get upset at a hunter harpy for speaking out of line.

The zonaw the duo had tackled looked surprised at being tackled by the duo, but it quickly flung them off its body with a simple swish of its arms. That didn't stop Gabrielle though, who regained her balance quickly as she glared right at the demon.

"Filthily, mangy, disgusting no nose!" She shouted in a rage. "I'll kill you for harming the princess!"

Mia nearly let out a squeak of surprise when she watched Gabrielle dive bomb right at the zonaw. Her talons aimed right at the chest of the demon as they shimmered in the light with a dangerous glint. Her target however didn't stay still for long as it jumped away from Gabrielle before her talons could pierce through its skin. That didn't stop the guardian harpy from attacking however, as she charged after the escaping zonaw with a fury in her eyes.

"Gabi, wait!" Mia cried out as she gave chase after her friend. "You don't wanna stray too far from the princess!"

Mia's pleading did little to stop the fury of the other

Guardian. Gabrielle kicked, slashed, and tried to ram her shoulder into the target of her anger. The zonaw was dodging every single attack with little effort. If it had a mouth, its lips would be forming an arrogant smile. The more it dodged her attacks the more Gabrielle snarled.

"No one hurts Princess Aello!" She screamed before suddenly pulling her right leg back and spun into a powerful roundhouse kick.

The kick hit its mark as her talons suddenly slashed into the face of the zonaw. It was brief, but three trails of what looked like black blood flew through the air before it landed on the ground below. Gabrielle grinned as she pulled her right foot back to the ground. The very tips of her talons covered by the black blood of the zonaw.

With a slow movement of its head the zonaw made eye contact with Gabrielle. Her talons had left their mark on its face with the three new cuts. If the demon had a mouth capable of lip movement, it would have been snarling in anger. Gabrielle on the other hand looked very smug and lifted her right leg up, mocking the zonaw.

"Aw, did I cut you too hard?" She asked. "Guess you'll need a new name then, disgusting piece of filth. How about…Scarface."

'Scarface.' A name that might have been commonly used in many of Aiden's stories and movies, but it fit the situation. If it had lips, Scarface would be scowling at Gabrielle for the new scars it had been given.

Scarface held its two claws up high, opening and closing them in unison as it eyed its enemy. The only words that Aiden could think of to describe the sound coming from the repeated movements of the claws was that it sounded like a rusty door opening and closing. Gabrielle didn't flinch from the sounds though as she took her own defensive stance.

Just as the two were about to strike at one another a shrill shriek exploded from behind them. Gabrielle gasped as she turned on a dime and noticed Mia trying desperately to push away one zonaw that had pinned her to the ground. The zonaw just tilted its head as it raised its right claw up high and opened it above its head.

"Mia!" Gabrielle shouted as she flapped her wings once before dashing to aid her friend.

The zonaw glanced up at the charging harpy and aimed its large claw towards her. Gabrielle growled as she threw her hands out and caught the claws just in time before they could clamp down. The guardian hissed in pain as the upper blades of the zonaw's claw cut into the palms of her hands. Blood rand down from her palms down her arms for a moment.

"Gabi!!!"

Mia, seemingly over her initial shock, charged with a fury towards the demon. Like Gabrielle before her she raised her legs up and opened her sharp talons wide before they were rammed into the body of the zonaw. The force from the impact was instant as the zonaw's body was kicked away from Gabrielle. The latter grunted in pain as she glanced at her bleeding palms.

"Dammit." She growled.

"Gabi, don't use your hands in this fight anymore." Mia said. "You're lucky that it didn't cut your hands in half!"

"I can handle it." Gabrielle responded as she clenched her hands tight. "These cuts are nothing compared to the ones from those wall demons last year."

"Can it birdbrains!" Kali shouted from afar. "In case you haven't noticed, these things are still alive! Kill them before they try to infect me!"

The group shared a collective sigh of frustration at Kali's shout. But she was right. The zonaws were still alive and they were blocking the way to the lab.

"We're wasting time!" Theresa shouted. "We're going to have to rush through them to get to the end! On my mark, rush forward and take down as many as you can!"

There was a bit of a reluctant nod from the group, save for Kali, at Theresa's plan. It was true that they were running out of time, but rushing head long into the enemy was a risk. Aiden almost wanted to question this action from his best friend, but then he saw it. The determined look in Theresa's eyes. He had seen it before from her. The last time he saw the fight in her eyes was in the harpy's den when she entered that strange Burning Form of hers.

For a split second there was silence in the hallway to the lab. But that silence died down as the sound of clashing weapons and claws rang out in a horrific song.

Aiden found himself in a deadlock fight with one zonaw that he inadvertently ran into. The only thing that kept the demon's claws from ramming through his body was Warfang. A grunt of fatigue escaped his lips for a moment as the zonaw gained the upper hand with the leverage it held over him.

Aiden didn't back down though. After all he had went through last year with the dragons and the harpy incident, he wasn't going to let a disgusting demon like this zonaw get the better of him. He summoned as much strength as he could to push back against the demon's claws before finally pushing them away from his blade.

He wasted no time in quickly reacting to the chance he had to attack. With a mighty swing Aiden brought his sword up and slashed the claws of the zonaw off with one strike. The zonaw glanced curiously at the stumps on its hands for a moment, but stared right back at Aiden.

"You little runt!" Kali shouted. "Hurry up and blast it with your magic before it reforms its hands!"

Every fiber of Aiden's being wanted to shout at Kali for barking out another order, but he was able to hold that desire back as he held out his left hand towards the zonaw.

"Flarnea!"

Just like the first time that Aiden felt the enhancing powers of

Kali flow through him, the same giant fiery beam was released from his palm towards the zonaw. The demon didn't have any time to react as the attack slammed right into its chest with a powerful impact. A small smile came to his lips as he saw the attack make its mark on his target. If it had a mouth the zonaw would have been screaming out in pain as the magical fire burned its way through the thick skin the demon had.

Aiden nearly gasped out in shock as he saw the Flarnea suddenly break through the body of the zonaw. Behind it came several more of its kind rushing to its aid. Aiden's attack though didn't stop with just the demon that it had pierced through. It continued to move forward as it reached another zonaw and slammed right into its chest as well.

A third zonaw tried to assist its brethren but just like the others it too was hit in the chest from the empowered Flarnea. The fiery beam seemed to have no mercy for the demons as they each tried to assist one another. Arms were burnt off, claws were shattered, and legs were burnt as they each tried to stop the beam of fire.

Aiden watched several zonaws fall from the attack. He winced though as the attack began to drain him. Kali's enhancements did help make him feel stronger, but his body was not used to using so much new power right away. Reluctantly he had to close his hand, stopping the Flarnea attack from erupting further.

The damaged caused by his attack had already laid waste to a small amount of the zonaws that the team had been facing. Aiden almost dropped to his knees though from using the attack for so long. The power he felt from Kali's magic. It was incredible. If he could learn to tap into that strength she passed onto him he would be able to do more than just last a few short rounds in a practice duel with Garrett.

"Over there!" Theresa shouted, pulling her swords from the chest of a zonaw she had slayed. "Make for the path that Aiden's Flarnea made for us!"

"Rexkin, your injuries though!" Seamus shouted.

Aiden blinked as he glanced back over to Theresa. True to what Seamus had said, Theresa's arms had been sliced into from the zonaws. Part of her shirt had also been ripped, and three slash marks rested on her left cheek. Theresa didn't seem daunted though, despite the pain.

"These wounds are nothing compared to what I went through last year." She said. "Move to the lab, now!"

The group didn't have to wait a second longer to move forward at Theresa's order. The white dragoness took charge as she held out Snow and Fire in her hands and charged ahead of the others. The zonaws that dared to cross her path were met with a swift and brutal attack from her swords. One zonaw had grabbed her right arm with its claws tightly. Despite the hiss from Theresa's lips, she refused to cry out in pain. Instead the white dragoness turned towards her attack and opened her mouth as a large white flame erupted from within her into the zonaw's face.

Aiden almost felt sorry for the demon taking the hit from Theresa's signature white fire. But given with what the demons had done to the human hosts that they had taken over he couldn't. Instead he steeled himself as he rammed Warfang into the heart of one zonaw that tried to approach him from the left.

"You disgusting vermin!" Kali shouted behind the others. "How dare you try to attack me?!"

Aiden glanced behind him for a moment as he watched the giant lamia take one zonaw in her tail. She hissed loudly for a moment as she slowly began to constrict the demon to a slow and painful death. Aiden felt a shiver run down his spine when he heard the cracking of the demon's bones echo throughout the hallway.

"Snake, would you stop complaining and move?" Garrett asked in annoyance. Kali gave him a dark look, but threw the demon she had in her tail away before slithering after the group once more.

It wasn't just Kali that was doing her part to get closer to the laboratory though. Everyone in the group had contributed to their efforts to reach their target goal. Seamus had used incredible wind magic, and healed when he could, against the demons that tried to pile in front of the team. The dakgrul that they had captured leaped onto several of them and bit into their necks and faces with ferocious sounds. Seamus had to whistle to call him away before he almost lost his head to a zonaw that approached him.

Liza was doing just as well as Aiden had with the power up she gained from Kali. She was lighting fast before, but her speed and agility at least put her on par with the zonaws that attacked her. She couldn't get a death-dealing blow on them, but she left several large slashes on their bodies when they tried to come too close to her.

Ryan's magic, which was already incredibly powerful, allowed him to blast away demons that tried to approach from behind. Aiden couldn't see them all, but each spell he cast was at least a different element from what he did see. Fire, ice, water, wind, and earth all were used against the zonaws as they were hit hard. It did little to kill them, but it kept them away for a brief moment.

After what seemed like hours fighting off the zonaws, they approached the door to the lab. Unfortunately it was blocked off by what looked like corrupted roots to Aiden. They were black and pulsing with a purple color that gave a hint of malice to it. Behind them, the zonaws continued to give chase to them. An audible groan was heard from the largest dragon.

"There's too many to kill at once!" Garrett shouted. "We need to end this madness, now!"

"Everyone, gather behind the dragons!" Theresa shouted. Kali was the only one who didn't bother to follow her orders as the group immediately got behind the Trinity.

Theresa, Seamus, and Garrett all stood together in unison. Their bodies each had several cuts on them, but they were determined to stand talk and continue to fight. In a blink of an eye the trio took deep breaths, then unleashed their fire breath at the roots that blocked their pathway.

The dragon fire began to burn away the roots that had blocked their way into the lab. A bright flash of light exploded as the roots began to burn away slowly. Aiden winced only for a moment, but the way into the lab was now open.

"MOVE!" Theresa ordered.

No one wasted a second in waiting anymore as they rushed into the source of where this mess had all started. The laboratory.

And what would happen in that room would be an event that would haunt Aiden for the rest of his days.

CHAPTER 16 - THE OVERMIND

*F*inally. At long last, the group arrived at their target's location. The laboratory. The source of all this chaos and death. The place where something went terribly wrong and pushed the once great Academy to the verge of being exposed. Floating before the group was the one thing that caused the Shadow Demons to be. The Overmind.

Aiden didn't know what to expect when they first laid eyes on the Overmind, but he had too admit that what he was looking at truly did fit the title of "Controller of the Shadow Demons."

The Overmind was a bloated, amorphous black object floating in the center of the room. It had several long tentacles, with razor sharp points and a distinctive neon pure purple color that swung around menacingly. At the center of the creature was a single, staring eye with a glowing green iris and sick yellow color where the white should have been.

As Aiden stared in shock at the Overmind his entire body began to feel cold. The appearance of this mass of shadows put together in such fashion was one of the most nightmarish things he'd ever see in his life. A chill ran down his spine as he watched the Overmind's tentacles whip back and forth in the air. Loud cracks erupted from each whip. It was enough to make the younger members of the group flinch involuntarily.

Behind them, the zonaws had followed. Though they were fewer than before, they still outnumbered the group as they began to circle around them. The group however, focused on the large object that floated endlessly in place. Its giant eye just staring off into nothingness. It slowly turned its gaze towards the group.

In the back of his mind, Aiden wondered, "What kind of person would dare think that they could control something like the monster that floated before them?"

He felt the cold hand of death nearby as he stared into the single eye of the Overmind. It was faint, but Aiden could feel the tremendous power that pulsed in the body of the giant eye. Everything that they had faced up to this point, the goblins, the harpies, Raven and Dimitri's demons and even the Teleranta paled in comparison to the power that surged through the Overmind.

"This...this is worse than I thought." Ryan said, his voice finally returning after the initial shock of the Overmind's appearance. "It's gathered so much power that it could break the shield protecting the Academy from the rest of the outside world!"

"And if that happens, the end of the human world as we know it." Seamus said with a disgusted tone. "Ivan...what the hell were you thinking?"

The Overmind's single eye just pulsed momentarily as it stared at the zonaws that had been gathered around the group. Its large tentacles moving back and forth before, to what Aiden could guess, was the voice of the being.

"...*Kill*..."

Behind them Aiden could hear the sounds of the zonaw's claws opening. Like two sharp blades grinding against one another. His body tensed as he held up Warfang. Beside him, he could hear Liza's breathing grow heavier as she too faced down a group of zonaws that were close to her.

"*..Kill...*" The Overmind's voice rang out once again. The zonaws wasted no time in attacking the group as they charged towards them. No one spoke a word as each held their weapons out in front of them, prepared for battle.

"Strike now!" Theresa ordered.

No one wasted a second arguing with her orders as they each clashed with a group of approaching zonaws. The song of metal against claw rang out once again as the huge brawl exploded once more.

No longer bound by the narrow hallways from before, the team was more mobile and free to do what they wished in combat. The ones taking the most advantage of this was the Trinity, mostly Garrett. The largest member of the Trinity took to the ceiling as his dragon wings allowed him to fly above with ease.

A grimace spread across his lips as he hefted his axe into his hands once more. Without uttering a word he dived towards a group of zonaws that had formed beneath him. The large dragon pulled his mighty axe back and with a single swing cut three zonaws in front of him in half.

Garrett landed on the ground without so much as a thud. He glanced at the pieces of the demons behind him. He laughed at the demons surrounding him before he lifted up his axe. The look in his eyes told the zonaws everything they needed to know as they drew closer and closer to him.

'Bring it on.'

Two zonaws leapt into the air at lightning speed, diving at Garrett with their claws open. Garrett quickly brought his axe up to block one pair of claws before he punch it right in the face with his left hand. The second one though, managed to slash past him and cut into his left shoulder.

The largest of the dragons swallowed a hiss as he glanced at the wound that had appeared on his shoulder. No one dared to wonder what was going through his mind as he stared at the fresh wound the zonaw had given him. For the first time in many years, Garrett bled. And that made him furious.

Smoke arose from his nostrils as he glared at the zonaw that had slashed his shoulder. That smoke soon began to turn into small embers as the pupils in his eyes became small slits. An audile low growl was heard from his throat as he turned to face his enemy.

"Your death will be excruciatingly slow, demon."

Garrett wasted no time as he charged the zonaw. In the blink of an eye he was in front of his target. He grabbed the zonaw by the face with his free hand. He growled in anger, ignoring the blood pouring down his arm from the shoulder as he lifted his prey off the ground.

Several more zonaw charged at Garrett and slashed at his back with their mighty claws, one even managed to grab his right arm with its left claw and clamped down. Garrett didn't react to the new set of claws on his body as his grip on the other zonaw tightened with each passing second.

The large dragon let out a massive roar of anger as he suddenly slammed his captured enemy into the ground with a 'crushing' sound. A small crater formed in place where the zonaw's head once was. Garrett growled as he turned his attention to the zonaw that had clamped down on his right arm.

"You're strong," a sultry voice purred. Garrett watched as a massive tail slid up and around the zonaw clamped to his arm, the creature began to squirm, but the tail quickly clamped around its head. With a small grunt, Kali tightened her grip on the zonaw, crushing it and causing it to go limp, releasing the dragon. She dropped it to the ground and flicked her tongue as she rose up to Garrett's eye level.

"So am I." she teased, drawing her long fingers across his cheek. They slid down to his arm, pausing next to the wound. A spark lit up at the tip of her finger and the skin began to mend itself.

"Since when does a Prime Demon want to tend to the injuries of others, snake?" Garrett asked, smoke still rising up from his nostrils.

Kali flicked her tongue, the tip brushing against Garrett's nose.

"An illustrious creature such as myself...always takes care of her toys." she hissed.

"Don't get any ideas, snake." Garrett said as he glanced to the zonaws behind them. "Besides, we have more work to do before facing the Overmind."

"Show me what you're made of, tough guy...and I'll teach you how to do even better." The demon hissed, leaning closer to his face.

As the two stared at each other the zonaws behind them gathered. Scarface, who had taken control of the forces, pointed its claws at Kali as ten of its kind charged and aimed to land on top of the prime demon's back.

"Behind you, snake."

The moment those words escaped his lips the giant tail of Kali quickly rose up and smacked the zonaws away. Her forked tongue slowly slipped through her teeth as she turned around to face the assassin demons.

"Let's see what you can do then, tough guy." She hissed as a sharp smile formed on her lips. Garrett didn't respond as he hefted his axe once more for battle. He and Kali both moved to attack.

Seamus and his dakgrul faired not nearly as well as Garrett did against their group of zonaws. Unlike his fellow dragon that was the living embodiment of strength, Seamus did not excel in close quarters combat. The dragon of magic didn't complain though as he hefted his staff up and swung it hard across the face of one zonaw that tried to get close to him.

The sound of fleeing footsteps came from behind Seamus as two zonaws leaped down at him and slashed into his back with their sharp claws. Seamus grunted in pain for a moment as he regained his balance. A soft chuckle escaped from his lips.

"Heh, it's been far too long since I fought any kind of demons like this." He said. His left hand began to glow with a strong magical power before he turned around and blasted the two demons with a force of fierce wind.

The magic attack was enough to send the demons flying, each one slammed into the wall with a loud 'thud' as they slowly slid down to the ground. Seamus spun his staff in both of his hands. Once he stopped spinning his staff he simply touched the bottom of it to the ground beneath him to send out electric shockwaves into another group of zonaws that dared to get close to him.

"You demons don't seem to get that with my magic, I can handle you." He said as he spun his staff behind him. "Bring it!"

Another zonaw charged at Seamus, this time with one claw open as it slashed his left shoulder. The dragon of magic grunted in pain for a moment as he swung his staff right at the head of the zonaw. The demon's head recoiled in pain as the end of Hurricane left a big mark in its cheek before it flew back into another zonaw.

Seamus turned to face another demon. But the moment his back was turned a third zonaw attacked and slashed his back with its large claws. Seamus, rarely caught off guard, growled in frustration as he felt the blood running down his back. His eyes glinted momentarily as he turned to face the attacker. Hurricane pulsed in his hands as he swung the mighty weapon at the zonaw.

The demon didn't allow itself to be smacked though as its claws quickly caught Seamus's staff before it could make contact. If it had a mouth it would be grinning in confidence as its claws refused to let go of Seamus's weapon.

The latter began to get annoyed as he tried to pull his weapon out of the zonaw's grip. As he tried to desperately free his weapon from the demon's hold, another zonaw attacked from behind as it slashed into his back with its right claw. Seamus grunted in pain from the attack, but didn't have time to retaliate as another zonaw attacked as well, slashing into his back just like the previous one did.

Just when things began to look bleak for Seamus as more zonaws gathered around him, the dragon of magic heard a familiar roar from his left. He glanced his head towards the sound and a small smile came to his lips as he watched the dakgrul he had captured leap into the air and pounce on one zonaw. The demon couldn't react in time as its attacker quickly bit down on its throat and applied enough pressure to break its neck with a single bite.

With the zonaw dead at its feet, the dakgrul raised its head up to face several more. The cat like demon let out a fierce roar as it pounced off his previous target to attack another zonaw. This time attacking with his right front paw as his claws tore into the skin of one demon before he launched himself into the zonaw holding Seamus' staff. The impact from the dakgrul's attack was enough to force the demon to release its hold on Seamus' staff as it tried to push its attacker off its body.

The dakgrul wouldn't budge however. He growled low as the acid drool from his mouth fell onto the face of his foe. The zonaw thrashed violently as it desperately fought to be rid of its attacker. The attempt ended in failure though as the dakgrul quickly bit into the neck of the zonaw just like the previous one and bit down hard.

Seamus blinked in amazement as the dakgrul pulled itself up from the fallen demon as it stared up at the dragon of magic. He took notice that the demon's lips were covered by the black blood of the zonaw, like a badge of honor for the cat like beast. A smile came to Seamus' lips as he gently scratched the top of the dakgrul's head.

"Good job. You've finally earned the right to have a name." The dragon thought for a moment, then nodded. "Malevo."

The newly christened Malevo nodded his head at the new name as he turned to face down the gathering zonaws. Seamus spun his staff behind his back for a few seconds before aiming the tip of it at the group.

"All right, Malevo. Let's get them!"

Malevo let out a loud roar as he charged towards the zonaws with Seamus by his side. A strange, but seemingly strong, bond was formed that day between the two beings. The first time that had ever happened in the history of the dragons.

Nearby, the harpies fought with a fierce ferocity against the vast numbers of the zonaws. Aello, with her lance whip, took the lead for her two guardians in the fight against the overwhelming horde of demons facing them. The youngest princess might not have been as powerful as her eldest sister, or as skilled at her middle sister, but she was still a harpy princess. And the training she had with both of her sisters gave her the skills needed to fend for herself.

Aello wasted no time in making her lance separate into its whip form. With a flick of her wrist she swung the whip towards one zonaw in an attempt to pierce through its chest. Her target didn't dodged away from the tip of the whip before running at her with both claws ready to clamp down on her shoulders.

The youngest princess didn't back down though as with another flick of her wrist she brought the whip back into its lance form and brought it up to block the claws of her attacker. She gritted her teeth as she felt the weight of the demon push against her weapon. Above the two, a loud shriek of anger exploded as Gabriella dived towards Aello's opponent.

"Get away from the princess!" She shouted. The zonaw glanced at Gabriella for the briefest moment as it pointed its left claw at the diving harpy.

Aello blinked in confusion for the briefest moment as she

watched the demon just point at Gabriella. A small audible gasp escaped her lips though when she saw a small ball of purple energy form in between the claw of the zonaw. Immediately knowing what the demon was up too she turned her head towards her diving guardian.

"Gabi, no!"

Her warning came too late though. A single concentrated beam of dark magic fired out of the zonaw's claw straight at the attacking harpy. Gabriella didn't have any time to react as the attack slammed into her stomach and sent her flying back into the air. The guardian harpy was slammed right into the wall by the beam, as she let out shocked cry of pain from the impact.

"Gabi!!"

Mia shrieked in shock as she flew off to aid her friend. Aello however, trembled as she felt an emotion that she was not all that familiar with, but knew all too well from her big sister's actions.

Anger.

"You. BASTARD!" She growled, pulling her lance away from her foe's claw before aiming the tip of it right at the chest of the zonaw. "No one hurts my guardians!!"

The youngest princess let out a screech of fury as she attacked the demon with a powerful thrust of her lance. The zonaw tried to move out of the way from the attack, but the lance's tip had already hit its target as the weapon pierced through its body. Aello growled as she pulled her lance out of her slain foe before turning her attention to where Gabriella had been sent. With a simple flap of her wings she flew right to her two guardians.

"Is she okay?!" She asked Mia. The look of rage from before had disappeared as it was replaced by concern for Gabriella.

"I can still fight…" The guardian hissed in pain as she managed to hover in place. Mia immediately grabbed ahold of her injured companion as she glanced over where the zonaw's beam had hit Gabriella.

"Princess s-s-he…she could have died from that attack." Mia whimpered out. Aello quickly examined Gabriella's stomach.

The zonaw's attack hadn't run through Gabriella, but it did nearly burn her skin and feathers off when it made contact with her. Aello let out a sigh of relief, but her eyes turned steely as she turned to face the vast amount of zonaws that were beneath the harpies.

"Get her to Seamus, she needs to be healed." Aello ordered. Mia nodded her head as she put one of Gabriella's arms over her shoulder. The former harpy turned back to Aello with a small frown on her lips.

"Be careful, Princess." She pleaded before taking off to find Seamus. Aello didn't respond as she kept her eyes locked on the demons below her.

"No one harms my guardians." Aello quietly said, right before flicking her wrist once as the mighty lance she held in her hand turned into its whip form once more. "You nasty creeps will feel the wrath of a daughter of Queen Lilith!"

Aello swung her weapon right at the first line of zonaws that were closest to her. The chains of her whip were quick to trip up the demons as they fell down one by one. With a flap of her wings the harpy princess landed on the ground. Another flick of her wrist and the whip rejoined into a lance once more.

With a wordless shout she charged at the nearest zonaw, ramming its tip into the chest of the demon. Aello's eyes glinted for a moment as she flicked her wrist once more as the lance turned back to its whip form once more. Using all the strength she could muster Aello swung her whip, with the demon still attached to the tip of the weapon, and smacked the zonaw into another one of its kind. That didn't stop Aello from continuing her assault as the young princess spun three hundred sixty degrees. All the while her lance whip continued to decimate demons.

Not uttering a single word Aello reformed her whip back

into its lance state once more. Bodies of the zonaws laid before her, broken and sliced apart. A gasp escaped from her lips as she realized what she had done. Aello had never taken such drastic actions against anyone, even foes, before like this. She glanced down to her weapon, which was coated in the thick blood of the demons. A part of her felt like she was about to faint at seeing her weapon coated with such a color.

A terrifying thought came to her mind. What if she was more like her sisters than she let herself believe?

The young princess sighed before turning back to find her two guardians. To her relief, she saw them reach Seamus in time for a quick healing spell.

However right behind Aello one of the larger zonaws had survived the onslaught of her weapon. The demon's usually life-less eyes flashed as it jumped into the air above Aello. The young princess turned at the last second to spot the demon dive-bombing her with its claws open.

"Aello!" A familiar voice shouted from the right. Liza's voice. Her athletic body allowed her to reach the conflict in time as she quickly blocked one of the claws with Gitanel. The zonaw's other claw though quickly grabbed ahold of Liza's left shoulder and tightened its grip.

Liza grit her teeth in pain from the razor sharp claw of the demon. She could feel her blood seeping through her shirt and down her arm as she felt the grip of her attacker squeeze tighter and tighter. Her right arm began to shake violently as her weapon barely could hold back the claw of the zonaw.

"Just...try it." Liza said through her clenched teeth. "You're never gonna beat me!"

The pain that Liza was feeling doubled once more as the claw pressed down even more on her shoulder. The athletic girl was forced to close her eyes as screamed out in pain as she felt the serrated edges of the claw nearly cut her arm off. The eyes of the zonaw shined with a sadistic glow as it prepared to finalize the job.

Just when it felt like she was about to lose her arm the pressure from the claw began to loosen up. Liza slowly opened her eyes to look up in confusion. What she saw made her gasp in surprise as she saw the lance whip wrapped around the neck of the zonaw. Both of its claws were trying desperately to pull away the whip that had begun to strangle it.

"Now!" Aello shouted. "Before it breaks out!"

Liza wasted not another second as she took her right arm and aimed the tip of her dagger right at the heart of the demon. The struggling demon suddenly stopped moving as Gitanel pierced its hide and reached its cold black heart. Its lifeless eyes just stared down at Liza and Aello. The former had a small frown on her lips as she shook her head.

"The human that you made into your host, I hope he has found peace…"

The zonaw went limp, as its claws fell to its side. Aello slowly released the demon from her whip as it took its lance form once more. She quickly grabbed ahold of Liza, who had nearly fallen over from the loss of blood combined with the pain she had felt from earlier.

"You shouldn't have used yourself as a shield!" Aello shouted. "You're not a dragon who can afford to lose some blood! You're a human!"

"Heh," Liza chuckled a big, despite the pain she was in. "You didn't think I was gonna let it cut off your arm, did you?"

Aello groaned in annoyance as she placed a hand over the wound on Liza's shoulder. She whispered the healing spell quietly as she began to mend the wound the best she could.

"You humans, why are you always so quick to throw yourselves into danger like that?" Aello asked. Liza let out a soft laugh as she stared right at Aello's hand healing her wound.

"Did you forget that me, Aiden, and the others ran across the state to find you when we thought you were in danger?" She asked. It was Aello's turn to laugh as she shook her head.

"I was perfectly fine then though. You're the ones who decided to come into our den."

Liza laughed a bit once more as she felt her wound slowly close up. Her muscles still screamed in pain from their encounter with the zonaw's claws, but she was no longer bleeding. She moved her arm in a circle, wincing in pain from the sore muscles.

"What are you doing?" Aello asked with a quirked eyebrow.

"Trying to get the pain out." Liza answered. "Whenever I strain a muscle I rotate my arm or leg in place for a bit to get the pain out."

"That...sounds painful." Liza laughed at Aello's obvious deduction.

"Yeah, it hurts like hell. But it will help me not focus on the pain for long." She turned her attention back to approaching zonaws. "Looks like we got some incoming demon scumbags to kill. You up to seeing who can kill the most?"

Aello rolled her eyes as she hefted her lance over her shoulder. Liza watched carefully as a small smile came to the princess' lips.

"You're on."

The duo rushed together at the zonaws that stood before them. Neither of them knew it them, but a strong team had been formed that day.

As they fought off their demons, Aiden and Theresa stood back to back as zonaws circled around them. Aiden glanced up above them, noticing one of the Overmind's tendrils was also floating above them. His grip on Warfang began to feel a bit sweaty as he turned his gaze back to the demons that had encircled them.

"Think you can transform into your true form and blast them away?" He asked Theresa. His answer came in the form of a small laugh from Theresa.

"I want to save that for when we battle the Overmind." She answered. The friendly tone that Aiden had grown up with had begun to mix with her Rexkin voice. "Besides, these zonaws are small fry compared to the Overmind. If I wasted all my draconic power on them before fighting their leader, I would be drained of power."

Theresa closed her eyes as she kept her swords up. In truth, she was not certain at how much power she had left after such a long trek. After what happened in the Harpy Den she had to come with the terms that she didn't have as much power as she did before now that she was in a human body with its limits.

If there was one silver lining to that incident, it was that strange 'burning' state of hers that somehow activated. The power was incredible, but short lived. If she could somehow tap into that source of energy again it would make the fight much easier against the numerous zonaws.

Theresa shook her head though as she dismissed the idea of tapping into that power again as she returned to reality. The important thing now was the fight they had to win before facing down the Overmind. With effortless movements of her hands, Theresa spun Snow and Fire in both hands before taking an offensive stance. The zonaws close to her charged.

Determined to not let what happened at the harpy's den re-occur Theresa brought her blades up to block two claws from the nearest zonaws. Her swords rang out a terrible song as she pushed the claws away from her. Theresa's normally calm eyes turned vicious as she pulled both her arms back before ramming them right towards the chests of the zonaws. The blades made their marks, piercing through the hides of the demons.

Theresa effortlessly pulled her weapons back before bringing up Snow to block another attack from the left. She swung Fire across the chest of the zonaw before kicking it away from her. Next she brought Fire up to block another attack before using Snow to slash across the chest of the attacker. The pattern repeated itself several times as Theresa began to push back the demons that dared to get close to her. The next demon that fell to her blades did so as both Snow and Fire created a cross slash over its body.

A small smile came to Theresa's lips as she spun her swords around in her hands. So far she was in control of the battle and didn't feel the same fatigue from last year affecting her. She glanced to her left, noticing a zonaw taking aim with both of its claws. She blinked in confusion at first, but immediately realized what the demon was about to do.

Theresa wasted no time with her next action. She took a deep breath, feeling the intense heat in the back of her throat form, and released a large stream of white fire towards the zonaw. The demon wasn't slow to respond though as it too released its own stream of dark energy towards the white fire Theresa spewed out.

The two attacks collided, swirling together in the middle of their power struggle. Theresa's eyes narrowed dangerously as she added more power to her fire, which began to overcome the demon's energy blast. Just when it looked like the battle of the two blasts would end with Theresa's overcoming the zonaws, a second zonaw joined the side of the previous one and opened its own claws firing out another blast of energy into the struggling beam.

If she weren't breathing fire Theresa would have gasped in surprise at the second blast. But she wouldn't let herself lose this battle as she dug her feet into the ground and added more power to her fire. The white flames grew stronger as they once again forced the dark beams away. From a far off view the two attacks looked like a disturbing light show as sparks of Theresa's fire and the demon's energy beam bounced away into the air.

The two attacks continued to clash with one another until finally an explosion went off from the colliding attacks. Theresa didn't flinch from the light of the explosion as she pulled her swords back up in front of her. She waited patiently, moving her left foot back slowly as she took an offensive stance. When the smoke cleared she blinked in surprise when both zonaws were gone.

"Theresa! Behind you!" Aiden shouted. Theresa glanced one eye over her shoulder to spot one of the zonaws pouncing at her back. The white dragoness quickly brought her wings out, flapped them once, and avoided the claws slicing into her back. Without wasting a second she quickly brought her tail out and wrapped it around the neck.

The white dragoness had a smug look on her face as she flicked her tail to the right as the zonaw was released from her tail. With a quick movement she combined Snow and Fire into their dual-bladed form and flew after the demon she had just thrown. The zonaw spun wildly in the air just before it hit the right angle to spot Theresa about to strike. Not wasting a word on the demon, Theresa swung her dual-bladed sword in multiple directions. She slashed up with the Snow half of her weapon, and slashed down with the Fire half.

As for the finishing touch to her slashing, Theresa separated her weapon once more into their single sword forms before slashing horizontally across the midsection of the zonaw. Theresa flapped her wings once and sent a gust of wind into her target. The force of the wind blew the demon away, and piece-by-piece its body fell apart, landing on the ground as Theresa's slashes had done their work.

Theresa laughed as she spun her swords in her hands.

"I still got it." She said with a small smile.

Her left ear twitched for a moment as she heard the sound of rushing footsteps. The white dragoness turned her body towards the approaching group of zonaws that had formed up to battle her as a group. Theresa spun her swords around once more before she flapped her wings and flew at them head on.

Nearby, Aiden was having his own battle against the zonaw

horde. In the back of his mind he cursed himself for always getting into a battle against seemingly endless opponents. The experiences with both the Goblins and Wall Demons still fresh in his mind, Aiden held his sword in both hands as he took a defensive stance when he bent his knees. His eyes moved back and forth as he kept a good view on the zonaws in front of him. They wouldn't be a problem if he acted smart and didn't rush headlong into battle against them.

The ones that worried him though were the ones behind him. He would have to be fast enough to turn on a dime and block their incoming attacks. And that is where Aiden felt his major flaw was in all his training. He had grown use the swift sword techniques that Theresa trained him in but he was by far the least agile of the group. Even Garrett was more agile than he was, and his major forte was his incredible strength.

And the zonaws were not only brutal but also very nimble with their movements. The odds were very much against Aiden and he knew that. But still, he kept his sword up as he prepared for the inevitable battle with the demons.

"Bring it." He said in the best macho tone that he could muster. The zonaws before him clamped their claws before each running at him. Aiden gritted his teeth as he braced himself for impact as Warfang clashed with one claw of the first zonaw.

Aiden pulled his sword back away from the zonaw before taking his left hand and firing out a Flarnea spell into the demon's chest. With that zonaw sent flying another one leaped into the air at Aiden and started to swing its massive claws at him. Aiden barely managed to side step the swipes as he was forced to move backwards from the advancing demon.

With a grunt Aiden hefted his sword up and parried the first claw from the zonaw. The demon swung its second claw at Aiden, just grazing the front of his shirt as the latter jumped away from the attack. Not wasting a second Aiden quickly spun

Warfang before thrusting the sword right at the demon's chest. His blade hit its mark stabbing through its pale flesh.

The zonaw grabbed ahold of Aiden's sword with its claws as it began to pull the blade away from its chest. It was that moment that Aden saw his chance to strike against the demon while its claws were busy grabbing his blade. He flung his right left hand right at the demon's face before grabbing it. The zonaw was too slow to react as his palm suddenly began to heat up as he suddenly released a point blank Flarnea right into the demon's head.

The intense power of his attack did more than just burn the zonaw's face. Instead Aiden's Flarnea spell had completely incinerated the head clean off the demon's body! The now headless body stopped moving as its arms went limp. Without missing a beat, the lifeless body of the zonaw began to fall backwards. Aiden wasted no time in grabbing the hilt of his sword and pulling it away from the lifeless corpse of the zonaw.

"Can't take the heat?" He asked with a smug expression on his face.

He would later realize that what he had said was a really bad move for him.

Behind him a zonaw had reached him, spin kicking him hard in the back with intense force. Aiden's eyes widened from the sudden pain from the kick as he dropped to his knees. The sudden attack was so unexpected that he could feel hot tears welling up in his eyes from the sudden blow. He mentally cursed himself for letting his guard down like that as he used Warfang to stand back up.

The moment he stood up though another zonaw had appeared before him. Not giving Aiden a chance to strike back the demon brought its knee into his stomach with a hard impact. Once again Aiden gasped out in pain, but didn't have time to regain his thoughts as one of the zonaws slashed into his back with its large claws.

Aiden hissed in pain as he felt the blood escape from the large slash mark on his back. He gritted his teeth as he tried to retaliate with his sword to the first zonaw that had struck against him, but it had already moved away from him by the time he swung his sword. A second zonaw struck behind him with another kick to his back, forcing Aiden down onto his knees again.

His eyes began to get blurry as the pain from the follow up kick began to seep in. Aiden had to force himself to not cry out in pain as he pushed himself to stand up. Hot tears burned in his eyes as he barely stood up. His lungs were screamed in pain and his muscles trembled as he turned to face another zonaw.

"I-I'm not done yet..." He mentally kicked himself for stuttering like that yet again. His entire body screamed in protest as he held his sword up once more. Just as he was about to swing his sword at the first zonaw he saw, he felt a new pain erupt from his right arm as one zonaw rushed past him with the tip of its claw slashing into his upper arm.

Aiden didn't have time to cry out in pain as he felt another one of the blades slash into his left arm at the same speed. The attacks didn't stop though as the two demons that had cut his arms turned and attacked once more. This time their claws clamped down hard right ontop of his arms. Aiden let out a short shout of pain as he felt the blades slash into his skin. If he was stupid enough to try to move they could have easily cut off his arms with just a simple movement of their hands.

The zonaw horde began to separate in front of him as they formed single filed lines. Scarface, who had taken leadership of the zonaws, approached down the path as its two claws glowed in the darkness with each step it took towards Aiden. A look of horror appeared on his face as Scarface stood in front of him.

Uttering not a single word Aiden closed his eyes and waited. He knew what was coming, and it was going to hurt. Hell, it might actually make him pass out from the pain. He flinched when he heard the sounds of Scarface's claws closing and opening repeatedly before it pulled its arms up and swung down at his shoulders.

CLANK!

Aiden's eyes opened up in shock at hearing the sound. It was then he saw it, the two dragon shaped pauldrons had appeared at the last moment before Scarface's claws could cut off his arms. Aiden nearly gasped in shock at their sudden appearance, but before he could ask how they appeared, a strange surge of power flowed into his body from the two pauldrons.

With this newfound strength, Aiden felt his wounds begin to close up slowly. His eyes glowed with a sudden new power as he quickly took Warfang in hand and stabbed the zonaw at his right with his blade. Once he pulled his trusty sword away from the demon he turned to its ally at his left. Aiden quickly turned the sword backwards in his hand before let out a single shout as his blade swung through the air before slicing the zonaw's head off like it was a hot knife through butter.

Scarface looked flabbergasted at the sudden strength of Aiden as its headless minion fell to the ground. It clamped its claws back and forth in anger as its lifeless eyes stared right at the newly energized Aiden. The latter glanced to his shoulders, his own eyes filled with confusion as the two pauldrons disappeared.

Just as soon as they disappeared, Aiden felt the immense pain from before return as his wounds opened up once more. He gasped for air as he used Warfang to balance himself before staring down Scarface. Sweat ran down his brow as he took in several big breaths. Whatever that sudden power that he felt was gone now, no matter how hard he tried to bring back the pauldrons.

Thankfully for him, a familiar voice rang out from the side.

"AIDEN!"

Theresa charged in fury at Scarface as both of her wings and tail were out. The white dragoness combined her swords into their dual bladed form once more as she flew upwards before tossing her weapon at the scare covered zonaw. Scarface leaped out of the way just in the nick of time as Theresa's weapon stabbed the ground.

The white dragoness was not sastified though as she dive bombed right into Scarface's chest with her head. The zonaw's lifeless eyes nearly bulged in shock from the sudden head butt that it gave Theresa a chance to attack once again. With her long tail, Theresa grabbed ahold of Scarface's neck and swung it away from her and Aiden.

Theresa let out a loud roar as she landed in front of Aiden, her back turned to him, as she grabbed her dual bladed weapon.

"T-Thes!" Aiden managed to sputter out even with the pain from his wounds. Theresa held out her left hand behind him and quickly whispered a quick healing spell as his wounds began to slowly heal up. Aiden stood up slowly as his lungs began to feel like they were on fire as the rest of his body screamed in agony.

"Stay close to me." Theresa told him. "Keep our backs together and take a defensive stance."

Aiden nodded at her order as he stood back to back with her. The two of them kept their swords up in front of them. The horde continued to circle around them, each step they took brought them closer. The odds beginning to look bleak, Aiden glanced over his shoulder back to Theresa.

"We need to regroup, get to the others." He said to her. Theresa glanced back at him and nodded.

"Hold on tight."

Before he could ask what she meant he felt her hand grab ahold of his. Just when he was about to feel his cheeks heat up he suddenly realized that his feet were no longer on solid ground. Theresa had taken off into the air, dragging Aiden by his hand as she flew away from the zonaws. The demons below gave chase however, determined to get their targets.

"Everyone! Regroup! Regroup!"

Theresa's order quickly reached the ears of the separated

team. Garrett and Kali finished the zonaws they were fighting before rushing off towards where Theresa was. Aello, with Liza in her talons, Mia, and Gabriella quickly flew back as well. Seamus, Malevo, and Ryan were quickly teleported to the duo as well with a simple magic spell.

As the team regrouped with one another they all turned towards where the Overmind floated. The shapeless eye stared right back at them as its massive tendrils swung back and forth violently. The zonaws continued to circle around them ever so slowly. Scarface took priority as it clamped its claws back and forth.

"This is taking too long." Garrett growled. Seamus sighed but nodded his head.

"Rexkin, he's right. We can't take them all at once. We need to focus on our true target here."

"As much as I agree with the two of you, we don't have any chance of attacking the Overmind with the zonaw horde still here." She replied as she glared at the controller of the Shadow Demons.

"We'll be dead before we can even attack it!" Mia shouted to Theresa. "We can't keep this up!" Besides her, Kali gave a short scoff.

"Typical bird brains. Without your numbers you are nothing more than fledglings."

"Not now, snake." Garrett snapped at her before the harpies could reply. The zonaw horde continued to creep closer and closer though as the heroes were surrounded.

"Any ideas?" Liza asked. Ryan took a big sigh as he held his staff up. The group looked at him in confusion as the top of his staff glowed with immense magical power.

"I was hoping to save this for the Overmind, but we don't have a choice here." Ryan held his staff high as the immense magical energy from the tip of it threatened to explode as more power flowed into his staff. Seamus, realizing what he was about to do, quickly pulled everyone down with his own spell to prevent the team from seeing the spell.

"MIND WIPE!"

A flash of blue white light exploded from Ryan's staff as it suddenly illuminated the room. The light was so bright that even he had to close his eyes momentarily as the spell erupted into the air. The zonaws glanced up at the ball of light that had floated into the air.

At first the ball of light did nothing but float there as it was. A perfect sphere. But appearances were deceiving. As the perfect sphere's surface suddenly began to bubble. The zonaws all took a step back for a moment, but before any could truly move the sphere suddenly exploded as lightning erupted from within the sphere. The bolts raced towards Scarface, hitting it square in its forehead before jumping from it to the next zonaw.

The chain reaction was instant as the spell spread across the entire zonaw horde. Lighting bolts each had smacked into the forehead of other zonaws. Aiden wanted to look up and watch, but he felt the strong grip of Theresa keep his head in place. All around them, the demon horde began to fall over, lifeless.

When the last demon fell, the group slowly glanced up as the bright ball above them died down. In front of them, Ryan sighed as he fell to his knees, taking in deep breaths.

"Ryan!" Seamus shouted as he and Malevo rushed over. "What were you thinking?! You know that spell is dangerous!"

"What even WAS that?!" Aiden asked in confusion. Ryan gave a short laugh as he shook his head.

"A necessary spell. I'll explain it later." He stared up at the Overmind. "We have more important things to worry about now…"

CHAPTER 17 - GRIM ODDS

"*...* *K*ill..." The Overmind's disembodied voice echoed. The voice alone was enough to send a chill down Aiden's spine. *"...Kill..."*

The massive tendrils of the Overmind flailed back and forth as each one slammed into the ground. Each time a tendril slammed into the ground Aiden could feel his body jump up momentarily before landing back on his feet. Just that alone was enough to show the incredible power of the Shadow Demon's leader. This was not going to be an easy fight.

Aiden gripped the hilt of his sword tightly as he watched the ever-shifting eye of the Overmind. He could feel his stomach twist into a knot as soon the eye began to spin around so fast that it looked like it was going out of control. The tendrils began to coil and lash out with just as much violence as before just moments as they all rose above the Overmind's body.

"KILLLLLLLLLL!!!!"

The entire team was forced to cover their ears as the Overmind's shriek exploded in the room. A pillar purple of magical energy enveloped the Overmind as it continued to shout. At first Aiden could make out the Overmind's body in the pillar, but the darker the pillar's color became the less Aiden could make out of the body until he could no longer see the Overmind's shape.

Another unholy roar erupted from within the pillar. The ground itself shook as pieces of the walls and ceilings began to fall down from the sheer force of power the Overmind. Aiden, Liza, Aello, and her guardians would have fallen over from the force of the cry had it not been for Theresa, Garrett, and Seamus holding onto their wrists. Even then, the Trinity were forced to dig their heels into the ground as the power of the Overmind continued to rise up.

Finally, after what seemed like hours, something emerged from within pillar of purple light. Two large muscular arms that reminded Aiden of the first prime demon slowly pushed their way through the pillar. The rest of the body soon followed suit, as the previous form of the Overmind was now no longer existent.

Aiden didn't know how to describe this new form. No matter how he looked at it the only thing that he could think of was that it was simply inhumane and words could not do it justice.

The Overmind's new form stood at least as tall as Garrett's dragon form. But, if Aiden had to be honest with himself, this new body of the Overmind looked even *bigger* than that. Its upper body was that of a gladiator with muscles covering the pectoral areas of the upper body. Below the strong upper body were two powerful legs, just as ripped and powerful as the top half over the Overmind. Behind the Overmind, a long and powerful tail swished back and forth. The tendrils of the Overmind had formed on its back, taking shape into what could have passed off as wings.

The most peculiar thing about the new form however was that it was inconsistent with its appearance. Unlike previous demons the Overmind's 'combat form', that Aiden had decided to dub, was constantly shifting back and forth between many different limbs, heads, wings, tails, and arms. The one thing that is consistent with its form is that it always has the single eye. That eye is located in the chest of the Overmind's new powerful form.

"U-Unreal..." Liza breathed out. Aiden had to give her credit. She was able to speak where he himself was at a loss for words.

"What the hell did it just do?" Ryan asked. "I've never heard of something like this!"

"First time for everything." Seamus replied, his grip on Hurricane became stiff. "This Overmind. It must have more power than any Overmind that came before it."

"H-How the heck do we defeat something like this then?!" Mia asked. "It's so powerful, and Queen Lilith isn't here to help!!"

"Well you don't have a choice, birdbrain." Kali responded as she coiled herself. "Besides, you don't need your nest mother. I'm here, and no one can match my perfection."

"You know nothing about her Majesty, you scaly, slimy, no good-" Gabriella started, but Aello placed a hand over her mouth.

"Now is not the time!" She said with a look at her guardian. "Save insulting the snake for later!"

Right when Aello had finished giving that order, The Overmind let out another bone chilling roar as swung its right fist down right at the team.

"MOVE!" Theresa ordered just as the fist of the Shadow Demon leader made contact with the spot the team once stood. When the fist made contact with the ground, a crater was created just with that one impact. Aiden had to mentally keep himself from gasping in shock as he turned to face the Overmind.

"There's no point in holding back anymore!" Theresa shouted. "Garrett! Seamus! Take your true forms!"

The two dragons wasted no time in obeying Theresa's order as a bright light exploded around the two. Both Seamus and Garrett had entered their true states. If it weren't a life or death situation, Aiden would be ecstatic to watch the fight. But now?

Now he was apart of the battle to be had with the great Overmind.

Instead he kept his mouth shut as Theresa took a step out in front of him. He reached out to her and placed a hand on her shoulder.

"A-Are you certain you want to do this? After last year you..."

"It'll be fine." Theresa responded. "I may not be as powerful as I once was when I was Theresa of the White Fire, but even if my power has become less since that time, I will fight with all I have." She turned her head back to him. "We don't have a choice Aiden, even if it's not much against the Overmind, fighting it in my human form would be pointless."

The same kind smile that Aiden had grown up with appeared on Theresa's lips once more as her wings and tail began to grow bigger. She closed her eyes as her entire body began to shift into a different shape once more.

"Remember. Don't look at the light." She told him. Aiden quickly brought up his hands in front of him as the bright light exploded around Theresa. Once the light died down, Aiden saw Theresa's beautiful dragoness form standing before him once more. Even in her dragoness form, her emerald green eyes were still filled with the same kindness as before.

Theresa lowered her neck down so that Aiden could hop onto her neck. Aiden gave a quick nod as he quickly jumped onto her neck and positioned himself. As Theresa rose up, a realization hit him.

"Theresa, I never had to fight while riding you!" He said. Theresa gave a short dry laugh.

"Well consider this a crash course!"

That didn't really help Aiden feel better.

The good news was that he wasn't the only one mounting up on a dragon. Nearby, Ryan and Liza jumped onto Seamus' back. Even Kali had slithered her way onto Garrett's back and wrapped her long tail around his neck. Aiden felt his spine shiver as he watched her smile deviously.

"Try not to make me fall, big boy." She said to Garrett. "Remember whose riding you." Garrett growled as he clenched his claws into the ground beneath him as the Overmind stared down the trio of dragons with those who rode on them.

"Stuff it, snake." He said. His massive tail slammed into the ground once as he lifted himself on his hind legs. Even seeing the massive size of Garrett's dragon form was not enough to help him feel calm as the Overmind's ever-changing battle form stared down the three massive dragons.

"Kill...KILL..." It said once more as its two arms suddenly took from of two giant meat hooks. With a single step from the great demon, the final battle for the Academy was on.

The Overmind was the first one to attack, with speeds that could rival even the dragons. With a simple swing of its left arm it brought the hook shaped claw towards Garrett's neck. The large dragon pulled his neck away to avoid the claw. Just as Garrett pulled his head back away from the first claw, the second tried to flank him from his blind spot.

Kali held out her arm and opened her hand. With a wordless shout she quickly casted a shield spell that reflected the second hook from striking Garrett. The Overmind stumbled back just a bit from the recoil of the shield. Garrett saw a chance to strike out. With a massive roar he lunged his claws towards the Overmind's arms and grabbed ahold of them. He wasted no time as he made an attempt to bite the throat of the Shadow Demon with his massive teeth.

The Overmind was quick to counter though. In a blink an eye its arms changed shape again from the strong meat cleaving hooks into long whip like appendages. A second wasn't wasted as the whip ends wrapped themselves around the strong neck of Garrett and held firm when the large dragon tried to rip off the whip bindings. The Overmind let out an unholy shout as its body shifted weight and tried to throw Garrett from the battle.

Aiden thought he was in some kind of weird dream as he watched Garrett's massive dragon form actually be thrown to the side by the whip arms of the Overmind. When his body made contact with the wall it created several large cracks within the foundation of the Academy. Aiden heard a hiss of displeasure as he watched Kali slither up towards Garrett's forehead. A displeased look on her face as she patted the side of his cheek.

"Come on now, big guy. You're not just gonna take this and let this disgusting creature get away with that, are you?" She asked. Aiden noticed there was a slight shift in her sultry voice.

Garrett growled as he forced himself to stand back up. His eyes glinted with anger. It happened in an instant as the largest dragon spewed out a torrent of hot fire at the Overmind. Any flammable objects that were within the reach of his fire immediately were set ablaze. The tip of his great fire breath almost burnt into the strange shadowy form of the Overmind, but a large magical shield erupted in front of the great demon before the fire could burn away at its target.

The Overmind's shield did more than just hold back the flame. With a simple flick of its left wrist, the shield quickly turned itself at an angle to send the intense flames into a wall nearby. Aiden looked dumbfounded as he witnessed the flames of Garrett literally melt away the wall.

"Oh that's just great!" Liza shouted, "That thing can reflect any attack that it wants!"

Garrett's fire breath came to an end as he clenched his claws into the ground. No one made his attacks look like they were child's play! He let loose a loud roar before bending his head down and charging straight at the Overmind with his horns aimed right at the great demon.

The Overmind's ever-changing arms once again turned into what looked like strong man arms on steroids as it grabbed

Garrett by his two horns. Aiden couldn't help but feel almost mesmerized at the sight as he watched the largest of the Trinity push his entire being against the grip of their foe.

Small embers flickered from his mouth as Garrett took each step slowly. From a distance it looked like every single one of his muscles was bulging the contest of power. The Overmind tilted its shadowy head to its side for a moment as it tried to lift Garrett off the ground.

"Garrett!" Theresa roared as she blasted out a torrent of white fire in an attempt to help him. The Overmind glanced at the racing fire and moved its right wing to block the attack.

As its wing held back the white fire of Theresa's, Kali slithered her way to the top of Garrett's head. The largest dragon glared at her as she promptly coiled herself there with a minor expression of concern.

"Come on now, big lizard. You can't tell me this is all you have." Her tongue slipped through her teeth a couple of times. "I mean, you should be far stronger than he is, right?" Garrett responded with a low growl before glaring right at back to the Overmind.

"I don't see you doing anything, SNAKE!"

With a loud roar Garrett broke free of the Overmind's grip. Before he can attack once more though the Overmind spun around so quickly that it's large tail smacked into his face. Kali quickly slithered over to his left horn and wrapped herself around it as the dragon nearly fell backwards.

"Enough of this! Seamus! With me!" Theresa shouted as she began to run at a ramming speed at the Overmind. "Aiden! Once I make contact, move in and attack!"

Aiden had no time to argue with her about that order as the white dragoness' speed began to increase. Seamus and she wasted no time in moving towards the Overmind. Aiden swallowed a bit as he held Warfang in both hands as Theresa rammed her head into the side of the Overmind. The force from the impact was enough to cause the Overmind's body to stagger, just enough for Theresa to move her head to the side so that Aiden could strike.

With as much strength as he could muster, Aiden swung his sword at the side of the Overmind. As Warfang sliced through the air Aiden prayed that his weapon would strike the hide of their foe. The tip of the sword made contact with one side of the Overmind's body, slicing into its skin like a hot knife through butter.

Aiden felt a small smile come to his lips when his sword made its mark. What looked like blue blood drizzled down the side of the Overmind slowly before it fell down on the floor. At that moment Aiden felt like they had this battle in their favor. But that thought was quickly pulled away when Theresa jerked her long neck away from the Overmind's left hand. Aiden had to brace himself as the white dragoness backed away from the Overmind's grasp.

What confidence Aiden had that they were going to easily win this battle was replaced by a sudden realization of horror. The slash mark that his sword had left in the side of the Overmind had stopped bleeding. He felt his pupils shrink in size as he watched as the sliced skin of the Overmind begin to patch itself together until the wound that he had left was nothing more than a minor memory.

"That…that's impossible…" Aiden barely managed to breathe out. "No living being can heal a wound that fast on their own!" Theresa growled low as smoke rose up from her nostrils.

"Overminds are no simple living beings, Aiden." She ducked her head quickly to avoid a punch. "They are in an entirely different league than other great demons!"

"Rexkin, to your left!" Seamus shouted

Theresa's head immediately turned to the left. The Overmind's large tail had transformed into a spikey club that was speeding towards her at full force. Theresa's green eyes shrunk as the massive tail of the Overmind smacked right into her face with incredible force. The spikes slicing Aiden felt his heart drop as he watched blood fly freely in the air from Theresa's skin.

"T-Theresa!" Aiden cried out as her almost lifeless head as it fell to the side.

In front of them, the Overmind spun its tail right back at Theresa once more. The club shape now taking the form of a blade as it raced towards her neck. Aiden desperately grabbed ahold of the sides of the neck of his best friend as he tried to get her attention.

"Theresa! It's coming back at us! Theresa, please! Open your eyes!! Theresa!!!"

The bladed tip of the Overmind's tail continued to race towards the white dragoness' neck. Aiden closed his eyes as he waited for the impact of the tail that would remove Theresa's neck from her body. His stomach twisted into a knot and his body tensed as he let out a loud scream.

Just when it looked like all was lost for the white dragoness, her eyes snapped back open. With a mighty roar she opened her mouth and grabbed the tail of the Overmind in her strong jaws. The bite was so sudden, so intense, that the sheer force of it was enough to sever the tail away from the Overmind's body.

Aiden opened his eyes the moment he heard Theresa bite down on the tail. A relieved smile came to his lips as he watched her rear her head back. White smoke escaped her nostrils before letting loose a powerful stream of white fire towards the Overmind's backside.

A small explosion went off the moment that her flame breath smacked into the back of the Overmind. The unholy shadow demon controller cried out in pain from the intense heat of Theresa's fire. The latter continued to breathe her deadly flames at her foe. An anger that Theresa rarely showed had erupted from within her emerald green eyes, as she did not stop her flames.

Only when the Overmind was forced onto its knees from the sheer force of the white fire did the white dragoness stop.

"Do you want some more, ugly?!" Aiden shouted from Theresa's neck. "That's what happens when you mess with a dragoness like Theresa!"

"Stop it Aiden." He blinked when he heard the stern tone in Theresa's voice. "It will take more than just one blast of fire breath to destroy an Overmind."

"But…"

"Use your eyes, whelp!" Garrett shouted from afar. "Did you really believe one attack would do the trick?!"

Aiden felt his stomach twist again before staring at the Overmind. While its back had been horribly burnt by Theresa's intense fire, he could see it. Up to six spots on the back of the Overmind began to boil and bubble. With a horrific cry of pain the Overmind reared itself upwards as the boils burst open as large spider like appendages formed.

The appendages were large, just as thick as Garrett's front legs. But the true horrifying part of the appendages weren't their size, but the tips. They were serrated, like a butcher's knife, and the very tip of the blade was a distinct purple color. With these new appendages, the Overmind forced itself back up to its feet as it turned back to face Theresa and Aiden.

"W-What the hell are those?" Aiden asked. Theresa gave a small growl as a response to his question.

"NOW IS NOT THE TIME!"

One of the Overmind's new appendages twitched back and forth momentarily, then lunged at Aiden and Theresa. With a flap of her mighty wings Theresa was able to dodge the tip. The Overmind didn't stop its attack though, as a second appendage shot straight towards Theresa's chest.

The white dragoness reared up on her hind legs and held her two front claws outward as she grabbed the appendage. She had a strong grip on it, but the muscular strength of the Overmind's new limbs caught her off guard as it began to push her backwards. Theresa let a snarl escape her mouth as she sunk her claws into the hide of the appendage. Aiden almost flinched when the blue blood of the Overmind began to pour out.

"Aiden!" Theresa shouted. "Fire a Flarnea at the leg!"

Not wanting to challenge Theresa's order, Aiden quickly placed Warfang in his left hand before holding his right arm out and aiming right at one section of the leg. Just like before the immense power up that Kali had given him coursed through his veins before it took the form of the fireball in his palm.

"Flarnea!"

At his command the fireball erupted into the large beam from before as it raced towards the section of the Overmind's leg. Aiden's eyes squinted as a bright light that erupted from his attack exploded when it made contact with the leg. In an instant the intense flames began to melt away the skin with its intense heat. The Overmind let out an annoyed roar before a second appendage began to aim at the spot where Aiden sat on Theresa's back. This didn't go unnoticed by Aiden though as his eyes spotted the appendage rising up. He glanced to the right, noticing Aello and her guardians were high above.

"Aello!!" He shouted. "Do you think you three can distract it?!" Mia gave him a look of horror at the suggestion.

"What?! You want to put Princess Aello closer to that thing!? Have you gone insane?!"

"Mia! Quiet!" Aello ordered. "Our survival is more important right now than just mine!"

The guardian nearly gasped at the order from Aello, but she did not argue. Aello turned her attention back to Aiden giving him a short nod.

"What do you want us to do?"

"Get close as you can to its face!" Aiden shouted, still holding the Flarnea spell as best as he could. "Make certain that it doesn't use its leg to strike at me or Theresa!"

Aello gave a short nod before flying off towards the Overmind. Gabriella and Mia nearly screeched as they gave chase to their princess. As the trio of harpies flew together, Aello readied her sword as she took off away from her guardians.

Once the princess had reached the head of the Overmind, she turned her sword from its blade form right to its whip form. With all the strength she could muster, Aello flicked the whip around the throat of the Overmind and began to pull.

The sharp blades of her whip sliced into the Overmind's skin as she pulled with all her strength. The Overmind turned its gaze toward Aello, as the harpy princess floated in place.

While it certainly wasn't enough to harm the Overmind to a great degree, it was enough to grab its attention for the moment. The second appendage that was previously aimed at Theresa slowly changed direction towards the young princess.

"Princess!!!"

Both of her guardians flew past Aello as they readied their talons before diving right at the face of the Overmind. Mia's left talon sunk itself into the right cheek of the Overmind while Gabriella's sunk into the left cheek.

Once both guardians had their grip in the Overmind's body they began to slash at its face with their claws. Each slash sent a piece of the Overmind's 'skin' flying into a different direction. With every slash they made their upper arms were soon covered with blue blood.

Soon the duo stopped slashing and jumped away from the Overmind's face as one of its ever-changing hands tried to grab them. Mia turned to Gabriella and gave a short nod before dive-bombing towards the Overmind's forehead with her fellow guardian.

Just when it looked like the duo were about to pierce through the skin of the Overmind's forehead, one of its appendages appeared from the left and effortlessly smacked them away from its body.

"Mia! Gabriella!" Aello screamed. "Get out of here before it crushes you!"

The Overmind soon turned its attention back to Aello. With a simple flick of its left hand it smacked her away from its body.

Aello let out a cry of shock and fear as she was sent back from the Overmind. The young harpy princess braced herself for the impact she was going to have with the wall behind her. She knew it was going to hurt, a lot.

"Oof!!" A sudden grunt came from behind her.

Aello's eyes opened when she felt something grab ahold of her body. The young princess blinked in confusion as she looked at her current surroundings. There with a strong grasp on her was Liza, still riding Seamus like before. The athletic girl gave a short smile at her.

"You sure your guardians got this under control?" The young princess rolled her eyes before shaking her head.

"You're lucky that they aren't trying to slice you open for even being near me, Liz."

"I don't think you'd let them." Liza retorted before the harpy princess flew out of Liza's grip. Seamus rolled his eyes at the two of them as Aello hovered in mid air beside them.

"You okay, princess?" The green dragon asked.

"I'll be fine..." Aello responded before grabbing her left arm in pain. "Gods Ozzy would be screaming at me for doing something like that right now..." Liza gave a short laugh before elbowing Liza in the side.

"She'd probably be screaming at the big monster that tried to hurt you...hey, if you screamed, how long would it take your sisters to get here?"

Aello cocked her head, lightly scratching her cheek.

"Uh...maybe thirty minutes, an hour? We're pretty far..."

Seamus shook his head at the two of them at the suggestion.

"That's not gonna cut it, kiddos. We're on our own here."

"Figures…" Liza grumbled. "I mean, what the hell can we do against this thing? It's huge!"

"Never give in!" Theresa roared from the left. The distraction was more than enough time for the white dragoness to rip off the appendage of the Overmind that tried to stab through her. A gush of blue blood poured out of the Overmind's appendage before it began to mend itself slowly from being ripped out.

Nearby, Garrett had recovered from his previous battle with the Overmind. Kali frowned as she gave his head a gentle pat with one hand as she coiled herself on the top of his forehead.

"You know, I normally do not like sharing things with scrawny humans and spell weavers, or even lizards like big boy here, but I've grown tired of this little game with this ugly shadow."

"Demon, now is not the time for your lies!" Ryan shouted at her. Kali didn't even bother to look at him as she folded her arms over her chest.

"If you all want to survive this battle with this ugly beast here, listen to me and only to me." She continued. "This kind of Overmind is physically stronger than many other kind of Overminds. Just attacking it one by one isn't going to do a damn lick of good for either of you. You'll be too tired before it even begins to put up a real fight against you with these constant attacks."

The lamia reared herself back a bit as her tail's tip waved back and forth slowly. A coy smile was on her face.

"But, this species of Overmind has one fatal flaw. It cannot focus on more than one target in its current state. If you truly wanna erase this disgusting thing off this planet, you must all confuse it by working together as a team." The lamia laughed. "I mean, that's what you're suppose to be, aren't you~?"

Garrett rolled his eyes at Kali's tone of voice before turning his attention to Theresa. Seamus followed suite as he took turned to the leader of the group. The white dragoness gave them both a short nod before beckoning them over together.

"The snake is right." She said with a small growl. "Attacking the Overmind one at a time isn't going to make this fight easier."

"Any ideas, Rexkin?" Seamus asked. "Now would be a great idea for one of your brilliant plans of attack!"

Theresa closed her eyes for several seconds. The white dragoness was lost in thought for a brief moment, but then opened her eyes with a new determination to win the battle.

"Yes. I do have a plan." She turned her head to Garrett. "Garrett, I want you and the snake to take the left side of the Overmind. Use your strength and her magic at the same time." Theresa's head turned towards Seamus next. "I want you to strike at the right with the harpies, Ryan, and Liza. Aiden and I will attack from the front when the moment is right."

"Now you're using that brain, lizard." Kali responded with a coy smile. "Just for your information? Try to aim for the most obvious weak spot on its body." Garrett gave a slow growl at the lamia.

"Can it, snake. Do no tell my Rexkin what to do."

Aiden almost gave a short laugh at Kali and Garrett's banter for a moment. It was like the two of them were meant to exchange quick retorts with one another. He kept his mouth shut though cause he did not want Garrett staring him down in anger.

"All right, everyone get into position!" Theresa ordered. "On my signal, attack with everything that you've got!"

"Right!"

The team quickly moved into their positions. As they moved, Theresa turned her head back to face Aiden. He felt a wave of relief flow over him as he saw the same friendly warmth within her emerald green eyes.

"Aiden, here's what we're going to do. When they strike from the sides, I am going to charge straight at the Overmind. The moment we're there I'm going to use all my strength to keep its arms from attacking. When I tell you too, I want you to strike at the giant eye that is on its chest."

Aiden felt like she had just asked him to do what seemed to be an impossible task. Just as he was about to protest the idea, he felt her snout nudge his chest with a simple touch.

"I believe in you, Aiden. I always have. And I know that you can deliver the finishing blow in this one assault."

Without another word the white dragoness turned her head back towards the Overmind. Its large appendages more than ready for combat once more as they flicked back and forth to strike out. Its ever-changing hands rose up in front as they took the forms of giant sickle blades.

A trail of smoke rose from Theresa's nostrils as she stared down the Overmind. Her claws dug into the ground beneath her. Her massive tail swung back and forth as her body's muscles tightened up.

Aiden felt his grip on Warfang begin to get damp. Time itself seemed to slow down as every one waited for the right moment to attack. The room had gotten so quiet that a simple pin drop would have been heard.

The Overmind reared itself back and let loose another unholy roar before aiming two of its large appendages towards Theresa. The white dragoness let loose a loud road before slamming her tail into the ground. That was the signal.

Garrett followed her roar with his own before grabbing one of the appendages with his massive front limbs. The sudden movement from the largest dragon caught the Overmind off guard for the briefest of moments. It nearly tripped over before turning its head towards Garrett. With what Aiden could have guessed to be a 'snarl' it aimed another appendage towards Garrett's chest.

What happened was almost too fast for Aiden to keep track of.

Kali, who throughout most of the fight did nothing to contribute, slithered herself onto Garrett's forehead once more. She clapped her hands together once and began to chant in what

Aiden could have only guessed was an ancient language for the Prime Demons.

A large stalagmite erupted from the ground right below the two appendages that had been aimed at Garrett and Kali. The stalagmite pierced straight through the hide of the large spider like legs without mercy. Aiden almost flinched when he heard the sickening sound of bone smashing through bone and muscle of the Overmind's appendages.

The attack was enough to make the Overmind cry out in sudden pain from this sudden attack. Now thanks to the stalagmite, two of its deadly back spines had been rendered motionless.

On the right side of the Overmind, Seamus took a deep breath before letting loose a large stream of hot fire. His attack made contact with the right arm of the Overmind causing a severe burn on the upper portion.

The Overmind's response was to turn towards Seamus with a deadly 'glare' before firing out a magical blast from its left hand to push against Seamus' flames. Their two attacks pushed back and forth against one another for a brief moment of time before suddenly exploding in the middle.

"Now, kiddos!" Seamus shouted.

At his command Aello, carrying Liza by her shoulders, and her guardians rushed through the smoke towards the Overmind. Not far behind them was Ryan, who was using his own magic to fly after the trio of harpies. Aiden could see the anger and determination in his eyes to bring this battle to a close and soon.

Liza held Gitanel at the ready. Once she, Aello, and her guardians were above the head of the Overmind, she glanced up towards Aello. With a simple nod she gave the okay to dive bomb at their target. Aello hesitated for a second, but dove downwards with her guardians not far behind.

The Overmind glanced up right at the moment that Liza took her dagger and rammed it into the top of the shadow demon's head. Aello released Liza by her shoulders, allowing the alethic girl to run on from one end of the Overmind's head towards the other. The entire time she dragged her Gitanel across the Demon's scalp. Her blade sliced through its shadowy skin as if it was a pair of scissors cutting paper in half.

As Liza ran across the head of the Overmind, Aello's two guardians attacked its neck with fierce swipes from their sharp hand claws and talons. The two of them each rammed their hand claws into the neck of the Overmind and flew around in a circle on its neck. Their claws, just like Gitanel, sliced through the Overmind's skin.

Aello whistled to get their attention before pointing towards where Ryan was. Mia and Gabriella both retreated from the neck of the Overmind as blood poured from the wounds they had inflicted there. Liza noticed Ryan as well and pulled Gitanel out of the head of the Overmind before running to the left side. She glanced up and watched Aello as she bent her legs and jumped away from the Overmind's head.

For a brief moment, she felt herself falling downward. But in that very moment, Aello's talons grabbed ahold of Liza's shirt and hung onto her. The athletic girl yelped as Aello pulled her away from combat.

"You owe me a new shirt!" Liza cried out. Aello rolled her eyes.

"Really?" Aello asked with a cocked eyebrow. She pursed her lips and glared to the side, "I save you for once and now I owe you?"

As the two of them flew away from the Overmind, Ryan arrived in front of the demon. The eldest son of the Grand Mage spun his staff behind him before aiming it right at the Overmind's face.

"Elemental Barrage!"

At his command a large array of various elemental attacks fired from the tip of his staff. The first was a jet stream of boiling hot water that scalded the Overmind's face with intense heat. The second was a blast of yellow lighting that, with what water was left, electrocuted the Overmind's face. After the lighting blast ten icicles rushed straight at the Overmind's head before they impaled its skin. Once the icicles had rooted themselves into the skin, Ryan snapped his fingers. At the command of the snap, the icicles exploded within the Overmind's face, causing shards of ice to tear through its skin.

Ryan's determined face did not falter as he watched the Overmind recoil in pain from the exploding icicles. He took a deep breath before he pointed his index finger right at the Shadow Demon.

"Ignituran."

A massive fireball erupted from the tip of his index finger as it soared straight into the face of the Overmind. Once it made contact with its target it triggered a large explosion that forced the Overmind to stagger back in pain from the intense flame. Ryan turned his back away from the Overmind as the explosion tore into the skin of the Overmind. Blue blood splashed against his back as the fiery explosion faded away.

"Now!" He shouted to Theresa and Aiden.

The white dragoness reared back and began to gallop full speed right towards their foe. Aiden almost slipped off her neck from the suddenness of the movement but managed to maintain his grip. He had little to no time to adjust to the speed that Theresa was running at though. Theresa was coming in close to the Overmind and she was coming in fast.

"Aiden! When I gave you the order, run towards its eye and stab it there!" Theresa ordered. Aiden felt him give an unconscious nod at her order, even though he knew she didn't see it.

Once they were in range of the Overmind's grasp Theresa let out a massive roar as she suddenly reared upwards. Her two front limbs grabbed ahold of the Overmind's massive front arms. The Overmind tried to pull out of her grip, but Aiden noticed that Theresa had dug her claws right into the Overmind's skin, securing a strong grip to ensure that it did not escape.

"NOW!" She roared out.

Aiden wasted no time in quickly standing up. What happened in the next few moments were all such a blur that Aiden didn't remember exactly how he kept his balance when he ran up Theresa's neck.

It was like he was on autopilot. Aiden just ran for all he was worth up Theresa's neck before her head came in sight. His eyes narrowed as he raced down her head and snout right at the giant eye that rested in the Overmind's chest. With Warfang in hand, Aiden leaped off Theresa's snout right at the eye.

Aiden let out the biggest shout he could as he aimed Warfang right at the chest eye of the Overmind. If he could land this one attack, maybe, just maybe, this would be the end of this climatic battle with the leader of the Shadow Demons.

Just as his sword's tip was about to pierce right into the eye though, Aiden noticed a strange pulse go off within its body. The ground began to rumble and crack apart as the Overmind suddenly broke free not only from Theresa's grip, but the stalagmites that Kali had summoned to hold several of its appendages in place.

"KILL!!!!" It roared out. *"KILL!!!!"*

An unseen shockwave exploded from the Overmind. The force of it was so intense that it managed to hit every single member of the group and send them flying back.

Aiden felt himself falling backwards, flying straight towards the ground where sharp rocks below waited to pierce right through his body. A sense of dread filled him as he glanced back just a bit to notice those rocks. He felt his entire body go numb as he prepared to be impaled through his body.

However instead of a sharp rock smacking into his body, a large white claw grabbed him from midair and pulled him close to its chest. Aiden didn't have to open his eyes to know that

Theresa had grabbed him. What he did open his eyes for though was the crashing sounds that came from her massive form smacking into the rocks for him instead. He winced as he heard larger rocks break apart from the massive weight of Theresa's dragon form.

The shock wave from the Overmind continued to expand and cause the entire lab to rattle and crack apart. Streaks of sunlight seeped through the roof above the more the lab shook apart. Debrief fell from the ceiling, nearly smacking into the fallen forms of the Trinity and the rest of the team.

Aiden tried to keep his eyes open, to see what the Overmind was doing, but he could not keep them open for long as a bright light seemed to engulf the Overmind, and Theresa's dragon form.

Had they truly lost this fight?

CHAPTER 18 - THE FINAL REVELATION

*A*ll he could see was darkness. Nothing around him seemed to exist. His five senses detected nothing - like he did not have them anymore, just emptiness - everywhere. Nothing was there.

Had he died? Had he ceased to exist? Where was he? He had no idea where he was, who he was, or why he was here in this endless void of darkness. It was all alien, before him was an eternal ever-expanding void.

For as long as he could remember, this was all there was. Was he someone before? Did he even live? If he did live, who was he? All of them were questions with answers that eluded him.

He didn't even know if he had a true body. If he did, it was long gone by now. Try as hard as he could, he couldn't remember anything - nothing was there.

It was just the emptiness before him, and within him a growing sense that he was empty too.

What seemed like an eternity of silence began to break apart. He heard something he thought he would never hear again.

Voices.

They were somewhere. And they were getting louder and louder.

Along with those voices were small rays of light shining into the eternal darkness. Had something changed? What was going on? Who were those voices? Were they friend, or were they foe?

Something was going on outside. Something that could possibly bring him out of this void, back to the real world.

* * *

"AIDEN! AIDEN, WAKE UP!"

The teenager groaned as he felt his eyes peel open at a snail's pace. Everything hurt. From his feet to his head the shock wave from the Overmind felt like a bullet train hitting him at full speed. If it hadn't been for Garrett's rigorous training exercises, Aiden would have been completely knocked out, or worse.

"Ow..." He groaned. Hot tears formed in his eyes from the extreme pain as he tried to move his arms. Even just the slightest movement sent shocks of sudden pain through out his body. "Everything...hurts..."

"Shh." Theresa's voice said from behind him. "Don't move. Let me handle this."

Aiden blinked in confusion when he heard her voice. It wasn't the tone she had when she was in her dragoness form, but rather her human form. He glanced down when he saw both of her hands resting on his chest. With a quiet whisper, she cast Emalla on his body.

The soothing wave of healing magic began to seep through his body like a river rushing down towards the ocean. He had become so used to this healing spell that he believed that the pain would disappear. Aiden winced as he tried to move his right arm out of her grasp.

"No." Theresa told him. "Your body is still in pain and the healing spell hasn't finished yet."

As much as he hated to admit it, she was right. He had jumped the gun in trying to move too soon while she was still casting the spell. He felt his cheeks turning red as Theresa held him close to her. It almost was embarrassing to have her tend to him every time he was injured. Aiden heard her give a short relieved sigh though as she whispered 'Thank the gods' under her breath.

"Thes...what the hell was that thing?" He asked. "The Overmind, did we, win?" Theresa didn't respond to his question right away. Instead she kept her hands over his chest and continued the healing spell. She didn't have to answer him right away. Aiden had a feeling he knew the answer she was going to give him anyway.

"No." She answered him. Aiden noticed that her leadership tone overtook her kind one. "I've been through too many battles with powerful demons like this before. These kinds of battles are never over that easily." Theresa grunted as the healing spell finished healing Aiden, banishing his pain . "And it's been a very long time since I've seen a demon use that kind of psionic wave."

"Psionic?" Aiden asked. Theresa nodded as she helped him stand up.

"Yes. It's something that massive demons use as a last ditch effort when they are feeling overwhelmed by their foes. It basically forces the opponent to transform into a weaker state." She glanced down at her shaking hands. A hiss escaped her lips as she clenched them. "Which means that it forced me, Garrett, and Seamus into our humanoid forms."

Aiden felt his heart drop into his stomach at those words. The dragon forms were easily their best bets for defeating the Overmind and bringing the nightmare of the Academy to an end.

A high-pitched screech came from their left. Aiden and Theresa turned to see Garrett standing tall in his humanoid form. The tallest of the Trinity rolled his eyes as a young lady stood there beside him. Both of them looked confused for a brief moment as they just stared at the woman.

"This. Is. TERRIBLE!" She shouted out in anger. "How dare that stupid idiot turn me into this...FRAIL THING!"

Aiden and Theresa could not believe it. Her words proved that it was Kali. Much like the dragons, she had been forced into a human form as well. Though it was far different from what Aiden would ever imagine for Kali if she were to take human form.

She was very tall, if Aiden had to guess she was about six feet tall, just shorter than Garrett and Ocypete. Aiden noticed she had a very curvy body, an hourglass figure, with wide hips and thick thighs. Unlike her demon form, her skin was a shade of light brown, just a tint lighter than the Harpies' and Garrett's. She wore a silken black material, wrapped around her in a way that almost resembled a dress.

Kali growled, and brought her hands to her chest.

"At least one thing wasn't suppressed by that bastard..."

Aiden felt his cheeks get even hotter before he mentally slapped himself to focus. Garrett rolled his eyes at Kali's reaction to her transformed human state.

"You're overreacting, snake." He said. "You act as if your demon form didn't have a human like appearance." Kali glared at him as her now regular tongue flickered through her teeth.

"Easy for you to say, lizard boy! My form was that of a true goddess, and now I'm forced to be in this...weak husk that mortals use for a body!" Kali's eyes grew misty with tears, either real or crocodile. Seamus, who was also in his human form like Theresa and Garrett, walked up with Liza, the harpies, and Ryan.

"Crying doesn't suit you, snake." Seamus said. "Besides, if you're gonna be in this world you'll have to learn how to blend in with everyone."

"Who says that I'm going to stay in this dreadful ugly place?!" Kali retorted. "Stuck in this frail body that humans are cursed with! And you three dragons just accept it easily! Gagh!" Theresa groaned as she shook her head at Kali's tantrum.

"I do hope you realize that there's something more important than what you look like." She pointed to where the Overmind was. "We still have an enemy to fight." Kali tried her best to hiss, but so sound came from her lips. No one ended up mocking her as they had all turned to look at the Overmind.

To Aiden's shock, the Overmind had shrunk from its previous towering form. It now stood roughly the same height as Garrett. If not his height exactly it was at only a bit taller than the strongest member of the Trinity.

The Overmind in its shrunken form still retained the ever-changing hands, tails, and spider like appendages extending from its back. It looked entirely different compared to the massive bulk it had before.

Long, thin to the point of emaciated, with an almost human face, but impossibly large eyes that never blinked, whose gaze followed their every movement. Its skin was stretched tight over rippling muscles, and its hands grasped at the air with long, dirty fingernails.

Every so often it would open its mouth to speak, but instead of a voice an unholy amalgam of sounds escaped in a gasping screech.

The harpies flinched in pain from the sound. Ryan gritted his teeth in pain. Aiden and Liza both placed their hands over their ears in an attempt to deafen the noise. The only ones who did not react to the mismatched cries were the Trinity and Kali. They stood there, staring down in recognition at the new shape of the Overmind - as if they had seen something like it before.

Once the amalgamation of sounds died down from the mouth of the Overmind, Aiden and Liza removed their hands from their ears. They both felt their bodies begin to stiffen as the Overmind's spider appendages stabbed the ground beneath the demon with the tips.

"It…it's way different from the way it was b-b-before." Aiden managed to spit out. "W-Why is it so much smaller but still j-just as strong?" His grip on Warfang began to feel slippery from his sweating palms. For the first time in his life Aiden knew the true meaning of fear, just by staring at this abomination.

"Kiddo, what you're staring at is the last ditch effort of any kind of Overmind." Seamus said. Garrett snarled as he spoke.

"This has to be it." He said as his grip on his axe tightened. "This has to be what many believed to be true among Overminds, that they have a secondary form. In a way, you could say that this is its 'True Form.' A form so nightmarish, that it has never been seen by any living eyes." Theresa blew out small puffs of smoke from her nostrils as she stared directly at the Overmind's newest form.

"I've heard tales, but I never once thought that they could be real." She whispered. Kali frowned as she folded her arms over her chest.

"You lizards have never really see this form before, because in the past your kind usually killed the Overminds with incredible overwhelming numbers." She explained, her tongue, despite not being forked, tried to slip through her teeth again. "In my home, these things are known in the demonic tongue as *Ishatarn*. In the mortal tongue, the closest word to it would be, Abomination."

Aiden felt his stomach twist into a knot at that one word. Abomination. He knew that word was associated with a disgusting monster with unrelenting power. Many of the RPGs that he played in his free time had different varieties of abominations that ranged remarkably in appearance.

None of them compared to the horrific being that was the Abomination Overmind now before the group.

The Abomination Overmind reared one of its spider-like appendages slowly. Aiden blinked for just a moment as a ball of magical energy, about the size of a basketball, appeared at the tip of the appendage.

"GET OUT OF THE WAY, NOW!" Theresa shouted.

The shout was so sudden that Aiden, Liza, and Aello each winced in surprise from it. Not wasting time, they jumped away from the spot, following the dragons, Ryan and Kali as the magical ball made contact with a piece of debris.

It was instantaneous.

The explosion was massive, blowing away anyone who hadn't managed to dive far enough. The room shook, debris tumbled from above as the light blinded everyone. As the dust settled, a massive crater appeared behind where the heroes had just stood.

"U-Unreal." Aiden managed to breathe out. That alone proved to be a difficult task as his entire body was now trembling in fear. "T-T-That...that attack was so small but it had that much destructive power?"

He stared back at the Abomination Overmind, it stood on its spider-like legs staring down at the group with malevolent filled eyes. Whatever sentience there seemed to be within the Shadow Demon leader was now long gone. It only had one objective now.

Kill.

Aiden felt himself weakly standing back up, his legs trembling in fear from the overwhelming power the Abomination Overmind held. A part of him dared to compare its power to that of Queen Lilith's own magic. Unlike the docile harpy queen though there was no chance in getting out of a fight against this monstrosity.

"*Rexkin*, what do we do?" Seamus asked. "Without our true forms, this fight will be a thousand times more difficult to win."

Theresa spun Snow and Fire around in both of her hands momentarily as she stared down the approaching Abomination Overmind. Their options were limited.

"We need to even the playing field." Theresa finally replied. "If it made sure that our power was limited to keep us from being in our true forms then our best chance at winning this battle is to force it to use a tremendous amount of power." Kali shook her head at Theresa's suggestion.

"Easier said than done, lizard. Abomination Overminds have a nearly infinite pool of magical energy."

"Well like Seamus said, our options are limited." Theresa replied as her two swords fused together to form Snowfyre once more. "If we fail here, the Academy falls, and the whole world will become a Shadow Demon's nest!"

The Abomination Overmind let out another unholy screech as its large spider like appendages twitched with intense power. Without a second of delay the disgusting demon lowered itself down onto the ground as its extra legs pointed at the group once again. Several more basketball sized magic balls formed at the tips before they fired out at them.

Garrett's eyes narrowed as he took his mighty great axe and swung it towards one magic ball. His weapon couldn't cut through the blast, but he was able to deflect it away into another part of the room. Just like before the attack exploded the moment it made contact with the wall.

Aiden felt himself almost lock up in fear as one of the attacks flew towards him. If it made contact with a part of his body it would explode. His left palm began to burn considerably once more as he felt what magic he had left form there. He glanced to Kali once more to see if she had used any magic herself. Just like before, she pointed a finger at him. The lamia demon grinned at him the moment he noticed her.

"Come now, mortal. Do try to make this interesting before you die."

Aiden just glared at her before aiming his left arm towards the Abomination Overmind's attack. It was for the briefest of moments, but Aiden felt the surge of the fire magic form as he shouted 'Flarnea' as it effortlessly erupted from his hand right at the Shadow Demon's attack.

Even with the power of Kali's magic enhancements the

Flarnea beam was barely enough to beat the Abomination Overmind's attack back. Aiden felt himself digging his feet into the ground as the magic orb slowly began to gain momentum over Aiden's Flarnea. Sweat ran down Aiden's forehead as the Abomination Overmind's attack gained in power over his Flarnea beam.

"D-Dammit!" He managed to swear as the orb nearly enveloped his attack. "It's too much!!"

"Not while I still breathe!" Aiden turned towards the source of the voice and noticed Ryan standing tall.

His staff in hand the eldest son of the Grand Mage began chanting. As he did, Aiden noticed a strange white aura of sorts rising around Ryan's body. As Ryan finished his chant, the staff he held in his hand shone brightly with an immense power. With no time to waste, Ryan pointed his staff right towards the orb and called out the spell's name.

"Bolt of White Light!"

The spell flew out of the top of his staff at an incredibly speed to the side of the magic orb that was very close to overpowering Aiden's Flarnea. At first Aiden couldn't tell what the spell looked like initially but the moment it struck the Abomination Overmind's orb he could see it clearly. Just as Ryan had called it, the attack was a large white lighting bolt blast with a loud crackling sound.

Aiden didn't have long to admire the pretty color of the attack though as it forced itself through the orb within a short time frame. The force of the magic lightning caused the orb to boil momentarily before exploding away from the group.

"Even with Kali's magic enhancements, the Flarnea was barely able to hold that attack back..." Liza managed to sputter out. "J-Just how strong is this thing?"

"Bah!" Kali scoffed. "You make it sound as though a perfect being like myself, is below this crazed Abomination Overmind. You know nothing of what real power is, small mortal."

"I don't see you trying to help us here you know!"

"Knock it off!" Seamus shouted to them. "We're in the middle of fighting for our lives here and the last thing we need is you two starting a cat fight!"

As he was yelling the Abomination Overmind let out another ear piercing screech of unholiness before taking a single step. Aiden couldn't even blink at the sudden speed erupting from the demon's body. In an instant it was in front of him and he registered the sudden feeling of a punch in his chest.

Aiden let out a loud gasp of pain from the impact, almost throwing up blood as the metallic taste filled his mouth. Before he could do that the Abomination Overmind grabbed his throat with its spare hand. The demon's weak physique gave the impression that it didn't have any body strength, but that was a perfect disguise.

The iron grip the Abomination Overmind had on Aiden's neck forced him to fight for any breath, however fleeting. He began to feel lightheaded, everything was going dark. It truly looked like it was the end for him in those agonizing seconds.

Just when it looked hopeless, Garrett's left hand grabbed the wrist of the Abomination Overmind, grasping it with incredible force. There was an audible 'pop' sound as Garrett's grip caused the Abomination Overmind to relinquish the grasp it had around Aiden's throat.

This was shortly followed by a bone-chilling shriek of pain from the Abomination Overmind as it grasped its broken wrist. As it backed away from the large dragon its spider like back legs rose up and aimed towards Garrett in retaliation.

The counterattack was swift and deadly as the spider legs jabbed towards Garrett's body with the intent to stab through his body. The tips hit their target, each one stabbing a different part of Garrett's body. The largest member of the Trinity stood his ground however despite each stab hitting a different part of his body. He did grit his teeth in frustration, and pain, as the top two spider legs stabbed right into his shoulders.

As Aiden sat there, recovering from nearly being choked to death, he watched in shock and amazement as Garrett kept the Abomination Overmind's attacks focused on him. The entire time Aiden had known Garrett he had never once liked him. And the feeling was mutual from Garrett. But yet here he was, taking these deadly blows to give Aiden enough time to recover.

The Abomination Overmind drew back its spider like legs one last time as they aimed towards Garrett's heart. With a wordless screech the tips of the legs dived towards the dragon with the intent of finishing him off.

Aiden could have sworn he heard a short scoff escape from Garrett's lips in that one second before it happened. Garrett, despite being a bloody mess, grabbed the four spider legs together with just one hand before their tips could pierce his chest. The Abomination Overmind made another screeching shout as it tried to pull its legs out of his hand, but Garrett refused to let go!

"You seem to rely on these too much, Abomination." He said. Aiden noticed that Garrett's voice had become raspy from the damage he had received from being attacked. "Allow me to show you, what **real pain is.**"

It all happened in an instant, as Garrett with just a simple tug of his left arm was able to rip off the spider legs from the Abomination Overmind's back. The sickening ripping sound exploded through the room, followed by a cry of pain from the Abomination Overmind.

Despite Garrett's impressive feat the controller of the Shadow Demons would not be beaten in such a brutal, but effective, way. After a few seconds the Abomination Overmind stopped screaming, simply glaring at Garrett for what it had done to its back legs. From the stumps of where the legs once were two gigantic bat-like wings grew from the stumps of the legs.

The Abomination Overmind let out a roar mixed with anger and pain as it took to the air above them.

"Gck...damn Shadow Demon." Garrett spurted out. The great dragon fell to one knee as the wounds he sustained finally began to take their effect on his human body. "If it hadn't reduced my power with that shock wave, these gnat bites would be nothing to me..."

"Oh, Honey, don't tell me you've blown your load already," Kali cooed as she slipped her arms around his neck. "I thought you were made of much stronger stuff than this..." she trailed off with a hiss, her tongue flicking across Garrett's cheek. The dragon threw a glare her way.

"I don't remember asking for your opinion, snake," he grumbled.

"I don't recall caring, dear dragon...." Kali retorted with a little laugh.

Aiden felt a bit of his spine shiver at Kali's little laugh. Even when she wasn't intentionally being evil, there were moments when just for a brief second it sounded demonic.

The prime demon turned her head towards Aiden. The small smile was gone as she made eye contact with him.

"Who said you could stare at me, mortal? I'll patch up Big Shot here. Go and attack that pathetic creature above us while I do so."

"You could help you know!" Aiden spat at her as she turned her attention back to Garrett.

Whatever brief annoyance Aiden had towards Kali disappeared though as the Abomination Overmind held its ever changing hands out towards him. This time the two hands took the shape of what looked like demonic versions of dragon heads before they unleashed a torrent of black flames at him. Aiden was quick to counter though as he fired out a powerful Flarnea attack at the flames. The two attacks made contact with one another before they both exploded harmlessly over the ground.

"Dammit!" Aiden cursed to himself as the Abomination Overmind flew in circles around the group.

The demon's two hands once more changed shape as they took on demonic versions of European dragon heads. The Abomination Overmind made some kind of gurgling noise as the eyes of the dragon heads opened up before streams of black fire spewed from their mouths.

Aiden pulled his left arm back and began to gather enough mana to use the Flarnea spell again. Once he felt the required mana in his arm reach its max potential he released the fire beam towards one of the black fire streams. He was certain that the attack would be enough to destroy the Abomination Overmind's attack the moment they made contact.

To his horror however the black fire didn't immediately die down when it collided with his Flarnea. Instead it began to smoother over the attack as it raced downwards towards his hand.

Nothing Aiden could have done to prepare himself for the pain of the attack would have made it less painful. The Abomination Overmind's fire hurt more than anything he had ever felt in his life before. Every single nerve in his left hand was screaming out in pain as the fire burned into his hand. It felt like his entire body had just been set ablaze just from a single touch from the demon's attack.

"AIDEN!" Theresa screeched out from the right.

The white dragoness rushed to his side, and with the use of her two blades, reflected the black fire of the Abomination Overmind away from him towards a wall. Her usually calm emerald green eyes filled with worry and fury as she turned to her friend.

Aiden screamed louder than he had ever screamed. He dropped Warfang to the ground as he tried to put the fire out on his left hand. But nothing he attempted to do worked. The fire refused to be put out and only seemed to spread further up his left arm.

Just when Aiden thought that he was going to lose use of his left arm forever, Theresa's hands grabbed his left arm in a firm grip. The pupils in her eyes had changed from the usual round sizes to tiny slits. With a hiss from her own lips, she moved her hands towards the spreading black fire.

It looked almost unreal to Aiden, but she had whipped off the fire with nothing but her hands. Aiden could barely see through the hot tears in his eyes but what he did see made him a bit astonished as Theresa simply blew her own fire breath at the black fire on her hands as it was smothered out by her flame.

The white dragoness hissed in pain momentarily as steam rose off her hands. They were not burnt but she did gain scorch marks on the top of her palms. She wasted no time as she turned back to Aiden and gasped.

Unlike Theresa, who got off light with minor burns on her hands, Aiden's left arm had third degree burns. The black fire of the Abomination Overmind had reached up towards his elbow. If Theresa hadn't taken the flame off his arm, Aiden might have burned to death.

"Aiden!" Theresa shouted before reaching towards his left arm carefully. "Oh Gods above…"

Aiden couldn't even give her a verbal response as just the presence of her hands near his arm made him tense in pain as he let out another cry. He got just a glimpse of Theresa in his eyes before glancing down towards his left arm and her hands. He knew that the pain wasn't just going to simply end.

He gave her a short nod and braced himself as she took hold of his arms as gently as she could. Aiden let out another cry of pain when she did, but didn't pull his arm away form her. With the burns he had gained from the Abomination Overmind he was willing to bet that if he pulled his arm away from her it would rip itself off.

Theresa also hissed in pain from the intense heat from his arm. But with a small whisper for Emalla the white dragoness stopped hissing from the pain as the healing magic slowly moved from her palms around Aiden's burnt arm. The magic may not have gotten rid of the pain entirely, but it began to fix the burnt skin on Aiden's arm piece by piece as the burns that were once on his arm began to vanish.

The skin on his left arm had been healed. But it looked raw and bright pink. It wouldn't be long though before not a trace of the burns remained on his arm.

It still hurt like hell though. As useful as Emalla had been in the past to treat any injury he had, it seemed like even its soothing touch wasn't enough to reduce the pain in it entirely. Even Theresa looked like she was in pain. Whether this came from using magic in an exhausted state or from the Abomination Overmind's fire Aiden couldn't tell.

Once the burns had been healed on his arm, Theresa released her grip on him. Steam rose from her palms, as more scorch marks had appeared now. Some of her hands even looked a bit red from the heat that Aiden's left arm had emitted.

"T-Theresa?" Aiden called out to her in apprehension. "A-Are you…"

"I'll be fine…" Theresa responded. Aiden noticed that her voice seemed more hoarse and rough than before. "I've suffered these kind of burns before. They're nothing." She raised her head towards him as her usually calm eyes were soon filled with worry. "What about you? Can you f-feel your arm?"

Aiden have never known Theresa to show fear in her life. This was the same girl he grew up with. The same girl that was willing to face down a roaring demon in the face and not flinch once. For the longest time he believed that there was no possible way that Theresa couldn't know what fear felt like.

"I…I can feel it yeah." Aiden said, trying to move it just a bit. "It's hella sore though."

"That's what happens when you get new skin on your arm via magic, kiddo." Seamus said as he approached them. "Your lucky you didn't lose your entire arm to that fire."

The green dragon glared back up to the Abomination Overmind. Aiden could see the disgust in his eyes. A small puff of smoke escaped from Seamus' nostrils, a trait that Aiden had grown used to seeing from the dragons.

"How dare that thing make a mockery of our fire breath?"

Aiden felt his entire body go numb at the question. The fire that the Abomination Overmind used against him was the very breath of the dragons themselves?

"That was...dragon fire?" He barely managed to ask. Theresa glanced away from him in shame. "That pain, it...it was unbearable!"

"I'm sorry, kiddo." Seamus responded. "I don't have the time to completely explain it, but think of it like this. Our fire breath works two ways, it can burn away at foes and it can smoother over other attacks."

"And right now, we don't have time to chat!" Ryan shouted from behind them as another blast of black fire flew towards the trio.

Seamus' eyes narrowed as he slammed the end of Hurricane into the ground and erected a small barrier in front of them. The barrier was enough to hold the flames back, but the power of these flames was enough to even make him flinch and twitch from the pressure the Abomination Overmind was exerting onto his shield.

His struggle to keep the barrier up did not last long however as Ryan's attack from earlier, the Bolt of White Light, flew towards the Abomination Overmind's right shoulder. The lighting spell was enough to pierce through the shoulder of the demon, causing it to recoil badly as its right arm jumped backwards. The dragon right hand aimed towards the ceiling and unleashed a black fireball that exploded when it made contact.

A small ray of light cut through the ceiling. The outside world was beginning to seep through the building as the battle raged on with the Abomination Overmind. Ryan cursed under his breath as he turned towards Theresa.

"We can't keep this fight going for much longer! If the damage gets even more out of control the entire Academy could be revealed!"

"You better stop blabbering then!" Mia shouted as she flew towards the Abomination Overmind. Elizabeth and Aello, the latter carrying Liza by her talons, not far behind the guardian.

The Abomination Overmind glanced towards the charging group and held out its left-arm at them. The dragon head shifted into a new shape, one of a long whip, as the demon pulled its arm back and swung with an intense force at them. The whip made a loud cracking sound that rivaled the boom of thunder as it grabbed one of Mia's talons.

The harpy let out a short shriek of surprise as the whip began to pull her towards the Abomination Overmind's body. The great Shadow Demon's right arm now began to mutate into some kind of large spike as it pointed itself right at Mia's stomach.

"Flarnea!"

Aiden watched in shock as a large stream of white fire smacked into the right arm of the Abomination Overmind, forcing the demon to move the arm upwards in an attempt to get away from the hot white flames of the dragoness.

Mia took her chance as she quickly used her freed talon to grab the part of the whip that had encircled around her ankle. With a loud harpy shriek she began to pull at the whip with her sharp claws before it eventually snapped.

As the whip retracted back towards the Abomination Overmind, Liza and Aello passed Mia before the latter quickly threw her friend straight at the demon. Liza shouted loudly as she brought up Gitanel and stabbed the dagger right into the shoulder of the Abomination Overmind with all her might.

Black blood erupted from the wound before the Abomination Overmind's very aura forced Liza to push away from its body. Aello quickly flew up to grab her by the shoulders before she could fall. The two glanced at one another before sharing a short nod as they faced down the Abomination Overmind.

Mia and Gabriella both took the chance to attack the Shadow Demon mastermind now as they dive bombed towards its back. The two of them pointed their claws straight towards where its makeshift wings met its back. Together they let out shrieks of fury, as their talons seemed to shimmer in the darkness.

"No wait!" Aello shouted. But it was too late.

The Abomination Overmind's eyes glinted momentarily as its body began to pulse with power. A black aura erupted around its body, just mere moments before the talons of Mia and Gabriella could pierce into its back. The two harpies had a brief look of horror on their faces before being forced away from the pure pressure the Abomination Overmind was giving off. Just the force of the aura alone slammed the two guardians into the wall of the laboratory with enough force to have incapacitated a mere mortal.

"Mia! Gabi!!" Aello shouted. She barely had enough time to notice that the right arm of the Abomination Overmind had transformed into a falchion sword like appendage. She gasped in shock as the sword swung towards her.

The young princess muttered under her breath for a second as her lance formed in her hand and blocked the strike from the Abomination Overmind's strike. Even her mighty weapon barely seemed to hold back the power of the sword arm as the lance began to tremble from the strength of the attack. Aello gasped as she felt her grasp around her weapon's hilt slip just a bit as the blade of the Abomination Overmind's sword nearly slashed through her weapon.

Liza wasted no time in throwing Gitanel towards the demon. The dagger's shiny blade glinted before piercing the throat of the great Shadow Demon. The Abomination Overmind made a gurgling sound before reaching towards the hilt of

Gitanel and slowly pulled it out. Liza shuddered at seeing her dagger being pulled out as its normal silvery color was now coated in the blood of the Abomination Overmind.

The great demon wasted no time in hurling Gitanel back at Liza. The blood-soaked dagger hissed as it flew, moving so fast it seemed to slice the air around it. Just as it seemed like the blade was about to pierce its owner, Aello appeared, bringing her wing down in front of Liza like a shield. However, harpy wings weren't as resilient as dragon wings. The blade sliced right through Aello's skin and embedded itself in her wing. The harpy princess's cry pierced the air as she collapsed into the blonde athlete's arms.

"Aello!" Liza shouted as the two fell to the ground. The pair landed in a loud 'thud' kicking up dust around them. The harpy princess whimpered, biting back sobs as tear rolled down her cheeks. She struggled to climb to her feet, but the pain left her unable to do so. The harpy princess hissed in pain as she tried to get up, but her body refused to move.

"Dammit all!" Seamus snarled as he swung Hurricane with all his might. A powerful twister formed from the swing and flew towards the Abomination Overmind with skin cutting winds. The leader of the Shadow Demons hovered in the sky, staring down the twister without a hint of fear.

It simply took a deep breath and let out a earth shattering roar that released a terrifying blast of wind that collided with Seamus' spell. The two wind forces clashed for a few moments before the shout over powered the twister and slammed right into Seamus hard enough to send him flying into a nearby wall.

"Seamus!" Aiden shouted. A familiar growl caught his attention from the left.

"Pay attention, whelp!" Garrett roared. "If you weren't focused on him you would see what the damn demon is doing!"

Aiden turned back towards the Abomination Overmind and gasped. It was already on the ground and a large aura of dark magic surrounded its body. For the briefest of moments the ever changing parts of its body stopped taking different forms as the all powerful demon began to pull in all of the power it had within itself.

It all happened so fast that Aiden barely had time to brace for the impact. A massive dome of energy erupted from the Abomination Overmind as it spread like wildfire. Aiden and Theresa both were sent flying the moment the dome touched them. Nearby Ryan had tried to stop the mass of energy from growing by casting a much larger Bolt of White Light into the dome, but the attack of the Abomination Overmind was far too strong for him to stop as it gained momentum and it sent him flying towards the wall as well. The energy from the dome was so great that it even began to overpower the mighty Garrett as it forced him back into a wall as well.

Kali flicked her finger once as a shield erupted around her body. The magic shield did its best to keep the dome from hurting the lamia demon, but it too began to crack under the pressure of the Abomination Overmind's overwhelming energy. Kali hissed in disdain as she was forced to endure the dome's incredible strength before it sent her flying right into Garrett's body.

"KILL!!!" The Abomination Overmind screamed. *"KILL!!!!!"*

In that instant, Aiden's eyes grew heavy and closed. Was this truly the end of it all?

*****

AIDEN GASPED as his eyes opened up once more. He could physically feel his pupils shrink as he realized where he was. It was the laboratory before the Shadow Demon outbreak. It was still as clean as it was before but it seemed grimmer than it was the last time saw it.

In the middle of the room stood Ryan's little brother, Lewis, holding his staff tightly. All around him were three giant glyphs of various sizes. Within the glyphs were several other different shapes as well. They included triangles, rectangles, crosses, diamonds, stars, and hexagons. The first circle contained the hexagons and stars. The second circle had the crosses and diamonds. And the third, and largest circle, held the triangles and rectangles.

Aiden glanced around the room momentarily as he looked for any other mages. There were several of them, each one chanting a spell of some kind. Their chant was so quiet that Aiden couldn't figure out exactly what they were saying. But his attention soon found itself on the tallest mage in the room. Ryan and Lewis' father, Ivan.

The Grand Mage had a scowl on his face as he watched the procedure of the chant. The glyphs around his youngest son pulsed with power as each chant grew stronger and stronger. It didn't take much to see that his patience with the spell was beginning to run thin as he hit the ground with the bottom of his staff.

"Can you tell what they are saying?" He asked his son, motioning to the caged Shadow Demons. Ivan's brows furrowed in anger. "You were able to tap into their language, do it again."

Lewis whimpered in fear as he glanced around at the caged Shadow Demons. The dakgruls, kelgraths, and even the turkskas made no kind of movement. He hissed in pain as a spark of magic from the glyph rose up and scorched his shoulder. The young teenager shook his head to the side as he stared back at his father.

"I...I can't. They're not speaking." He managed to splurt out. The response from Ivan was not a pleasant one.

"Try. Harder." He ordered. Lewis flinched a bit in fear.

"D-Dad, I-I'm honestly trying to-" Lewis started, but a lighting bolt from Ivan's staff cut him off as it hit the ceiling of the laboratory.

"You are not trying hard enough!" Ivan snapped. "You

somehow were able to understand that damn cat in just a few seconds. You managed to break through a barrier we have been trying to achieve for months! Now try, **again**."

What Ivan said next made Aiden's stomach twist in an a sickening knot.

"Or you will always be a failure."

Aiden felt his mouth going dry watching the scene play out in front of him. If Lewis could turtle up at the very sound of his father's harsh tone he would. The young mage glanced back to the caged demons once more. There was an audile swallow from his throat as he held his hand out towards the cages. Aiden could see Lewis' body trembling in fear as a small ball of white light formed in the palm of his right hand.

The caged shadow demons at first did not react to the magic he was casting. A look of dread filled Lewis' eyes. The young mage whimpered as he desperately pointed his hand at the closest dakgrul. Aiden watched in shock as Lewis' eyes flashed with a blue white light.

"Turn." He ordered. His voice meek and timid. The dakgruls at first just made some kind of noise, as if it was scoffing at Lewis, before turning away. Lewis, in an act of desperation, spoke out once more. "**Turn**." He ordered, his voice becoming deeper in the process.

This is when all Hell broke loose.

One dagrul had turned to face Lewis when he gave the order. It stood up slowly and made a low growling sound at Lewis, but that growling soon came to an abrupt halt when it spotted the light in Lewis' palm. The cat like shadow demon jumped to its paws and slowly began to move forwards the cage to face Lewis. Behind it many more of its kind joined the dakgrul. As if they were in a hypnotized trance.

In the corner of Aiden's eye he spotted Ivan grinning. Lewis, now filled with a new confidence, turned towards the kelgraths' cage. The young mage once again barked his order to the shadow demons, which resisted at first but they too eventually fell in line.

Lewis turned to the turkskas' cage and ordered them to look at him as well. The demonic worms let out a pained hiss of anger as they turned towards him.

"Well done, Lewis." Ivan praised his younger son, all the while clapping his hands slowly. "You've done it. You've discovered the answer."

Several mages began to clap, most half heartedly, at the achievement. The smallest of confident smiles grew on Lewis' lips at the praise he received from his peers and father. But no one would have expected that what should have been the greatest achievement for the Academy would turn into the greatest of all nightmares.

One of the glyphs stopped glowing momentarily before it began to change colors in rapid succession. Lewis blinked in shock as the the second glyph began to change color as well before the third and final glyph joined the previous two in changing colors as an immense amount of magical energy began to grow out of control.

Several mages rushed towards the glyphs in an attempt to regain control of the magic. But the energy that the glyphs were giving out were too much as they forced them away with just a simple push of power.

"D-Dad! What's going on?!" Lewis cried out. Ivan gritted his teeth as he turned to look at the rest of the mages.

"Don't just stand there you fools! Get in there and regain control of the glyphs!" He ordered.

At the order of the Grand Mage the rest of the mages rushed towards the glyphs in an attempt to regain control. As this was happening, the Shadow Demons began to make loud roars and noises. Some of them even trying to break free from their cages. Lewis closed his eyes tightly as he grabbed the side of his head with one hand.

As the Shadow Demons roared the glyphs below Lewis' feet continued to spiral out of control. Each time the mages tried to regain control of the energy they were created with a jolt of lighting from the glyphs. Some ended up dying from the pure shock of power from the glyphs' uncontrollable power. Finally, a jolt of lighting smacked Lewis right in his heart. The young mage's eyes shrunk in fear and pain as the magic of the glyphs poured into his body.

"Lewis!!!" Ivan shouted. The latter turned back towards the Grand Mage, his eyes filled with terror.

"D-Dad I-I..." Lewis stammered as the symbols of the glyphs appeared over his body. Hot tears ran down his cheeks as his body jolted. "I can't...s-stop!"

"Dammit, Lewis!" Ivan snarled. "You will regain control of the magic of the glyphs and you will stop this madness!"

Nearby, the Shadow Demons were slowly starting to destroy their cages with their repeated rammings. Not too far from them the sleeping Kali began to stir as well. The more violent the Shadow Demons became the more power was poured into Lewis' body. The young mage fell to his knees as the immense power began to seep out of his eyes as rays of energy now.

Swirls of dark magic began to form over Lewis as the darkness spread like wildfire over his body. The last word Lewis was even able to scream out as the magic overtook his body sent shivers down Aiden's spine.

"KILL!!!!"

That very shout alone was enough to break the cages that held the Shadow Demons as pools of darkness began to form on the floor of the room. Now free to do what they wished, the Shadow Demons rushed out of their cages towards the mages. Several of the dakgruls had already pounced on the poor souls that were close enough to them before they began to bite down and slash at their bodies. Kelgraths rammed their tusks into mages that were foolish enough to get close to them. And the turkskas had burrowed their way into the ground to begin their strikes.

Nearby, Ivan used his staff to destroy five dakgruls that tried to get close to him and any mage that was smart enough to run. The Grand Mage hissed in disdain as he watched what used to be his youngest son float into the air as the dark magic began to take a spherical shape. His eyes filled with anger and disgust he turned towards the mages that were still trying to subdue the escaped Shadow Demons.

"Retreat! All of you!" He ordered. "Get all the students out of the classrooms and towards the Grand Hall! Move!!!"

The last thing Aiden saw of this vision was the sight of fleeing mages as the Shadow Demons slowly began to take control of the laboratory while pools of darkness opened up and more of their kind joined into the fray.

*****

Aiden gasped as his eyes opened. Now he understood everything that had happened. Slowly he rose up from where he was laid, right beside Theresa, who was in pain. Aiden glanced around the laboratory. All around him his friends laid in pain from the overwhelming power of the Abomination Overmind. Seamus was sprawled on the back of his dakgrul, who just like him had taken a nasty hit from the dome. The harpies and Liza were gathered together in one spot, each one trying to help the other stand up before succumbing to the pain that rippled their bodies.

Not far away from Seamus was Ryan. The eldest son of the Grand Mage had taken a blow to the head as blood ran down past his bangs. His body twitched a bit as he tried to lift himself up, but he slumped down to the ground in pain. An audible grunt escaped his lips to signify that he was still alive.

Garrett and Kali had gotten off the lightest compared to the rest of the team. Kali, who had hidden behind Garrett's back, had several scrapes on her legs and arms. But to a Prime Demon like herself these scrapes were nothing. Garrett had several cuts and gashes on his arms, legs, and across his cheeks. Aiden had to guess that he had been hit by some sharp debris that had flown past him. Blood still ran down his body though as even the great dragon of strength hissed in disdain and anger.

Theresa slowly pushed herself up from where she was with her hands. She glanced back to Aiden, who had taken his time to stand up.

"Aiden..." She barely managed to say. But he didn't respond to her voice as he took one step forward towards the Abomination Overmind. The Shadow Demon's cries were so filled with hatred and rage now sounded completely different to Aiden, who had discovered the truth.

Aiden's eyes were filled with pity for the Abomination Overmind. He shook his head as he continued to walk towards the Shadow Demon leader.

"I understand now." He said, each step he took made his body feel like it was rejuvenating, "Why this all happened. Why I could understand the conversation between Malevo and the kelgrath. Why I saw events that happened in the past. Hell, I even know the true reason why this whole thing even started. I finally understand..."

He stopped the moment he was only a few feet away from the Abomination Overmind's dome of energy. His eyes filled not with anger, hatred, or fear. But sadness. Sadness for the truth.

"I know everything..." Aiden spoke softly as he held Warfang in both of his hands. "And I will end this nightmare for you..."

A warm red light surrounded Aiden's body as the two shoulder pauldrons formed. Aiden glanced around to make certain that no one was watching before he indulged in the power of the armor. It brought a new source of strength to his tired muscles. Even Warfang glowed with a bright golden light as the sword itself seemed to become alive in that very moment.

With a deep breath Aiden held the sword up in front of him and aimed carefully at the Abomination Overmind. The latter let out one last roar of defiance and anger as it released a powerful energy blast from its mouth towards Aiden.

Warfang slowly rose up towards the energy blast. Aiden closed his eyes as he simply waited for the right moment. The sword gave a short pulse of power before a torrent of flames erupted around the blade. He waited for a few more moments before his eyes opened up. Aiden gritted his teeth as he released the Draconic Firestorm straight through the energy blast.

The fiery dragon took form once again and charged towards the Abomination Overmind. For the first time throughout the entire battle with the demon a look of dread filled its eyes as the flames engulfed the Shadow Demon leader. A wailful howl was all that was heard as the mighty dragon flames burnt away at the dark magic of the Abomination Overmind.

As its last cry rang out throughout the hall, a chain reaction to those Shadow Demons still connected to the Abomination Overmind took effect. All over the Academy the demons began to fall like dominos. Some demons fell over dead, some burst into flames, while others just disintegrated into nothing.

The mission had been accomplished.

"Aiden!" Theresa shouted as she ran towards him. By then the shoulder pauldrons had disappeared from his body. Aiden felt his cheeks reddening as she held him tightly. "Don't you ever do something like that again! You still can't control the Draconic Firestorm!"

"T-Theresa, I'm fine, really…" Aiden managed to mumble out. The dragoness ignored him before placing her cheek against his own.

"I don't care. You shouldn't use that spell yet. It is more than you can handle." She frowned as she glanced towards where the Abomination Overmind was. "It's over now…"

For once in his life, Aiden actually had to correct Theresa.

"I don't think so." He said. The white dragoness looked at him in confusion as their friends approached them. "Theresa…I saw it. Everything. The truth about what really happened here, what started all of this."

The team turned their attention where Aiden was looking at. The smoke slowly began to leave as a figure could now be seen directly where the Abomination Overmind once was. Ryan's staff fell to the ground as it made a loud audible clang upon contact.

It was Lewis. Who had curled himself up in a ball, his eyes covered in hot tears as he rocked himself back and forth in place. He spoke only two words, words that would haunt any man to the end of his days.

"Kill…me…"

CHAPTER 19 - THE FATHER'S SINS

"*L*-LEWIS!!!" Ryan screamed. The elder brother ran towards his little brother, gathering him into his arms. The latter flinched a bit as tears ran down his cheeks.

"K-Kill me...k-kill me..." He repeated. His voice weak, trembling, full of fear. "K-Kill me..."

"Shh, it's gonna be okay!" Ryan told his little brother. His own eyes filled with tears as he gently held Lewis. "It's gonna be okay, I'm here now. I'm right here little brother..."

Aello and her harpies covered their mouths with their hands. Liza dropped her dagger. Seamus' eyes filled with disbelief. Garrett snarled in anger. Even Kali looked shocked at the sight before them. Theresa and Aiden just stared at Lewis in disbelief.

He looked so fragile.

From the way he appeared it was clear to all of them that Lewis had gone through all the domains of Hell and back again. His clothes were tattered, his body anorexic, lines under his eyes. Even though the room was quite warm he couldn't stop trembling. Tears ran down his cheeks as he desperately clung to Ryan, repeating the same words over and over. Kill me.

"It's gonna be okay...it's gonna be okay." Ryan gently rocked Lewis back and forth.

A new voice broke the silence.

"So, you were finally able to do it."

Everyone turned towards the staircase with shock and anger at the Grand Mage, Ivan, walking towards them. The head of the Academy wore a smug expression that became more clear with each approaching step.

"I knew you dragons would be able to do this task. That you would be able to find your way here and destroy the cause of the Shadow Demon infestation." Ryan's eyes snapped open as he glared at his father.

"Dad! What is the meaning of all this?!" He demanded. "What did you do to Lewis?! Why was he the Overmind?!"

Ivan glanced at his eldest son before turning his attention to Lewis. A look of displeasure crossed his face.

"So, you found your brother?" He asked.

"Cut the crap!" Aiden shouted. "I saw it all, you sick bastard! I saw what you were doing here!"

Aiden felt his own eyes well up in angry tears as he glared at the Grand Mage. His sword arm trembled in fury, while the rest of his body shook with anger.

"You were trying to find a way to control the Shadow Demons! You were experimenting on them! You tried to find a way to control them without any repercussions and when your youngest son revealed that he could understand what they were saying, you sacrificed him for your own selfish gain!!!"

Ivan's face remained motionless. Aiden trembled in anger as he continued.

"Don't act like you're not guilty you son of a bitch! I saw it all! Throughout this entire ordeal I was getting visions, dreams, and I was able to understand what the demons were saying sometimes! At first I thought I was going crazy or that they were somehow getting to my head, but now? Now I know why. It was your son calling out for help! To free him from the Hell that you had put him into when the magic you tried to use to control the Shadow Demons went wrong! It transformed him into the Overmind! You turned your own son into a slave of the dark magic!"

Aiden's voice echoed in the room. Ivan stood there, eyes closed as the teen's voice slowly died down. Not far from Aiden was a snarling Seamus, his lips revealing that his teeth had reverted to fangs.

"Ivan…" Seamus growled. "Is it true? Did you allow this? You, the Grand Mage of my Academy, caused this tragedy?"

Ivan let out a long sigh before opening his eyes. The Grand Mage turned to face the group. His eyes steely and cold.

"Yes. I am the one who made this happen." He said, clenching his fists. "And I do not regret it."

"You don't regret turning your own son into a living experiment?" Kali asked, her tongue escaped through her lips as she began to retake her true form. "And humans think we demons are monsters."

"I see that you are free, Prime Demon. It's interesting that a creature of your stature would bother being a part of this group."

Kali hissed at Ivan, but her hissing came to an end when Garrett pulled her by the wrist. The Grand Mage glanced back to his sons. Ryan was holding Lewis close to him as his younger brother trembled like a leaf in the wind. Ivan shook his head for a few seconds before speaking.

"I do not take joy in what I did." He said. "But you must understand, I had good intentions."

"Intentions?!" Aello shrieked. "Isn't Lewis your son?! You were supposed to protect him, make him feel safe! That's what a parent does for their child isn't it?!" Everyone watched as Aello's eyes filled with tears. The harpy princess clenched her fists back and forth as her talons dug into the ground below her.

"But instead you put your own child through a terrible ordeal!

What kind of parent does that?! He's your flesh and blood isn't he?! How could you subject him to such a thing?!"

"P-Princess please…" Mia begged, but Aello paid no mind as she continued.

"My people have been portrayed as monsters, as cautionary tales to your kind ever since the days of the Ancient Kingdoms! But we never would subject our own daughters to being used as an experiment for some sick gain like you used your own son for! How can you even call yourself a father?!"

Ivan did not respond to her, but simply stared at his two sons. The Grand Mage let out a long sigh and shook his head.

"You have no idea what it's like." He slowly spoke, each word filled with venom, "To be gifted with something as incredible as magic, but then be told there are limitations of what you can and cannot do."

"That's no excuse!" Seamus shouted. "The rules of the Academy were set for a reason, Ivan!"

"Set by you and men who died long after you left this place." Ivan said coldly. "Rules I have lived by for all my life. Obeying them like some kind of trained animal. Never allowed to explore outside the rules, to see what truly could be done with our true potential."

Ivan flicked his wrist and a magic tome floated towards him. He slowly took the tome in his hands, turning the pages to the section on the Shadow Demons. He scoffed.

"Demons, Shadow Demons, and Prime Demons. Monsters they're often called. You and the old masters said that they were beings that take control of the mind of the mage and use them for their own personal gain. Through the means of the dark arts." Ivan slowly turned a page to a spreadsheet on the Overmind demons. "But I know that these facts are wrong, Dragon of Magic. I have seen the kind of control one can hold over demons."

The realization of what Ivan meant hit Aiden like a ton of

bricks. He clenched his left hand as he glared at the Grand Mage. He could feel the anger inside his chest begin to boil like molten lava.

"You talked to Dimitri, didn't you?" Just even saying the name of Raven's master made him feel like he was spitting bile. Ivan's eyes shimmered at the name before he turned his head to Aiden.

"You know him?"

"We've run into him a couple of times before." Aiden's voice was filled with venom. "But what does he have to do with this?" Ivan gave a short laugh.

"Dimitri used to be a professor at this Academy. One of the brightest. I was a student here when he first arrived as a small boy. He came from Russia, not certain what part of it though, he never spoke of it. But through his years as he moved from student to master, he always showed some kind of interest in demons and the dark arts. This was unusual since all of the students at this place are taught from day one to never ask about the dark arts, much less indulge in them. I always thought it was because he was such a curious student."

Ivan sighed as he closed the tome before continuing his story.

"Over the years, Dimitri began to change. He went from asking random questions to secretly studying the dark arts. He nearly got caught a couple of times, but this did not deter him. He wanted to learn and he did exactly that. I like to think he stopped studying the dark arts the day he became a professor."

Ivan gave a short laugh as he placed the tome down on the ground before him.

"He approached me and another associate of ours when he believed he had found a way to control demons without falling victim to the seductive powers of the Dark Arts. We initially brushed it off as a farce.

History had taught us that no mage could control demons. But that day, he completely shattered history - he had control

311

over a demon. Using his own free will." Ivan smiled slightly. "It was stunning. Our darkest fear was not real."

"That's a load of crap." Seamus snarled. "Not only is that a direct violation of the rules of this Academy it also would have set off alarms designed to sense dark magic being used."

"I thought the same thing, Seamus. So did my associate. But I tell you this - what he did that day was real. The Demon obeyed his every command. There was no trace of dark magic or mind control at all. It was a hundred percent under his control. It did not break lose, or make demands! It was groundbreaking!" Ivan's voice turned sour. "But my associate took the same position you have taken. He deemed the discovery too dangerous. He believed any mage with that kind of power would not only attempt to rule over all the other demons but would also attempt to control the modern world. He ordered Dimitri to dismiss the demon, and to never speak of the matter again. For a while Dimitri obeyed the rules."

The Grand Mage sighed.

"But then came the day he took a student under his wing. A young boy with jet black hair."

"Raven." Theresa spit out. "We're well aware of him."

"Yes, Raven. He was so filled with hatred and distrust that I'm amazed he stayed with us as long as he did. I think it was because Dimitri took an interest in him. He said it was because he saw himself in Raven's eyes. But I think the truth of the matter is that he saw a pupil that could take advantage of the dark arts and use it to his own whim. Just like he could."

An audible hiss of disgust escaped from Kali's lips.

"You spell weavers, you're all the same. Always thinking that just because you can access some power, that you can control it. Is it any wonder that this mortal and his student left this boring Academy."

"I can not say for certain why they left the Academy, but it was around that time that I began to wonder. What if Dimitri was right?" Ivan frowned. "What if the old rules were always holding us back from achieving true greatness? I had to know. But unfortunately, the research that Dimitri did was destroyed, or he took it with him. Either way, I was left with nothing and had to start at square one."

"Do you mind telling me how you were able to summon Shadow Demons in the first place?" Seamus growled. "The last time I checked, there was no tome explaining the process."

"Ah yes, that was a problem I must admit. It took me months of scouring through old documents and scrolls in the library, to see if there was any clue. But then, as if it was placed before me, I found it. This very tome." Ivan gestured towards it. "It was if someone had left it there for me to discover. With the secrets within, I could finally begin to understand."

"Understand WHAT?!" Aello shouted. "That you are a crazy evil man that would do harm to his own kin?!?"

Ivan gave the young harpy princess a dirty look as he hefted his staff and pointed it towards her. Mia and Gabriella, despite their injuries, moved in front of their princess with snarling lips. After a few seconds the Grand Mage scoffed, pulling his staff back up.

"If I wanted to, Harpy, I could blast you into ashes with the simple flick of my wrist. But that'd be a waste of my power." He turned back to where Ryan and Lewis were as he continued. "There is one thing that you are wrong about though. I never wished harm on my own sons. They are my flesh and blood, my legacy to this world. To me, they are the most precious things within these walls."

"Then why...." Ryan stammered as his body shook in anger. "Why would you force Lewis to go through with this? Why would you make him into that...that THING?!"

"...You don't understand." Ivan replied. At this Ryan jumped up and stared his father down. "Understand what?!" Ryan's eyes were filled with angry tears. "That you forced your own son into an experiment?!"

"It's not as if I planned for this to happen, Ryan." Ivan frowned. "I wanted to find a way to control the Shadow Demons without use of dark magic. That is what I set out to do. I brought those who believed that we could achieve this goal into my fold as he began our experiments. For months we failed, trying to command the Shadow Demons without the use of dark magic. But Lewis…"

He trailed off for a few moments before staring at his youngest son. A somber look filled his face.

"Lewis was able to do what we could not do. He was able to understand one of the Shadow Demons. I don't know how he was able to do it. But Lewis' magic has always been special compared to all the other students. Something about him makes him so vastly different from the others that he can understand Shadow Demons. With that potential we could forever change the way we look at magic! He may not be the brightest or most skilled mage, but my son's unusual talents have paved the way for all Mages. "

"And what gave you the right to force him into this?" Theresa asked as she stepped up now. "What kind of father would go and put his own son through a disgusting experiment such as this?!"

Ivan's hands began to tremble. Whether it was from anger or sadness, Aiden could not tell. And quite frankly, he did not care. Much like the others he could not see the rational reasons behind all of this. He was too furious to even notice that he had clenched his left hand so hard that blood was pouring out of his fingers.

"It's not as if I wanted to use him right away." Ivan said with a calm town. "I gave him the option of helping with my experiment. Since he was able to make some form of contact with the demons, I thought it would be best if he helped finished what I started."

"Is that why you called him a failure to his face?" Aiden asked, his tone much darker than before. "At first I was confused when I was able to understand the Shadow Demons, and why I saw visions of what this Academy was like before the Shadow Demons took over, but I understand now. It was Lewis trying to tell me the truth. I saw his memories, I saw what you made him do. You made him feel so small and insignificant because he wasn't doing it right!"

Ivan turned to Aiden with a furious expression. "I had no choice! You have no idea how long Project Overmind took just to research! Without Lewis' strange ability to connect to their minds, we wouldn't have been able to learn that there could be established contact!" He gestured towards his youngest son. "Lewis may not be the most powerful mage, the least talented, but he has a gift. A gift that I can use to make things easier for my people! If my work with the Overmind Project can help us learn the secret to controlling demons without the need of the dark arts, or even those bands of magic you have over that Dakgrul there, then I will take whatever path I must in order to ensure that we can maintain control over them!"

A force of wind began to pick up around Seamus' body. His pupils turned into tiny slits of anger as his draconic powers began surge. If his tail had reappeared behind him, it would be lashing back and forth in anger. As he stared down at Ivan his fingernails began to grow into sharp claws.

"That's your reasoning?" He asked in a dark menacing tone. "You sought to control the demons without the use of dark arts? What did you gain from this experiment, Ivan? There are many mages, who were your students and professors, now dead within the halls of your school. And now your son, he's scarred for life. Can you really rest easy at night knowing that you might as well have sacrificed your son's happiness for your own pathetic goals?"

Ivan went silent at this question. He glanced back to his youngest son, who was still curled up in a fetal position as he shook his body back and forth in fear. His eyes filled with tears as they poured down his cheeks like a waterfall.

"Kill me...k-kill me..." He whimpered. "S-So many...s-so many voices..." As Lewis whimpered in fear, his father turned away from him.

"...Do not speak to me as if I do not know what I have done, Dragon of Magic." Ivan closed his eyes. "It haunts me, every moment within these walls, what I did haunts me. My actions were unethical, unforgivable, and I nearly lost my youngest child in the process. No, not just my son. I nearly lost the entire Academy. And now, I have potentially scarred Lewis for the rest of his life."

Aiden blinked in surprise at the admission from Ivan. At first it sounded like he was not going to take any of the blame for what he had caused his youngest son to go through. Aiden could feel himself slowly calming down, but he continued to watch Ivan like a hawk.

The Grand Mage reopened his eyes as he stared down at the ground.

"But...I've come too far to give up now. It's still possible, to achieve what I set out to do. To find a way to control the Shadow Demons."

"You don't know when to give up, do you spell weaver?" Kali asked with a disgusted hint. "You plan on reusing your precious little brat to reignite the experiment. Well, I can tell you this, it will never work. No matter how many attempts you make, what happened here will happen again."

"No! No it can work!" Ivan shouted as he turned to the group. "I know what went wrong, what I need to do! I won't even have to use Lewis again! He'll be safe from them from now on! I can assure you that what happened here won't happen again!"

"Father, are you even hearing what you're saying?" Ryan asked with bile in his throat. "You plan on starting this crazy experiment again after it cost us nearly everything we have!" He gestured to the laboratory. "Look around at what's happened! Not just this room, but all of the Academy! You've jeopardized our entire existence! You put your own flesh and blood on the line, allowed him to become an Overmind, and you want to continue with this grand delusion that you could control Shadow Demons?! What more do we have to sacrifice until you achieve this goal?! They almost got out! What's stopping them from getting out if you attempt this again?! Our barriers were almost broken!"

"Barriers can be refortified. We can learn from our mistakes. We can prevent all this slaughter from ever happening again!" Ivan argued back.

"It will ever happen again!" Seamus shouted out as he swung his staff once, a gust of wind smacked Ivan in the cheek hard. "Grand Mage Ivan, as the Spellweaver, I hereby strip you of your title as the head of this Academy. You are to step down, effective immediately."

Any sensible person would not challenge a direct order from Seamus. But Ivan had lost all sense of himself and he retaliated with his own wind attack at the dragon of magic. The wind forced Seamus to brace himself as it pushed against his body.

"I will not give up my position! Nor will I give up my goal!" He shouted. "I will finish what I started! I will find out how Dimitri can control the demons without being controlled by them! Even if it means I must use my sons to further my project!!!"

At that moment, the anger inside Aiden exploded. Not waiting for a word from any of his friends he charged at Ivan in fury. The pain he felt from his fight with Lewis had faded away like a bad memory as he tackled Ivan to the ground.

The Grand Mage let out a surprised yelp as the two of them crashed to the ground. Aiden, now sitting on top of Ivan's chest, dropped Warfang to the side as he pulled his right fist back and threw a powerful punch into Ivan's cheek. There was an audible gasp from Liza as Aiden punched Ivan again, this time with his left hand.

"How. Dare. YOU?!" Aiden shouted in anger as he began to rotate which hand was punching Ivan. "You used your own son in an experiment, you nearly lost your Academy, and you want to continue these sick experiments by acting like they never happened?!"

"Aiden! Stop it!" Theresa ordered. For the first time in his life Aiden disobeyed her as he continued to punch Ivan over and over again. A fierce fire filled his eyes as each punch was filled with more anger and hatred for the Grand Mage than the last.

"Lewis nearly died! Hell, he wants to die! And it's all because you brought him into this sick game of yours! You played to his emotions! Called him a failure so he would try harder to impress you!!"

Ivan's face, which was now covered in bruise marks, began to swell from each punch Aiden had thrown. The teenager stopped punching momentarily as he glared down at Ivan.

"You used your own son's talents to fulfill a childish goal! You're not fit to even be in the same room with him!" He reared his right hand back, which was soon covered in magic flames. "I'll make you pay for what you've done to him!"

"AIDEN!" Theresa, Seamus, Liza, and Aello shouted in unison as he threw the punch towards Ivan's face.

Just when it looked like the attack was about to hit its mark, a giant hand grabbed ahold of Aiden's wrist and stopped him. The teenager gritted his teeth as he tried to pull his arm away. He knew who it was that was holding him back.

"That's, enough, whelp." Garrett said with clenched teeth. "You've made your point."

"Like hell I have!" Aiden snapped. "I can see it in his eyes! He doesn't care at all what will happen to this place! As long as he accomplishes his goal, he will continue to experiment with the

Shadow Demons! He needs to be taken care of, right here, right now!"

"Calm down and listen to me - right now." Garrett responded. "The strength you're using it's enough to kill him. I taught you to use this strength to protect others. To keep them safe from monsters like him. But right now you're allowing your anger to cloud your mind."

Garrett slowly pulled Aiden's arm back. The latter tried as hard as he could to fight back against the dragon's immense strength, but even with the new surge of power erupting from his body he could not break free of Garrett's iron grip.

"If you kill him, you will be no better than he is. You'll be even worse. You'll become a true monster."

"And he's not?" Aiden asked as he felt his strength to ebb away. "He's responsible for this Hell on hearth here in the Academy. The blood of innocent mages are on his hands! He has to pay for what he's done!"

"And he will." Garrett replied. He had pulled Aiden's arm back far enough to keep the fist from ramming right into Ivan. "Listen well, whelp. Theresa sees more in you than this. By letting yourself be taken in by anger at what he's done you are no better than him. Do not let his sins turn you into a monster like he is. Be the better human...no, be the better man. Relent. Now."

Aiden could feel his entire body tremble in anger and frustration as Garrett help his right arm in place. If he resisted any longer, there was a good possibility that the dragon of strength would snap his arm in two. But the longer he stared at Ivan, the more he wanted to hit him. He glanced towards the others for a moment. Each of them watching with concerned expressions as his arm hovered over Ivan's face.

When his eyes made contact with Theresa's emerald green eyes though, he felt the anger inside him stop bubbling. Theresa's eyes. They were filled with worry. He could see that she was mentally begging him to stop before he wound up killing Ivan.

Those emerald eyes that were so filled with courage, concern, and happiness.

"...I..." Aiden stammered as he glanced back down at Ivan. "I just..."

"I know. You want him to pay for what he's done to this place." Garrett said as he released Aiden's arm. "But this is not the way. Deep down inside, you know that."

Garrett's words surprised Aiden. From the very beginning of his time with the big dragon all he ever heard from him was how he was not worth his time to train, how he was a whelp, and just how terrible humanity was. But for the first time, Aiden could see that he was just like Seamus and Theresa. He cared for those around him.

"Are you calm now, whelp?" Garrett asked as his tone returned to being flat. "Because you're going to have to get off this slime ball."

Aiden shook his head as he stood up and began to walk away from Ivan. He only took a few steps before the Grand Mage gave a short, almost melancholy, laugh.

"Now I know why you looked familiar." He managed to wheeze out from his mouth. "You were just like the man who forced Dimitri to never speak of controlling demons again. It's almost funny. You followed well into his footsteps."

The Grand Mage's words sent a shiver down Aiden's spine. Something about it, it didn't feel right. He was just like the mage that stopped Dimitri when he lived here? He looked familiar to Ivan? Who was he talking about? The teen began to turn around with the intention of asking the former leader of the Academy what he meant, but Theresa had already grabbed his shoulder.

"Don't Aiden." She told him. "He's clearly no longer in his right mind. With what he allowed to happen in this once grand Academy, I don't think he ever will be again."

Her voice was soft, almost cheerless. They had won a great victory, sure, they managed to stop Shadow Demons from breaking out of the Academy and heading out into the world. But at what cost? As the group began to regather, with Garrett now carrying Ivan over his shoulder, Liza cleared her throat.

"How come Aiden was able to punch the dude?" She asked. "I mean before he was so powerful that he could bend reality to his whim if he wanted to." Seamus gave a long sigh to her question before he spoke up.

"I think in his mind, and possibly what heart he had left, Ivan knew that he was in the wrong. He could have easily overpowered the kiddo if he chose to. But he didn't. A piece of him must of realized that what he did here? It's unforgivable. And he will carry that sin with him till the end of his days."

"Kill me...Kill me..." Lewis' whimper echoed throughout the room. Ryan gently helped his little brother stand up as he holstered one of his arms over his shoulders.

"It's okay little brother...it's okay." Ryan tried his best to reassure him. "We're gonna make everything better now..."

As the group trekked through the stairway that lead to the laboratory and through the destroyed hallways and rooms of the Academy, no one spoke a word. It all felt empty, hollow, meaningless after what they went through.

If there was one word to describe how Aiden felt in that very moment, it was despair. Nothing felt right to him. It was suppose to be a great victory for the team. They may have possibly saved the entire modern world from being overrun by Shadow Demons. But it paled in significance to what he witnessed happening in this place, the path that the Academy's leader took to obtain his personal goals. The innocent lives that were lost due to what Ivan had done. The destruction of their home. It didn't feel like stopping it was something to celebrate.

In the very moment when the team was within sight of the Academy's grand hall the realization hit Aiden hard. The fantasy life that he had always imagined, those games that he played for what must have been endless hours before, the amazing worlds where he wanted to be apart of? He never once took into account how in those worlds, it wasn't fantasy.

To those characters he always admired, from reading books, watching their shows, or even just playing a video game, it wasn't some sort of make believe world. It was real life.

In the end, many of their battles had very bittersweet victories. And that was the only way Aiden could use to describe how he truly felt in that moment. Bittersweet. Lewis' life had been saved, freed from the magic that caused the Shadow Demons to run free. But Ivan's actions had ruined any chance of it ever being a truly happy success.

As the rest of the student body rushed to meet their saviors, Aiden swore to himself that he would never forgive Ivan for what he had done.

No. It's not that he wouldn't ever forgive him. It was that he couldn't ever forgive him. Ever.

"I still can't believe this happened." Ryan said as he watched his father placed in a cell the mages had made to resist any magic. "I would never imagine in a thousand years that my own old man would not only attempt to gain control over demons, but would use his own flesh and blood as a means to do so."

"It's not the first time a person did something terrible in order to achieve his goals." Seamus replied with a frown. "I wish I could tell you that he will recover his sanity, Ryan. But with what he allowed to happen in this place, let alone what he did, he's lucky he isn't facing a Tribunal like in the old days."

Ryan gave a short dry laugh at Seamus statement as he shook his head.

"No offense, Spellweaver, but I'm kinda grateful we don't live in those times anymore. I'd rather not see all the life energy pulled out of my father's body."

"Even with all that he's done?"

"Yes. I know it sounds odd, but I would never want to see my father be turned into a lifeless husk." Ryan's expression turned melancholy as he stared down at the ground. "No matter what, he'll always be my father. And I know that someday he'll realize his terrible mistake. And when that day comes, I hope to God above that we can begin fixing the bridge he's destroyed."

Seamus gave a sigh as he shook his head at Ryan's optimistic approach. The dragon of magic had seen enough similar cases before to know that when a mage lost their mind, they normally weren't given a second chance. But for the sake of his son, he would not mention those cases. How could he do such a thing? He saw the hope in Ryan's eyes. The belief that one day the former Grand Mage could and would redeem himself.

"There is one little problem." Seamus said as he and Ryan headed back towards the main hall. "With your father locked up, the school is without a Grand Mage." Ryan gave another dry laugh.

"The school has a lot more than just that one particular problem, Spellweaver Seamus. It lost a lot of professors, students, and materials needed for learning."

"True, true. But I've been around much longer than you can possibly imagine, bucko." Seamus stopped as they stared out at the students and surviving professors below them.

"The one thing that's never changed since is that humanity always manages to find a way to move on after any tragedy." A small smile replaced his frown as he patted Ryan's back gently. "I think the only person who can truly lead this place now, is someone who dared to stop the madness caused by the Grand Mage. No one else is more suited than you to be the Grand Mage now, Ryan."

Ryan blinked in surprise at Seamus' praise as his cheeks went a bit pink. Clearly he wasn't use to praise by someone who was clearly more skilled at magic than he was. That or his father barely ever gave him any kind of praise.

"I appreciate your high opinion of me, Spellweaver. But I am the son of the man who nearly sent this place into Hell. Why would they trust me when you could be the Grand Mage?"

"Ha. I would make a terrible Grand Mage. Besides, I've already got one group that I gotta stick around with and take care of. Course, I'll be sure to come back and check up on this place more often. I owe that much to the mages I helped start this place with after all."

The eldest son of the previous grand mage frowned as he glanced at the group of students and professors below him. All of them stared back at him with lost and confused expressions. In the middle of the gathered group, his girlfriend gave a small smile when their eyes made contact.

She was the first one to point her staff up in the air. Several more staffs from the student body soon joined her staff in unison. The surviving professors hesitated for a few seconds before they too raised their staffs. Each of the tips of the staffs glowered with a bluish white light that pushed away the grim darkness from Ivan's reign over the Academy.

Ryan sighed before giving a short nod at the mages below him. He sent a short look of confirmation to Seamus, who gave him a thumbs up. Ryan took a deep breath before he addressed the survivors below him.

"My fellow mages. What happened to our fine Academy may go down in the books as the darkest day for us. Our former Grand Mage not only broke the vow to never study the Dark Arts, but he performed one of the most heinous crimes a person could commit. Subjecting his own son to an experiment in an attempt to control demons." There were a few murmurs from the gathered mages as Ryan continued pacing back and forth. "It brought shame down on his name, my name. A name that my little brother and I unfortunately share with him. His actions can never be easily forgotten or forgiven. I know that you are all wondering now what we must do. How do we recover from the

325

greatest tragedy our kind has faced since the fall of the Ancient Mage Kingdom?"

He stopped pacing before taking a deep breath. The mages below watched as Ryan chose his next words carefully.

"Rebuilding will not be easy. We have lost many innocent mages to this dark event, and many good professors valuable to this school. Those of us that are left will be facing the greatest test we'll ever have. Continuing their legacy as students, and teachers of the ways of magic. This will not be simple. It will not be easy, but we have to rebuild this great school that the Spell-weaver and our forefathers created for us. Then we will begin looking for new students. I know that together we'll get through these dark times. This I promise you."

Ryan held his staff in front of him before giving a short smile to the mages below him.

"Will you follow me?" He asked. For the briefest of moments the survivors said nothing. One of the professors stepped forward before speaking out.

"What your father has done, those are his crimes alone. Not yours. You already have proven you are more than capable of succeeding him, young Ryan." He knelt down on one knee before lowering his head. "As far as I am concerned, you have always were meant to be the true Grand Mage of this Academy."

Ryan was flabbergasted as the rest of the survivors began to kneel in respect for their new Grand Mage. He coughed nervously for a few moments before turning to Seamus. The dragon gave a short laugh, nodding his head.

"Like I said, you're the Grand Mage this school needs right now. Look at them. They need a leader they can trust. A leader that saw what went wrong within the halls of their Academy. A leader who will make certain that what happened here never happens again." Seamus smiled as he placed one hand on Ryan's shoulder. "And that, buster, is you. I have a full belief that you will be able to bring this great Academy back to its former glory again."

As the mages all cheered for Ryan to be their Grand Mage, the rest of the group broke up and began talking with one another as they waited for Seamus. Each one had a different take on what had happened.

The harpies were still in shock over what they had just seen take place. No one could fault them for their reactions. They had spent their entire lives in a flock where the most important bonds were between mothers and daughters. There was not a single member of that flock who would even once think about turning on their daughters.

Aello was more bothered by this event than her two guardians. Her entire life she had idolized and loved her mother. She had never once even entertained the thought of her mother taking advantage of her talents like Ivan had done with Lewis. The harpy princess gripped her arms tightly as she stared away from the group.

"How...how can someone be so cruel to their own flesh and blood?" She asked. "Why would a parent turn their child into...into that thing?"

A gentle hand placed itself on her shoulder. She glanced the hand's owner for a moment as her eyes began to fill up with tears. It was Liza. She had a look of distraught sadness on as she gently squeezed Aello's shoulder.

"I wish I could tell you that this never happens..." Liza said softly. "That Ivan is the only rotten apple in the bushel. But the truth is this. There are so many people like him in the human world. Many of them doing things I dare not speak of, but sadly they exist."

The look of horror in Aello's eyes were enough to make any heart break. Liza bit her lip. She was hesitant to speak about this, but dug up enough willpower to do so.

"But even though there are those who treat their children

terribly, or use their children for selfish goals, there are parents who do not do that. Much like your own mother they raise not with fear, manipulation, or anger, but with love, respect, and wisdom. Those are the real parents of humanity, not monsters like that bastard."

Aello sniffled a bit as she placed one hand over Liza's. The harpy princess' body trembled a bit before she spoke out.

"My kind has a phrase for those who treat their offspring like that..." She said, *"Elterak stalo."* Liza noticed that she almost made a gagging reaction to even saying the word. "If I had to do a literal translation of the phrase, it simply means, 'Empty Void.'"

Aello's guardians flinched at the phrase for a moment as the clenched the ground with their talons. It clearly was not a phrase that was spoken often around the den. They glanced away in fear and disgust at the term.

Liza frowned as she gently pulled Aello into a comforting hug. The princess blinked in confusion.

"Your mother would never do what that...monster did." She said. "You know what a true parent's love is like. You and I both know she would never do such a thing."

Aello's eyes teared up a bit as she hid her face in Liza's sleeve. A few hiccups could be heard from the princess.

Nearby Garrett and Kali were in discussion. The prime demon, still in her human form, hissed a bit as several of the survivors glanced at her.

"Stupid spell weavers." She said with a tone of disgust. "It's because of them that I can't get back home. And now they dare to look at me like they have the permission to even stare at my beauty?"

"Shut it woman." Garrett said with a groan. "You are new to them. Many of these mortals have not seen a demon before."

"Prime Demon." Kali responded, her now human tongue trying to flicker between her teeth. "Please keep in mind my rank, lizard. It's very rude to forget important information such as that."

"It's easy to forget such meaningless things like that from your kind." Garrett folded his arms. "But why do you say you are trapped here? If your magic is so great, snake, you should be able to easily escape back to your precious Hell."

Kali scoffed as she placed a hand over her chest at the suggestion. If her tail was still there, it would be coiling in anger and frustration.

"Would that I could, dragon boy. But sadly, not even I have the power to bring a portal to my home world. Not yet anyway."

"And here I thought you were suppose to be this all powerful prime demon that wanted to be praised as some kind of goddesses."

The lamia gave the meanest kind of glare she could muster in her human form at Garrett for that statement.

"How dare you, lizard? I am a goddess while you are nothing but a speck!"

"So you say. But from the looks of it you're stuck here in this world and have no clue as to where to go or even stay." Garrett cracked his neck before continuing. "And unlike your realm, the mortals of this world have no clue about your kind nor about your 'position' as a high ranking demoness. Nor are they aware of the actual gods that have long been forgotten. So if you went spouting your mouth about any of the demon gods or the benevolent gods, you would become an outcast in this world."

"I can handle myself, lizard." Kali hissed.

"Perhaps. But I doubt you know how to truly survive in this world of mortals. You do not know their ways of life, what they do with their spare time, or how their societies work. You're alone here, snake."

A small sneer grew on Kali's face at his words. If she could the Prime Demon would be coiling around herself right now in anger, frustration, and disgust at the truth in Garrett's words.

Her tongue gently slipped through her teeth, as best as it could, as she stared right into the dragon's eyes.

"And what do you suggest then, lizard? That you'll be my protector in this world? Don't make me laugh."

"Hardly." Garrett replied. "You're too much of a liability to this world if you're allowed to roam free. And since the rest of my group here doesn't seem capable of keeping you in check, I'll be the one that will keep an eye on you."

"And just what makes you think that you can do that?"

"You and I share similar views about humanity. They're greedy, weak, and destructive. I keep myself from setting their cities ablaze because I honor my King of old, and my Rexkin. I will stay true to my honor by respecting their wishes and protect them from any harm. You're not going to wander this world free to do what you wish, Kali."

There was a tense moment of silence between the two of them as they exchanged glares. But a sly smile slipped across Kali's lips at Garrett before she laughed ever so softly.

"Oh lizard, you are indeed an interesting one. The same goes to your little group of friends that you travelled with to get to the Overmind. They're actually fun. The most fun I've had in over the last hundred years." She gave a dainty laugh. "How about this, lizard? I'll stick around with your group. Now don't worry I'll behave myself and refrain from showing the pitiful low life humans the punishments they deserve from being in the same presence as myself. However I expect you to realize that I am a hard girl to please."

"And you expect me to worry about that?" Garrett replied with an annoyed look.

"I expect you to keep me entertained."

The two of them shared one more glare of mutual dislike for one another before giving a short nod. It wasn't exactly the best way to start off a new friendship between two beings but for now it would have to do. The most important thing was that they established some kind of understanding about how things were going to work.

Nearby, sitting on a small stool, Aiden was distraught over the events of what had happened. The horrors he had seen in the Academy etched into his mind. He didn't know if he could ever be rid of them. The dead bodies of the students and staff members that weren't fortunate enough to survive. The terrifying demons that roamed the hall. The stains of blood that were splashed on the walls of the hallways. What Ivan had done to his youngest son and the rage that Aiden had felt when he lost all control in that one moment.

How could he ever move on, after everything he'd seen?

His body couldn't stop trembling as the events kept playing in his head over and over. The battles. The demons. The close calls with death. But the one image that seemed to be permanently burned into his mind was the state they had found Lewis in. How skinny he was from being the source of the Overmind's power. How his eyes were wide as dish plates and that he repeatedly asked to be killed over and over again. It would have driven anyone else insane just thinking about it.

Aiden felt like that he was going to go insane as well. His mind began reeling over and over with the realization that everything that had just happened in the Academy did not result in a happy ending. The number of the mages had gone down considerably, Ivan had been locked away for his sins, and Lewis was going to be placed in some kind of special care in an attempt to fix the psychological damage inflicted on him by the grand mage.

The trembling from his body continued to grow more frequent now as the thoughts refused to leave him alone. Try as hard as he could, Aiden was unable to push them away. He could feel his blood begin to boil over in a mix of emotions that he didn't think could rush together. Anger. Fear. Sadness. Confusion. All these emotions just merged together in a way that he swore he never imagined they could.

In the moment when it felt like it was going to become too bleak for him, a gentle hand reached his cheek and stroked it. The boiling mix of emotions that Aiden had felt before began to diminish. He had become quite familiar with the soft skin of Theresa's human form lately when he felt weak or angered. His eyes began to close as Theresa's hand gently stroked his cheek.

"Oh Aiden…" She said in a quiet voice. "I know what you must be feeling right now after what we just went through."

"Do you?" He asked, his voice sounding a bit darker than it usually was. "Do you really know what it is that I am feeling right now?" His eyes opened up slowly as he stared into her own emerald green eyes. "Do you know what it's like to feel like you had completely failed?"

"Failed?" Theresa blinked in confusion. "What are you talking about? We managed to stop a great disaster from breaking out."

"You know what I'm talking about." Aiden replied as he unconsciously clenched his hands. "We may have stopped the Shadow Demons breaking out of this place and spreading across the world, but was it worth it in the end?"

He stood up from where he sat, but kept his head hung low in place.

"When I think about what we just faced in there, I can't help but feel like it was for nothing, Theresa. The dead bodies of the mages that were slaughtered by the Shadow Demons, the husks that were used for those that emerged from chrysalides, the blood on the walls, and Lewis' state, I can't help but feel that what we just went through and what we just did was nothing. We failed to make everything okay. Everything is wrong. The mages are small in number, the former Grand Mage is insane, and Lewis may never recover!"

He angrily kicked the stool he was sitting on in a bout of frustration and anger. Tears forming in his eyes at the thought of them being unable to craft a happier ending for the Academy. Once again his body trembled with a mix of emotions.

"How can we call this operation a success when what we went through lead to nothing but one bad reveal after another? It shouldn't be a success unless we managed to not only stop the demons but were able to save everyone?"

Theresa let out a small sigh of sadness at his question. The white dragoness reached back to her long flowing hair and began to tie it up in a ponytail once more. She carefully chose her words to answer his question completely.

"I told you before. I know exactly how you're feeling, Aiden." She said, "The frustration, the anger, the sadness, and the doubt you're feeling, I've felt it all before. Long before I became Rexkin I went on several missions like this. Where we planned to save all the lives that we could and that things would be okay in the end. The first mission I went on? Every single person that we were trying to save died. I was so distraught that I nearly quit being a fighter because I could not believe that we were unable to save even a single life."

Theresa took his hand in her own before squeezing it with care.

"My own Rexkin, a powerful warrior in his own right that I thought would never falter, was the one that taught me two valuable lessons that day. Sometimes you cannot save everyone and plans do not go the way they should." She gently pulled his hand up and held it in place as she squeezed it ever so gently. "Those are lessons I had yet to teach you myself. And I regret that you had to learn them in this way. I should have told you a long time ago that even dragons do not always succeed in every mission they undertake."

She let out a sad sigh at the bitter memory from her ancient past. A small smile slipped onto her lips once more though as she stared right into Aiden's eyes.

"I thought just like you did when I was younger, Aiden. That we could save everyone in a mission, it's a nice ideal to have. But the truth of the matter is that you can not predict how a mission will go. Not fully at least. Things will happen that you just can not control. You can spend hours coming up with the perfect plan that you believe will end with everything ending with no innocents lost. But truthfully anything can happen and usually does."

She gently placed her forehead against his own, despite having to stand up on her toes to do so, before giving a short laugh.

"I know it's hard to come to terms with this reality, but in many ways this was more of a victory than it was a complete failure my friend."

"But…"

"How can I count it as a victory?" She finished for him. "It's simple Aiden. Not only did we managed to keep the Shadow Demons from breaking out into the world but we managed to save the mages that weren't slaughtered by them and were able to save Lewis from being the Overmind for the rest of his life." Theresa gave the same warm genuine smile that she was known for before continuing. "It may take him time to recover, and he may never be the same again, but you spared him from a far worse fate than death."

A small smile finally crept to Aiden's lips at her words. Once more her natural talent at being able to cheer him up had come into play. He still felt bad that they hadn't been able to save every person that had died in the halls, or even managed to make Ivan fully understand the error of his ways, but she was right. They did managed to get the best outcome they could have from what they went through.

"Thes? Thanks." He said with a grateful heart. Theresa smiled before ruffling his hair up a bit.

"You're welcome. Now stop being all broody. We already have Garrett doing that for the group, and the last thing I need is you doing the exact same thing."

"H-Hey, watch the hair!"

"I hate to interrupt," Ryan said as he approached now. "But I do wish to speak with all of you before you leave us."

"Ah, Grand Mage Ryan." Theresa said. "That's a title I think I can get used to saying from now on." Ryan blushed a bit in embarrassment.

"Please, it's still all too new to me to actually be called that just yet." He scratched the back of his head a bit. "Besides, you were the ones who pretty much did everything in the final moments of our mission to secure the Academy."

"Don't sell yourself short, slick." Liza said, with Aello and her guardians not far behind her. "If it wasn't for you we would have bitten the dust quite a few times. Your magic gave us an edge."

"Ahem." Kali scoffed. "His spells are powerful, but do keep in mind who was the one who truly helped all of you be able to succeed."

"Quiet snake."

Ryan rolled his eyes as Garrett managed to pull Kali back in line once more. He turned his eyes towards Seamus' dakgrul, Malevo, the latter demon tilting its head in confusion at his stare.

"I know that you somehow are able to keep him from attacking all of us right now, Spellweaver Seamus, but tell me. What do you plan to do with him?"

"Malevo?" Seamus glanced at the demonic being for a moment before shrugging. "I figure I'll end up with him either hidden in a spot where no one can find him, or I'll figure a way to make him change his shape from his current form to a cat of some kind."

"Can you really make other beings take different shapes?" Gabriella asked. Seamus flashed a toothy smile at her for a moment.

"You bet I can. It's not that hard to do. Besides, I use magic to create alternative human shapes all the time."

"And what if he breaks out of your control?" Ryan asked. "What father was trying to do, control the Shadow Demons, it's not that different from what you're doing with this dakgrul here."

"True, I do have control over Malevo. But the difference here is that I'm not interested in controlling an entire horde of demons. Nor do I have any intention to use the dark arts to control this fella. The spell I cast on him is entirely different and can only be used on one demon at a time." Seamus gave a gentle stroke to Malevo's head. "Besides, I can use this guy to help us understand how to create a protection spell against the acid they have in their mouths."

"Just as long as you keep that thing around his neck." Aiden said with a groan. "The last thing we need is to have a demon trying to kill us in our sleep."

"Oi. Don't underestimate my magic, kiddo."

Before their little argument about if Seamus could keep Malevo under control could continue, a loud noise came from where Ryan and Seamus had placed the former Grand Mage. The group fell silent as the subject reared its ugly head once more.

"What are you going to do with him?" Theresa asked.

"He'll be held accountable for his actions." Ryan frowned. "We'll hold a trial for him, decide how heavy the weight of his sins are, and then either keep him locked away for the rest of his life, or try to get him rehabilitated as well."

"And Lewis?" Aiden asked hastily.

"He's...he's going to be a tougher case." Ryan admitted. "My little brother went through a nightmare, one that he should never have been apart of. I can only imagine that what he's been through was so traumatizing that he may never recover." He closed his eyes before continuing. "But I won't give up on him. Not when I know that he is stronger than what our father had placed him through. Even if it takes me till the end of my days, I will find a way to help my brother survive what he experienced."

"Noble words." Theresa said, "I do hope that you are able to achieve this, Ryan. If there's anyone that can manage to fix what your father has done to this once proud place, it is without a doubt you."

As the two of them exchanged words, Aiden felt a nagging question eating away at the back of his head. What Ivan had said to him after he finished beating him with his bare fists. It bugged him.

What did Ivan mean that he was exactly like his acquaintance? Why would he say such a thing? Just who was the person that stood against Ivan and Dimitri's wishes to understand the Dark Arts? Did he really have that much in common with this person?

"Aiden?" Ryan called out to him. "Aiden did you hear me?"

Aiden blinked in surprise before he shook his head. In his time of wondering and pondering, he had drowned out the conversation that Theresa and Ryan were having. He turned his head back to Ryan, a bit embarrassed that he was practically ignoring the new grand mage.

"S-Sorry, I didn't mean to do that." He said sheepishly. "I was just pondering some questions."

"No need to apologize my friend." Ryan gave him a smile. "It's a good thing to wonder and question things." He cleared his throat. "Aiden Russell, you were the main key contributor in the final battle with the Overmind. You saved my little brother from being destroyed, and exposed the dark lies that my father had committed before. You my friend, deserve a reward for such a thing."

"T-That's really not necessary." Aiden replied. But Ryan shook his head.

"But it is. If it wasn't for you, my brother would have died as the Overmind and my father would have sacrificed one of his own sons for such a disgusting goal. As Grand Mage, it is my honor to reward you in someway."

He snapped his fingers as two mages rushed along up to his side.

"These two mages here, are some of the best weapon creators

in the Academy. If you wish it, I could empower your blade more, or perhaps create you something to go along with your sword. A shield perhaps?"

"Ohhh, now that's a generous offer there kiddo." Seamus said. "Magic shields are some of the best defenses a guy can ask for. And it would go perfectly with your sword training."

"I..." Aiden blushed in embarrassment at the praise that he was getting from Ryan and the offer he had presented to him. A shield? He could never in a million years imagine that anyone would willingly offer an award to him. "I don't know I mean...are you certain that it's okay?"

"Honestly, you deserve much more than just a shield my friend." Ryan admitted. "If I could give you everything you desired in this world I would. Your act of saving my little brother alone is more than enough to justify you getting a gift from our Academy."

Aiden glanced over to Theresa for a second, as if he was seeking her approval. She shook her head at him.

"This is your choice, Aiden. The offer was given to you and you alone."

With those words etched into his mind, Aiden turned back to Ryan and the two mages that were beside him. Theresa was right. It was his choice. And Ryan, who had praised him for saving his little brother, was more than happy to give him this chance at a magical shield.

"Well...o-only if it won't be too much of a problem to create."

"Not at all my friend." Ryan smiled. "It will take some time for the shield to be complete, but when it is done it will be delivered to you with the best magic spells for transfer that we have."

"A good move, Kiddo." Seamus said. "Trust me when I tell you this, magic shields like those don't let you down at all."

Theresa rolled her eyes at Seamus before giving Aiden's shoulder a squeeze. He smiled a bit before letting her take over again.

"It has been an honor, Grand Mage." She said. "I hope that you and your people will be able to rebuild your school and that the next time we visit it will be under much better circumstances."

"The honor is all mine, my lady." Ryan replied. "You all were apart of saving my home. If it weren't for you, I may not even be standing here right now. And that is something that I can never forget."

With his staff in hand, Ryan opened up a teleportation spell for the group to use back to Virginia. An expression of happiness and sadness mixed on his lips as he glanced one last time at them.

"With this, you will return to your home state. As you know, time works differently in here. And I can imagine that over there the whole ordeal here was a mere hour at the most in the outside world. When you return, I ask of one simple favor for you. Treasure your family. Even if they drive you crazy and make you question their choices at time, do remember this. Families are always there for one another. A lesson my father has forgotten, but I will not."

For some reason Ryan's words seemed to hit Aiden just right. Before his life changed around the moment he was given Warfang, Aiden had begun to question his own father's actions and insistence that he act more mature. Before Aiden had brushed it off as if his father wanted to control his life and not allow him to be happy, but after seeing what Ivan had done to his youngest son it dawned on Aiden that there was one simple truth to his father's actions.

Unlike Ivan, he loved Aiden. And only wanted the best for him.

As the group walked towards the portal to return to Virginia, with Kali in hand, Aiden smiled.

"I should be more grateful." He thought. *"Dad's only looking out for me. Maybe when we get back I'll take him up on his golf lessons."*

And with that one thought, Aiden left the Academy with his friends to return back to their home. He made a promise to himself. From now on, he was going to be more considerate to his dad. After what he went through and what he saw from Ivan? Aiden could confirm one very important thing.

Connor was ten times the man Ivan was. Even if Aiden knew that when he returned, a slew of yard work waited him.

EPILOGUE

Not too far away from the Academy, Dimitri and Raven watched from the roof of another building. Though the eyes of regular mortals could not see it, they could. The dark aura that had engulfed part of the Academy had faded away. Dimitri sighed.

"So they were able to do it after all." He mused.

"A shame, Master." Raven said as he clenched his fists. "I was kind of hoping that they would not be able to do so. I would have loved to see the last of those weaklings be killed by the Shadow Demons, then watch as the innocent civilians here would be torn by their power."

"You and I both know that such a thing would prove to be more hindering to our plans than helpful, my dear apprentice." Dimitri replied. "As much as I want the world to be brought to its knees, we can not afford to do so. Not when we are so few in numbers."

The elder mage scratched his chin momentarily as he chose his next words.

"And we must begin to fuel these numbers soon. The Great One wishes an army of followers to our cause."

Raven flinched at the mention of this 'Great One.' Though he could be stoic and almost uncaring about anything at times, the mere mention of that title sent a shiver down Raven's spine. One that was a combination of both fear and respect.

"Y-Yes, the Great One." He said meekly. "I do hope that he is not upset about what has happened here." Dimitri scoffed.

"You worry too much my young ward. Our lord has a plan for everything, and I am certain that he did not want Shadow Demons to break out and ruin everything. Not when we are so close to accomplishing our goal."

"Of course, Master."

Dimitri turned around and narrowed his eyes. Hidden in the shadows were two beings.

"The two of you know what to do next, do you not?"

Though their facial details could not be seen in the shadows, the two beings were without a doubt female. The two of them gave the mage nods of understanding, not speaking a single word. A sly grin came across the lips of Dimitri as he clapped his hands together.

"Excellent." He said. "With this little annoyance out of the way, we can begin our plan. Start recruiting, all three of you. This world will fall, and from its ashes, our Great Lord's ideals will resurrect it to the point where we will rule over all!"

To Be Continued In
   "The Exiled"

*E*nglish Dragonic Pronunciation

AFRAID KITHOR (KIT-HOR)
    After Foful (fo-ful)
    Again Bentia (bent-e-a)
    All Span (span)
    Allow Spenzer (spen-zer)
    Although Spafiveenarre (spa-five-en-air)
    Always Spaveteran (spa-ve-ter-an)
    Am Ka (car)
    An Ki (key)
    And Tim (tim)
    Any Kif (keyf)
    Air Floia (flow-e-a)
    Abandon Fiekona (fee-kon-a)
    Are Guo (goo-o)
    As Guto (gu-to)
    Be Lo (lo)

Because Lokhan (lo-kan)
Been Lowen (low-en)
Before Bealom (bear-lom)
Being Lowing (low-ing)
Believe Demanda (de-man-da)
Bird Beasttee (be-st-tee)
Born Feiry (fair-e)
Brother Stragna (stragna)
Bugger Liaron (lair-on)
But Xou (zoo)
By Heel (heal)
Bye Heel (heal)
Can Toa (toe-a)
Calm Queet (queat)
Care Hito (hi-to)
Careful Hitokan (hi-to-kan)
Carry Titoa (ti-toa)
Chosen Denengar (de-nen-gar)
Claim Nevi (ner-vi)
Crap Xot (zot)
Currant Cresion (crez-e-on)
Current Cresion (crez-e-on)
Cyclone Featheroo (fef-e-roo)
Day Veek (v-k)
Dark Rappra (rap-pra)
Decide Hoaliea (hol-e-a)
Dictionary Diarra (die-a-ra)
Discussion Iletian (il-et-ian)
Did Highroal (high-rol)
Die Pearoo (pair-roo)
Differ Haven (hay-ven)
Dispose Depoa (dep-po-a)
Do Jey (j)
Down Tuggr (tug-gr)

344

Dragon Drakon (Dra-kan)
Earth Gitanel (Gi-ta-nel)
Eight Ipoy (i-poi)
Eighth Ipoyo (i-poi-o)
Eighty Ipoyven (i-poi-ven)
Eleven Difer (dif-er)
Ember Em (m)
Enough Aimabel (aim-a-bell)
Eve Dect (det)
Even Dectven (det-ven)
Female Jilbecken (jil-bec-ken)
Fifth Hityo (hi-ti-o)
Fifty Hityoven (hit-ti-o-ven)
Fire Beut (be-oot)
First Guyger (guy-ger)
Five Hity (hit-ti)
Flow Spatter (spat-ter)
Friend Jid (jid)
Foe Laco (la-co)
For Uranni (you -rain-ne)
Forest Teena (teen-na)
Forth Uranio (you-rain-ne-o)
Forty Uraniven (you-rain-ne-ven)
Four/For Uranni (you -rain-ne)
Fourth Urannio (you-rain-ne-o)
Garden Jeadit (gee-dit)
Get Gag (gag)
Give Kilo (kil-lo)
Glad Sient (si-ent)
Go Sie (sigh)
Good Singl (sing-l)
Guardian Familiu (fam-a-lee-u)
Guess Deed (deed)
Had Tid (tid)

Happen Foulger (foul-ger)
Have Tieg (tieg)
Heal Emalla (e-mal-la)
He Gan (gan)
Hell Hilk (hilk)
Hello Kaby (kar-be)
Help Ihan (ir-harn)
Her Gar (gar)
His Gos (gos)
Him Go (go)
Hold Petir (p-tear)
Hope Jetoo (jet-oo)
Home Dunu (dun-oo)
How Tyan (tie-an)
Huh Rye (rie)
Hundred Weloect (we-lo-et)
I O (o)
Idea Kipit (kip-it)
Idiot Kalen (kal-en)
If Of (of)
In On (on)
Is Os (os)
It Ot (ot)
Just Golt (golt)
Know Xorea (zor-e-ar)
Land Piane (p-ain)
Langue Opilain (of-fil-e-an)
Let Heardl (hear-dl)
Leader Rexkin (rex-kin)
Life Doll (dol)
Lighting Ragnatorm (rag-na-torm)
Like Cuay (q-ray)
Live Dollvie (dol-v)
Lives Dollvies (dol-ves)

Long Whyt (white)
Luck Valo (val-o)
Male Becken (bec-ken)
Mana Kotura (ko-tu-ra)
Many Zane (zain)
Master Kinsaur (kin-saur)
Memory Lockieo (loc-key-o)
Might Tenara (te-na-ra)
My Min (min)
Name Cert (kert)
Never Sandra (san-dra)
Next Gon (gone)
Nice Fasy (fa-c)
Nine Leo (lee-o)
Ninety Leoven (lee-o-ven)
Ninth Leoo (lee-oo)
No Yed (yed)
None Rikie (ric-key)
Not Reo (ree-o)
Now Rew (ru)
Of Ewra (oo-ra)
Off Ewrana (oo-ra-na)
Oh Gad (gad)
Okay Pomain (po-main)
One Zon (zon)
Our Zo (zo)
Or Li (lee)
Other Keddit (ked-dit)
Over Zitter (zit-ter)
Past Beta (bay-ta)
Peace Avena (A-ve-na)
Petition Gemala (ge- ma-la)
Piss Vaoo (var-oo)
Planet Soaku (so-ku)

Poor Fraw (fraw)
Prevent Joarhand (Jo-ar-hand)
Previous Joarietin (jo-ar-e-tin)
Pronounce Joyerition (joy-er-i-tion)
Prop Dryan (dry-an)
Really Funnel (fun-nel)
Release Joinne (join-ne)
Relax Elgane (el-ga-ne)
Remember Canoain (can-o-ain)
Right Ritted (rit-ted)
Rope Ohnalga (oh-nal-ga)
Sake Litin (li-tin)
Sad Ditin (di-tin)
Scary Zanatone (zan-ar-tone)
Second Poite (poi-te)
See Lon (l-on)
Separate Tineat (ti-n-eat)
Serenity Sinotu (sin-o-to)
Serious Silowin (sil-o-win)
Seven Youao (u-a-o)
Seventh Youaoo (u-a-oo)
Seventy Youaoven (u-a-o-ven)
Shelter Wyen (y-en)
Should Shumbel (Shum-bell)
Six Dren (dren)
Sixth Dreno (dren-o)
Sixty Drenven (drenven)
So Ceo (c-o)
Some Merm (merm)
Sorry Forfit (for-fit)
Speech Stutak (stu-tak)
Spirit Shimera (shim-er-ra)
Stand Keya (key-a)
Still Tair (tear)

Stop Nomaran (no-ma-ran)

Sword Ladbe (lad-be)

Take Yakki (yak-ki)

Tantrum Onergall (o-ner-gall)

Tell Kidon (ki-don)

Ten Wari (wa-re)

That Hubo (hub-o)

The Aba (a-ba)

Them Abam (a-bam)

There Abaren (a-ba-ren)

These Abasen (a-ba-sen)

They Abat (a-bat)

Thing Ittye (it-tie)

Third Itin (it-tin)

Thirty Itinven (it-tin-ven)

This Bah (bah)

Though Fiveenarre (five-en-air)

Thousand Veinatim (vein-a-tim)

Three Itoa (it-toe-a

Through Ficenarre (thick-en-air)

To Ter (ter)

Together Tergaggar (ter-gag-gar)

Tomorrow Teragain (ter-a-gen)

Too Ter (ter)

Torture Deertom (deer-tom)

Turn Goar (go-r)

Twelve wave (twa-ve)

Twenty Twaven (twa-ven)

Two Ter (ter)

Under Quake (quake)

Understand Quakekeya (quake-key-a)

Up Vuat (voo-at)

Was Ghan (gr-han)

Water boakuo (bo-koo-o)

Way Vun (voon)

Warrior Eltraga (El-tra-ga)

We Tolua (to-lu-a)

What Bouk (book)

When Bein (bee-in

Where Beian (be-arn)

Why Quic (quick)

Will Dagal (dag-gal)

With Sammoo (sam-moo)

Would Umbel (um-bell)

Wow Fair (fare)

Yeah Sear (see-er)

Year Quiv (quiv)

Yes Seah (see)

You Yokee (yo-key)

Your Yokeer (yo-keer)

(an) Before

(ed) After

(er) After

(ex) Before

(im) Before

(ing) After

(less) After

(ly) After

(r) After

(s) After

(teen) After

(un) Before

(y) After

The Mage's Sin

First Edition

ISBN:

Publisher

Broken Tower Press

United States

6261 14th Avenue South

Suite 201

Gulfport, Florida 33707

Phone: 813-924-4717

Copyright Broken Tower Press, May 2017

A Subdivision of CHR Publishing

All Rights Reserved

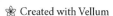 Created with Vellum

ABOUT THE AUTHOR

Living with the stories in his head from the time he could talk, Charlie Rose describes himself as a writer, first, last, and always. In his spare time he can be found on the internet or playing one of his many different gaming systems. He loves animals, Tolkien, and stories - in all their forms. He also loves to hear from his fans. If you want to talk you can reach him by email at chroseiv@hotmail.com.

He looks forward to hearing from you soon!

Books by Charlie Rose
Book 1: Dragonera: The Adventure Begins
Book 2: The Harpy's Den
Book 3: The Mage's Sin
Book 4: The Dangerous Traitor (upcoming)
Book 5: Bane of Dragons (upcoming)
Book 6: The Return of the Dragon King (upcoming)
Book 7: The Final Truth (upcoming)

Made in the USA
Monee, IL
23 August 2020

Made in the USA
Middletown, DE
28 March 2016